P9-DMZ-184

Goodnight Nobody

ALSO BY JENNIFER WEINER

Good in Bed

In Her Shoes

Little Earthquakes

Goodnight Nobody

a novel

JENNIFER WEINER

ATRIA BOOKS
New York London Toronto Sydney

1230 Avenue of the Americas
New York, NY 10020

This book is a work of fiction. Names, characters, places and incidents are products of the author's imagination or are used fictitiously. Any resemblance to actual events or locales or persons, living or dead, is entirely coincidental.

For information address Atria Books, 1230 Avenue of the Americas, New York, NY 10020

Permissions acknowledgments appear on page 373.

ISBN-13: 978-0-7434-7011-7
ISBN-10: 0-7434-7011-7

First Atria Books hardcover edition September 2005

10 9 8 7 6 5 4 3 2 1

ATRIA BOOKS is a trademark of Simon & Schuster, Inc.

Manufactured in the United States of America

For information regarding special discounts for bulk purchases, please contact Simon & Schuster Special Sales at 1-800-456-6798 or business@simonandschuster.com

For Frances Frumin Weiner

"Each suburban wife struggled with it alone. As she made the beds, shopped for groceries, matched slipcover material, ate peanut butter sandwiches with her children, chauffeured Cub Scouts and Brownies, lay beside her husband at night—she was afraid to ask even of herself the silent question—'Is this all?' "

—Betty Friedan, *The Feminine Mystique*

"Sighed Mayzie, a lazy bird hatching an egg:
'I'm tired and I'm bored
And I've kinks in my leg
From sitting, just sitting here day after day.
It's *work!* How I hate it!
I'd *much* rather play!
I'd take a vacation, fly off for a rest, if I could find
  someone to stay on my nest!
If I could find someone, I'd fly away—free . . .' "

—Dr. Seuss, *Horton Hatches the Egg*

"Well I had a dream and in it
I went to a little town
And all the girls in town were named
Betty."

—Laurie Anderson, "Smoke Rings"

PART ONE

The Good Mother

ONE

"Hello?" I tapped on Kitty Cavanaugh's red front door, then lifted the brass knocker and gave it a few thumps for good measure. "Hello?"

"Mommy, can I ring the doorbell?" Sophie asked. She stood on her tiptoes and waved her fist in the air.

"No, it's my turn," said Sam, kicking his sneakered feet against one of the half-dozen perfectly spherical pumpkins beside Kitty's front door. Halloween was a week away, and we'd only gotten around to carving our single jack-o'-lantern the night before. It had come out crooked and its right side had rotted and caved in overnight, and it looked like we had a sadistic stroke victim parked on our porch. When I'd lit the candle, all three kids had cried.

"*My* turn!" said Jack, shoving his younger-by-three-minutes brother.

"Don't push me!" cried Sam, shoving back.

"Sophie, then Sam, then Jack," I said. Two degrees in English literature, a career in New York City, and this was where I'd ended up, standing on a semi-stranger's doorstep in a Connecticut suburb with uncombed hair and a tote bag full of bribe lollipops, wrangling three kids under the age of five. How had this happened? I couldn't explain it. Especially not the part about getting pregnant with the boys when Sophie was just seven weeks old, courtesy of an act of intercourse I can barely remember and can't imagine I'd condoned.

Sophie reached up, pigtails quivering, and rang the bell. A dimple flashed in her left cheek as she gave her brothers a smug look that said, *This is how it's done.* Nobody answered. I looked at my watch, wondering if I'd heard Kitty wrong. She'd called on Wednesday night, when the boys were in the bathtub and Sophie was sitting on the toilet, applying lipstick and waiting her turn. I was kneeling in front of the tub, my shirt half-soaked, a washcloth in my hand, scrubbing playground grime from underneath their fingernails and enjoying one of my most persistent and vivid daydreams, the one that began with two men knocking on my front door. Who were they? Police officers? FBI agents? I'd never figured that out.

The younger one wore a beige suit and a clipped inch of sandy mustache, and the older one had a black suit and thinning black hair combed over his bald spot. He was the one who did the talking. *There's been a mistake,* he would tell me, and he'd explain that, due to some glitch I'd never quite fleshed out (Bad dream? Alternate universe?), I'd wound up with someone else's children, living someone else's life. *Really?* I would ask, careful not to sound too eager as a woman—these days, she was usually the lady from the Swiffer commercial who danced around to the Devo song, happily dusting—stepped between them, hands planted on her capable hips. *There you are, you little scamps!* she would say to the children. *I'm so sorry for the inconvenience,* she'd say to me. *No problem,* I'd graciously reply. And then she'd say . . .

"Telephone."

I looked up. My husband stood in the doorway, with his briefcase in one hand and the telephone in the other, staring at me with something that was either disdain or its close first cousin. My heart sank as I realized that getting slopped with the boys' bathwater was the closest I'd come to showering that day.

I reached for the phone with one soapy hand. "Can you watch them for a sec?"

"Let me just get out of this suit," he said, and vanished down the hall. Translation: *See you in an hour.* I stifled a sigh and tucked the telephone under my ear.

"Hello?"

"Kate, it's Kitty Cavanaugh," she'd said, in her low, cultured voice. "I was wondering whether you were free for lunch on Friday."

I'd been too shocked to stammer out "Sure" or "Yes." I'd wound up saying "Shes," even though lunch with Kitty Cavanaugh wasn't high on my to-do list. As far as I was concerned she represented everything that was wrong with my new hometown.

I remember the first time I'd seen Kitty. After a morning of unpacking I'd driven the kids to the park our Realtor had pointed out. I hadn't washed my thick, curly brown hair in three days and was looking more than a little disheveled, but the other mothers wouldn't mind, I thought, as I pulled into a parking space. As the kids and I walked through the white picket playground gates, we saw four women seated on the green wooden bench by the seesaws: four women wearing the identical shade of dark pink lipstick; four formidably groomed, exquisitely fit, terrifyingly capable-looking women. Each one had a monogrammed paisley silk diaper bag slung across her shoulder, like a Pink Lady jacket. Or an Uzi.

"Hi!" I said. My voice seemed to bounce off the pebbled rubber mats underneath the slides and echo through the swing set. The women took in my outfit (loose, syrup-stained cargo pants, finger-paint-smeared sneakers, one of my husband's washed-out long-sleeved gray T-shirts with one of my own violet short-sleeved shirts on top), my messy hair, my makeup-free face, the belly and hips I'd been meaning to do something about for the past two years and, finally, my kids. Jack looked okay, but Sam was clutching his favorite pacifier, which he hadn't used in months, and Sophie had pulled on a tutu over her pajama bottoms.

The buff-looking blonde in the middle, in camel-colored boot-cut pants topped with a zippered fleece vest, raised her hand and gave us a semi-smile. Her name, I'd later learn, was Lexi Hagen-

Holdt, and she looked exactly like what she was—a former all-state athlete in soccer and lacrosse who'd worked as a high school coach before marriage and had started training for a triathlon six weeks after she'd had baby Brierly.

The brunette next to her had shoulder-length light brown hair perfectly streaked and styled, and eyebrows plucked into perfect arches, then dyed to match; she gave us a half of a wave. Her full lips twisted sideways, as if she'd tasted something sour. This was Sukie Sutherland, in Seven jeans and high-heeled, pointy-toed suede boots—the kind of outfit my friend Janie would have worn out clubbing and I never would have attempted at all.

"Hi!" said the redhead—Carol Gwinnell—at the far end of the bench. She sported a pumpkin-colored sweater with a long skirt in swirling shades of red and orange and gold. Her little gold earrings were clusters of bells that jingled and chimed, and she wore sequined purple slippers trimmed in gold braid. Carol's husband, I would shortly learn, was head of litigation at one of the five biggest law firms in New York City. Carol and Rob and their two sons lived in a Bettencourt and had a summer house on Nantucket, which I guess gave her the right to dress like she was going to a Stevie Nicks concert if she wanted to.

Finally, the fourth woman deigned to approach us. She knelt down gracefully in front of my kids and one by one asked them their names. Her straight, thick hair fell to the center of her back, a glossy sheet of chocolate brown held with a black velvet band. She had lovely features: full lips, a straight, narrow nose, high cheekbones, and a neat little chin. Given her hair, and her golden complexion, I would have expected brown eyes, but hers were wide set and a blue so dark it was almost purple. The color of pansies.

"And I'm Kitty Cavanaugh," she said to my children. "I have twins too."

"Kate Klein," I managed, thinking, *Don't fall for it, you little bastards.* Of course, my kids were charmed. The boys let go of my leg and smiled at her shyly, while Sophie stared at her and said, "You're so pretty!" I tried not to roll my eyes. The last time Sophie looked at me that intently, she hadn't said that I was pretty, she'd told me I had a hair growing out of my chin.

I plastered a smile on my face and made a series of mental notes: figure out where to buy a perfectly cut suede jacket; find out where these women got their hair blown, their teeth bleached, their eyebrows plucked; and try to locate the other overwhelmed, undergroomed, bigger-than-a-breadbox mothers like myself, even if I had to cross state lines to find them.

The ladies had gone back to their conversation, which seemed to concern the student-teacher ratios at the town's competing private schools. It had taken three more playground visits, twenty minutes spent listening to Sukie talk about reorganizing her pantry, and a trip to Mr. Steven, the local hairdresser, before Kitty and I had had an actual conversation, about what kind of baked goods I should bring to the Red Wheel Barrow annual holiday bake sale. "No nuts, no dairy," she'd told me. I'd nodded humbly and managed to keep from asking, "How about crack? Would crack be okay?"

Our second talk had been less successful. We'd been standing side by side at the swings on the playground one summer afternoon. Kitty was wearing a pink linen sundress, simple yet elegant, a look (and a fabric) I hadn't attempted in years, and I was wearing my usual—grubby pants and a cotton tank top—feeling overweight and underdressed and entirely inadequate. *It's this town,* I thought, tugging at my waistband with one hand and pushing Sophie with the other. Back in New York I'd get the occasional whistle from a construction worker, an appreciative glance from a guy on the street. Sixty miles out of the city and I was Shamu in a sweater set.

I had been daydreaming out loud about a vacation I'd probably never take, describing some resort I'd read about in a travel magazine in my gynecologist's waiting room. Private open-air bungalows . . . individual swimming pools . . . fresh-cut pineapple and papaya set out on the terrace every morning . . .

"Can you bring kids?" Kitty had asked.

Startled, I'd said, "Why would you want to?"

"Phil and I take our daughters everywhere," she'd said primly, giving little Madeline a push. "I would never, ever leave them."

"Never ever?" I'd repeated—a little sarcastically, I'm afraid. "Not even for a Friday night at the movies? Not even to go out to dinner? Or for a light snack?"

She'd shaken her glorious hair, a tiny smile—a smug smile, I thought—playing around her lips. "I would never leave them," she'd repeated.

I'd nodded, plastered a smile on my own face, eased Sophie out of the swing, mumbled, "Have a nice weekend" (without realizing until much later that it was Tuesday), hustled all three kids into the van, stuck a DVD into the player, turned up the volume, and muttered the word "freak" all the way home.

Since then, Kitty and I had had a nod-and-wave acquaintance, smiling at each other across the soccer field or the dairy aisle of the grocery store. I didn't want it to go any further than that. But I'd said yes—or "shes"—anyhow. Oh, well. *Mindless assent,* I thought, and shoved a wayward curl behind my right ear with one shampoo-slick hand. It was what had gotten me three babies and a house in Connecticut in the first place.

"I think we have a friend in common," Kitty said.

I wiped my hands on my thighs. "Oh? Who's that?" For one giddy moment I was completely sure that she was going to say Jesus, and that I'd be stuck listening to a soliloquy about her personal relationship with the Savior and how I needed one myself.

But Kitty answered my question with another one of her own. "You were a journalist, right?"

"Well, that's putting it a little strongly," I said. "I worked at *New York Night,* and I covered celebrity addiction. Not exactly Woodward and Bernstein stuff. Why?" *Here it comes,* I thought, bracing myself for the invitation to edit the nursery school newsletter or do a quick polish on the Cavanaugh Christmas card. ("Dear friends!

Hope this season of comfort and joy finds you well. It's been a blessed year for the Cavanaugh Clan . . .")

"There's something . . . ," she began. Just then Sam dunked Jack under the water. "Mommy, he's drownding the baby," Sophie observed from the toilet seat, where she was twisting her hair into a chignon. I bent down to drag Jack upright. He was spluttering, Sam was crying, and Kitty said we'd talk on Friday.

At least, I was pretty sure she'd said Friday. Positive, almost. I took a deep breath and lifted the knocker again, noticing the way the Cavanaugh house gleamed under the cloudless blue sky. The hedges were trimmed, the leaves were raked, the windows sparkled, and there were charming arrangements of bittersweet and miniature pumpkins in the window boxes that complemented the dried-red-pepper wreath on the door. *Gah.* I gave an especially forceful knock, and the door swung open.

"Hello?" I called into the dim, echoing entryway. No answer . . . but I could see lights gleaming from the kitchen at the end of the hall, and I could hear music playing, one of the Brandenburg Concertos, which were undoubtedly more edifying than the polka tunes my kids enjoyed. "Kitty? Hello?" I called again. Nothing. The wind kicked up, sending a drift of brown leaves rattling against the hardwood floor. I was starting to get the proverbial bad feeling about this as I wiggled my cell phone out of my pocket, called information, and asked for the Cavanaugh listing at 5 Folly Farm Way.

The operator connected me. Inside the house I could hear Kitty's phone ringing . . . and ringing . . . and ringing.

"Nobody's home," Sophie said impatiently, bouncing up and down in pink sneakers that did not quite match her orange overalls.

"Hang on," I said. "Hello?" I called into the house. Nothing.

"Mama?" Sophie reached for my hand. The boys looked at each other, their foreheads drawn into identical furrows, plump mouths pulled into matching frowns. The two of them were all curves and dimples and alabaster skin that flushed when they were overheated or upset. Their lashes cast spiky shadows on their cheeks, and their brown hair curled into ringlets so beautiful I'd cried at their first haircuts . . . and second . . . and third. Unlike her brothers, Sophie was tall and lanky, like her father, with olive skin and fine brown hair that tended toward snarls, not ringlets.

"Stay here. Right here. On the porch. On the pumpkins," I said, in a burst of inspiration. "I want tushies on pumpkins until I say it's okay. And don't close the door!" Sophie must have caught something in my tone because she nodded. "I'll watch the babies."

"We're not babies!" said Jack, with his hands balled into fists.

"Stay here," I said again, and watched Sophie scowl at her brothers as they copped a squat on one of Kitty's perfect pumpkins. I held my breath and walked inside. The Cavanaughs had the same house we did, the Montclaire (six bedrooms, five full baths, hardwood floors throughout). The investors in our development were Italian, plenty of the residents were Jewish, and yet the homes all had names that made them sound like members of the British Parliament. Evidently nobody would buy a model called the Lowenthal or the Delguidice, but if it was the Carlisle or the Bettencourt, we'd be lining up with our checkbooks.

I tiptoed through the entryway, into the warmly lit kitchen, where the solemn notes of the cello and an antique clock's ticking filled the air. No dishes in the sink, no newspapers on the counter, no crumbs on the kitchen table, and no lady of the house that I could see. Then I looked down.

"Oh, God!" I clapped my hand against my mouth and grabbed on to the countertop to keep myself from sliding to the floor. Kitty had gone for the same upgrades that Ben and I had picked. Her countertops were granite, her floors were pickled maple, and the French doors leading to the garden had leaded glass insets. There was a Sub-Zero refrigerator and a Viking range, and between them was Kitty Cavanaugh, facedown on the floor with an eight-inch carbon-steel Henckels butcher's knife protruding from between her shoulder blades.

I ran across the kitchen and knelt in a pool of tacky, cooled blood. She lay arms akimbo, white shirt and hair both a sticky maroon. I felt dizzy as I leaned over her body, queasy as I touched her sticky hair, then tugged at the handle of the knife. "Kitty!"

I'd watched enough cop dramas to know better than to move the body, but it was as if I were floating outside myself, unable to stop my hands as they grabbed her slender shoulders and tried to pull her up into my arms. The music swelled to its crescendo, strings and woodwinds sounding in the still, copper-smelling air as her torso came loose with a sickening ripping sound. I let her go. Her body thumped back onto the floor. I clapped my hands over my mouth to keep from gagging, and stifled another scream.

"Mommy?"

I could hear Sophie's voice, which sounded like it was coming from another planet. My own voice was shaking as I called back, "Just a minute, guys!"

I got to my feet, wiping my hands convulsively against my pants, and whirled around once, then again. It wasn't until I'd slammed my hip against the breakfast bar that I finally forced myself to hold still and think. Should I call the cops? Get my kids? What if whoever had done this to Kitty was still in the house?

Cops first, I decided. It took me what felt like forever to work my hand into my pocket, extract my cell phone, and dial 911. "Yes, hello, this is Kate Klein, and I'm visiting my friend Kitty Cavanaugh's house at Five Folly Farm Way and she's . . . um . . ." My voice broke. "She's dead. Somebody killed her."

"That address, please?" asked the voice on the other end of the line. "Your name?" I gave it. Then I spelled it. When she asked me for my Social Security number and date of birth, I hissed, "Just send someone! Send the police . . . send an ambulance . . . send the Marines if they're around . . ."

"Ma'am?"

My voice trailed off as I saw a square of creamy, heavy-stock stationery beside Kitty's telephone. I saw ten digits that froze the blood in my veins.

A Manhattan area code, the same number he'd had when I'd known him, the same number I'd dialed all those times when we'd lived down the hall from each other, the number that I'd struggled almost daily ever since to keep from dialing again.

I think we have a friend in common . . .

Without even thinking I hung up the phone, reached out with one shaking hand, and grabbed the note. I crumpled it and crammed it deep into my pocket. Then I shoved my bloody hands under Kitty's kitchen faucet, dried them on her cheery fall-leaf-printed dish towel, and ran down the hall on wobbly legs.

"Mommy?" Sophie's narrow face was pale, and her big brown eyes were wide and solemn. Sam and Jack were both holding her hands, and Sam had his thumb stuck in his mouth. Sophie looked at the blood on my pants. "Did you get hurt?"

"No," I told them. "No, honey, Mommy's fine." I fumbled a Wet One out of my bag and took a few hasty swipes at the stains. "Come on, Sophie," I said, and I gathered the boys into my arms, feeling the fierce engines of their hearts beating hard against my skin as I carried them down to the edge of the driveway and we sat there, waiting for help.

TWO

"Excuse me," I said, raising my voice above the crackle of the scanner, the radio tuned to the all-conservative talk station, and the cluster of cops muttering by the Mr. Coffee. "Stan?"

Stanley Bergeron, Upchurch's chief of police, gave a distracted nod. He'd parked me on a wheeled metal chair in front of an empty desk with a cracked rotary phone, beneath a yellowing sign-up sheet for Weight Watchers at Work, none of which was making my heart brim with confidence. Neither was the receptionist-slash-dispatcher, scratching her scalp with the tip of her pencil and pretending to type while hanging on every word that was uttered.

Be cool, Kate, I told myself. *Don't act guilty, or they'll think you are.* But it wasn't going to be easy. Some people crack their knuckles when they're nervous. I crack jokes. I took a deep breath and tried for a tone of detachment. "Hey, can you at least tell me if I'm under arrest? Because, not to be flippant, but if I'm in jail it's really going to mess up the carpool schedule."

"You're not under arrest, Kate," Stannie rumbled. Stan was short, barrel-chested, and jowly, with a basset hound's watery brown eyes and a droopy dun-colored mustache. He'd been a member of the New York City Police Department until September 11, when he'd traded high crime and the threat of terrorism for sleepy little Upchurch, where a big day might involve writing a speeding ticket or two, rousting teenagers from the local lovers' lane, and chasing down one of Lois Kenneally's champion corgis, who had a tendency to wander. Stan and I had gotten to know each other during my first six weeks in Upchurch, when, thanks to my failure to master the extremely expensive and very sensitive alarm system, he'd been out to my house on Liberty Lane almost every other day.

"We just need to ask you a few more questions," Stan said.

"What else?" I asked, trying to sound like my heart wasn't in my throat, like I wasn't still shaking, like I couldn't feel the crumpled note in my pocket bearing my former crush's phone number swelling and throbbing like a tumor. I'd thought about going to the bathroom and flushing it down the toilet. But what if it got stuck? Then I'd imagined tearing it into shreds and eating it. But what if I got sick? Better to just wait it out. I shifted in my seat, imagining I could hear the paper crackle when I moved.

In the three hours since I'd staggered out of Kitty Cavanaugh's house, I'd called Gracie, my babysitter, to come take the kids home in my minivan. Then I'd been driven to the police station, where I'd filled out my statement and had my fingerprints taken. I'd explained three different times to three separate people why my fingerprints were on the knife's handle. My interrogators had included one cop who'd grunted in disgust and said, "Geez, lady, don't you watch *CSI*?" I'd widened my eyes and said, "Is it on Noggin? Because if it isn't, probably not."

I pulled on the beaded barrettes that were holding my bangs out of my eyes. Mr. Steven had sold me on layers, but because he'd declined moving into my house and styling my hair each morning, I always had at least two inches of oh-so-trendy choppy bangs hanging in my eyes any given moment. As I reclipped them, I inquired, "Do I need a lawyer?"

Stan shrugged. "Why would you need a lawyer? You're a witness, not a suspect. You don't have anything to hide."

"Or do I?" I intoned. Stannie stared at me. "Just kidding," I said. Stan's face fell. "Please. Like I've got time to go around plotting

murders. My husband's been in California for a week. I've barely got time to empty the dishwasher." I looked at my watch, hit redial on my cell phone again, and hung up without leaving a message when Ben's voice mail answered. I'd already left half a dozen messages—none of which he'd returned—that were variations on the pertinent theme: *I stopped by Kitty Cavanaugh's house and found her dead on the kitchen floor with a knife sticking out of her back. Now I'm filling out a statement at the police station. Please call. Please come home. Please call me and come home as soon as you can.*

My husband was out in Los Angeles for some big Democratic confab, soliciting new clients for his political consulting firm. If you've lived anywhere in the Northeast for any of the past three election cycles and seen an ad where one of the candidates appears in jiggling slow motion, or in grainy mug-shot black-and-white looking like he might have little boys' body parts stashed in the basement freezer, chances are you've seen Ben's work. He's got two senators, three representatives, the governor of Massachusetts, and the United States attorney general as satisfied clients, the word "hotshot" permanently preceding his title, and more than enough money to keep the five of us safely ensconced in this bedroom community forty-five minutes outside of Manhattan, where the least expensive house costs more than a million dollars, where all the cars have four-wheel drive, and where I haven't made even a single friend.

I shifted on the chair again as the elementary school crossing guard consulted with a fellow in blue polyester, who I was pretty sure was the postman. I wondered if everyone in town who wore a uniform had shown up for the occasion.

I pushed the note deeper into my pocket. I'd washed my hands twice, but my fingertips were still black with the police department's ink. Stan, meanwhile, was mumbling on the telephone. The receptionist set down her pencil and slid a mirror and a tube of mascara out of her desk drawer. She tilted the mirror, pretending to fix her eyes, while staring at the action in the corner. Finally, Stan hung up the phone, had a quick word with the crossing guard, nodded at the mailman, hitched his pants up under his belly, and sauntered over to my desk.

"Do you know Evan McKenna?"

My heart froze. Oh God. *They knew.* Somehow they knew I'd taken the note with Evan's number on it. In about five seconds Stan's friendly smile would vanish, and he'd pull out the handcuffs. I'd be arrested. Thrown in jail. I'd never see my kids again. My husband would divorce me and eventually remarry, someone tasteful and appropriate, a slender blonde with a decent backhand who'd fit right in to this town he'd chosen, and my brother-in-law would spend the rest of his life saying, "Told you so."

I rubbed my hands along my thighs. "Why do you ask?"

"His name came up on her caller ID."

I felt myself relax incrementally. "I knew someone with that name in New York. We were . . ." I twisted my inky fingers. "We haven't been in touch in years."

Stan nodded, dropped his bulk into a chair, and wrote something down.

"So he's not a suspect?" I blurted, before an even worse thought occurred. "He's not . . . he isn't . . ." Interesting. All the years I'd been wishing grievous bodily harm upon Evan, all the fantasies I'd had about him expiring in a manner both excruciatingly painful and humiliating enough to ensure that his passing would appear in "News of the Weird," and now that he might actually be in danger, I couldn't stop shaking.

Stan ignored both of my questions. "What does Mr. McKenna do?"

"Models," I said.

Stan didn't crack a smile. "His occupation?"

"He was an investigator, when I knew him. He did freelance work for insurance companies, workmen's comp claims, and . . ." My voice trailed off. "Divorce cases. Surveillance. Cheating husbands . . .

oh!" So maybe I was a little slow. You'd be too, if you hadn't gotten a full night's sleep in four years. I jumped to my feet so quickly that one of the barrettes flew out of my hair. "Maybe Kitty hired him because her husband was cheating on her! And her husband found out and killed her!"

Stan stared at me. So did the postman, and the young patrol officer I recognized from the elementary school crosswalk. In my fantasy, the handcuffs and the smug brother-in-law were gone, and Stan was clapping me heartily on the back, saying, *Brilliant, Kate, you solved the case!* Instead, he merely flipped to a fresh page in his notebook. "Do you know Philip Cavanaugh?"

I shook my head and picked my barrette up off the floor.

Stan scribbled something. "Let's back up. When Kitty called she said she wanted to talk to you about something. Do you know what?"

I shook my head again. "I have no idea. I'm sorry. I wish I could be more helpful, but really, I didn't know her well at all."

"You don't know what she wanted to discuss."

"No. Have you talked to her husband yet?"

Stan licked his thumb and flipped to a fresh page in his notebook. "Why do you ask?"

"Isn't it always the husband?"

He rubbed his cheek. "Always?"

"Well, in my experience as a journalist, it's always the husband."

Stan was now staring at me with his mild brown eyes like a second head had sprouted out of my neck.

"On Lifetime Television for Women too. Husband. Always. Unless it's the boyfriend."

He started writing again. "Did Kitty have a boyfriend?"

"I have no idea." I shrugged. "If she did, she must've had amazing time management skills. You know, with two kids . . ."

The front door swung open, and a police officer walked in, holding tightly to the elbow of a tall, handsome man of about forty, a man with silvery blond hair and a gray flannel suit who looked like he'd forgotten how to walk.

"Excuse me," said Stan, hustling over to the two of them. The receptionist abandoned the pretense that she was doing anything other than eavesdropping, setting down her mascara wand and tilting the mirror to follow the action. Stan grabbed the gray flannel man's other elbow and steered him around the corner, into his own office. The door closed with a click behind them, but not before I could hear the man start shouting.

"My wife," he was saying. "My *wife.*" His voice broke. I shut my eyes, remembering the weight of Kitty's body, the nauseating tearing sound her shirt had made when I'd pulled her off the floor. I looked at my watch again. Almost three o'clock. Soon Kitty's daughters would be home from school. Who would be there to tell them the news? Where would they go?

I listened as hard as I could. Stan's voice was low and soothing, his New York accent reminding me painfully of home. I could only catch a word here and there, but I could make out all of Philip's. "My fault," I heard him groaning, as the receptionist strained forward, wide-eyed and breathless. "All my fault."

They let me go fifteen minutes later, with instructions not to leave the state and to call if I heard anything from Evan McKenna.

"I will," I told Stan, "but I don't think he'll call me. We don't talk," I said.

"Things change," said Stan.

The crosswalk officer, a pink-faced kid with a buzz cut who looked all of nineteen, drove me back to the scene of the crime. I ducked my head and racewalked past the news vans already parked in front of the Cavanaugh house and into Gracie's car. I'd barely made it to the end of Folly Farm Way before my heart was hammering so hard I was afraid to keep driving. Evan McKenna. After all this time.

I pulled out my cell phone and began dialing the number I

hadn't realized I still knew by heart. Three digits in, I hung up. What would I say if he answered? *Hi, it's Kate Klein. Remember me? You broke my heart? Anyhow, I know we haven't spoken in years, and oh, by the way, I guess you knew Kitty Cavanaugh, and she's been murdered and the police need to talk to you.*

I put the phone in my pocket, set my hands on the steering wheel until they stopped shaking. I left a message for my best friend, Janie Segal, and told her to call as soon as she could. Then I drove myself back home.

THREE

The next afternoon, after I'd schlepped the kids to Little People's Music, fed them grilled cheese and pickles for lunch, and read to them from *Where Did Grandpa Go?*, a treacly watercolor book written by two psychologists to "aid young readers as they process loss and grief," I piled them into the van, along with the requisite two tons of extra clothing, Wet Ones, Dora the Explorer stickers, and juice boxes, and went to the Upchurch Community Park.

I'd lived in Upchurch for almost eight months and, by my own clear-eyed estimation, hadn't done one single thing right. I'd worn my customary cargo pants to the Red Wheel Barrow Preschool open house, when all the other mothers were in skirts and boots with heels. I'd yelled, *"Son of a bitch!"* when Sophie slammed my thumb in the car door, even though Rainey Wilkes, whose son was in my kids' nursery school class, merely uttered, "Fudge!" after her husband, Roger, backed over her foot in the parking lot.

But none of this compared to the disaster that was my twins' third birthday party.

Back in New York, where Ben and the kids and I had lived in a two-bedroom apartment with a sliver of a view of Central Park, it would have been a perfectly appropriate fete. I'd invited all of the kids in the boys' nursery school class to join us on Liberty Lane, plus half a dozen friends from New York, including Zeke, who had two mommies, and Jonah, who had two daddies, and May, whose single mother had adopted her in China the year before. I'd bought a piñata, baked a cake (from a mix, but I'd thrown in chocolate chips and a packet of pudding), and served it with punch and soda, cut-up vegetables, and a bowl full of Cheez Doodles. Ben and I had shoved our couches against the walls to make more space in the living room. For entertainment there was fingerpainting, pin the tail on the donkey, and, for the adults, Janie in a short black dress, mixing mojitos and discoursing voluminously and obscenely on her latest beau's lack of bedroom skills.

Everybody seemed to have a good time, although I did notice that the other Upchurch mothers were keeping their kids away from the Cheez Doodles as if they were severed fingers and asking lots of questions about whether there were artificial dyes in the punch. I also saw a few of the kids staring at our back yard and asking where the pony rides were, or when the men were coming to set up the bouncy castle. I'd figured they were kidding. They weren't.

I found that out two weeks later, when we attended a party for one of their nursery school classmates. It was held at the Upchurch Inn, and it featured a catered spread with a smoked fish buffet, a sushi chef, and a life-sized ice sculpture of the birthday boy. No plastic forks or pin the tail on the donkey, no nontraditional families, no partially hydrogenated snack foods or artificial anything, and no talk of inept cunnilingus over punch. The entertainment was also a cut above what we'd offered. The father, a sports agent, had set up a half-sized basketball court in the parking lot and had somehow prevailed upon the entire starting lineup of the Knicks to make the trip to the suburbs and play H-O-R-S-E with the party guests. And lose.

Ben didn't say a word, but I knew how upset he was from the way his lips were pressed together, and how he jabbed at the radio buttons extra hard as we drove home.

"I didn't know!" I protested, as the kids, wiped out from the excitement of the four-tiered birthday cake, the personalized goody bags, and the thrill of meeting the seven-foot-tall center, snoozed in their car seats. "Honest to God, if I'd had any idea, I would have hired a clown!"

Ben sighed noisily.

"Or a circus!"

"You're with those women all day long. You didn't know?"

I shrugged. "I'm sorry," I told him.

"Next time, ask someone" was all he said.

I promised that I would, even though I didn't think it would help. The die had been cast. If our disastrous birthday party hadn't sealed the deal, Sophie's a cappella rendition of "Don't Mess with My Toot-Toot" at the Red Wheel Barrow's "Every Child Is Talented" show would have done it. Not only had the teacher sent a note home about the need for "more appropriate lyrics" for future performances, they'd had a schoolwide conference about it, complete with a child psychologist from Greenwich on hand to answer any questions the kids might have had about what constituted a toot-toot and who was allowed to touch theirs.

"Don't mess with my toot-toot," I sang, piloting the minivan into a parking spot. "Don't mess with my toot-toot. I know you have another woman. So don't mess with my toot-toot."

I did feel a twinge as I climbed out of the driver's seat in the town park's parking lot, wondering what kind of morally deficient opportunist would leverage a neighbor's murder to improve her social standing. I wasn't even sure it would help. I wasn't at the bottom of the Upchurch mother totem pole; I wasn't even on the pole. I could barely see the pole. If one woman announced that she was using recycled-paper diapers, the mother next to her was using cloth, and the woman next to her was using cloth diapers she'd personally sewn. If one mother was allowing her child to eat only organic food, then Mommy Number Two was feeding her kid organic vegetarian cuisine, and the mommy after her was an organic cruelty-free vegan who gave her children only cucumbers and carrots grown in her backyard, nourished with mulch she'd composted herself.

Not that the Tal-bots, as I sometimes called them, were empty-headed, muffin-baking Martha Stewart clones. Marybeth Coe, prior to Powell and his big sister Peyton, had been a bond trader. Carol Gwinnell had managed an art gallery in SoHo. Heather Leavitt had been in the arbitrage department at Goldman Sachs before retreating into the wonderful world of cloth diapers, handcrafted wooden toys, pesticide-free snacks, and scheduling every second of her children's lives for maximum enrichment. Preschoolers in Upchurch took tumbling classes and ice-skating lessons. They went to craft circles and learned tennis. They studied at least one instrument and two languages apiece. The girls went to dance class, the little boys played T-ball, and all children of both genders played soccer (with practice twice a week and games every Saturday) through the fall and the spring.

The parents behaved as if this were perfectly natural, as if, in fact, this were the only way they could imagine raising their young. I couldn't figure out why. Maybe after they'd delivered their babies, a malevolent lactation consultant had sprinkled Super-Mommy dust onto their pillows, or had bent and whispered into each sleeping ear, *From now on, the only thing you will care about is breast-feeding, toilet training, Mommy and Me Pilates mat classes, and whether the kindergarten's better at Greentown Friends or Upchurch Country Day.*

I didn't stand a chance. Even if I'd only had one child on which to lavish my energies and intellect, even if I were thin and pretty and motivated enough to do my makeup plus an hour of exercise every morning, and my idea of a really good time were arranging eensy-weensy cubes of cut-up tofu in the shape of the Cyrillic alphabet at mealtime. Even if I had the kind of kids who lent themselves naturally to such an endeavor.

The other Upchurch toddlers had never seen so much as a minute of television. They didn't have tantrums that made us late for school, or scream for Kentucky Fried Chicken, inevitably mispronounced as Kenfucky Fried Chicken, or occasion parent-teacher conferences because of their talent-show choices. Oh, well. I smoothed my pants and opened my door just as Lexi Hagen-Holdt pulled in beside me in her SUV, a brand-new model so high off the ground, and with so many oversized windows, that it looked like a mobile greenhouse. I looked at myself in the rearview mirror—chapped lips, shiny skin, unruly wavy brown hair, and too much excitement on my face. I tried to replace it with more appropriate sorrow before I opened the door.

"Oh my God!" Lexi said in her hoarse voice, extracting Hadley from his car seat without a single scream or struggle with a recalcitrant bucker. "Did you hear?" She settled the toddler on one slim hip, tossed her streaked, straightened hair over her shoulder, and pulled her pristine diaper bag from the snack-cracker-free carpet beneath the car seat. "I watched the news for hours last night, and I still can't believe it!"

Lexi walked briskly into the park, and I followed her as my kids scattered, the boys in the direction of the metal-and-plastic climbing structure and Sophie for the swings. I sat down on the bench that in my post-baby suburban life had replaced the popular girls' table in the cafeteria, a bench where I'd never dared sit before, and I waited until I was sure all the mothers could hear me before I ducked my head modestly and said, with just the right tremor in my voice, "I found her."

"Oh, no," murmured Carol Gwinnell. I saw Sukie Sutherland and Marybeth Coe hurry over to the bench. Marybeth's eyes were red, and Sukie's hair was swept into a hasty ponytail.

"Tell us everything," Lexi said, patting my shoulder sympathetically and almost certainly leaving bruises. Lexi wore what I'd come to think of as the Upchurch mommy uniform: a snug (but not slutty) long-sleeved T-shirt topped with a cardigan or a suede jacket; pressed, boot-cut wool trousers; shoes that were styled like sneakers but were made of suede and nylon mesh and cost about three hundred bucks.

I took a deep breath. "Kitty called me Wednesday night to ask if I could bring the kids for lunch."

"You two were friends?" asked Carol Gwinnell, her earrings jingling.

I shook my head, wondering why she'd asked. These women saw me in the park or the library or the school parking lot every day. They had to know that Kitty hadn't been my friend any more than they were.

"So why was she calling you?" asked Sukie Sutherland.

"I don't know," I said, digging the toes of my grimy sneakers into a pile of crimson leaves. "I have no idea."

There were more questions. The ladies wanted details. She was in the kitchen? On her front or her back? Was the door unlocked? Had anything been stolen? How did she look? Had the police said anything? Were there any leads? Was this a random crime, or someone with a grudge? What were the police doing? Was the family offering a reward? And what about Kitty's daughters?

"They're at my house," said Sukie. Sukie and I had been struggling for cordiality ever since the day we'd met, when she'd told me her kids were named Tristan and Isolde, and I'd laughed, thinking she was kidding, and she wasn't. "Philip didn't think they should spend the night in the house where . . . you know." She tugged at her ponytail. "Where it happened. He's taking them to his parents' house tomorrow."

"Do you know the Cavanaughs well?" I asked.

Sukie shrugged. "We're neighbors, and the girls are in Tristan's class at Country Day."

"Do you have any idea who could have . . ." I lowered my voice as I saw that all of our kids were within earshot. "You know."

Sukie shook her head. Her big brown eyes were shiny. "The police talked to me, but I don't think I was much help. I bet," she murmured, flicking an invisible bit of lint from her long-sleeved pink T-shirt, "that it might have something to do with her job."

"Wait . . ." said Carol.

"What?" asked Lexi.

"Kitty had a job?" I asked. This was a shocker. As far as I knew, none of the Upchurch mommies had jobs.

"What was it?" asked Lexi, easing her shoulders in circles, probably already planning her afternoon workout. "What'd she do?"

"She was a writer," Sukie said. "A ghostwriter."

"For who?" I asked.

"Do you guys ever read *Content*?" Sukie asked. Everyone nodded. So did I, even though the truth was that I didn't really read *Content.* My husband and I subscribed, as did practically every person I knew of a certain age, class, and degree of education. Every week I'd mean to read it, but the issues full of cutting-edge postmodern fiction written by twenty-three-year-olds, cartoons that required careful deliberation before you'd get the joke—provided there was one—and political exposés about countries I couldn't find on the map would end up stacked underneath the coffee table gathering dust until, in a fit of guilt, I'd toss them into the recycling bin. "You know that column 'The Good Mother'?"

"Laura Lynn Baird's column?" I asked.

"Laura Lynn Baird's byline," said Sukie. "Kitty was the one who actually wrote it." She smoothed her ponytail and looked at us. "It was all over the Internet this morning."

Like I had time to get online. Like I could even remember where in the house my laptop was located.

"I can't believe it," Marybeth Coe exclaimed. I couldn't either. Laura Lynn Baird was a conservative bomb-chucker, a telegenic blonde with a pageant queen's smile, a sailor's vocabulary, and politics that made Pat Buchanan look like a moderate. It had been big news when the normally left-leaning *Content* had hired her. "We're looking for writers to shake things up," the editor in chief, one Joel Asch, had told one of the morning news shows that Ben taped religiously and made me suffer through before we went to sleep. "Laura Lynn Baird is possessed of that rare combination: a fine mind and a witty, engaging voice," he'd said. He'd sounded, I'd thought at the time, mildly surprised to discover those two qualities coexisting in a woman.

"The Good Mother" appeared every month, but I'd only read it once or twice because it made me so angry I could feel my blood pressure rising with each word. The good mother, according to Laura Lynn, was one who gratefully retreated to "the sanctuary of hearth and home" after the birth of her children and wouldn't venture forth again until her offspring had attained the age of majority. Laura Lynn was opposed to mothers who "warehoused their children in day care," critical of "affluent, educated women, so-called feminists, bored with the routines of domestic life, hiring dark-skinned immigrants to care for their babies, mouthing platitudes about sisterhood while paying them under the table." As far as I knew, she hadn't yet expressed her opinion of mothers who hired the occasional sitter for a Saturday night, but I could bet that she wasn't a fan.

"Kitty wrote that stuff?" I asked.

Sukie nodded.

"Did she believe it?"

Sukie shrugged. "She wrote it. That's all I know."

"Did anyone else know that Laura Lynn Baird has a ghostwriter? Before it hit the Internet?"

Sukie's face was unreadable as she fiddled with the strap of her diaper bag. "I don't know," she said. "But the police asked me the exact same thing."

The mommies murmured uneasily, digesting this surprise. I don't know whether they were more shocked to learn that Kitty had written for someone as infamous as Laura Lynn or that one of us had worked outside the house at all.

"How is Philip?" asked Carol Gwinnell.

"I saw him in the police station yesterday," I said. "He seemed pretty shaken up."

"Well, why wouldn't he be?" asked Lexi.

"Philip's lived in Upchurch forever," Sukie said.

"Old family," said Carol Gwinnell.

"He was the best-looking guy in my sister's class at Upchurch High," Sukie said with a little smile. "We actually dated a little bit. A million years ago."

Lexi squinted toward the swing set, holding baby Brierly against her chest in a brightly colored handwoven Guatemalan sling. "Hadley?" she called. Her voice had an edge, and her rosy cheeks were more flushed than normal. "Hadley?" She swung around wildly. "He was right over by the slide a minute ago . . ."

All of us got to our feet, and I looked around instinctively for my own brood, exhaling when I saw Sam and Jack bobbing up and down on a seesaw and Sophie singing to herself on a swing.

"Mommy!" Hadley waved at his mother from the other side of the picket fence. Lexi sprinted across the playground and scooped her son into her arms.

"Don't!" she said, hugging him hard. "Don't you scare me like that!"

Hadley, who'd probably just wandered off to pick his nose in private, stared up at his mother, then burst into tears.

"I thought you were lost!" Lexi said as Hadley wailed. We gathered around her, patting her back, telling her it was okay, that we were all safe, that everything would be fine. I don't think any of us believed it. Ten minutes later trick or treating had officially been canceled. We'd agreed to have a party at Carol's house instead, said our goodbyes, gotten into our air bag–equipped, steel-reinforced cars, and driven our children back home.

FOUR

My cell phone rang as I was tossing two bags of instant rice into the microwave.

"Hello?"

"Birdie?" The voice on the other end was tentative and quiet. My father, Roger Klein, had always been more confident with his instrument than with words. When he played his oboe, his tone was the purest I'd ever heard, but his voice could have belonged to a fourteen-year-old schoolboy with a crush. He still called me by my little-girl nickname, and it always made my heart melt a little.

"Hi, Dad." I slammed the microwave door, hit the buttons, grabbed plates from the cupboard and paper napkins from the drawer, and looked into the family room, where the kids were happily entranced by *Bob the Builder,* and hopefully would be for another eighteen minutes.

"How are you doing?" he asked. "Have they caught anyone yet?"

I ripped open a bag of Shake 'n Bake. "Not that I know of."

"Ten-ten WINS had a story about it. Her name was Kiki?"

"Kitty," I said, cracking eggs one-handed. "Kitty Cavanaugh. And guess what? She was a ghostwriter for Laura Lynn Baird!"

"Who?"

I sighed and grabbed a package of chicken. "You know, she's one of those blond conservatives who's always shouting at someone on

CNN. She's got a column in *Content* called 'The Good Mother,' and Kitty was the one who actually wrote it."

Roger wasn't impressed. "Are you being careful?" he asked. "Are you using your alarm and locking the doors?"

I slid the chicken into the oven, kicked the door with my foot, pulled the rice out of the microwave, and surveyed the refrigerator for a vegetable my kids might actually eat. "We're being careful, Dad. And I'm fine."

"Do the police have any suspects?"

"Not as far as I know. Maybe it was someone who was after Laura Lynn. People hated her."

After we'd gotten home from the park, I'd planted the kids in front of a DVD, swallowed my guilt, and spent ten minutes online. My first Google query had yielded no fewer than ten thousand hits for Laura Lynn Baird. Some of them were approving posts from hard-core fans. Others—many, many others—were from weblogs and online magazines whose authors had actively and publicly wished for her demise. "Or maybe Laura Lynn's the killer. Every time I saw her on TV, she looked like she was two seconds away from biting somebody's ankle. Maybe Kitty got uppity," I guessed. "Maybe she said that she thought drug dealers should actually have trials before being sent to the electric chair."

My father laughed. I considered a bag of baby carrots in the vegetable crisper. If I dumped enough ranch dressing on them, I might get lucky.

"Listen, Kate," said my father. "I've got a concert tonight, but I could rent a car and drive up afterwards."

And do what? I wondered, putting the dirty dishes into the sink. *Use your oboe to beat murderers back from my door?* "Nah, we're fine. Ben's coming back tomorrow afternoon."

"Daddy's coming home!" cheered Jack and Sam, racing into the kitchen, wearing jeans and striped shirts from the Old Navy clearance rack, waving plastic swords at each other.

"You should call your mother," my father said.

"And where might I find Reina these days?"

He cleared his throat. "Still in Torino. I faxed her the clippings about the murder, and I know she's worried too."

Then why hasn't she called? I thought but didn't say. Instead, I promised I'd try ringing her in Italy when I had a free moment. I said goodbye, hung up, clicked *Bob the Builder* into oblivion over the boys' shrieks of protest, and supervised hand washing for dinner.

FIVE

The earliest thing I remember is my parents singing together. My father would be at the piano, which was draped with a lace scarf and covered with gold-framed pictures of the divas: Callas, Tebaldi, Nellie Melba, and my mother, of course. I'd be belly-down underneath the piano on the pink and ivory fringed rug, with my coloring books and my crayons. My mother would stand behind him, one hand resting on his shoulder. She'd sing Mozart arias with her heavy eyelids half-closed, pianissimo, the kind of vocalization, she told me, that was hardest for the soprano to master. Even when Reina sang softly, her voice was bigger than I could ever be, huge and rich and thrilling, a living thing that pushed at the walls and the ceilings and took up all the space in the room.

I could feel her voice, and my father's admiration: love and lust. I couldn't name it at four years old, or six or eight, but by the time I was ten or so, I knew enough to slip out of the living room after the first song. I'd lock the door of my bedroom, flop facedown with my book, plug my headphones into my ears, and blast Blondie and Pat Benatar, but I could still hear them: the notes vibrating in the overheated air, and then the silence, more intimate than if I'd actually caught them doing it. *"Mi chiamano Mimi,"* she would sing—her favorite aria, one she'd never performed, a part for a lyric soprano, not a coloratura, the ones who sing the highest parts and some of the showiest ones. Still, I knew, my mother dreamed of playing Mimi, of dying beautifully every night on stage. *"Il perchè non so."*

My mother, Reina, was born Rachel Danhauser in Kankakee, Illinois. She renamed herself when she moved to New York City at twenty-one with nothing but two hundred dollars and every recording Maria Callas had ever made. (She also had a full scholarship to Juilliard, but that's precisely the kind of detail my mother tends to leave out of her life story, especially when she's telling it to reporters.)

My parents met at Juilliard, where my father was teaching and my mother was a graduate student. I've imagined the scene many times: my father, a thirty-six-year-old bachelor, hair already thinning, glasses perpetually askew over his mild brown eyes, having achieved as much fame and fortune as any oboe player can hope for, because while there are superstar singers, virtuoso violinists, millionaire pianists who play solo performances to sold-out concert halls around the world, there has never really been a breakout oboe player, unless you stretch and count Kenny G, which my father does not. And there was Reina, her five feet nine inches enhanced by three-inch heels, her hair a tumble of dark brown curls; towering, magnificent Reina, sheet music clutched to her chest, folding pointed crimson-painted nails into a fist and knocking at his rehearsal room door, asking, sweetly, if he could accompany her. (I can even imagine them consummating their love beneath a sign reading PLEASE DO NOT EMPTY YOUR SPIT VALVE HERE, but only after I've had a few drinks.)

I was born the summer after my parents' first wedding anniversary, and after forty-eight hours in Lenox Hill Hospital, they brought me home, to the rent-controlled prewar apartment building on Amsterdam Avenue that, since time immemorial, had been inhabited almost exclusively by musicians. Leases were handed down like heirlooms. A bassoonist leaving for the Boston Symphony would bequeath his two-bedroom to the new second-chair cellist; a tenor departing for London would hand down his studio to the new assistant concertmaster at the Met.

The air in our building was full of music. Fugues and concerti poured through the heating vents, arpeggios and glissandos filled the hallways. As you rode up in the elevator, you would hear the trill of a flute, or a mezzo-soprano working on one phrase of an aria; the brassy *wah-wah* of trumpets, the mournful, lowing notes of a cello . . . but it had been years since a baby's cries had joined the choir.

The neighbors must have gathered around me, gazing down at a baby wrapped in a pink blanket, looking for signs of the talent I undoubtedly possessed. *Those fingers,* Mrs. Plansky the clarinetist might have said. *A pianist, maybe?*

Look at her lips, my father would interject. *Woodwinds. Maybe the French horn.*

No, no, Reina would say, clutching me proudly. *Have you heard her cry? The notes she can hit? E above high C, I swear it!* And she'd beam down at me, false eyelashes fluttering. (Somehow I know that even two days after giving birth, Reina would have been wearing her false eyelashes.) *My daughter is going to sing,* she would say, and all of them would nod almost unconsciously in agreement.

A singer, they would repeat, like two dozen fairy godmothers giving their blessing. *A singer.*

It would have been easier if I hadn't been able to sing at all, if I'd been completely tone-deaf, if I couldn't have carried a tune in a bucket. The hell of it was, I was good, just not good enough. I had a fine voice for high school choirs and college glee clubs and, eventually, for winning fifty bucks' worth of free drinks singing karaoke at the local bar. I had an ideal environment, and the best instruction that could be bought or bartered for. But to my mother's eternal dismay, I didn't have an opera voice.

My singing career, such as it was, ended when I was fourteen, two weeks before I would have auditioned for the High School of Performing Arts.

"Can you have your mother come up for a minute?" Mrs. Minheizer asked at the end of the lesson. Alma Minheizer was seventy-two, small and pink-cheeked, with a corona of fluffy white hair and a wall full of framed photographs of her own performances around the world. She'd been one of my mother's teachers, fifteen years before, when Reina had first moved to New York. I went downstairs to fetch my mother, who was home, for once. She'd made a big point of telling me that she'd turned down Queen of the Night in San Francisco in order to be home for my audition.

"What's this about?" she demanded from where she was posed on the couch, perfectly lipsticked, eyebrows plucked into dramatic arches and glossy curls piled high, with a lap full of sheet music and her calendar. She'd been chatting to her agent—in Italian, naturally—and wasn't happy to be interrupted. I shrugged, walking with her to the elevator, holding Mrs. Minheizer's door, and leaving it open so that I could make out most of what they were saying. I slumped against the wall, then sat on the floor, trying to make myself invisible. Easier said than done. I was five feet eight inches tall, with my mother's figure—big breasts that I disguised under shapeless sweaters and baggy sweatshirts, heavy hips that no amount of dieting or aerobics would ever diminish, my mother's full lips and thick curls. She wore hers flowing over her shoulders, or arranged in a complicated updo. I wore mine hanging in my face, which did a pretty fair job of disguising the zits on my forehead. I had Reina's looks (or I would, when my skin cleared up), but I didn't have anything even close to her sound. I knew it, and Mrs. Minheizer knew it too.

". . . never be better than adequate," I heard her say. I sank down further on the carpeted hallway floor, giddy and queasy with a mixture of shame and relief. Someone had finally told Reina what I'd suspected, what a dozen other teachers had hinted at but hadn't h[illegible] the courage to come out and say . . . and because it w[illegible] heizer, who'd been, in her day, one of the l[illegible] world, Reina would have to listen.

"Alma, that's absurd," my mother said. I could imagine her lifting her chin in an imperious gesture, and the gold and ruby bracelets she wore clinking on one plump wrist.

". . . know how hard this life can be. If I had a daughter—"

"Well, you *don't.* I *do.*" Even back then, Reina spoke primarily in italics.

"If I had a daughter," my teacher continued, her voice smooth and quiet and absolutely serious, "and she could do anything else—write, or paint, or teach, or work in a bank—I'd tell her to do that. You know what our life is like! There are a hundred singers for every slot in the chorus, never mind the principals. If you're not the best of the best, there's no place for you."

There was a pause. Some murmuring. "So she'll practice," said my mother.

"She does practice," Mrs. Minheizer said. "I've never had a more diligent student than Kate."

I could picture my mother dismissing my diligence with a wave of her hand. "She can always practice harder." She slammed Mrs. Minheizer's door harder than she had to and strode down the hall, white lace sleeves fluttering, lavender chiffon skirt swishing, in a cloud of perfume and indignation.

"What'd she want?" I asked, pushing myself to my feet.

Reina made a dismissive noise in the back of her cosseted throat. "You need to practice harder," she said.

"Mom . . ." I took a deep breath to steady myself while she pressed the button for the elevator. "I don't want to sing anymore."

She stared at me, black eyebrows aloft, as if she'd never heard those words before and didn't know what they meant. "I'm sorry?" Her stiff eyelashes fluttered. "I beg your pardon?"

"Mom, I hate it," I said. This wasn't exactly true. I liked crooning Bessie Smith and Billie Holiday songs in the privacy of my bed-[illegible]m. What I didn't like was the endless cycle of reaching and fi[illegible]ort and trying harder and falling short again, the way I'd [illegible]nd watch while Mrs. Minheizer would compose her face carefully and pause before saying anything. In that pause, I'd feel her weighing her words, parsing the difference between what she wanted to tell me and what she would actually say. I'd lived with the real deal long enough to know that I was a pretender. I'd heard my mother. I'd heard her students too, heavy-hipped, double-chinned girls, unfashionable and unremarkable until they opened their mouths and their voices were so ethereal, so transcendent that, like magic, they became beautiful.

"I'm no good," I mumbled.

"Kate, I won't *hear* this."

"You know I'm not," I said, the words tumbling out, loud and reckless in the high-ceilinged hallway. "I don't have it. If I go to the auditions at Performing Arts, they're going to laugh at me, and if they take me, it'll just be because I'm your daughter."

My mother's face softened for an instant, probably because I'd paid her a compliment. Then she jabbed the button for the elevator again with one crimson-tipped finger. "We'll find you another teacher."

"Mom, I've been through every teacher in the building!"

"There are other buildings," she said grimly. The elevator doors slid open. She got on. I stood in the hallway.

"Kate."

"No."

"Kate, you're being—"

"No."

She must have seen something in my face that convinced her I wasn't kidding. The doors slid shut on her disappointment, but by the time I'd walked down the stairs, Reina had regrouped. She stood in the doorway, gave me a tremulous smile, and held something toward me like a peace offering. I wasn't sure whether to laugh or cry when I looked down and saw my father's third-best oboe in her hands. "You have *talent,*" she called toward my back, as I pushed past her and half ran down the hall to my bedroom, where I flopped on my bed and opened my copy of *The Mists of Avalon.* "Kate, you *do*! And maybe you won't be a singer, but you shouldn't give up on *music*!"

I won the battle but lost the war. I canceled my audition at Performing Arts with the promise that I'd continue with my voice lessons until I left for college. Reina and Roger grudgingly enrolled me in Pimm, an all-girls school on the Upper East Side that was, I later realized, chosen because it was the only other high school they'd ever heard of (and the only reason they'd heard of it was that a senior there had been killed in a rough-sex-and-cocaine romp in Central Park that had been all over the headlines the year before). Pimm was full of sleek girls with trust funds who'd heave up their celery sticks in the echoing marble bathrooms every day after lunch. They'd all known one another since their preschool days and weren't in a big hurry to welcome a brunette, trust-fundless interloper who wore a size in the double digits and never made more than the occasional foray into their top two pastimes—shoplifting and bulimia.

I pretended not to care, but I did, of course, especially when I would watch my parents making music together. I pretended not to mind that my mother was out of the country more than she was in it, but of course I longed for her, even when I was fifteen and required by law to sneer at anything that came out of my mother's mouth.

"I'll be back by June," Reina told me the afternoon I arrived home from school and found her in the bedroom with her scuffed leather trunks with their brass padlocks open, getting ready for a three-month stint at the Staatsopera.

"Vienna?" I asked, hating the sound of my voice, hating the way I looked like her and how it seemed such a cruel joke that the instant I opened my mouth to sing, the best I could hope for was "adequate."

"Vienna," she confirmed. Her dimples flashed as she smiled, and her hair gleamed: she'd had the color touched up that afternoon, the way she always did before a long trip. "They've given me a contract for three operas, and you know how rare that is!"

"Three months is a long time," I said, my voice cracking. "You'll miss the school musical." We were doing *West Side Story,* with boys brought in from Episcopal, and I'd landed the part of Anita, a coup due mostly, I figured, to Pimm's lack of altos. But somehow the low-cut blouse and long black wig had given me a confidence I'd never felt in all my years of voice lessons. I'd been imagining opening night, my mother handing me a dozen red roses, her eyes wide with astonished approval. *Kate, you're really good!* she'd say.

Reina sat down on the satin coverlet on her bed, rubbed a scuff mark off the toe of one glossy black leather boot, then took my hands in hers.

"I'll miss you so much, you have no idea, but I have to do this now." She got to her feet and kept packing, boots drumming against the hardwood floor, skirt belling around her, and as she piled clothes and books and compact discs into her trunks, she explained about biology, about time, about how a singer has only so many years before her tone and control start to go. "First I'll lose my flexibility, and then . . ." She shuddered, a grimace of distaste pursing her painted red lips. "Character roles and fund-raising."

"Maybe you could come back for the weekend," I suggested. "For *West Side Story.*"

"You know what flying does to my voice," she said. I hung my head. No Reina on opening night, no Reina for the Spring Ball, which I actually had a date for.

She snapped the latch of the trunk shut, then gathered her perfume bottles on the dresser, her long nails clicking against their cut-glass sides. Then she brushed my bangs out of my eyes. I squirmed away. I wanted her to hold me. I didn't want her to touch me. I didn't want her to leave. I didn't want her to ever come back.

The next morning I ignored her when she tapped on my door at six a.m., and pretended not to hear her whispering my name. I lay facedown on my bed, a copy of *Lace* under my left cheek, and thought about whether things could have ever been different. If I'd worn the makeup she'd bought for me, the soft leather boots and suede coat instead of baggy jeans and sweatshirts, would she have stayed? If I'd called myself Maria Katerina instead of Kate, if I'd practiced until sheer force of will had transformed my voice, my instrument, into something rare and beautiful, could it have kept her on the same continent as my father and me?

I pushed myself off the bed and looked down at the street, my forehead resting on the cool windowpane, my knees digging into the milk crates where I kept my novels, chewing at the ends of my ponytail as a limousine pulled up to the curb and my mother walked out the door. I watched as the driver spent fifteen minutes wedging all of her luggage into the trunk. I saw my father kiss her, then step back into the dark little doorway, handing her over to the driver, and her future: another airplane, another country, another opera, another three months of dying every night. The driver held the door. My mother shaded her eyes and looked up at my window. *I love you,* she mouthed. I bit down hard on my hair as she blew me a kiss.

SIX

When I walked out onto the porch and into another perfect Connecticut afternoon the next day to collect the newspapers, I heard a car roaring down our cul-de-sac. My heart lifted as a bright red Porsche Boxster veered into the driveway. It was, I thought, the perfect car for a woman who drove maybe once a month. Badly.

"Janie!"

"So much for safety in the suburbs," said my best friend, scowling at me from behind her designer sunglasses. She wore a chocolate brown suede skirt that ended just above her knees, a soft cowl-neck cashmere sweater, and bright red cowgirl boots. Her hair was long and light brown streaked with honey and amber, her small mouth was glossed a shiny pink, her close-set eyes were artfully enhanced with liner and mascara, and her handbag and earrings probably cost more than my first year of college.

She sauntered up the stairs and peered into the house. "Hello, rug rats."

"Aunt Janie!" said Sam, who loved Janie.

"Janie!" crowed Jack, straining forward with his arms outstretched. Jack loved Janie even more than Sam did.

"Hello," said Sophie, air-kissing Janie's left and right cheeks in the manner of socialities the world over. She loved Janie more than both of her brothers put together, but even at four, she was too sophisticated for gushing. I led Janie and the kids into the kitchen, where we were working on a Welcome Home, Daddy banner to hang over the front door.

"Ooh, craft time!" Janie said, picking up a crayon and examining it like it was an artifact from another planet. She brushed glitter off a chair and took a seat. "Can you guess who brought you presents?"

"Aunt Janie!" shrieked the kids.

"Do you know who loves you more than your mother and father put together?"

"Aunt Janie!" they shouted.

"Guess who's having dinner at Per Se Friday night with a guy she's been out with three times and suspects might wear a toupee?"

"Aunt Janie!" said Sam and Jack. Sophie crinkled her nose. "What's a doupee?"

"Pray you never have to find out." Janie tapped Sophie's nose with the crayon and produced three gift-wrapped boxes from her Birkin bag.

The boys got remote-control race cars that they promptly began racing across the kitchen floor. Sophie got another custom-made outfit for her Uglydoll. Uglydoll was a rectangular blob of blue fur with buck teeth, yellow eyes, and small, protuberant ears that Janie had given to Sophie when she was born. I watched in awe as Sophie unwrapped a miniature cowboy hat, a lasso, bandanna, tiny cowboy boots, and a pair of chaps. "Chapter two hundred and thirty-seven," Janie growled in the gravelly southern drawl she'd assigned the toy years ago. "In which I ride a mechanical bull to glory."

Sophie giggled with delight and ran upstairs to dress her doll in his new finery.

"Got anything to drink around here?" Janie asked, rummaging through the frozen peas and chicken parts until she found the vodka she'd left on her last visit. The refrigerator yielded an empty carton of orange juice—a carton I swore had been full that morning. I waited until Janie's back was turned, mixed her a vodka and Pedialyte, and led her into the living room.

"So let's review," Janie said. She sank into the couch. (The decorator Ben had hired turned out to have had a vastly different view of what the word *overstuffed* meant than I did. I'd been thinking something comfortable in nubbly, washable linen. I'd ended up with a nine-foot sectional with taupe cushions so wide and deep you had to practically swim your way out of them.) Janie took a long swallow of her drink and winced, but luckily didn't ask me what it was. "You abandon me in Manhattan in favor of this hellhole."

"Give it credit," I said, smoothing the tassels on a throw pillow. "It's a hellhole with an excellent school district."

"The women here are a bunch of dopes who can't stop reproducing—and talking about it," Janie continued with a shudder, "like the whole world wants to hear about their sore nipples."

I made a noncommittal noise, knowing what had my friend so freaked out. On her first visit to Upchurch, Janie had been cornered at the nursery school craft fair by Marybeth Coe, who'd described to her at great length how she was raising her newborn son without diapers by "getting in touch with his natural rhythms" and placing him atop what had formerly been a salad bowl when she sensed he was ready. Janie had proclaimed herself scarred for life by the experience. It had taken her weeks, she'd told me, before she could eat vinaigrette again.

"You're at least twenty miles from the nearest Saks, not to mention good deli," she continued. "Oh, that reminds me . . ." She rummaged in her bag and tossed me a gift-wrapped knish. I opened it up and took a big, blissful bite as the rant continued.

"You ditch me for bucolic little Bumblefuck, this allegedly safe haven, and the next thing you know, you're stumbling over dead bodies."

"I didn't stumble over her, I found her."

"Same difference," said Janie, shiny lips pursed in distaste.

I shrugged. It was so good to have Janie around that finding a dead body almost seemed like it wasn't too high a price to pay. "Can you stay?"

"Well, I think I should," Janie proclaimed, taking another swallow of her drink. "I don't think you guys are safe here all by yourself."

"And you're going to defend us?"

She reached into her bag again. "Mace," she said, showing me the spray can. "Straightening iron. All-day lipstick. BlackBerry. If the killer shows up, I'll just CC him on all my edit memos and bore him to death."

"Sounds like a plan," I said.

Janie and I had met nine years ago, when we'd both landed interviews to be fact-checkers at *New York Review,* the nation's preeminent literary magazine (at least, that's what the masthead said).

"In here," whispered the mousy woman administering the test. There were two desks in the stuffy little room. The one closest to the door was occupied by a slender girl in a chic black suit that, unlike mine, probably had not come from the clearance rack at Century 21. She was bent over her pages so that I could only see the tip of her nose and her beautifully streaked hair.

The woman handed me five paper-clipped pages, two blue pencils, a dictionary, and a thesaurus. "Use standard proofreading marks, please," she whispered. "You have thirty minutes."

I sat behind the desk on a chair covered in stained gray fabric, tucked the novel I'd been reading on the subway into my purse, and tried not to be disappointed. I'd majored in English at Columbia and then, because that didn't make me quite unemployable enough, I'd picked up a master's degree in American literature and done all of the course work toward a Ph.D. Ever since leaving Columbia, I'd been temping in law offices, living at home, sending off resumes to any magazine that I thought would have me, and dreaming of writing a book of my own without actually doing any writing. On Friday nights I'd go to the library and take out a dozen novels from the new release shelf to last me through the week. On Sunday nights my father and I, and Reina, if she was home, ordered in Chinese. I'd date every once in a while—an SAT tutor I'd met in the video store, an MBA candidate whose mother played bassoon with my dad. It was a quiet kind of existence, not unhappy, but not particularly exciting. Sometimes at night I'd turn off my lamp and lie motionless in my bed, in the darkness, listening to the sounds of buses and taxis on the street, the sound of voices calling and laughing, and I would think, *I am waiting for my real life to begin.*

I wiped my hands on my skirt and looked around the *Review*'s offices. I'd expected something more impressive from the magazine that had published some of the most important fiction of my lifetime: a cozy, dimly lit sanctuary with mahogany desks and secret nooks, hidden corners and shabby armchairs where the geniuses would sit with their deep thoughts and their tumblers of whiskey. Instead, I'd found a falafel cart guarding the door on Forty-fourth Street and, up on the seventeenth floor, grids of humming fluorescent lights and cheap-looking blond wood desks, which lent the space all the romance and mystery of a podiatrist's office.

The test turned out to be an essay on the geography and climate of a place called Pago Pago. Was that even a real place? Was this story something the *Review* would publish? Had published?

The girl with the great hair pushed her chair back from her desk. "In *Beauty and the Beast,*" she asked, "did Beauty ever sleep with the Beast?"

I was nonplussed. "Is that what your test is about? *Beauty and the Beast?*"

"Nope. Pago Pago. I was just wondering. Do you know?"

I set my pencil down. "The fairy tale or the TV show?"

"TV show." She was petite, I saw, with close-set hazel eyes and a lower-case letter C of a nose that I recognized as the work of Dr. Kornbluth, an Upper East Side plastic surgeon who'd performed nose jobs on at least half a dozen members of my high school's graduating class. The nose was set in a lively, mobile, intelligent face, with a flashing grin that promised mischief.

"Sorry, I never watched it."

"Oh, well," she sighed. She kicked her crocodile pumps onto the floor and cracked all the joints in her toes. I gave her a look that I hoped combined cordiality and *please be quiet and let me concentrate.* I still couldn't believe I'd landed this interview, and I wasn't going to let myself get distracted. A few minutes went by. "In Pago Pago," I read, "the median temperature is seventy-two degrees." *Median or mean?* I wondered, grabbing my dictionary. *And was that different than average?*

"If you had a gay bar," the other girl mused out loud, "what would you call it?"

"I. Um. I'd have to give it some thought."

She twirled a lock of honey-streaked hair around her blue pencil. "I'd call mine The Glistening Pickle," she said.

"That's a good one."

"Or The Bent Whisker," she said. "That'd be good too. Or—"

"Okay!" I said heartily. "Well, listen, this is very interesting, but I really need to concentrate."

"Why?"

I set my pencil down and took a deep breath. Maybe this was part of the test. Maybe there were cameras hidden in the ceilings. Maybe this weirdo was a plant, and somewhere down the hall, the *Review* editors were watching to see how I'd respond. If I handled the situation with dignity and aplomb, I'd be whisked through a secret passageway to the real offices, where John Updike and Philip Roth would offer me whiskey and congratulations, and two first-class tickets to Pago Pago.

"Because I really want this job," I said, speaking slowly and distinctly, in case the ceiling was listening.

"Really?" she asked, as if the concept of wanting a job was novel to her.

"Yes. Don't you want to work here?"

"I guess," she sighed, twirling more hair around the pencil. "My father thinks I should find something. He says it's a disgrace that my only job's been my nose job," she said, touching the feature in question. "But the way I see it, any job I get is just a job that's been taken away from someone who really needs one." She smiled at me brightly. "Like you!"

"Yes. Right. Well . . ." I bent back over my pages. *Tuna canneries provide the principal employment in Pago Pago.*

"He's the Carpet King," said the girl.

I looked up with my hands balled into fists.

"My father," she said, and cracked her toes again. "Sy Segal. The Carpet King."

My hands unclenched as the name registered. "Doesn't he own this magazine?"

"I think so," she said. She'd slipped her pumps onto her hands and was making them dance a jig across her desk. "Or maybe it's that he owns the company that owns this magazine. It's hard to keep track."

"So he could just tell them to give you a job."

"And you too!" She grinned, pulled her hands out of her shoes, and wheeled her chair over to my desk so we could shake. "I'm Janie Segal."

"Kate Klein," I said. "And I should really get back to work."

"Oh, sure. Of course. Go right ahead," Janie said.

There was silence. I picked up my pencil again. *Tutuila's harbor is surrounded by dramatic mountains which plunge straight into the sea.*

"But first can I ask you a question?" Janie inquired. "Why do you want to work here?"

"Please! Are you kidding? It's . . ." I breathed the name with the reverence instilled by nine years at Columbia and an equal amount of time spent poring over its annual Young Fiction Issue with alternating waves of jealousy and awe rolling over me. "It's the *Review*!"

"Feh," said Janie. "I'd rather read *People.* In fact, I'd rather work at *People.*" She fixed me with her hazel eyes. "Do you think they're hiring?"

"Um . . ."

"Wait!" She stabbed one finger in the air. "Idea!" She crossed the room to my desk and picked up the telephone with her manicured, long-fingered hand. "Yes, in New York City, the editorial offices for *People* magazine." While she was holding, she grabbed a memo pad. "Write down your phone number," she whispered. "Managing editor, please," she rapped into the telephone, and then paused. "Voice mail," she stage-whispered to me.

"You know, I really don't think we should be—"

She silenced me with one upraised hand. "Yes, hello, I'm calling from the offices of the *New York Review.* I've been working with two very fine researchers who, regrettably, we won't be able to hire. They're both experts in popular culture and modern celebrities and, as you know, we at the *Review* pride ourselves on never writing about any celebrity who isn't a politician or a dead transcendentalist."

"Oh, my God," I groaned, clutching Pago Pago to my breast.

"Their names are Jane Segal and Kate Klein, and their home telephone numbers are . . ." She recited our numbers. "Thank you in advance for your help," she said, and set the phone down. "There!" she said, looking pleased with herself. She picked up her purse and her coat.

"Aren't you going to finish?" I asked, pointing toward Pago Pago. A random sentence jumped off the page. *Until 1980, one could experience the views from the peak by taking an aerial tramway over the city harbor.* Was *tramway* one word or two? I didn't know. I wasn't sure I cared.

Janie gave me a pitying look that encompassed the dingy eggshell paint on the walls, the disreputable light brown carpeting, the water cooler gurgling in the corner like an old man with indigestion. "I think I'd rather die than work here."

"But . . . ," I spluttered. "Norman Mailer! Tom Wolfe! Saul Bellow! Jerzy Kosinski!"

There was a framed copy of the first two pages of *The Scarlet Letter* on the wall, the sole literary touch in the room. Janie stood on her tiptoes and used the reflection in the glass to reapply her lip gloss. "Last time I checked, they're all married."

"Jerzy Kosinski's actually dead."

"See? That's even worse." She smoothed her hair and picked up my coat and purse. "Come along, grasshopper. Let's blow this taco stand."

She reached for the doorknob. I sat back down defiantly, picked up my blue pencil, and circled the word *tramway.* "No," I said. "No thanks. You go ahead. I'm going to finish this."

"Kate," she said. Her voice held an edge of impatience, but her eyes were kind. "Look around. Ugly cubicles, pretension, and no single men. Do you really want to work here?"

I thought about it. All of my professors had spoken about the *Review* the way believers spoke about heaven, the way country music fans talked about Branson, the way my mother described the Met. My father would have been thrilled if I'd landed the job. But did I want to work as a fact-checker? I wasn't sure I'd ever considered the question, and when I did, the answer surprised me.

"No. Not really. No, I don't."

"Then come on!"

"I can't," I told her.

"Oh," she said. "Okay." She slowly buttoned her coat and started humming.

"Good luck," I said.

"Good luck to you too," she said, and started humming louder. Then she started singing. "When I was young . . . I never need-ed anyone. And making love was just for fun . . ." She shook her head sadly. "Those days are gone."

"Excuse me?"

"All by my-sellllf," she sang. Not softly. "Don't wanna be . . . alll by *my-self.*"

I couldn't help it. I started laughing. Her voice was beyond terrible, and she was loud, loud, loud. "Janie—"

"All! By! My! Self!" she sang at top volume. Someone knocked softly at the door. I doubted it was either John Updike or Philip Roth. "Excuse me. Could you keep it down in there?"

"All by myself," Janie sang mournfully. I put down my pencil, picked up my coat, and followed her out the door.

In my living room, years after we'd left the *Review* together, Janie stared at me with a familiar look of mischief in her eyes. "So where is Ben?"

"In California," I said. "Business trip. Home tomorrow." I picked her glass up and took a hasty swallow. Janie lifted her eyebrow. I looked back at her defiantly and drank some more.

"Is that post-murder-discovery nerves or something else?" Janie inquired.

"It's . . ." I cleared my throat. "Um. Evan McKenna."

Janie's expression darkened. "I thought we pinkie-swore never to speak his name again."

"We did, and while it pains me to break a pinkie swear, the thing is . . ." I held the little pillow against me and told her everything—how I'd found Evan's name in Kitty's kitchen, how the police had found his number on Kitty's caller ID.

Janie got so excited that she shoved herself out of the couch and started bouncing in her high heels. "Oh my God! What if he's the killer! Then he'll get the death penalty!" She whipped out her cell phone. "Does this stupid state even have the death penalty?"

"I'm not sure. But Janie—"

She shushed me and started to dial. "Sy knows someone in the governor's office." She stopped dialing and stared out my window. "I think it's the governor, actually. Maybe we can be the ones to pull the switch, or give him the lethal injection, or whatever!"

"Janie!" I grabbed the phone away from her. "Listen! I don't think Evan killed her."

"Oh." She frowned. "Then who did?" She sat back on the couch. "Maybe it was that Marybeth woman." She nodded, looking pleased with herself. "A woman who'd raise a child without diapers is capable of anything."

Sam and Jack came racing into the living room with Sophie wailing behind them. The boys, I saw, had used a bungee cord to strap Uglydoll in his western wear to the top of one of the cars. "Chapter two hundred and thirty-eight," growled Janie, "in which I am hijacked by a band of pint-sized ruffians."

I freed the doll, consoled Sophie, and sent the boys into the Uncooperative Corner, then glanced at the clock. Somehow, it had become five thirty, and I'd forgotten dinner.

"There's more. Kitty was a ghostwriter for Laura Lynn Baird."

Janie's eyes widened. "You're kidding me!"

I shook my head. "It was all over the Internet this morning."

"But not the magazines yet, right?" She scrambled for her phone again. "I shouldn't be surprised," she said. "Everyone's been saying that there's no way Laura Lynn could be doing everything she's been doing unless she cloned herself. Every time I turn on my TV, there she is, yap-yap-yapping about affirmative action or something. I always figured she was outsourcing her columns to some twenty-three-year-old in a think tank in Madras, not some mom in the suburbs." She caught her breath.

"Because no mom in the suburbs could string two sentences together," I said dryly.

"Present company excepted," said Janie. "God, this is a fabulous story. Fabulous." Her bobbed nose wrinkled as her editor's voice mail picked up. "Segal. Call me." She got to her feet, fingers already flexing for the keyboard. "Where's your computer?"

"Janie, listen to me." I pulled her back onto the couch. "Do you think you could get me an interview with Laura Lynn Baird?"

"Huh?" She gaped at me. "Why?"

"Because . . ." I took a deep breath and tried to think of what to tell her that would get me what I wanted. "Because if Evan's involved in this somehow—"

"Oh, no." Janie held up her hand and shook her head. "Oh, hell no. You wasted enough of your life on that man-shaped pile of dog poop. If it turns out he did it, I will lead the parade. And I'm making you be grand marshal." She paused thoughtfully. "Grand marshals get the good hats."

I tried again. "Maybe Laura Lynn knows something that she hasn't told the cops. And Kitty was my friend."

She glared at me. "You told me you didn't have any friends out here." She sniffled. "You said I was your one and only!"

Strike two.

"It's my community," I finally said. "My neighborhood. It's where my kids live."

Janie placed one hand gently on my shoulder. "When the pod people took over your body," she asked, "did it hurt?"

"Okay, you know why? Because there's a murderer running around, which even you have to admit is a little alarming, and you know what else? I'm bored." I stared at her defiantly, knowing that I'd just spoken the dirtiest word in the Upchurch lexicon. As far as my fellow mommies were concerned, saying you were bored was admitting to being about two steps away from drowning your babies in the bathtub, something so sinful and forbidden you could never 'fess up to it. But here I was, 'fessing. "I'm bored, and this murder, while horrifying, is also the single most interesting thing that's happened here since the Langdons next door broke ground for their guesthouse and cracked their septic tank. It's interesting, and I want to find out more."

Janie sat back, looking satisfied at last. "That's my girl," she said.

SEVEN

Once upon a time, there was a woman who'd lived in New York City, then moved to Connecticut with her baby and her husband—a woman not too different from me, or Kitty Cavanaugh. Except Laura Lynn Baird was famous, and she didn't have to deal with boredom. When her son was born, she'd kept working (although, paradoxically, much of that work seemed to involve flying around the country or appearing on television to tell other women that they were bad mothers if they had jobs that took them outside of the home).

I parked my minivan in front of 734 Old Orchard Lane in Darien, Connecticut, checked my lipstick in the rearview mirror, and tucked my bangs behind my ears. Janie had worked her magic, getting Laura Lynn on the phone with me. "H-hello," I'd stammered. It had been years since I'd interviewed anyone except a potential babysitter. I'd fumbled through the basics: I was working on a tribute to my departed neighbor and colleague, and I would be deeply appreciative if Laura Lynn, busy though she must be, could possibly spare—

Laura Lynn cut me off. "Ten o'clock, tomorrow morning. I can give you twenty minutes." Click.

The dashboard clock said 9:54. I pulled a sheaf of papers out of my bag. I'd printed every single one of "The Good Mother" columns, and I'd highlighted pertinent passages the night before, after

I'd put the kids to bed. "Feminism's Big Lie is a two-headed Hydra, a snake that whispers into the modern woman's ears that her own happiness is primary, that having it all is possible, and that both can be achieved without her children suffering, or even noticing," Laura Lynn Baird–slash–Kitty Cavanaugh had written. "The truth, as any woman who's honest with herself knows, is that children were meant to be raised by their mothers. In this case, and for a finite number of years, biology really is destiny. Shame on the woman who exchanges her role as the dispenser of good-night hugs, consoling kisses, and lullabies for the transitory pleasures and cocktail-party cred of the corner office and the fancy title. And pity the working-class child-care provider who doesn't realize that the real villain in her life isn't a stereotypical sexist pig, but the woman wearing recycled-fiber clothing, eating organic produce, and calling herself your sister even as she profits from your off-the-books, under-the-table toil."

Heady stuff. It was hard to imagine Kitty, with her pleasant smile and inoffensive chatter, writing it. I tucked the pages back in my bag, called home to make sure that nothing was burning or broken, and exited the car, making my way up Laura Lynn's crescent-shaped driveway, stepping onto her pillared porch, and knocking on the green front door. At ten on the dot, a tanned, bony hand snaked out of the six-inch gap between the door and the jamb, grabbed my sleeve, and pulled me inside.

"You're Kate Klein?" Laura Lynn Baird snapped.

"Yes," I said.

Laura Lynn had looked slim but imposing every time I'd seen her on television, gleefully trashing some Democratic congressman or feminist lawyer. In person, she was tiny, a flat-chested androgynous sprite the size of a starving fifth grader, clad in a pink Chanel suit with tufted cream trim at the hem of the skirt and on the jacket pockets. She had on cream-colored pumps, a double strand of pink pearls, and pearl and gold earrings. Her obligatory blond tresses, dyed the color of straw, had been blown out and sprayed until her entire head looked like it had been stuck under a broiler and crisped.

"Come," she instructed, tightening her grip on my arm, drawing me into a cloud of hairspray and sour coffee breath, and leading me into a living room, a high-ceilinged space sparsely furnished with a few pieces of leather and metal furniture as hard-edged as she was. "Sit." She pointed, and I perched on a corner of a white suede love seat. There was a trio of panel-style television sets hanging on the wall like paintings. They were flanked by floor-to-ceiling bookshelves filled with hardcovers. All the conservative heavy hitters were there: Ann Coulter and Peggy Noonan, Bill O'Reilly and Sean Hannity, the Michaels (Medved and Savage), and her fellow Lauras (Ingraham and Schlessinger).

I stared at the titles, blinking at the yellow Post-its stuck to the spine of each title, each bearing two numbers and the words "How High" and "How Long."

"The *New York Times* bestseller list," Laura said. "I like to keep track."

I looked around for the baby paraphernalia—the bouncy seats, the Exersaucer, a couch cushion stained with spit-up—but couldn't find any. I did, however, see a framed eight-by-ten of her father, Byron "Bo" Baird, posed in front of an American flag. Bo Baird, with iron-gray hair and a complementary steely gaze, had owned twenty-eight newspapers nationwide at the height of his powers, each of them more right-leaning than the next. He'd dined with presidents and advised senators before dropping dead at the age of seventy-eight in a bed he turned out to be sharing with a woman who, regrettably, was not his wife. I'd been in high school when it had happened, but I remembered the late-night talk show hosts having a field day. The rumors—never confirmed, but extremely persistent—were that not only had Bo expired on top of another woman, he'd been wearing her high heels at the time.

"I've got twenty minutes," Laura Lynn said, making a production of looking at the gold watch on one itty-bitty wrist. "And before we get started, I want to make one thing clear: Kitty Cavanaugh was not my ghostwriter. We worked together. Those goddamn fucking bloggers are already getting it wrong, big surprise, the *Times* had it wrong this morning, my lawyer's already drafting a cease-and-desist motion . . ." She paused for breath and snatched a can of Diet Coke from an LLB-monogrammed ice bucket on the chrome and glass coffee table. "You saw the obit?" she barked.

"I . . . uh . . ." I fumbled through the slurry of broken crayons and juice-stiffened napkins at the bottom of my WGBH totebag and pulled out a notebook with a pink, glittery cover featuring Hello Kitty. It was Sophie's—the only thing I'd been able to find on short notice.

"O-bit-u-a-ry," she said, pronouncing each syllable as if she were speaking to someone who'd just come back from her lobotomy. "In today's so-called paper of record." She snatched the offending pages off the coffee table and tossed them at me. "Connecticut Mother, Writer Slain," said the two-column headline on page B-6. "Katherine Cavanaugh, a Connecticut woman who worked in the editorial department of *Content* magazine writing 'The Good Mother' column beneath the byline of conservative social critic Laura Lynn Baird, was found dead in her kitchen on Friday afternoon. Mrs. Cavanaugh, thirty-six" was all I saw before Laura Lynn grabbed the newspaper out of my hand.

"Don't read it," she rapped, her jaw clenched and tiny eyes glittering. "It's all lies, lies and bullshit, typical liberal smear garbage. My lawyer's already spoken to their ombudsman—oh, excuse me," she said, her husky, clipped voice heavy with sarcasm, "their ombuds-person. Gotta be gender neutral these days, right? Right?" She threw back her head, exposing a scrawny, corded neck, and made a noise that must have sounded like laughter when she was on TV.

"How long had Kitty been, um, working with you?"

"Five years, six years, something like that," she said.

I wrote it down. "How did you meet her?"

"We were introduced," she said. "Joel Asch, he's the editor in chief of *Content,* had been her professor at Hanfield. He spoke highly of her, I interviewed her, she seemed intelligent, and capable enough, so that was that. There you go." She tapped her foot on the hardwood floor. "What else? What else?"

I blurted out the first thing I could think of. "Where's your son? Is he napping?"

"He's at the park with my mother. She takes care of him when I'm working," she said. She lifted her chin and narrowed her eyes at me, daring me to call her a hypocrite.

"Oh."

"And when I travel. I used to take him with me—he was more portable when he was little—but it just got to be too much. Last year I was on the road one night out of every three. That was why Kitty was so perfect," Laura Lynn said. "I supplied the politics, the ideology, the spin. She provided some of the details. You know. All that messy domestic stuff. Dirty diapers and drool." She whipped one manicured hand through the air. I imagined I could hear the air whistling in its wake.

"So . . ." I wanted to ask *who did the writing,* but I knew I couldn't. So I said, "How did you divide the labor?" *There,* I thought. *Much better.*

Laura Lynn shook her head in frustration. Not a single hair moved. "We'd talk on the phone, or we'd email. I'd give her ideas, we'd have conversations, and then she'd send me the final product. When you think about it, I was doing her a real service," Laura Lynn said.

I couldn't help raising my eyebrows at that one, and I tried to camouflage my disgust as deep interest. "Oh?"

"I believe in earned equality," she said. I recognized the catchphrase from one of her TV appearances. "And unlike the so-called feminists"—she hooked her spindly fingers into air quotes and lifted her lip in a sneer—"I actually support women."

"Oh?"

"Absolutely," she said, nodding vigorously. "You see, a woman like Kitty, a mom with two kids . . ." She drummed her fingers on her knee, looking disconcerted, even upset, for the first time in our conversation. "She had two kids, right?"

I nodded.

"Two kids, in the suburbs, what other work could she possibly do? She couldn't go to an office, couldn't go back to school. I allowed her the luxury of staying home with her children, and a chance to have a voice in the world!" she concluded triumphantly.

Hv voice in world, I scribbled, keeping my eyes assiduously on my page, knowing that if I risked looking at Laura Lynn, my face would give me away. "So she worked from home?"

Laura Lynn nodded, sighed audibly, and glanced at her watch again. "That's right. After that first time we met in the city, it was just easier for us to do it on the phone or with email."

"That was all right with your editor? With . . ." I looked at my notebook. "Joel Asch?"

"Anything was going to be okay with him. He loooved her. He might have been fucking her, for all I know," she added, her voice suddenly vicious. *So much for sisterhood,* I managed to keep from saying.

"Did she agree with your point of view? Your take on motherhood?"

Laura Lynn scowled at me. "Well, of course she did. Why wouldn't she?"

I wrote it down without answering. I wasn't touching that one. It was probably true. A woman who'd tell an almost stranger, "I would never leave my children," with her face and eyes glowing, like she was in the grip of some religious passion, or insane—probably would buy what Laura Lynn was selling.

"Look," Laura Lynn continued, leaning forward and laying one hand on my knee for emphasis, "I would have been perfectly happy with a double byline. Honest to God. But the editors felt . . ."—she gave a tiny shrug—"that my name was the draw, and that sharing the credit would just muddy the waters. And Kitty was fine with it. Really. Especially once we got the book deal."

"Book deal?"

She gave another impatient exhale and cracked open another can of soda. "We sold our manuscript three weeks ago," Laura Lynn said. "At auction. Six houses were bidding." She held her soda can like a microphone. "A collection of essays about the contested nature of motherhood in modern-day America. We got a seven-figure advance."

"Did you have a title? I'd like to mention it at the memorial service."

She blinked at me as I congratulated myself on my quick thinking. "*The Good Mother.* Of course."

Of course.

"And we were both going to have bylines!" Laura Lynn concluded, as if that fact alone put her halfway toward sainthood. "Make sure you mention that. Well, you know. It would say, 'By Laura Lynn Baird with Kitty Cavanaugh.' "

I nodding, remembering a line I'd read in a hundred different detective stories: *follow the money.* A seven-figure advance meant that there was plenty of money to follow. "I don't want to get too personal, but would you mind telling me how you planned to split the advance, and the royalties?"

"Well . . ." Laura Lynn set down her soda can and fiddled with her pearls. "We hadn't quite finalized it." She gave me a wide-eyed look. "But it was going to be fair. You can be assured of that. See, I believe in treating women fairly, and in paying them fairly."

I nodded and wrote that down too, then kept nodding as Laura Lynn expounded on her views of motherhood (pro), feminism (con), and a woman's impact on the world (significant and favorable, provided she attended to her children first, thus effecting change on a micro level, but from little acorns spring great oaks, and there would be no need for gun control, campaign finance reform, or government regulation of the Internet, if only the mothers of the world would do their job).

"Jane Segal said you found the body," Laura Lynn said. "Was

it . . . was she . . ." She tilted her soda can back and forth, then raised her hands to her necklace. "Did she suffer?" she finally asked. Her pearls chattered between her fingers.

"I don't know," I said.

We sat in silence for about ten seconds before Laura Lynn chugged down the remnants of her soda and set down the can. "Gotta go," she said, wiping her lips with the back of her hand. "I'm taking the train to D.C."

I knew my cue. "Did Kitty ever mention someone named Evan McKenna to you?" His name seemed to hang in the air like a mobile. If I looked up, I'd see it dangling over my head.

"No," said Laura. "Why? Who's he?"

"Nobody," I said. "He's nobody." As always, his name twisted through my heart. *Nobody.* How I wished that it were true.

She got to her feet. "So, listen, I'm sorry for your loss. Was Kitty a good friend of yours?"

I shook my head. "I didn't really know her that well. Just from the playground, or the supermarket, or soccer games."

That admission seemed to relax Laura Lynn. "That's a shame. She was nice," she said. "Very reliable. Very thorough." She paused, perhaps realizing that what she'd said sounded more like a reference for a cleaning service than a eulogy for a departed colleague. "You know what Kitty was? She was a *good mother.* Just like the column said."

I got home at five past eleven, which gave me fifteen minutes to debrief with Janie, fifteen minutes for research, and ten minutes to get myself to the Red Wheel Barrow for the eleven forty-five pickup.

Typing "Laura Lynn Baird" and "Good Mother" and "book deal" into my favorite search engine caused it to spit out a dozen stories. Laura Lynn had, indeed, landed a deal "said to be well into the seven figures" for a collection of essays on motherhood previously published in *Content,* plus "additional original material." All the articles got all three of her names right, and a few of them even resurrected the scandal of her father's death, but I couldn't find any mention of Kitty Cavanaugh or any cowriter, ghostwriter, or other assistance, anywhere. I jotted down the name of the agent and the editor, Googled their phone numbers, and glanced at the clock: 11:28. My fingers hovered over the telephone. *Screw it,* I thought, and dialed.

Dafna Herzog, Laura Lynn's literary agent, had a raucous laugh that she used midway through my spiel about how I was a neighbor of Kitty Cavanaugh's and that I'd recently spoken to Laura Lynn Baird. "Oh, God," she said, and chuckled ruefully. "My new favorite client."

"I don't mean to pry."

"Pry away," she said, and kept laughing. "I've gotten about twenty calls from reporters already this morning. The dead ghostwriter. What a story!"

"So you knew about Kitty?"

"Let's put it this way. I made an educated guess that Laura had assistance for those *Content* pieces. She's a hell of an advocate—you know?—and of course she's great on TV, but when it comes to putting pen to paper, or fingers to keyboard . . ." She chuckled again. "She can do sound bites, but not paragraphs or chapters, God forbid."

"No talent?" I ventured.

"No time," Dafna said. "So I figured there was someone, but I didn't know for sure until I saw it in the *Times.*"

"Laura never told you she'd be working with another writer."

"I guess that was kind of an unspoken assumption on my part," Dafna said. "Which is to say, I didn't ask, she didn't tell."

"And in terms of the financial situation . . ." I paused, but Dafna outwaited me. Finally I asked, "How much was her advance, exactly?"

"Seven figures, with bonuses," Dafna said. "That's as specific as I'll get."

Fair enough. "Laura Lynn told me that she and Kitty were going to split the money."

"That," said Dafna, "would have been between Laura Lynn Baird and your friend. The deal I negotiated was only for Laura."

Deal only for Laura, I wrote. "You know, I think your client lied to me," I said.

Dafna practically exploded in laughter. "Well, mazel tov! You just lost your virginity!" she chuckled. "Listen, Laura Lynn was—is—a writer. At least, she'd like to be one. Writers lie. They embroider. They dissemble. Not to put too fine a point on it, they make things up. And what was Laura Lynn going to tell you? I'm a greedy monster who was going to keep it all? Poor thing," she spluttered, "now she's really on the hook. She'll probably have to set up a college fund for the ghostwriter's kids. Is there anything else I can help you with?"

Eleven thirty-two. I decided to go for it. "Do you think Laura Lynn Baird could have killed Kitty?"

I braced myself for another hailstorm of laughter. It didn't come. "For the money, you mean?" Dafna asked. "If she thought that Kitty was going to sue her, or expose her somehow? I guess I'd say that people have killed each other for a lot less money than what we were talking about." She paused. "Boy, wouldn't that be some story?"

"Some story," I repeated. "So what happens to the book now?"

"Hard to say. Now that it turns out Laura didn't technically write those pieces by herself, your dead lady's going to get author credit for sure. It'll build interest. Given the—uh—recent events. Anyhow," she concluded, "call back if there's anything else you need." Click.

It was eleven thirty-four. Information gave me the switchboard for *Content,* and the receptionist put me through to Joel Asch's office. "What is this regarding?" she asked dubiously, after I'd introduced myself as Kate Klein from Upchurch, Connecticut.

"Kitty Cavanaugh. She was a friend of mine." I paused, considering, and decided, *What the hell.* "I was the one who found the . . . who found her. Her body."

"And, so . . . what is this regarding?"

Good question. "Well, I know she wrote for *Content,* and that Joel was the one who hired her . . ." I paused.

"Yes," said the woman on the other end of the line. Her voice sharpened. "But what is this regarding? What do you want?"

"Just to talk to him," I said limply. "To talk to him about Kitty."

"I'll give him the message."

"Thanks," I said, reciting my name and my telephone number. Eleven thirty-seven. I set the phone down and sprinted to the minivan. If I was late again, I was going to get another lecture and another ten-dollar-per-child fine from the school's director, Mrs. Dietl, who had the curling gray hair and warm blue eyes of a cookie-box grandma and the heart and soul of an ATM machine.

Suspect, I thought, zipping out of the driveway and narrowly missing the mailbox, picturing Laura Lynn's corded neck and skinny fingers strangling a can of Diet Coke. I had an honest-to-God suspect.

I pulled out of Liberty Lane, onto Main Street, zipping over a pile of pulpy gray and crimson that had formerly been a squirrel. "Frankie and Johnnie were lovers. Oh, Lordy, how they did love," I sang. "They swore to be true to each other. Just as true as the stars above. He was her man, but he done her wrong." I didn't realize how loudly I'd been singing, or how wide my mouth must have been open, until I whizzed past a police car parked at the corner of Folly Farm Way and noticed the pink-faced officer staring at me. Oops. I shut my mouth and picked up my cell phone, which had started beeping insistently. One missed call. I hadn't heard it ring, but that was no surprise. Upchurch cell phone reception was notoriously crappy, because the town fathers and mothers had refused to permit a tower anywhere near their quaint little country paradise. I punched in the numbers for voice mail and felt my hands tighten on the wheel in a death grip as I heard my name. "Kate," said a voice I hadn't heard in seven years. There was a burst of static, loud noises in the background. ". . . it's Evan McKenna. We need to talk."

EIGHT

Janie and I didn't get hired by *People* magazine, but thanks to Janie's persistence, my good grades, and, I suspect, the eventual behind-the-scenes machinations of Sy Segal, we landed jobs as copy editors/wannabe reporters at *New York Night,* a weekly magazine just shy of being a tabloid whose bread and butter—or gin and tonic—were the drug- and alcohol-fueled antics of young celebrities. Not that we ever got to meet any of these young celebrities, although if Sy had been less insistent on the matter of her employment, Janie could have partied with them all night instead of working all day.

We'd sit at a pair of battered desks with cigarette burns on the tops and mousetraps underneath. Our job was ensuring that the reporters spelled the stars' names correctly and got the histories of their addictions in the right order. "Charlie Sheen!" a reporter on deadline would shout, and it would be up to one of us to come up with the actor's correct age and place of birth, the titles, costars, and grosses (foreign and domestic) of his last three movies and/or television shows, and, most important for *New York Night*'s purposes, who he'd been dating, what he'd been taking, and where he'd gone to kick it.

After a few months at the job, we each developed our own reliable sources. Janie had a quasi-phone-sexual relationship with a janitor at an exclusive rehab in Minnesota: she called him Loverboy, checked in with him at lunchtime every day, sent him expensive boxes of chocolates and promised him they'd spend eternity together as soon as her divorce went through.

I didn't have Janie's flair as a writer, or her easy way of cajoling hard-nosed publicists to give up the dirt. I had Mary Elizabeth. She'd been one of the most abusive—not to mention inebriated—of my Pimm classmates. Sophomore year she'd put a maxi pad on my seat in geometry class and let me go around for the rest of the day with it taped to my butt. The year before, she'd told me that Todd Avery at Collegiate had asked for my phone number, and I'd spent a month without straying more than six feet from the telephone as I waited for his call. Two months shy of graduation, she'd gotten expelled for the one-two punch of spiking the girls' basketball team's water bottles with Finlandia and performing unmentionable acts with one of the gym teachers in the broom closet. Mary Elizabeth had eventually gotten it together enough to get a GED, but she'd flunked out of Wesleyan, been asked to leave Penn, and burned through her trust fund before she turned twenty-three, at which point she'd eloped with one of the cloggers from the touring company of Lord of the Dance. At twenty-eight she'd come to her senses and joined Alcoholics Anonymous. The week I'd started at *New York Night,* she'd called me out of the blue, per step nine (making direct amends to those she had harmed). Sensing a shot at a byline, I'd shamed her into calling me each week to confirm details of famous people she'd seen at spas and rehab clinics she frequented.

Our boss was a woman named Polly, who wore glasses thick enough to stop bullets and seemed to live in the newsroom. She was there when we arrived in the morning. She was there when we left at night. Not only had we never seen her leave the building, we'd never seen her in the bathroom either. Janie and I had long discussions about this with Sandra, the mealworm-pale book critic who took great joy in pronouncing any book where the girl got the guy "ridiculous." Sandra had choppy brown hair that looked like she cut it with toenail clippers, an MFA from a prestigious university, and a five-hundred-page manuscript, which, presumably, did not include a happy ending, reposing in a shoebox underneath her bed, beneath letters from the thirty-six literary agents who'd rejected it. The three of us finally agreed that the less we thought about our boss's excretory habits, the better.

Polly's boss, the managing editor, was a man named Mark Perrault, who was notable only because once a month or so, when the layout guys had caused him to miss deadline again, he'd emerge from his office and attempt to throw his chair across the photographers' desks. Unfortunately, Mark, while not technically a little person, was barely five feet tall and probably weighed less than the chair did. He'd wrestle the chair up to chest level, all the while spluttering "How much *longer* am I going to have to put *up* with this *goddamn fucking incompetence,*" lurch forward a few steps, and then, with a tremendous, whistling *"Argh!"* fling the chair a disappointing foot or two in front of him, while Janie and I would huddle by the vending machine, shaking with silent laughter.

"You know what we should do now?" Janie asked one night, over the hot fudge sundaes at Serendipity 3 she'd insisted on to celebrate her father's most recent divorce.

"What?"

"Move!"

I raised my eyebrows. "Don't you already have a place?" Janie, as I knew perfectly well, lived in her own suite in her father's Park Avenue apartment, an eighteen-room palace with its own elevator that had been photographed for *Metropolitan Home.*

"Oh, come on," she said. "We can't live with our fathers forever!"

"I think you living with your father is a little different from what I've got going on."

"Nevertheless," said Janie, pulling a copy of the *Village Voice* from a handbag that had cost several baby alligators their lives. "Look, a two-bedroom in Murray Hill for eighteen hundred a month! We can totally afford that!" She circled it in lip liner, then squinted at the page. "Where's Murray Hill?" Her eyes widened in alarm. "It isn't Brooklyn, is it?"

I struggled for a reference point she'd understand. "It's sort of near Grand Central Station."

"Great! Let's go see it!" She whipped out her cell phone.

"Well, first we have to see if it's even still available, and then we have to make an appointment—"

Janie held up her hand for silence. "Yes, hello, to whom am I speaking? Achmed? Achmed, this is Janie Segal of the carpet Segals."

I shook my head, even though I knew resistance was futile. In the months since we'd met at the *Review,* I'd become Janie's plus-one at all of the fabulous functions she attended. During six months of black-tie bashes at the city's museums and concert halls, and drinks afterwards at bars and nightclubs all over town, she'd never once made me feel like the fat, frumpy sidekick she kept around as a kind of human moat between herself and the guys who were forever asking her if she wanted a beer or wanted to dance or would mind giving them her number. We had fun together, whether we were buying five-dollar earrings at the flea market on Sixth Avenue and Twenty-fifth Street or dining on braised veal cheeks at a fund-raiser at the Museum of Modern Art, and then singing karaoke in Chinatown afterwards, still wearing our gowns.

Janie finished with Achmed and hung up the phone triumphantly. "We can see it Saturday afternoon!"

I licked my spoon clean and set it on my napkin. "I've actually got plans."

She put down her phone. "Do you have a date?" she asked. "Can I come?"

I stared at her. "Can you come?" I repeated.

"I could pretend to be your sobriety counselor!"

"Janie . . ."

She pushed aside the melted remains of her nine-dollar sundae. "And when they bring the wine list, I'll be like, 'Oh, no, we won't be needing that!' And I'll say how you really aren't even supposed to be dating, but that your therapist gave you a special dispensation. And then—"

"Janie!" I held up both hands. "No, you cannot come on my date and pretend to be my sobriety counselor." I paused to take a breath. "I don't actually have a date."

"Oh. So what are you doing on Saturday?"

"I'm . . ." Oof. It was going to sound pathetic out loud, but I plunged ahead anyhow. "I'm going to rent a movie and order Chinese food and help my father pay his bills."

"Oh," said Janie. "Well. That sounds nice." I saw her expression become wistful, and knew that unless I moved quickly to stop it, she'd break into "All By Myself."

"Do you want to come?"

Janie leaned forward eagerly. "Could I?"

"Well, sure."

"And on Sunday we'll pack!"

"We should probably find a place first . . ."

"Oh, right, right," she said, writing the words "wear comfortable shoes" in the margin of the *Voice.* She tapped her lip liner pencil on the page, considered, then wrote "buy comfortable shoes."

"I'll lend you some sneakers," I said. The next week, we'd both fallen in love with a big two-bedroom apartment in the West Village—"On Jane Street!" Janie said. "So it's, like, meant to be!" It had a bath and a half and a dishwasher, a kitchen big enough for two people to stand in, eastern exposures, and oversized windows that flooded the space with light.

We moved in on a sunny Saturday morning in April, the first warm day of spring. I'd packed my boxes and labeled them Kitchen, Bathroom, Bedroom, and Books. Janie had followed my example, begging free boxes from the local liquor store, and even packing and labeling them herself. The three stacked at our building's front door read Cosmetics, Wrapping Paper, and Bracelets. Not perfect, but it was a start.

We lugged the boxes into the elevator, down the hall, and into our new digs. Janie had brought along a CD of Abba's greatest hits. She plugged in my boom box, popped in the Abba, and blared it loud enough for the whole building to enjoy.

I'd gotten almost all of my things into my little room in half a dozen trips, so I was helping the movers drag Janie's boxes off the sidewalk, while Janie, outfitted in specially purchased overalls, work boots, and a T-shirt that read "You Wish," stationed herself in the kitchen. From there she could keep an eye on the movers unpacking her china for eighteen, wait for 1-800-Mattress, and supervise the installation of the all-new stainless steel appliances she'd ordered, even though we were only renting and Janie had freely confessed that she knew how to cook only microwave popcorn and toast with melted Emmentaler cheese on top.

It was a perfect afternoon. The sky was blue, and the sliver of the Hudson I could see between the buildings was sparkling. It looked like everyone in New York City, or at least everyone in the Village, was out and about, carrying balloons, pushing babies, licking ice cream cones, and many of them felt compelled to comment on our stuff.

"Moving day!" a dozen of them had said. Or, "Howdy, neighbor!" Or, "Don't hurt yourself with that," as I struggled to lift a box Janie had labeled Other Boxes and thought to myself that telling someone not to hurt herself was not even close to offering to help her. By five o'clock that afternoon I'd vowed that the next person to say something stupid was going to get a piece of my mind. So when a deep male voice remarked, "Are you moving into four-B?" into my ear, I straightened my aching back and said, without turning around to look at who that voice belonged to, "No. I'm actually committing the crime of the century. Don't tell anyone, okay?"

"Your secret is safe with me," the voice promised. "In fact, I've got a guy on Eleventh Avenue who can move this stuff for us. We'll split the profits and run off to A.C."

"A.C.?" I asked.

"Atlantic City, baby," the man said.

I put my hands against the small of my back and turned around, smiling in spite of myself at the thought of hightailing it down to New Jersey. The man smiling back at me was tall, with close-cropped dark curls, flashing green eyes, and a cleft in his chin. "They'll never find us," he promised. I felt my face flush as he knelt down and started flipping through the compact discs in one of the milk crates I'd scavenged from my former bedroom. He plucked out a copy of Billie Holiday's *Commodore Master Takes,* then one of *The Essential Ida Cox.* "Are these yours?"

I nodded. Then I cleared my throat. "Yes."

He looked at me closely. "You got *Blues for Rampart Street?*"

I nodded again. "I've got everything," I said, wishing I'd found time to put together an ensemble like Janie's, instead of wearing an old Spoleto Festival T-shirt and my least-flattering jeans.

"You like the blues."

"I like girl singers," I said. "All those sad old songs . . ." My voice trailed off while he flipped rapidly through my CDs and whistled in appreciation before plucking one and brandishing it at me. My heart sank as I saw Debbie Gibson's face staring back at me.

"Electric Youth?" he asked.

"It was the eighties!" I protested.

He shook his head and hefted the crate under his arm.

"Come on, I'll help you."

I picked up Janie's box of boxes and followed him onto the elevator. He had strong shoulders, sinewy forearms, and a pale strip of milky skin under his hairline, like he'd just had his hair cut.

I hit the button for the fourth floor. "Hey, we're neighbors," he said. His smile widened. He was looking at me like he'd known me my whole life . . . or, I thought, feeling my cheeks heat up again, like he'd already seen me naked, and liked what he'd seen.

Oh, God. I raised my eyes, studying the lit numbers far too intently as he started whistling "Wild Women Don't Get the Blues." I imagined hitting the emergency stop button and how, once the elevator stopped moving, the lights would somehow magically dim, and my neighbor would reach for me, his fingers just skimming my shirt. "Come here," he would say, in his deep voice, in a tone that wouldn't permit refusal, and I'd step into his arms, and I'd press my face to his chest, inhaling the sweet scent of his skin as he slid his hands down my back while nibbling at the side of my neck, saying . . .

"Hey."

I blinked, shook my head, and found the elevator doors open and the handsome guy staring at me. "It's our stop."

"Oh, yeah! Right! Four-B, that's us!" At the apartment door we both reached for the doorknob at the same time. I almost fell into the foyer and Janie's antique iron headboard.

"So what's your name?" he asked.

"It's Kate." I swallowed hard. My throat felt dusty, and I'd apparently forgotten the rest of my name.

"Kate," he said, and nodded, as if this pleased him. "I'm Evan McKenna. Four-A."

"Nice to meet you." There. I'd gotten a complete, socially appropriate sentence out of my mouth without babbling or mentally molesting him. Progress! I set the box into the hallway closet and put my hands in my pockets.

He cocked an eyebrow at the mess, the suitcases and boxes leaking crumpled newspaper and packing peanuts onto the floor, the movers sweating and cursing as they shoved the headboard along the hall to Janie's bedroom.

"So how many of you are there moving in here?"

"Huh? Oh, um, just two. Me and my roommate Janie. Janie Segal of the carpet Segals." Shit. Now why had I said that?

"Janie Segal of the carpet Segals," he repeated.

I nodded. I'd decided that speed was not my friend.

The eyebrow lifted higher. "Did she have some kind of reversal of fortune?"

"Oh, no, no," I said, shaking my head more vigorously than I had to. "She just likes to keep it real, you know. With the Village people. Well, West Village people. Ha ha."

Evan—Evan! Had there ever been a more beautiful name!—surveyed the mounds and piles and teetering stacks of Janie's belongings. "Do you guys need more help?"

"Oh, no, no, we're fine, we've got it . . ." Just then, there was a loud crash from the kitchen, followed by some even louder cursing. Evan and I hurried into the kitchen, where Janie was on her hands and knees.

"Damn!" she said, picking up the pieces of a broken soup bowl. "So much for our service for eighteen."

"Careful with that," I said, kneeling down beside her as she picked through the shards. "Hey, Janie, this is Evan McKenna. He's our neighbor."

She raised her head, swept her index finger dramatically beneath each eye, then looked at him . . . then at me . . . then at him again, as something in her bedroom crashed to the floor with a wall-rattling bang.

"Very pleased to meet you," she said. She stood up, gave Evan's hand a brief shake, and bounded out of the room.

"Huh," said Evan, watching her go.

"Yeah, she, um, she's a little . . ." God, he was handsome! Like a *General Hospital*–era Rick Springfield, only without the mullet. Just then, as if I'd willed it, or as if Janie had read my mind, the Abba was replaced by the opening notes of "Jesse's Girl."

Evan grinned. "Are you ladies Rick Springfield fans?"

"I love this song," I babbled. "I wrote Rick Springfield a fan letter when I was twelve, I think, and he sent me back an autographed picture. My mom always called him Rick Springsteen."

"Rick Springsteen," he repeated.

"Yeah," I said. "She's an opera singer. She doesn't like any music that was composed in the last fifty years," I said. "Well, I guess I should, you know, get back to it."

"Let me put on something better."

I stared after him. Then I opened a box labeled Hairspray, which turned out, unsurprisingly, I guess, to contain about two dozen half-empty cans of hairspray. I'd started sweeping up the broken bowl when Rick was replaced by Bessie Smith's bemused crooning, courtesy of Janie, playing DJ in the living room.

"Comes a rainstorm, get your rubbers on your feet. Comes a snowstorm, you can get a little heat. Comes love, nothing can be done."

My heart lifted and thrummed in my chest as Evan hummed along. It meant something. It had to.

"Comes a fire, then you know just what to do. Blow a tire, you can get another shoe."

I sang softly, tipping the dustpan into the trash can. "Comes love, nothing can be done."

"Hey." I looked up. Evan was looking at me . . . really looking at me, with that grin still on his lips. "What?"

"Hold still," he said. He reached out with two fingers and deftly plucked something out of my ponytail. "You had this stuck."

I looked down into his palm, where a curled pink feather rested. "Wow. Huh. Wonder where that came from?" My guess would have been Janie's feather boa, which I'd removed a few hours before from a box labeled Feather Boas, but I wouldn't have been able to say so even if I'd wanted to. He was staring at me, I was looking at him, and my mouth was dry, and my heart was pounding, and . . .

Evan pulled a beeper out of his pocket. I hadn't noticed that it was ringing. "Oops," he said. "Appointment. Gotta run."

"Oh. Sure! Okay, um, nice meeting you . . ."

He waved at me, edged through the thicket of Janie's stuff, and then out the door, leaving me standing there, staring after him, my heart in my throat and a feather in my hand.

• • •

The movers had left Janie's nine-foot mirror in a baroque gold frame leaning against the wall. My heart sank as I studied myself two hours later. Why couldn't I have worn a little foundation, I thought, gazing at my flushed cheeks and shiny forehead . . . or lipstick . . . or a bag over my head? A bag would have solved all my problems, although it would have made it difficult to schlep boxes around.

I yanked at the hem of my shirt and sucked in my cheeks. The SAT tutor I'd dated had had a bit of an overbite and an unfortunate tendency to spit when he talked. The MBA candidate was handsome but a head shorter than I was. A guy like Evan McKenna would have never looked at me twice—if he hadn't noticed my music first.

I tucked my unruly hair, still damp from a shower I'd taken that morning, up into a twist. He must have seen something in me, even if I couldn't see it myself.

"Vietnamese or Thai?" asked Janie, waving a sheaf of takeout menus. "Senegalese? Laotian? Cuban-Chinese?" She closed her mouth as she caught sight of me in the mirror. "Oh, so it's like that, huh?"

"Like what?" I asked innocently, even while I was trying to remember where I'd packed my lucky black sweater.

"Don't play dumb with me, sister," Janie said. "You've got it bad."

"I don't know what you're talking about," I said. "And Cuban-Chinese sounds great." I slipped past her into the kitchen. We had beer in the refrigerator, six six-packs we were going to give to the movers, plus tips, when they came back with Janie's living room furniture the next day. I took the coldest one out of the back, combed my hair, located my sweater, borrowed Janie's lipstick and mascara and one of her bracelets, and proceeded down the hallway to 4-A. I took a deep breath, licked my lips, and smiled as the door swung open.

"Hey . . ." The witty remark I'd been preparing died in my throat as I looked up at the most beautiful woman I'd ever seen. She had russet hair that hung in waves almost to the small of her back, and almond-shaped aquamarine eyes, the kind of cheekbones that looked like they'd been carved, and upturned lips full and soft as pillows.

"Yes?" she asked politely, as her eyes flicked once, up and down, taking me in with a single pitiless glance and instantly dismissing me: *no threat here.*

"I'm sorry, I must have the wrong apartment."

I looked for a number by the door and got ready to apologize when Evan appeared in the doorway. "Hi, Kate!"

I thrust the beer out at him. "Hi. Um, I wanted to thank you for, uh, helping us."

"You didn't have to get us anything," he said.

"Oh, it's nothing." *Don't panic,* I thought. Maybe she was his sister. Or just a friend. Or a lesbian, one of those hot makeup- and miniskirt-wearing ones who'd recently been discovered by *New York* magazine. Or—

Evan looked at me kindly. With what I hoped wasn't pity on his face. "Kate, this is Michelle," he said, placing his hands on her shoulders, with the look of a man who's just cashed in a winning lottery ticket. "My fiancée."

"Nice to meet you," I said, and tried to smile. Michelle ignored my efforts.

"Yum," she drawled, plucking the beer out of my nerveless fingers.

"Say thank you, Michelle," said Evan.

"Thank you, Michelle," she recited, and turned on her heel. Evan gave me an apologetic shrug. I could hear music in the background, not Billie or Bessie but something loud and atonal and repetitive, like a CD that was skipping.

"That was really nice of you." When he smiled, his eyes crinkled in the corners. "So I guess I'll see you around."

"Sure," I said. "Sure thing."

"Kate," he called, as I started back down the hall. When I turned around, he was still smiling. "Atlantic City," he whispered. "Don't forget."

Back in our apartment, the living room was lined with empty boxes, and Janie was hanging her coats in the front closet.

"So?" she asked.

"So what? I just brought the guy next door some beer."

"Is that what the kids are calling it these days?" she asked, hanging a plastic-wrapped full-length shearling coat next to something she'd told me was sheared beaver.

"Janie, he's just a nice guy!"

"Umm-hmm," she said, pulling a fluffy white stole out of its plastic bag.

"And," I sighed, pulling more coats out of Janie's box and hanging them, "he's living with the most beautiful woman in the world. And she's kind of a bitch."

"Oh, dear." She shook her head. She'd twisted her hair into a bun that she'd anchored with a pair of lacquered chopsticks. "Well, look. Better you find this out now than get your hopes up."

"My hopes weren't up," I said.

"Oh, grasshopper," she said, and gave me a hug, almost skewering my eyeball with her chopstick. "What a bad, bad liar you are."

NINE

"Like I said, miss, I don't want to question her," Stan Bergeron explained patiently from my driveway the next morning as I made my way downstairs in my bathrobe. "This isn't official. I'm just checking in."

"Not without a lawyer," said my best friend, standing at my front door with her arms crossed over her chest, a stance that would have been more imposing if she hadn't been wearing pink silk pajamas and giant raccoon-shaped slippers and had my kids peeking out from behind her legs.

I yawned. It was ten o'clock in the morning, a good four hours past when I normally woke up, but I hadn't been able to sleep until after two in the morning. I'd wanted to call Evan back but couldn't think of an excuse to leave the house without the kids, and there was no way I'd be dialing the former love of my life while under the roof I shared with my current husband. When I finally dozed off, I'd had terrible dreams, nightmares of being lost in a library where all the books had Kitty Cavanaugh's byline and, when I opened them, the blank pages slowly filled with blood. "I'm looking for something a little different," I told the librarian, who was Mrs. Dietl from the Red Wheel Barrow. She tapped her watch face and held out her hands for the books. "Late again," she said.

I rubbed my eyes and surveyed the situation. Janie appeared to have things well in hand, with a few minor exceptions: the kids were still in their pajamas (judging from their hands and faces, they'd enjoyed a breakfast consisting entirely of syrup), and there was a police cruiser parked in my driveway. "Hey, Stan."

He nodded at me fearfully as I edged past Janie. "Good morning, Kate. I just came by to give you an update."

"Um, excuse me? Law-yer? Was one of those syllables not making sense to you?" Janie inquired.

"It's okay," I told her.

"It is not," she said. "If you talk to the police, you need a lawyer." She rolled her eyes and turned to Sophie. "Did I watch ten seasons of *NYPD Blue* for nothing?"

"No way!" Sophie said. She had Uglydoll under her arm, dressed, I saw, in his police uniform ("Chapter 108: In Which I Join the Force").

"You don't have to say anything!" Stan called. "You can just nod."

I nodded. "What's going on, Stan?" I asked. "Did you find out who did it?"

"No." Then he brightened. "But we found Evan McKenna!"

My heart leapt like a stupid fish at the sound of his name. "Good!" I managed. "Good for you!"

"Is he a suspect?" Janie asked hopefully.

"We won't know until we question him," said Stan. "He was down in Miami."

"He says," Janie muttered. She raised her voice. "How about the husband?"

"The husband?" Stan repeated.

"Is he a suspect?" Janie asked.

"Nooo . . ." Stan said, dragging the word out. "No, he's got an alibi. He was in the city all day."

Janie flipped her hair over her shoulders. "Well, there you go. Sounds like you've eliminated everyone. Maybe the butler did it."

I glared at her.

"Has Mr. McKenna been in touch with you?" Stan asked.

I started to answer, caught Janie's finger-across-the-throat gesture, and shook my head instead. Stan stared at me. "Let us know if you hear from him," he said, and wandered back down the driveway to his patrol car. I watched him as he backed out over my hydrangeas.

"Well!" Janie said. "If that's Connecticut law enforcement at its finest, might I suggest the name of a few Realtors?"

We sent the kids upstairs to get dressed. Back in the kitchen, I started in on the sinkful of dishes while Janie helped herself to coffee.

"So, Sherlock," Janie said. "What next?"

I shrugged as well as I could with my hands full of silverware.

"Call Evan back, I guess."

"In my presence, and not from your house," Janie said. "We'll find a nice quiet pay phone somewhere else."

"Why a pay phone?"

"So after they arrest him there's no record of you consorting with criminals."

"And why do you want to be there?"

She rolled her eyes. "Hello! I have to be there so you don't pledge your undying love to him—which, if you'll remember, didn't work out very well the last time—and run away and ditch me with the rug rats."

"Don't pretend you don't secretly dig them," I said, even as the memory of the last time I'd pledged my love to Evan McKenna twisted in my heart like a straightened paper clip. I bent down to put the silverware in the dishwasher while Janie flipped through the newspaper.

"Who were Kitty's friends in town?" she asked.

I scrubbed a frying pan and thought about it. I knew who Kitty hung around with, but I wasn't sure they were really friends. I'd never heard them talk about the things that friends would talk about: their marriages, their parents, their former lives, preparenthood. In fact, most of their conversations seemed to revolve around scintillating topics such as whether the organic milk they sold at the local convenience store was really organic.

"I don't know," I said slowly.

"You don't know who her friends were?"

"I don't know if she really had any. Maybe everyone else was afraid of her," I said. "Lord knows I was." I squirted soap into the dishwasher. "I should probably talk to the sitter," I said. "If she worked, she had to have a sitter. Someone who was in her house. Someone who saw her, and her husband, and her kids."

"Sitter. Excellent." Janie tossed me the phone, and I called Sukie Sutherland, who seemed to know everything, to ask if she knew the sitter's name.

"Lisa DeAngelis," Sukie said, and rattled off home and cell phone numbers. "Why?"

"Well . . ." I hadn't considered that Sukie would want to know why I was trying to get in touch with Kitty's sitter.

Luckily, she gave a cool little laugh. "Don't be ashamed. You're only the third person who's called me to ask for her number. Listen, a good sitter's hard to find."

I saw the lifeline, and grabbed it. "Do you think she's got any time left? I'm desperate for a little help."

"If I were you, I wouldn't wait too long to call."

"Great. Thanks. I'll see you at the park!"

"See you there," Sukie said, and hung up.

"Good job," Janie said, nodding her approval from behind the Business section. "Call her up. See if she's free. I'll hang out with the kids."

"Don't you have to go back to the city? And work?"

She waved the concept away as though it were a fly. "I'm supposed to write a trend piece. Gray is the new black, black is the new pink, belly buttons are the new nipples." She drummed her fingernails on the table. "Hmm . . . Ass cleavage is the new cleavage?"

"Works for me," I said. I closed the dishwasher, hit the buttons for heavy wash, and wiped my hands on my bathrobe.

"Excellent. Only, Kate? No offense, but you might want to let me help you pick out an outfit before you go."

TEN

In most other towns in America, the opening of a chain coffee shop isn't that big a deal. When Starbucks wanted to come to Upchurch, it occasioned no fewer than three town meetings that packed the town hall's auditorium, a month's worth of outraged letters to the editor of the *Upchurch Gazette* decrying the "degradation of our downtown," and a demonstration on Main Street, where the protestors held placards with red slashes through mugs beneath the words *No Corporate Coffee.* Evidently, they were perfectly satisfied with Tea and Sympathy, where you could buy lapsang souchong for four dollars a cup, crumbly scones, and Danish that could have doubled as doorstops.

The town selectmen finally decided that Starbucks could open, but it couldn't have a sign out front, because a sign would compromise the quaint character of Main Street. Thus, the Secret Starbucks, on the corner of Maple and Main, with nothing but the smell of roasting House Blend to give it away. It was like a speakeasy, in need of only a password to get you through the unmarked glass and metal door.

I sidled inside, dressed in Janie's suede stiletto boots and light blue cashmere sweater—a size medium, which I couldn't have comfortably fit into even before I'd breast-fed three babies—and a clean pair of cargo pants that had been modified to show the small of my back and about two inches of my butt crack ("I need to test my theory!" Janie had said. I'd nodded my consent, then snuck into the bathroom to change my underwear, so that now the pants revealed the small of my back and two inches of faded grayish Hanes Her Way briefs.)

Janie had trailed my minivan in her Porsche. We'd found three broken pay phones before locating one that worked, but Evan's phone just rang and rang before voice mail picked up and Janie cut the connection before I'd said a word. "No leaving incriminating messages," she said. She'd gotten behind the wheel of the van to take the kids back home, tossed me the keys to her car, and told me to call her when I was done interrogating the sitter.

Once I'd placed my order, I scanned the room looking for—I'll admit it—a busty blonde, because that was the image the words "twenty-four-year-old babysitter" had conjured: every suburban mommy's nightmare; every suburban daddy's happy dream.

Under different circumstances, Lisa DeAngelis, with her big blue eyes and buttercup blond hair, might have fit the bill. But when she gave me a listless wave from her table in the corner, she wasn't looking like anyone would be begging her to pose in lingerie any time soon.

"Kate?" she asked tonelessly.

"Hi," I said, and wobbled over to her table in Janie's boots. "Can I get you anything?"

Lisa pointed at a plastic cup in front of her that seemed to be filled primarily with whipped cream. Her eyes looked glazed, whether from sleeplessness or something chemical, I couldn't tell. Her hair was pulled back in a listless ponytail at the nape of her neck. A canker sore bloomed in the corner of her mouth; a pimple was flourishing in the center of her forehead; and the tiny gold stud in her left nostril was surrounded by puffy, infected-looking red flesh. She might have had a drop-dead figure, but since she wore baggy gray sweatpants and an oatmeal-colored sweater, it was impossible to tell.

"Thanks for meeting with me," I said. She shrugged.

"I've got some free time now?" she said. She had the habit remembered from my own younger days of turning every statement into a question. "Now that . . ." She sighed and stared into her coffee cup. I was grateful that she wasn't staring at me, the way the three baristas and the six other patrons all seemed to be. The sweater and the boots, I thought sadly, had been a mistake.

"Well, if you're looking for kids, I've got 'em!" Oy. "There's Sophie, my four-year-old—well, she's four going on forty—and my twins, Sam and Jack, are three . . ." I shut my mouth as a tear made its way slowly down Lisa's check. "Are you okay?"

I handed her a napkin. She wiped her eyes, then blew her nose. I slid more napkins across the table.

Lisa blinked, wiped her cheeks, then tilted her head back and fanned at her lashes. "I still can't believe it?" she said.

Just the opening I'd been waiting for. "It is unbelievable," I murmured.

She spun her cup in a circle. "She was nice, you know?" she said. "She'd talk to me. And there was never any *Oh, could you please unload the dishwasher?* or *Oh, if the kids nap, can you fold some clothes?* They had digital cable, and TiVo, and actual ice cream in the freezer. Ice cream just for me," she said. "The girls had that sugar-free whole fruit stuff."

It figured. I could remember Kitty on the playground peeling fresh clementines for her kids. When mine had asked for a snack, I'd been reduced to offering them each a breath mint.

"I should have . . ."—Lisa paused and wiped her eyes—"appreciated her more, you know?"

"How long had you known her?"

"Three years?" she sniffled. "Since the girls were in nursery school? I'd do three days a week, Mondays, Wednesdays, and Fridays, from one to six thirty. When she went to the city, she'd take the one twenty-two, and she'd be home by six, almost always, and she'd always call when she was going to be late."

"How often did she go to New York?"

Lisa twirled her cup around the table some more. "Depends. Sometimes a lot. And sometimes she'd just be home. She had a computer in the bedroom. She'd work there." I looked down at her hands and saw that her fingernails were bitten to the quick, her cuticles were ragged and scabbed.

"Do you know what she was doing in the city?"

Lisa shook her head. "She never told me. I never asked."

Never told. Never asked. Very interesting. According to Laura Lynn Baird, Kitty had worked from home. They'd collaborated by phone and by email—the perfect, flexible part-time gig for a stay-at-home mother who'd told me she never left her kids. So if Kitty wasn't going into the city to work, what was she doing there? I had an idea. A guess, at least.

"Did she dress like she was going to work or going to . . ." *Meet up with a mystery man in a midtown hotel for hours of illicit passion and overpriced liquor from the minibar?* "Do something else?" I concluded.

"I don't know," Lisa said, after she'd paused for a long look at my underwear-baring ensemble. "She just wore clothes. Skirts and sweaters. Normal things."

Ah, yes. Normal things. I remembered them well. "I'll bet you've got intuition," I said, using one of Janie's techniques: when in doubt, flatter. "Anyone who's good with kids—and I've heard great things about you—you must have kind of a sense about people."

Lisa shrugged, but I could see from the faint flush in her cheeks that she was pleased. Or maybe not. Maybe she was just having some kind of allergic reaction to underwear.

"What was your sense of Kitty?" I asked. "Was she happy, or anxious, or bored? Do you think she could have been . . ." I paused, gathering myself. "I don't know. Maybe having an affair?"

Lisa's flush deepened. "I don't know," she said. "I really have no idea." She picked at the cuticle on her left thumb until she'd drawn a bead of blood. "How many hours a week are you looking for?" she asked.

It took me a minute to remember why I'd ostensibly asked her out for coffee. "Oh, um . . . ten? Fifteen, maybe? It would be really basic. You'd just have to watch the kids. You wouldn't have to do any housework or even answer the phone." I paused to sip my drink and regroup before asking, as casually as I could, "Did you ever answer Kitty's phone?" *Good one, Kate,* I thought. Subtle. Like a fart in an elevator.

She shook her head . . . and I saw she was starting to look puzzled. "She said to just let voice mail pick up, so that's what I did. You don't have voice mail?"

"Well, we do, sure, but sometimes, I guess, the personal touch is nice." Oh boy, was this going nowhere fast. So much for my career as Kate Klein, ace investigator of suburban wrongdoings from eight-thirty to eleven forty-five on Mondays, Wednesdays, and Fridays. I stared into Lisa's eyes, trying to pin her down with my gaze so that she wouldn't bolt or, worse, start talking about babysitting again.

"You know, I used to babysit when I was your age," I said. Flattery hadn't worked, so maybe empathy would. "I loved it, except sometimes the fathers would think it was, you know, their constitutional right to try and hit on me." This was, of course, a complete fabrication. I had picked up the occasional babysitting gig when I was in high school, but none of the fathers had so much as shaken my hand for too long, probably because they were all musicians and Reina could have ruined their careers with a look. Also, I doubted that my bad skin–baggy sweatshirts–slouch combination was much of a turn-on. "I guess times have changed," I said, before I got a good look at little Lisa and saw that her flush had deepened and that her lips were trembling.

"I . . . ," she whispered. *She has a computer in the bedroom,* she'd said of Kitty. How would she know that, unless the lady of the house had shown her? The lady, or the man of the house?

I leaned across the polished wood table and lowered my voice. "Did something happen between you and Kitty's husband?"

She shook her head wordlessly and pressed her lips together as two large tears plopped onto her gray shirt.

"Have the police talked to you?" I asked.

She nodded, sniffling.

"Do you need a lawyer?"

She shook her head. "Phil—Mr. Cavanaugh—he got me one. Kevin Dolan? He's a friend of theirs?" She blew her nose on a recycled paper napkin. "I shouldn't have . . . ," she whispered.

"Shouldn't have what?"

Her neck was a pliant white stalk beneath the straggling ponytail as she cradled her head in her hands. I leaned even farther across the table and managed to knock her drink onto the floor with my right breast. "Shouldn't have what?" I asked again, ignoring the crushed ice seeping through the suede of Janie's boot.

She shook her head again and got to her feet so fast that her chair tipped over, hitting the Secret Starbucks floor with a bang that startled all three of the baristas. Then she spun around on her sneakers and ran out the door. *Well,* I thought, tossing out the dregs of my drink. *Well, Kate, that went just fabulously.*

ELEVEN

"Question for you, my friend," Janie said to Evan one night over dinner. We'd been in our Jane Street apartment for six months, and we'd made it our project to work our way through the cuisines of the world, or at least the ones represented by New York eateries that delivered. Tonight was Greek, and we were feasting on a spread of souvlaki, grilled grape leaves, and taramasalata on warm grilled pita bread. Janie served herself more olives and feta and asked, "Do you have a job, or what?"

Evan grinned and swallowed a last mouthful of moussaka. "She thinks I'm a wastrel," he stage-whispered to me across the table.

"Isn't that a bird?" asked Janie.

"No, that's a kestrel," I said.

Janie glared at us. "Please don't try to educate me. And don't change the subject."

"Wouldn't dream of it," he said, getting up to clear our plates and stack the Styrofoam-packed leftovers neatly in the refrigerator. "Do you know," he asked, decrumbing Janie's placemat, "that the verb form of *butler* is *buttle*?"

"Do you know," Janie asked sweetly, "that the verb form of *fiancé* is *affianced*? Speaking of which, have you and Michelle set a date yet?"

Evan shook his head. "We can't even agree on a place. Or a season. She wants Malibu in the summertime, I want New Jersey in the fall." He grinned at her. Michelle was off in Miami shooting swimsuits for a catalogue, and Evan was mine—well, ours—for the weekend. This had become our routine. Michelle would leave and, in her absence, Evan would adopt us. We'd come home from work with our arms full of research (i.e., the tabloids) to find him hanging around the mailboxes.

"Hello, ladies," he'd say. "What news, what news?" Janie would roll her eyes and make faces at me while I'd fill him in on which celebrities had been arrested/incarcerated/shipped off to rehab, and what they'd done to deserve it. He'd trail us into the elevator, talking in what I think was meant to be a Cockney accent—"Carry your bags, mum? Shine your shoes, guv'ner? Take that package? Take a message? Need any 'elp?" Once we were up in the apartment, he'd flop onto the floor or whatever piece of furniture was empty—our couch, my bed—and magically regain his ability to pronounce the letter *h.* "So!" he'd say cheerfully. "What's for dinner?"

We'd order out, or sometimes we'd cook. Evan's specialty was stir-fry, I could make pastas and casseroles, and Janie had her old reliable cheesy toast. Evan and I would try to stump each other with increasingly obscure blues songs, swapping tapes and compact discs back and forth and arguing over the meaning of Nina Simone's self-imposed exile and whether her cover of "Need a Little Sugar in My Bowl" was, as Evan maintained, superior to all others.

At midnight, Janie would kick him out, except for those precious handful of nights when he fell asleep on the couch and I'd convince her to just let him sleep. After she'd gone into her own room, I'd pull my comforter tenderly up over his shoulders, brushing his hair off his forehead. Once—only once—I'd dared to bend down and brush my lips against his cheek, knowing that what I was feeling was the very definition of *unrequited.* As soon as Michelle came back, she'd claim him like he was a piece of luggage she'd left on the carousel. He'd amble back down the hall with a friendly wave and a "See ya, pal," and that would be the end of it.

That night, Evan returned to the table bearing a waxed-paper bag. "Baba au rhum!" he announced.

Janie poked at hers skeptically. "Don't think you're getting out of this. I still want to know what you do for a living, and I can't be bought off with pastry."

"I can," I said, and took a bite.

Evan handed out fresh napkins and gave Janie what was meant to be an inscrutable look. "I am a man of constant sorrows," he said, with his wineglass in his hand.

"Constant sorrows pay the bills?"

"I'm a man of many talents," Evan said. "A jack-of-all-trades."

"A jack with a trust fund?" Janie asked. "There's nothing wrong with it," she reassured him. "I've got a trust fund!" Like he hadn't figured that out. "But I work," she said, and then repeated it. "I *work.*" Like the two of us spent our days toiling in the salt mines instead of sitting in ergonomically designed chairs in a climate-controlled office typing search strings like "Chris Farley AND hookers AND cocaine" into the LexisNexis database.

"I work too," Evan said easily. "I freelance."

"Freelance writer, freelance musician, freelance proofreader . . . ?" Janie asked.

"That," said Evan with a grin, "is for me to know and you lovely ladies to try to figure out." He finished his dessert, gave Janie a showy smack on the cheek, then bent down briefly and kissed my forehead, allowing me a tantalizing whiff of his skin. He smelled so clean, I thought. "Gotta go," he said, tipping his glass into the sink and walking out the door.

Janie watched him go, hazel eyes narrowed, rubbing one finger against the diminished bridge of her nose. "He's dealing drugs," she finally said.

"No," I said. "No way."

"Well, how else do you explain it?" she demanded. "We come home at night, he's here. We leave in the morning, he's here. I came home for lunch last week . . ."

"Lunch?" I asked, deadpan.

"Okay, sex," said Janie. "We're walking back to the elevator and who should stick his head out of his door? He's always here, except when he's taking off for three days in a row and says he's on quote-unquote vacation, or we're playing Scrabble and his beeper goes off and he not only leaves the room or the apartment, he leaves the building to answer it. He's always got money in his pocket, and I know for a fact he's not going to an office—"

"So you just jump to the conclusion that he's selling drugs?"

"Well, it does explain a lot of things," she said. Her finger was back against her nose. "Although I can think of one other possibility."

"What's that?" I asked, even though I wasn't sure I wanted to know. As far as I was concerned, Evan was charming, sweet, funny, sincere, and, best of all, genuinely interested in me, plus he kept me supplied with bootleg recordings of Diana Krall. Except for the minor obstacle of being engaged to somebody else, he was perfect . . . and I wasn't ready to hear news that would burst my bubble.

"Maybe he's not selling drugs," Janie said. "Maybe he's selling . . ." She paused dramatically and widened her eyes. "Himself!"

"Oh, come on," I said, and started wiping the perfectly clean table.

"It happens!" Janie said.

"I'm sure there's some other explanation. You know, a rational one," I said, tossing the sponge in the sink. Meanwhile, my mind had instantly conjured up a classified ad for Evan, something that would run on the back pages of the *Village Voice—Handsome, charming, well-built twenty-eight, available for fun and games and maybe more . . .*

"Then why's he so mysterious about it?" Janie asked. "If it's legit, why won't he tell us?"

I turned on the water to drown out the sound of her questions, because I knew that she was right. If Evan had a legitimate job, there was no reason he wouldn't tell us about it.

• • •

Michelle came home the next day, and Evan disappeared, and I tried to walk as fast as I could past their apartment door, certain that if I slowed my pace, I'd hear things I didn't want to hear. Two days later, there was a languid knock at our door, and when I opened it up, Michelle was there, resplendent in leather pants and a boned bustier—the exact thing, I thought sourly, that I normally wore for lounging around the house.

"*Hola,* Michelle," said Janie.

Michelle frowned. Lately, she'd been styling herself *ME-shell.* Janie had made a major point of pronouncing it the plain old American way—or, worse, calling her Micky.

"I'm having a Halloween party," Michelle announced.

"Fun!" said Janie.

"Great!" I added.

"Around eightish on Saturday night," she said. "It's a costume party. Can you bring some beer? And some food and stuff? And help with the coats?"

"You know, there's people you can hire," Janie began.

I cut her off. "We'll help."

"Great," said Michelle. "Eightish. Did I say that already?" She flicked at her long turquoise and silver earrings and wandered off down the hall. Janie scowled. "That is one presumptuous beeyotch."

I set down the Ruth Rendell book I'd been reading and asked the question that had been plaguing me since my first encounter with Michelle. "Why is he with her? Is it just because she's beautiful?"

Janie straightened her blouse, smoothed her hair, and assumed a professorial attitude. "It's not just because she's beautiful. It's also because she's smart."

"Smart?" I scoffed. I hadn't spent as much time in their apartment as Evan had in ours, but the only Michelle-centric reading material I'd glimpsed was a magazine called *Hair Style Monthly.* Michelle didn't watch anything on television besides Madonna's videos, didn't listen to any music except Madonna's songs, and didn't talk about anything but herself, her hair, her skin, and, most recently, the series of oxygen facials she'd embarked upon just like her idol. "She spent three weeks in Paris and she still thinks Bain de Soleil is spelled exactly the way it's pronounced."

"Not smart smart. Man smart," Janie said. "She never lets Evan think that she's a sure thing. She's always leaving. Thus, he's always chasing after her. As long as she keeps herself unattainable, he'll keep trying to catch her."

"Even though she's boring?"

"Even if she's boring, the chase is exciting," Janie explained. She rubbed her nose. "Also, she could be double-jointed."

I groaned and threw my book at her. Janie caught it, then looked at me sternly. "Forget him," she said.

"I don't—"

She held up her hand. "Kate, I see how you look at him. You're going to get your heart broken. She's got him hooked, and he's not interested in breaking it off. Find someone who deserves you."

"She doesn't deserve him," I muttered, even though I knew that what Janie was telling me was true.

"Probably not," Janie said. "But as my father's four ex-wives have remarked, frequently in front of judges, life isn't fair." She slung her arm around me, then steered me toward her bedroom. "Come on, let's find you a costume."

"So tell me," drawled Michelle, tilting her fine-boned face to its most photogenic angle and pursing her lips in a dramatic pout. "What was college like?" Michelle had come to her party as a sexy witch, with a lot of dark red lipstick, high-heeled lace-up black boots underneath a black satin and tulle dress with a tattered hem, and a pointed hat perched at a fetching angle. Given that there'd be a room full of Michelle's fellow models, all of them dressed as sexy somethings—a sexy nurse in an abbreviated white uniform; a sexy cop with handcuffs dangling from her hot pants; a sexy French maid in fishnets and a starched wink of an apron—I'd decided to not even compete, ignored Janie's entreaties, and gone as a pirate. Not a sexy pirate, either, unless you thought that boots, an eyepatch, a plastic hook, and a stuffed plush parrot I'd duct-taped to my shoulder spelled "Do me."

"It was great," I said. "I really loved my classes and having time to just read."

Michelle didn't look impressed. Then again, I wasn't sure I'd ever seen Michelle looking anything other than bored. Bored and lovely, of course. "Maybe I'll go someday," she said, picking a fleck of dried mascara out of one extralong eyelash. "When I'm too old to model anymore. Where'd you go?"

"Columbia."

She stared at me with cool aquamarine eyes. "Maybe you could call someone there, and I could go too."

"Well, that's not normally how it works. Maybe you could talk to an admissions officer."

Michelle smiled, a sly, satisfied smile. "Make sure it's a boy admissions officer," she said, and patted my arm. "I won't have any problems." She peered down at me. "What are you supposed to be, exactly?"

Before I could answer, she'd spotted someone more interesting, waved, and sashayed away. I took a gulp from my glass of rum-spiked cider.

"Arr," I said, and looked around. The apartment was crowded with bodies, all of them far more beautiful than mine. To my left, a stunning blonde in a psychedelic print minidress and white go-go boots was gesturing with her Marlboro and complaining that her booking agent had grabbed her ass again. To my right, a gorgeous brunette with café con leche skin, a tumble of glossy black curls, and a spiderweb inked on her cheek was telling everyone within earshot that she hadn't eaten anything but cabbage soup for the past ten days. I carefully sidled upwind of her and looked at the door. I was wondering how to escape, when two more long-legged lovelies with about six guys in their wake came striding arm and arm through the

door. They pulled off their coats, revealing matching Daisy Duke outfits (minuscule cut-off denim shorts, sleeveless shirts knotted to reveal flawless midriffs, not much else) and piled their outerwear into my arms. I edged my way through the throng to the bedroom, thinking I could dump the coats on Evan and Michelle's bed.

"Hey! A little privacy, please!"

I blinked in the gloom as the tangle of limbs and hair turned into two extremely attractive people having energetic sex in a position I wouldn't have previously believed physically possible.

"Sorry, sorry," I said, staring long enough to make sure that the guy with his legs pretzeled around the woman's neck wasn't Evan. Then I hastily backed out into the living room again with my cheeks flushed and my stuffed parrot wobbling on my shoulder.

"Michelle," I called, over the Madonna dance mix blaring from the stereo. "I'm going to take these coats next door."

She gave me a dismissive wave. Free at last, I hurried into the hallway, and smack into Janie, who was exiting our apartment dressed as a sexy pope (big hat, rosary beads, not much else).

"Oh, no," she said, shaking her head. "Uh-uh. There are . . ." —she shook her head and whacked my hip with her censer, sending a gust of incense billowing into the hallway—"one, two, three, four, five eligible guys there."

"Yeah, and about thirty eligible models."

"Never mind them," Janie said. "You are not going to hide in your bedroom all night."

"Can I just drop these coats off?"

"Thirty seconds," she said, tapping her wrist. "I'll be watching. Now, have you seen my altar boys?"

I shook my head and waited until her back was turned before I slipped into my bedroom, a tiny space that barely had room for a bed, a little table for my lamp with its rose-colored glass shade, and all my books. Oh, sweet relief. In the dark I tugged off my boots, pulled off my parrot, tossed the coats in the corner, and got ready to hide underneath the pale-pink-and-cream-striped comforter with my book when I noticed the shape of a body underneath the sheets. A male body, prone and mumbling. I made out a few words—"crank" and "street" and "Chaplin." *Okay,* I thought, edging backwards. Some homeless guy must have snuck in with the Daisy Duke contingent. Nothing I couldn't handle. I grabbed a can of volumizing hair mousse in case I needed to defend myself, thinking that I'd just close the door, call the cops, and—

The body sat up. "Ahoy, matey," it said. I flicked on the lights and saw Evan in my bed. "Sorry if I scared you," he said.

I set down the mousse, feeling my heart hammering. "What are you doing in here?"

"I couldn't stand the music," he said, making a face like he'd bitten something sour. "I put on Elvis Costello. I put on the Clash. Then the party people show up, and it's all . . ." He started humming his best approximation of "Vogue." "I can only deal with that in very small doses. So come on," he said, patting the comforter. "Get comfortable."

I pulled off my hook and plopped down beside him.

"Do you like my costume?" he asked.

"Well, let's see." I checked him out, happy for the excuse to stare at him. He was dressed in jeans and a long-sleeved T-shirt. "Um . . ."

Evan shook his head mournfully. "I thought you of all people would get it. Come on!" he said, adjusting a pair of thick horn-rimmed glasses. I shrugged apologetically.

"I'm Robert Downey Jr.," he said. "I've been passing out all night, and you're the first one to find me. My costume," he said. "My brilliant, brilliant costume."

"Poor you," I said, arranging myself cross-legged with my back against the wall. My bedroom, while tiny, was my favorite place in the apartment. It had everything I needed: a wide, low comfortable bed covered in the highest-thread-count sheets I could afford, a little table with my lamp and two photographs in silver frames: a head shot of my mother from the year I was born, all ivory skin, raven curls, and perfect profile, and a picture of the three of us at Tanglewood when I was five. Before we'd moved in, I'd planned on stacking my books on plywood and cinderblocks the way I had in college, but Janie had told me that Sy was redecorating and had given me three gorgeous six-foot-high mahogany bookcases with glass doors. My secondhand paperbacks and battered textbooks looked shabby inside of them, but my salary didn't permit me too many hardcovers.

Evan leaned over and lit the candles next to my bed, and the shadows flickered across his face. "You should've gone as Margot Kidder," I told him, leaning back against the headboard. He'd opened the window a crack, and I could feel cool night air on my cheeks. The glow of the moon filtered faintly through my curtains, and I could smell smoke from somebody kindling the first fire of the season in their hearth.

"Who do you think I was last year?" he asked. "I can't repeat myself, Katie!"

"Of course not," I said, savoring the warmth I felt when he said my name. He'd started calling me Katie a few weeks before, and it gave me a jolt of pleasure whenever he said it. I'd been a Kate and a Katerina, but never a Katie.

He shifted on the bed, and I could feel his breath against my cheek as he reached over and pulled my eyepatch over my head. Then he put it on, turning his head left and right for my inspection.

"Very nice," I said. I was surprised to hear how normal my voice sounded. "Piracy becomes you."

"So what are you doing in here?"

"The conversation was getting too intense," I said solemnly. "There's only so much talk of particle physics a girl can take."

He shook his head. "I know," he said. "They're awful, aren't they?"

"But highly decorative," I said, leaning back into the pillows.

"I used to like parties," he said. "My parents would have great ones. I'd pass out the drinks and then, when things were rolling, I'd go around picking up the empties, and if they weren't quite empty, I'd drink 'em. Scotch, rum and coke, white wine . . ." He shook his head. "My parents could never figure out why I was so grumpy the next day. Guess they'd never seen a nine-year-old with a hangover. How about you?"

"My parents went to parties," I said. "My mother used to drag me to these fund-raisers . . ." I sat up straight, indicating Reina's practiced gesture, the way her gaze would unerringly find me, even if I was hiding behind a cluster of battleship-sized basses, or a potted plant, the dramatic gesture she'd make. " 'Please say hello to my *beautiful* daughter, Katerina,' " I intoned in my best Reina voice.

"So what's wrong with that?"

I couldn't tell him what was most wrong with that—a few hundred pairs of eyeballs swinging toward me in unison when I was a pudgy eight-year-old, a gawky twelve-year-old, a slumping, sullen, zit-besmattered fourteen-year-old, and thinking, so hard I could practically hear it, *beautiful?* I pulled a pillow onto my lap and held on to it hard.

"Well, for starters, I can't sing, and everybody at these things wanted to know if I could. They expected me to be able to. And she'd sing . . ." I stopped for a moment, remembering a dozen parties in a dozen gilt and marble reception halls. "Reina, a song!" someone would call. My mother would do a few minutes of obligatory demurral, waving away requests with a plump, bejeweled hand. Then she'd sing for twenty minutes. Plus encores.

"But you can sing," Evan said.

"Oh, no. Not me. No."

"Yes, you can."

Now I was blushing so hard, I was sure I was glowing. "No, I don't sing."

"Yes, you do," he said. His voice was low and teasing. "I've heard you humming in the elevator."

I winced. "Well, humming. That's not singing."

"And you sing in the shower."

"What?"

"The walls are thin," he said. "Don't be ashamed! I like Bon Jovi too!"

Oh, God. "That was Janie," I lied.

"Was not," he said. He rolled over onto his side, propping up his head in his hand and staring at me with his unpatched eye. There was one hair sticking up from his right eyebrow, and my fingertips wanted desperately to smooth it. "Sing me something," he said.

If the room hadn't been so dimly lit, if he hadn't been in my bed, if there hadn't been rum in the cider, I would have said no, forget it, and found a way to change the subject. But what did it matter? He would never be mine, I thought, staring at his face in the rosy glow of the candles, and I could make a fool of myself or impress him completely, and he'd still be going home to sleep with Michelle at the end of the night.

"I'll make you a deal," I said. "I'll sing you something if you tell me what you do for a living."

He plumped the pillow. "You really want to know?"

"You really don't want to tell me?"

"Fine," he said, and grinned at me. "Deal. But you have to go first."

I sat up, straightening my spine and adjusting the red silk scarf I'd tied across my head. Then I thought, *Why not?* I'd never have a chance like this again. I pulled off the scarf and unpinned my hair, letting the damp curls tumble over my cheeks and down my back. I could hear Mrs. Minheizer's gentle voice in my head, telling me how to use my core, how to use my mouth and tongue to shape the air that would carry the sound, how to let the music come not from me but through me.

I held the parrot in my hands like a microphone. "Welcome to the Stuffed Parrot Lounge," I intoned. "My name is Katie Klein, and I'll be here all week. Tip your waitresses. They work hard." Then I took a deep breath and started to sing.

"My funny Valentine," I sang softly. "Sweet comic Valentine. You make me smile with my heart . . ." I could see Evan, out of the corner of my eye, gazing at me raptly, with his total attention, holding himself perfectly still as my alto—a little reedy, but clear and sweet—rang through the room.

"Is your figure less than Greek? Is your mouth a little weak? When you open it to speak, are you smart? Don't change a hair for me. Not if you care for me. Stay, little valentine, stay. Each day is Valentine's Day." I let the last note hang in the air. *Adequate,* my mother would have said, if she was feeling generous. Evan tugged me back beside him by the hem of my loose white blouse. Then he started to clap.

"Wow," he said. "Wow *wow.* You're amazing, do you know that?"

I shook my head, blushing again. "I'm not amazing."

"You're just full of shit, is what you are," Evan said. "Why don't you go on auditions, or sing with a band or something? Did you study music in college?"

"I'm not that good."

He wasn't listening. "I can't believe you can sing like that. I can't believe you're"—he reached over and tapped my chest, right above my heart—"carrying that around with you."

"Okay," I said, hoping he couldn't see me blushing. "Your turn. Spill."

He suddenly got very interested in toying with the horn-rimmed glasses he'd pulled off to make room for my eyepatch. "Well, it's kind of a secret."

"Not drugs?"

"No, no, nothing illegal. I work part-time. I do freelance investigations. Like if someone files a workmen's comp claim, and the company thinks they're faking, I trail them for a few days, see what they're doing, see if they're really wearing a neck brace all day long or if they're meeting ladies at a merengue club. Or marital work. Pre-nups, custody arrangements, stuff like that."

"Really?" That would certainly explain the strange absences and the hush-hush phone calls.

"I also manage a small investment portfolio," he said.

"So you do have a trust fund!"

"Not exactly," he began. "I won some money on TV."

"Doing what?"

He mumbled his response toward my comforter. "*America's Funniest Home Videos.*" Then he lifted his head. "But don't tell Michelle I told you. She thinks it's déclassé. She wants me to pretend I was on *Wheel of Fortune.*"

I started laughing. I couldn't help it. "*America's Funniest Home Videos?* Is that the show where somebody's always getting hit in the crotch with a golf club?"

"Katie, Kate, Kate," he said, shaking his head. "You're being very unfair. Sometimes it's somebody getting hit in the crotch with a Wiffle ball bat."

"But there's usually a crotch involved, right?" He didn't say yes, but he didn't say no either. "So were you the hitter or the hittee?"

"Neither," he said. "I was the lucky guy in the front row of my sister's wedding when her bulldog started humping the priest's leg."

I stared at him. "I know you're kidding."

"Not kidding," he said. "Look it up. It was called 'Ringbearer Bulldog Goes Berserk.' And just for the record, the priest completely deserved it. He gave my sister a really hard time just because she was a lesbian in college."

"Was that her official minor or something?" I asked. The door swung open, admitting a wedge of unwelcome light.

"Evan?"

I squinted until I could make out the peaked point of Michelle's witch hat.

"Oh, hey, babe," he said, so warmly that I felt my heart shrivel into a chunk of the wadded-up tinfoil.

She shook her finger at him and pouted. "What are you doing hiding in here? People are dancing."

"I'll be out in a minute."

"Bye, then." She closed the door, leaving us in semidarkness.

"Well," said Evan.

"Well," I repeated. "Back to particle physics. And don't worry," I said, "your secret is safe with me."

"I'll bring you some snacks," he said, swinging his legs out of the bed. "Or a study guide."

He pulled my eyepatch back over my head and settled it over one eye. "Have fun," I told him.

"You too," he said, and closed the door gently behind him.

TWELVE

"It's . . . devastating," said Philip Cavanaugh. He was sunk into an armchair in his living room, which was full of white-on-white flower arrangements and thick with the cloying scent of lilies. As I watched, he lifted one hand slowly and touched his index finger to the center of his lips. Then his hand drifted back down past his coffee cup and landed in his lap.

I'd called Janie as soon as I'd gotten outside the coffee shop to tell her of my misadventures with Lisa DeAngelis.

"Shtupping the sitter," Janie had said, over the sounds of Sam, Jack, and Sophie singing "Five Little Monkeys." "How revoltingly cliché. So what now?"

"Call the police?" I guessed.

"Why not have a chat with the merry widower first?" said Janie.

I looked down at my outfit. "I don't think I'm really dressed for a sympathy call."

"*Au contraire!* You'll lift his spirits! Go on. I've got everything under control here." She paused. "The kids still take naps, right?"

"Right."

I figured that it wouldn't do to show up at the widower's house empty-handed, so I cruised to the Super Shopper on Route 9 and bought an apple pie and a gingham-checked tea towel. Back in the van I liberated the pie from its plastic clamshell, wrapped it in a towel and drove to the scene of the crime. I would have swung home to heat it up and make it look even more authentically homemade, but someone—probably me—had left a plastic cutting board in the oven. The month before I'd set the oven to preheat and didn't realize what had happened until the smoke alarm went off and I opened the oven door to reveal a smoking, dripping, gooey mess. I'd run the self-clean cycle twice since then, but still, everything I baked tasted faintly of burnt plastic, including the roast I'd prepared when my brother-in-law and his girlfriend came for dinner.

My knees shook as I lifted the Cavanaughs' brass knocker. I'd had a whole song and dance ready to get me through the front door—*I just wanted to convey my sympathies in person, such a tragedy, such a terrible thing*—but I found myself so lost in my memories of what had happened the last time that door had swung open, that when Philip Cavanaugh answered my knocks, I couldn't say anything at all. No matter: he'd merely nodded, taken the pie, and led me into the living room.

"Devastating," he said again, and blinked his pale watery eyes, a motion that seemed to sap his energy entirely.

I nodded, looking around the living room, a twin of my own that Kitty had transformed into a warm, clean, welcoming space, the kind of room you'd want to spend time in. Her walls were painted a creamy cappuccino brown, and she'd chosen chocolate brown leather sofas, accent tables painted buttery yellow, and burnished wicker baskets for the toys and books and magazines. There was an Oriental rug in crimson and gold that even my untrained eye could recognize as the real item, not one of the mass-produced department store numbers that graced my own floors, and big gold-framed paintings on the walls, seascapes in a primitive style, where the sun was lemon yellow, the sea was turquoise blue, and the beach was dotted with red umbrellas that bloomed like poppies.

Philip followed my gaze. "Kitty's mother did those."

"They're beautiful."

"They're Cape Cod. Where she's from," he said hoarsely. "We'd take the girls back there for two weeks every summer. I can't . . ."

His voice caught, and he blinked again. "I can't . . . believe . . ." Nor could he muster the energy to complete the sentence. I looked away as he wiped his eyes, focusing on the photographs in painted wooden frames that lined the mantel. There was one of Kitty and the girls, each of them holding a wedge of watermelon and grinning, and a wedding picture, with Kitty cool and lovely behind her veil and Philip beaming beside her.

My plan—such as it was—was simple: pretend that Kitty and I had actually been friends. Pretend that she'd opened up to me, and maybe Philip would do the same.

"I've always loved that picture," I murmured, pointing at the mantel, realizing that while I'd been staring at the walls and the pictures, Philip Cavanaugh had been staring at me. More specifically, he'd been staring at my chest, shown off to eye-popping advantage in Janie's too-small sweater. I crossed my legs, wishing for Lisa's sweatpants. When I looked up, Philip's watery gaze had drifted down to my thighs. His jaw hung open, and I could hear him breathing through his mouth. *Ick.* Philip wasn't a bad-looking guy. All of the elements were there: the blue gray eyes, the silvery blond hair, the solid cheekbones and the height, the narrow hips and broad shoulders, but it was all a little soft, a touch unfocused, a little blurred around the edges. He'd probably spent his whole life hearing *Oh, you look just like Robert Redford!* But up close, he didn't. He looked like Robert Redford's younger, not-terribly-bright second cousin, the one who'd have a few too many cocktails at your grandfather's birthday party and think it the height of hilarity to slip an ice cube down your back when it was time to dance.

Could I imagine him pawing the sitter in the car on the way home? Indeed I could. Could I imagine him whispering in the sitter's ear, *If Kitty wasn't around, we could be together,* and asking whether she knew anyone with free time and low morals who'd do the deed? Possibly. What I couldn't figure out was why someone as cool and collected and lovely as Kitty had married this mouth-breather in the first place.

Philip cleared his throat noisily, and I settled on another tactic—flirting my heart out. I licked my lips and tried to remember what it was like to look enticing to a man who hadn't seen you splayed on a table, sweating and cursing and attempting to push out an eight-pound baby. It was like asking someone who'd spent the last five years defrosting fish sticks to whip up a salmon en papillote.

"Have you heard anything from the police?" I asked in my softest, most come-hither voice.

He shook his head.

"When I was at the police station"—I smoothed my pants and toyed with a lock of hair, dropping my already low voice half an octave—"you said . . . that is, I overheard you saying that it was all your fault."

He blinked his watery eyes at me again. *"Content,"* he croaked. "That columnist Kitty worked with got hate mail . . . death threats. There are unbalanced people. Crazies." He shook his head. "She said nobody knew her. Ghost . . . writer. Nobody knew." Tears splashed down his stubbly cheeks. "She liked it. Liked . . . flying under the radar. Being . . . invisible. But I think . . ." He rubbed his hands up and down the sides of his face, filling the room with a rasping, sandpapery sound. "Somebody found out."

Which, of course, was what I thought he would say if he was trying to throw me—or the cops—off his trail.

"Any somebody in particular?" I asked.

He stared at me, mouth slack, trying to decipher the sentence. I tried again, leaning forward, touching his hand with mine. "Was there anyone who'd bothered her, or called the house, or come here before?"

He shook his head.

"My fault . . ." he said. "I should . . . have insisted."

I pulled a Starbucks napkin out of my pocket and handed it to him. In slow motion, he folded it, then dragged it across his eyes.

"I'm so sorry," I murmured. "So sorry for your loss." I wanted to ask him a dozen things: *What was your wife doing in New York? Was it work or something else? Was Kitty having an affair? Were you shtupping the sitter?* Instead I leaned forward and tugged at the hem of my sweater, putting the already-straining fabric tight against my breasts. "Remind me again how you met Kitty."

"At . . . the office," he said. "She walked in . . ." His eyes filled with tears even as they stayed locked on my bosom. "She was so . . ."

Beautiful, I filled in.

"Alive," he said. "Curious about everything. Asking questions . . . looking around."

Asking questions, I repeated in my head. *Looking around.*

"I loved her," he said. His eyes were slipping shut again.

"I'm so sorry," I said, and got to my feet, thinking about what Lisa had told me. "I should be gettig home." I wiped my hands on my pants. "The last time I was over—" Oops. "I mean, not the last time, obviously, but earlier this month, Kitty and I were upstairs and I think I might have dropped my earring in the bathroom. Do you think it would be all right if I ran up there to take a look?"

He shrugged, then nodded. I thanked him and walked sedately back to the foyer. My breath was coming quick and fast as I dashed upstairs, tiptoed past the powder room, and eased open the door to the master bedroom. Lemon yellow walls, a white lacy comforter, two dozen ornamental pillows at the head of the bed, the kind that would have to be removed every night and repositioned each morning. I crept across the room to the dressing table, thinking that Kitty had had way better taste than I did, and she was much tidier too. There was a heavy mirror in an ornate wrought-iron frame, a profusion of cut-crystal perfume bottles on a mirrored tray underneath it, a curvy little seat with a plush upholstered cushion. Her comb and hairbrush were lined up side by side, along with a pot of loose powder and a brush, a wicker box of tissues, a pink crystal barrette that looked like it belonged to one of her daughters. No laptop. Maybe the police had confiscated it.

Her dresser was covered with more gold-framed photographs. I saw Kitty and Philip, beaming at each other in their wedding finery; Kitty in a hospital johnny with a plastic bracelet around her wrist, an exultant smile on her face, and two tiny blanket-wrapped babies in her arms; Kitty with her daughters again at the Red Wheel Barrow's annual bake sale, each one of them proudly holding a pie.

I shoved my hair out of my eyes and eased open the top dresser drawer. I wasn't sure what I was hoping to see—a ribbon-tied stack of love letters with a New York City zip code and a signature that wasn't Philip's? A book labeled "My Diary" with an entry from October naming the killer, and perhaps offering a detailed physical description and a Polaroid? I worked my way through the drawer, unearthing a packet of birth-control pills and a bottle of aspirin, lip gloss, hand cream, laminated fold-out maps of New York and Washington, and finally, a photograph in a frame that matched the ones on the wall. I turned it over in my hands and saw Kitty and a pretty, dark-haired woman, both of them in their early twenties, with their arms around each other's shoulders, smiling at the camera as the wind blew through their hair. It took me two tries before I was able to slide the photograph out of its frame and read what was written on the back: "K and D, summer '92, Montauk."

I put the picture back in its frame and went back to the drawer, digging until I found a piece of the same creamy stationery on which she'd written Evan's phone number, with the words *Stuart 1968.* What was that? A place? A name and year? I refolded the paper and put it back.

Finally, near the back of the drawer, I pulled out a postcard with a shot of the Statue of Liberty, addressed to a P.O. box in Eastham, Massachusetts. "Dear Bonnie," it read. "New York City is everything I could ever want and more. We are together now. Happier than I can even believe. All my love always." No signature, no stamp. Whoever had written the card had never sent it.

"Did you find what you were looking for?"

I whirled around and saw Philip standing in the doorway, holding on to the jamb as if he'd topple over without its support, with a wolfish look in his glazed eyes.

"Your earring," he said. "Did you find it?"

I shook my head, suddenly aware of the king-sized bed that seemed, somehow, to be growing by the minute, stretching wider and wider until it took up every centimeter of space in the room.

Philip attempted a lecherous smile. It sat unsteadily on his face, like garnish on an oily salad plate. "I like your shoes," he said. The instant the words were out of his mouth, his leer slid away and was replaced by grief and bewilderment. He looked old, and tired, and very, very sad.

"I'll show myself out," I said, putting the postcard back in the drawer and taking a hesitant step toward the door. "I just want you to know how sorry—"

Philip moved with a speed I never would have suspected from a man punch-drunk with sorrow. In three swift steps he crossed the room, fell to his knees, wrapped his arms around my waist, and pressed his face hard against my belly. "Tell me something," he said, his words coming fast, right on top of each other. "Was she happy?" I could feel the warmth and wetness of tears against my legs. "You were her friend. You knew her. Was she happy?"

This poor guy, I thought, forgetting for the moment that, if my theory were true, Philip Cavanaugh had been consoling himself in advance with the babysitter, and his wife might have been traveling to New York for some extracurricular activities of her own. He sounded so desperate. I was reminded of my father wandering through our apartment with his oboe in his hand, the way he did every time my mother went away.

"You were her friend," Philip said again. In that moment, I found myself wishing desperately that it had been true. I rested my hands on his shoulders, cleared my throat, and looked down at his bowed blond head as his hands loosened their desperate grip on my hips and migrated over to my ass.

"Stay with me," he wept. "Stay with me, please. I don't want to be alone."

Okay, Kate, I thought. I patted the top of his head gently, as if he were a large dog I suspected might bite. Don't panic. Be calm. Ask yourself the question that's gotten you out of tougher times than these: WWJD? What would Janie do, if she found a bereaved and possibly drugged widower sobbing and—oh, dear—tugging at her pants?

"Philip," I said, twisting my torso incrementally, first left, then right, then left again, until he'd loosened his grip. "I have to go now," I said, and patted his head again. "I have to go back to my children."

"I'm sorry," he muttered. He dropped his hands, letting them hang limply by his knees.

"Oh, that's okay," I said. I grabbed my purse and my coat. "If there's anything I can do . . ." I scribbled my phone number on a scrap of paper, hoping against hope that he wouldn't misinterpret the gesture, and made it down the stairs as fast as I could.

Back in the car, I turned on the heater, gripped the steering wheel hard until my hands stopped shaking, and did a few neck rolls. Once my heart had stopped pounding, I pulled out Sophie's notebook and wrote down what I remembered from the picture and the postcard. Then I flipped to a blank page and wrote, "Asking questions. Looking around." What had Kitty wanted to know? What was she doing in the city three days a week? And who had she been before she'd met Philip, had her babies, and turned into the most formidably perfect mother in Upchurch?

THIRTEEN

I parked the minivan in the garage and stuck my head into the living room. The kids were playing cheater's Candy Land, and Janie was slumped on the couch. Her pink silk blouse was untucked and missing two buttons, and her low-riding jeans had a rip on the cuff.

"Thanks for watching them," I said, then took a closer look. "Are you all right?"

"Little bastards zipped me in their tent," Janie said, pushing herself upright and running her hands through her tangled hair.

I glared at my children. "Did you guys do that?"

Sophie giggled. Sam and Jack stared at the game board.

"Say you're sorry."

"Sorry," they chorused, as Janie waved their apology away and staggered toward the stairs. "May . . . need . . . transfusion. Never . . . having . . . kids." So much for my plan of loading everyone in the van and driving to the pay phone to call Evan again. I sent all three of the kids to the Uncooperative Corner and got to work on dinner—fish sticks and frozen sweet-potato fries on a baking sheet in the oven, frozen peas and carrots bubbling away on the stove. Sam and Jack watched me from their perch, arguing over which one of them would get the red plate, and I spent five minutes going through my cabinets until I'd located a second red plate, at which point they both decided they wanted white plates instead. Sophie turned up her nose at her meal until I dug a jar of wasabi sauce and pickled ginger out of the refrigerator, gave her a set of chopsticks, and told her it was deep-fried sushi.

At eight thirty, when Janie and all three kids were sleeping, I fixed myself a plate of fish sticks and sweet-potato fries and poured Chardonnay into a plastic cup. I set my dinner on the coffee table, pulled the Hello Kitty notebook out of my purse, and curled up to read. "We are together now." What did that mean? Who was the brunette in the picture, and could I plausibly arrange a trip to Montauk to find out?

When I opened my eyes again, it was ten o'clock. There was a pair of wheeled suitcases leaning next to the front door, and my husband—tall and thin and intense, with a shadow along his cheeks and his tie pulled askew—was nuzzling my neck. "Do you know there's a strange woman passed out in the guest room?"

"Your lucky day," I said, yawning.

"Don't get up," he whispered, kissing my neck again. I ran my hands over his thick black hair, touched his face lightly, then traced his belt buckle with one fingertip. Janie and the kids were sleeping, or at least quiet, the washing machines and dishwasher were running, which would mask any telltale grunts or sighs, we were both awake, and I wasn't having my period, so yes, there was a chance we could have sex for the first time in . . . I thought back. And back. And back some more. Yikes. What if I'd forgotten how?

"I felt terrible I couldn't be here for you," he said. Not so terrible that he didn't have an erection pulsing behind the fly of his pinstriped pants. I yawned again, then eased his zipper down. "It must have been awful."

"It was scary," I said, as he slid his hands under my tight sweater. "And they haven't arrested anyone yet, I went to see Philip Cavanaugh, and . . ."

"Oh. Oh, baby." He'd unhooked my bra and had one hand squeezing each of my breasts. First the left one, then the right one, then both at the same time, like he was comparison shopping. I sucked in my breath.

"She was a ghostwriter," I said as he yanked off my pants.

"Touch me," he panted, taking my right hand and pressing it against the front of his pants, in case I was confused about where he wanted to be touched.

"For Laura Lynn Baird, you know, that scary-looking, blond—" He pressed his lips against mine, whether out of passion or a desire to shut me up, I wasn't sure. I kissed him back as he straightened up and put his hand on my neck. The pressure was light but undeniable. I sighed, bent down, and fell to.

"Oh, God," he gasped. "Oh, God, Kate, that's so good."

I bobbed my head up and down with my hands on his hips. "You know," he gasped, "I heard something about Phil Cavanaugh once."

"Mmph?"

"Some woman. Him and some woman. Oh, God, don't stop."

I lifted my head and took a quick breath. "When?"

"Last summer," he said. His head was lolling back against the couch pillows. "The guy who told me—Denny Simon, from the bank, remember?—he said they were hot and heavy last summer. Oh, God, like that. Just like that."

Last summer, I thought as Ben lifted me back onto the couch. *Interesting.*

"Anne something. Or Nan something. Or—Kate," Ben said, tugging my sweater over my head, popping off two of the buttons. "I need to be inside you." The buttons pinged on the floor, and I made a mental note to retrieve them before we went up to bed. Sophie and Jack knew enough to put strange objects into their mouths, but Sam wasn't a hundred percent yet, and I'd already made one trip to the emergency room this month when he'd stuffed a dried cranberry up his nose.

Ben slid his hand up my thigh. I closed my eyes.

"Oh. Oh." Not the sitter, then, but Anne or Nan somebody. And maybe the sitter too. I had to admire Phil's energy. Then I wondered if it had been payback. Maybe Kitty had been trysting in New York when she was supposed to be ghostwriting, and while the Kitty was away . . .

"Oh," I gasped as he eased my legs apart. "Oh, honey, wait. My diaphragm . . ."

"I'll pull out," he panted.

The last time I'd fallen for that one, we'd had Sam and Jack nine months later. "It'll just take a second." He groaned but sat back on the couch. I wrapped the afghan around my waist and raced up the stairs. The diaphragm was where I'd left it, in the medicine cabinet, and I felt encouraged: at least it wasn't visibly dusty. I found a half-full tube of spermicide, squirted a double layer around the edge, then filled the diaphragm itself with the clear goop. *Better safe than sorry,* I thought, one foot on the toilet seat. I eased the diaphragm in, picked up the afghan, and scurried back downstairs, where my husband sat. He'd taken off his shirt and tie and his pale body was completely naked except for black socks and a copy of *The Economist* in his lap. I flung the magazine aside, ran my hands through the sparse black hair on his chest, and settled myself on top of him, thinking that it was sort of like riding a bike: no matter how long it had been, you never forgot how.

"Oh," he sighed. "Oh."

"Don't talk," I said, rocking my hips and pressing my fingers against his lips.

"Why not?" he asked, taking my index finger between his teeth and biting down lightly.

I grabbed his shoulders and closed my eyes. "Because it's interfering with my ability to pretend you're that cute doctor on *ER.*"

"Very funny," he said, rolling me onto my back. I sighed at how good I felt, how complete. It was, I realized, the first time since I'd found Kitty's body that I hadn't been completely occupied with thoughts of the murder. And of course, with that thought, I began to think about Kitty and Philip again. Ben's breathing speeded up. I clutched at his back. "Oh, God!" he said in a strangled whisper. He bit his lip to keep from crying out, and his hands dug into my hips as he shuddered.

"See," I said, wriggling out from underneath him a few seconds later, "good things happen when you come home from work when I'm still awake."

He rested his sweaty cheek against mine. "I know. And I'm sorry. It's been so long."

"I think Chevy Chase's talk show lasted longer than you did." I curled up in a corner of the couch, still flushed and breathing hard.

"You can do better," he said, pulling me against him. I felt him smile against my cheek as he wrapped his long, thin legs around my not so long, not so thin ones.

"Al Sharpton's presidential campaign?"

"Al Sharpton's campaign actually lasted quite a while," he informed me, easing me onto my back and stroking slowly between my legs. "His legitimate hopes of attaining the presidency may have been short-lived, but the campaign went on forever."

"Don't stop," I murmured as my eyes slipped shut. It felt so good, so good . . .

"Mommy?"

"Mommy's busy," my husband called over the back of the couch. *Too late,* I thought, wrapping the afghan around me and getting unsteadily to my feet. Nothing kills the mood quite like a four-year-old who can't sleep.

"Mommy, Sam says he needs a drink of water," Sophie said, stepping down the stairs. "But I told him, 'No water after bedtime because then you'll wet the bed.' But then Sam said . . ." She peered at the diamonds of bare flesh that peeped through the holes of the afghan. "Where are your underpants?"

"Hang on a minute, Soph," I said, tucking the afghan more tightly around my bare legs, then lifting her in my arms. "See you soon," I whispered to Ben. But by the time Sam had been given his water and escorted to and from the bathroom and Sophie had been lullabied back to sleep, my husband was passed out in his boxer shorts, snoring on top of the quilt.

My rotten luck. I brushed my teeth, folded my afghan, and looked longingly at the shower. It was late, and I'd be exhausted in the morning, but I was still too turned on to sleep.

With three kids and no time, I'd gotten masturbation down to a science. A fast science, I thought, five minutes later, as I leaned against the wet tiled walls, panting and shuddering, with the handheld nozzle thrashing like a possessed snake where I'd dropped it on the shower floor. It was sad, I decided, as I turned off the water, but I'd probably had more fun with the shower than with Ben. In fact, I was pretty sure that since we'd moved to Upchurch, most of my orgasms had been of the DIY variety: an indictment of suburban living if ever there was one. Were there any married couples with children who still had fulfilling sex lives? Or were all of these perfect Upchurch mommies secretly like me, feeling like they were just playing a part, like they'd wandered into some stranger's bedroom farce, sleeping with their husbands occasionally, lusting after the hunky Little People's Music instructor obsessively, and still falling asleep thinking of their exes?

FOURTEEN

"Tell me there's no hope," I'd begged my best friend on a Monday morning as Janie and I sat at our battered metal desks at *New York Night.* Our work space was overflowing with the day's newspapers, the week's tabloids, and dozens of promotional tchochkes (coffee mugs, T-shirts, a stuffed pig that squealed a movie title when you squeezed its belly).

"Can't," she said crisply, hitting enter and send and shipping off some staff writer's latest opus—six hundred words on celebrities who had sex in public bathrooms. "There's always hope."

"Like what? Michelle could lose all her limbs in an industrial accident? Even if she was just a torso, she'd still be better looking than me. Even if she was just a head."

"Not true," Janie said. "Although she would be considerably more portable. And again, I remind you: A, you're beautiful, and B, physical beauty is both fleeting and not the point here. The point is Michelle's unattainability and, I suspect, Evan's deep-seated fear of commitment, which has manifested itself as an engagement to a woman who's never going to actually walk down the aisle with him."

I stared at her. "You think she's going to dump him?"

Janie opened her mouth, shut it, then shook her head sadly. "I give up," she said.

I sighed, then rested my head against my own keyboard and

started banging it gently against the keys. Nobody seemed to notice. The music editor didn't miss a word in his conversation; Sandra the book critic didn't look up from the manuscript she was scowling at. Five minutes later, Polly cruised by and dropped a photograph on my computer keyboard. "You're up," she said.

I studied the photograph. It was slated to run on our back page, which, in the very height of wit, was called the "Back Page" and always featured a celebrity caught picking a wedgie or scratching indelicately in his or her hindquarters. This week's picture was of a cluster of a dozen drunk-looking people, one with his hand obligingly down the back of his pants, plus girls in jeans and stilettos dancing on the table. My job would be to figure out who everyone was and write a witty yet accurate caption. *Okay,* I thought, squinting at the faces. Rapper, rapper, model, model, celebrity, publicist, celebrity publicist . . . My heart stuttered in my chest. There was an elbow in the picture, an elbow and a little bit of arm. The side of a hip, a flash of cheek, and a headful of long red hair.

I knew that arm. I knew that hair. Hadn't I spent months fantasizing that their owner would perish in a tragic accident, leaving me a clear field to console and, eventually, marry her fiancé?

"Hey, Polly," I called, struggling to keep my voice steady. "When was this shot?"

"Last night," she yelled back. "At the Mercer Kitchen."

I bent back over the picture with my pulse thudding in my ears. Michelle was supposed to be out of town. That's what Evan had told us. Up in New Hampshire, paddling a canoe and climbing mountains for an outdoor gear catalogue. I straightened up, heading toward the back of the newsroom, where the photographers worked, with the picture in my hand. "Was this cropped?" I asked. Pay dirt. The uncropped version of the shot, which the photographer obligingly printed for me, revealed that skinny, ivory-colored arm was looped firmly around the waist of a handsome man with chin-length dark brown hair. The man was nuzzling the redhead's neck, and he was most assuredly not Evan McKenna.

I racewalked over to Janie's desk and brandished the picture in her face. "Look," I told her. "Look at this."

She looked. "God," she murmured. "You'd think one of his three publicists would tell him not to scratch his ass in public."

"Not the rapper," I said, pointing. "Here. This arm. Right there. Who's that?"

She stared at me. "Oh, fun! Is this like Where's Waldo for adults or something?"

"Look," I said again, and showed her the uncropped version of the picture. Janie studied it carefully. "Oh, my," she said. "Oh, dear." She put the picture aside and walked me back to my desk. "Okay, you need to listen to me."

But I couldn't. I was jittery, bouncing on the balls of my feet. "She's cheating on him!" I said. "And when he finds out . . . and they break up . . ."

Janie shook her head. "How's he going to find out?" she asked.

I looked at her. I hadn't thought this part through. "I'll tell him?" I guessed.

"No, you won't. You ever heard the expression 'Don't shoot the messenger'?"

I nodded.

"You know who you are if you tell him? You're the messenger." She pressed her hands together and cocked her index fingers up at my heart. "Bang, bang."

"But . . . but someone has to tell him. We can't let him marry someone who's cheating on him!"

Janie shook her head sadly and pressed her freshly lipsticked lips together. "Not our job," she said.

"So what do we do?"

She picked up the photograph and tapped its edge on her desk. "We wait," she finally said. "We consider the possibility that he might already know."

I started to shake my head. "Why would he stay with someone who was cheating on him?"

"Remember what I told you. It's the thrill of the chase. The unattainable." She considered. "And let's not forget the make-up sex."

I pulled the picture out of her hands and studied it carefully. Maybe I was wrong. Lots of girls had thin hips and red hair. Even if that skinny arm was attached to Michelle, the fact that she was back in New York, unbeknownst to her boyfriend, and at a party with another guy didn't necessarily mean anything, although it certainly strongly suggested it. But maybe she'd just come home early. Maybe Evan knew all about it. Maybe it was no big deal. Still, I had to be sure.

"Nope, sorry, she's still up in New Hampshire," Evan said, when I called and asked whether his intended might be available to help me pick out an outfit for a product launch party. "I could give you her cell phone." "Thanks," I said, and hung up.

Ten minutes later I was on the phone with Michelle's agency, telling them that I was calling from *New York Night* and that we were doing a photo spread on new trends in lingerie. "I've got a blonde and a brunette, just need a redhead," I said. "About five ten, a size four—"

"Four?" the booker asked, sounding skeptical.

"Two!" I said. "Oh, and, um, I don't know quite how to put this, but we're not looking for a rocket scientist. The last shoot we did, the model wouldn't stop talking about some Thomas Pynchon book she'd just read."

"Five ten, size two, not a genius," recited the booker. "I'll messenger you half a dozen cards this afternoon."

"That's great. And the shoot's tomorrow morning, so whoever you send, they have to be available and in New York now."

"Got it," she said, and hung up. An hour later I was flipping through a stack of tall, gorgeous, available, nonbibliophilic redheads. Michelle was card number three.

Calm, I told myself, even though I was sweating and flushed and starting to get a headache. I washed down three Advil with a swig of warm coffee as Janie sent the words "Don't be the messenger!" over to my screen nineteen times.

My next step was figuring out who Mr. Wavy Hair was. A phone call to the publicist in the picture answered that. "Travis Marx. He's the Pantene man."

The whole day was starting to feel a little unreal. "Beg your pardon?"

"Pantene shampoo and conditioner? He's their hair model. Mr. Pantene. Best follicles in the business. Why? You guys want to book him?"

"Maybe someday," I said. "Who's his agent?" I swallowed more coffee and made two more phone calls. The gullible agent was all too happy to give me the Pantene man's home address, ostensibly so I could send him clippings of ads that had appeared in *New York Night.* Then it was time to hit the pavement.

In the months since he'd revealed his work as an investigator, Evan had occasionally solicited our help. He'd show up at our front door on Saturday morning in jeans and a baseball cap with a notebook in his hands. "I need you in the lobby of the Algonquin," he'd say, handing me a pair of sunglasses and a man's photograph. "This charming fellow says he's spending his Saturdays doing volunteer work in a soup kitchen. The soon-to-be-ex-wife isn't so sure." I'd sit in the lobby, sipping Diet Cokes and looking for the man, and when the man checked in, glancing furtively over his shoulder, hands trembling as he pulled a wad of bills from his pocket, I'd snap a few pictures, call Evan on his cell phone, and we'd go out for brunch.

Or "Equinox," he'd say. "I can't believe he found a way to work even less," Janie complained, but eventually we'd pull on workout gear (oversized sweatpants in my case, skintight Lycra in Janie's) and gossip on the treadmills until a woman allegedly suffering from whiplash and herniated disks showed up in a hot pink unitard for high impact aerobics. Or "Dalton." That day he'd arrived up at the offices of *New York Night* at lunchtime with a plastic bag containing a corned beef sandwich, saddle shoes, and a plaid skirt. "You're looking for a girl named . . ." He consulted his notebook and scowled.

"Lockhart. Ugh. Why do rich people give their kids such stupid names? Anyhow. The nanny's supposed to meet her; Mom thinks she's been letting Lockhart take the subway home by herself."

I fingered the skirt dubiously, imagining my winter white thighs underneath it. "Couldn't I just pretend to be one of the mothers?"

"You could," said Evan, grinning at me, eyes sparkling beneath his thick eyebrows. "But that would be a lot less amusing for me." So I ate the sandwich and slipped into the bathroom. ("Do I even want to ask?" Janie inquired as she smoothed on another coat of mascara.) Thirty minutes later I was hanging around outside the school. At three-fifteen little Lockhart breezed past me, a backpack almost as big as she was bouncing on her scrawny shoulders, and headed for the subway, sans nanny.

I thought about asking him why Michelle couldn't help him, why she couldn't be the one on the treadmill, or in the lobby, or in the plaid skirt outside the school. But the answer was obvious. Michelle was the kind of woman you'd notice and remember. As for me, it turned out that I had a talent for invisibility, developed over years of living with Reina. I knew how to melt into the shadows, how to stand quietly in a corner, how to pull up a newspaper and make myself completely inconspicuous. Just say the magic words—*My beautiful daughter, Katerina*—and I'd be gone.

At five o'clock that night I slid the photograph of Michelle and the Pantene Man into an envelope and presented myself at the midtown offices of a car rental company. By six I was parked across from a limestone building on the Upper East Side, slumped behind the wheel of a nondescript Neon, staring at the door to Mr. Pantene's apartment. I had a knitted cap pulled low over my forehead, my winter coat to keep me warm, and I was provisioned with a turkey and cheese sandwich and a bag of chips, two bottles of water, a disposable camera, and an empty plastic pitcher in which to pee, should that become necessary.

It didn't. I was ready to wait for hours—all through the night if I had to—but this one was an easy layup, a home run, a touchdown. At nine o'clock that night Michelle and Travis came sauntering down the street, arm in arm, heads thrown back, laughing. She wore a short black-and-white-striped dress that whipped around her perfect thighs and no hat or coat or mittens, in spite of the cold. Maybe she had guilt to keep her warm. Mr. Pantene wore an everyhipster's black turtleneck sweater and black jeans. I watched as Travis held the door open and Michelle whispered something in his ear before slipping inside. I snapped pictures of everything, including his hand lingering at her hip.

Two hours later I'd had two sets of prints developed, dropped off the car, and made my way back to our apartment. Janie was waiting for me with a bowl of popcorn and a stiff vodka and grapefruit juice.

"All true," I said, sliding the photographs across the kitchen counter.

"You can't tell him," she said.

"I wasn't—"

"You can't, Kate. Here." She handed me the glass. "Drink." She led me to the couch. "Sit. Reflect on what I've told you. Bide your time." I nodded numbly and sipped my drink. "If it's meant to be, it'll be."

"And if not?"

Janie shrugged, slid the photos into a drawer and gave me a kind smile. "You'll always have me."

Janie and I had big plans for New Year's Eve, honed through weeks of planning and discussion. Fancy restaurants were too crowded, takeout was too pathetic, and the one time I'd accompanied her to Sy's place to ring in the new year, I'd felt so out of place (not to mention roughly twice the size and infinitely more broke than the other female attendees) that I'd befriended the coat check girl and spent the entire night helping her hang and retrieve furs.

So this year we were going to Big Wong in Chinatown for

Peking duck and dumpling soup. After dinner, we'd go to the Lo Kee Inn on Mott Street and sing karaoke until the ball dropped in Times Square. "With your voice and my choreography, we'll probably get a record deal!" Janie said. (I'd agreed to learn her dance steps but had drawn the line at donning a Tina Turner wig.) After much hesitation, I'd called Evan the week before to invite him. "Sounds like fun," he said, but he and Michelle had plans: dinner and dancing at Windows on the World.

"Have a good time," I'd told him. Janie and I backed up all of our computer files and called our parents to wish them a happy New Year. Then Janie pulled me into her bedroom and handed me a pink sweater and a pair of sparkly high-heeled, hot pink sandals. "You know what my New Year's resolution is? To get you laid."

I frowned at the sweater. "Can't you just decide to lose ten pounds like everyone else?"

She shook her head. "I'm already perfect," she said and pushed the shoes into my hands. "Sy lent me his car and driver."

I pulled the sweater over my head, remembering how the last time Sy had lent her something (specifically, use of his Miami Beach condo for a weekend), Sy hadn't actually known about it until after the fact.

"No, really! I asked him!" she said, steering me toward the bathroom.

I lent her a necklace, beads of Murano glass my mother had brought me back from Italy. She lent me some earrings, platinum and diamond hoops whose cost I couldn't bring myself to think about. We spritzed each other with perfume, toasted each other with the bottle of cheap champagne the owners of *New York Night* had given us in lieu of a holiday bonus, and headed out into the cold.

By eleven o'clock, we'd completed our Tina Turner medley ("Proud Mary" with a segue into "Private Dancer," complete with Janie in a silver-fringed minidress and complementary wig) and climbed off the stage, sweaty and breathless and fifty dollars richer, to the enthusiastic applause of two hundred liquored-up revelers.

"Told you we'd win!" Janie said as we wiggled through the crowd, accepting high fives and glasses of champagne on the way back to our table.

I grinned back at her, then whirled around, glaring. "Did somebody just pinch my butt?" I shouted.

"That was me," Janie shouted back, shaking her fingers joyously. "Happy New Year! I'm going to powder my nose!"

I waved her goodbye and threaded my way through the crowd back to our table, where there were two vodka and cranberry juices waiting.

"From the gentleman at the bar," the waitress said, pointing. I followed her finger and my heart stopped. Unless my eyes were deceiving me and I was experiencing some sort of acute New Year's Eve desire-induced hallucination, Evan McKenna was sitting at the bar, in a tuxedo, without a tie. Alone.

"Evan!" His name burst out of my mouth, a lot louder than I'd intended. Here he was, as if I'd imagined him into being. Only in my daydreams he wasn't drunk, I thought as he got to his feet, staggered left, leaned against a barstool to steady himself, tugged at his cummerbund, and finally lurched to our table. Onstage, a quartet of guys who barely looked old enough to drink launched into "Ninety-Nine Luftballoons" as Evan listed, then righted himself again.

"Kate," he said, trying for a smile as he collapsed into a chair. Clearly, he'd spent a long night drinking somewhere, and I doubted it had been Windows on the World. He had a baseball cap pulled over his hair. He smelled like he'd been marinating in Scotch, and he looked utterly miserable. "Thought I'd find you here."

"And here we are." I smoothed Janie's pink sweater against my chest. "Aren't you supposed to be at dinner?"

"Supposed to be," he said. His green eyes were bloodshot, and his words weren't quite slurred, but they were definitely a little mushy around the edges. "I like your shirt." He reached out and ran one finger along the neckline.

My heart was hammering in my chest. "Are you all right?" He

stared down at the table. "Evan?" I reached out tentatively and laid my hand on top of his. "Did something happen?" His lips trembled. He pressed them together.

"Hey! You!" called a grinning guy in a tuxedo with a forty-ounce bottle of Coors in his hand. "Proud Mary!" he said, and gave me two thumbs-up. I gave the guy a quick smile and didn't remove my hand from Evan's.

"You go on," Evan said, getting to his feet. "I don't want to wreck your night."

"No, no, it's okay, we're done. We did our thing. Our thing is done. What are you doing here?"

He slumped back in his chair again. "Michelle and I were supposed to meet at the apartment at six. She never came home," he said. I swallowed hard and only barely managed to keep a cry of *Thank you, God!* from exiting my lips. My heart felt as if it were expanding in my chest, growing bigger and bigger and lighter and lighter until it would lift me right out of my seat and I'd float above this smoky, crowded, noisy room, over the chairs patched with duct tape and the fraying carpet, above the stage flanked by two television screens and a smoke machine, through the roof, and out into the clear night sky.

I bent down to murmur in his ear, the very portrait of the solicitous gal-pal, a true friend. "Do you think she's all right? Do you have any idea where she is?"

"I know," he said. He grabbed one of the drinks and drained it in two long gulps. "I know." His voice cracked on the final word, and he barely seemed to notice when I laid my free hand between his shoulders, patting him gently, making soft crooning noises over the karaoke. *Remember this,* I told myself, feeling the warmth of his skin under his cotton shirt, breathing in the smoky air of the bar, memorizing every mirror and neon light, the smell of fried dumplings and cheap champagne, the sweet scent of the fake smoke they pumped onstage as a tiny Asian girl in a blue satin dress sang. "Once upon a time, I was falling in love, now I'm only falling apart."

"Yeah . . . well . . ." He shook his head. My palms were tingling, and my heart was beating too fast. He'd come all the way downtown to find me. Just like Daniel Day-Lewis in *The Last of the Mohicans.*

Evan stared at me with his glassy bloodshot eyes. "Pretty," he said, in a tone I'd only ever heard in my daydreams. His eyelids drooped. "You look so pretty tonight."

We both looked up as Janie cleared her throat. "What have we here?" she inquired, plopping down in her chair and readjusting her wig.

"Hi, Janie," said Evan.

She stared at him. "Jesus. Did you get the license plate number of the truck that ran you over?"

I cut my eyes at her, hoping to psychically communicate the pertinent facts—that Michelle had ditched him on New Year's Eve, that he appeared to have learned of the presence of Mr. Pantene. Unfortunately, Janie wasn't psychic. "What's going on?" she asked, fiddling with the spaghetti strap of her fringed minidress.

Evan flinched, then got to his feet. "Excuse me," he said blearily, and headed off into the crowd.

I watched him as he staggered away. "What happened?" Janie demanded. I told her what he'd told me.

Janie grabbed my hands and stared up into my eyes. "Okay, Kate. You need to listen to me," she said.

I knew what she was going to say—another version of her don't-shoot-the-messenger/don't-shit-where-you-live lecture—and I didn't want to hear it.

"His heart has been broken," she began. "He's lonely. He's hurting. He's vulnerable. By the looks of his pupils, he may be abusing prescription painkillers. Do not—I repeat—*do not* sleep with him."

"I wasn't going to sleep with him," I said, even though that was, of course, exactly what I'd been planning on doing. This was my shot. On a level playing field, there was no way I could compete with a six-foot-tall redheaded model imbued with the allure of the unattainable. But if Michelle had broken Evan's heart and run off with the shampoo boy, if he was drunk, despondent, and maybe even drugged, then there was a possibility I could stand a chance.

I got to my feet. "Be right back."

"Kate . . ." Janie stared up at me, hazel eyes beseeching. "I'm serious!"

"Bathroom!" I said, and started walking, faster and faster, my high heels sliding on the carpet. I rounded the corner when I felt someone grab my bra. Firm fingers yanked me backward hard, then released the strap, which thwacked painfully against my back.

"Ow!"

"I'm sorry if I hurt you," Janie said, "but Kate, I will burn this village in order to save it."

I gaped at her. "Huh? Am I the village in this analogy?"

Janie tugged at her wig. "Hang on . . . let me work through it. Yes. You are the village. Yes. Now listen to me. Give it time. Don't throw yourself at him. Be patient."

I whispered, "Gotta go," thinking that patient was for girls who looked like Janie, and opportunities like tonight were made for girls like me. Evan was slumped outside the bathroom at the end of a dim little hall. I took his hand and pulled him through the door marked Emergency Exit that had been propped open with a chair, out into an alley, out into the night.

We spilled onto a street filled with New Year's Eve revelers, tourists in Statue of Liberty foam headbands, women teetering in tight dresses and high heels, bellowing bunches of guys clutching one another with bottles dangling from their fingers, bottles of beer, bottles of wine, more champagne. Evan pulled me onto a side street lined with import shops with red cloth awnings and gold-fringed paper lanterns blowing in the wind. Everyone, it seemed, was planning on staying open all night. "Where's your coat?"

"I didn't bring one," I said, leaning close to his cheek so that he could hear me. I should have been cold, but I wasn't, even though I could see our breath condensing in the frigid air as we spoke. "Janie has her father's car . . . we weren't going to walk anywhere, and we'd just have to carry our coats around all night . . ."

He pulled me into the vestibule of a Chinese pastry shop and there, underneath the glow from the plate-glass windows, in front of the trays filled with flaky gold red bean paste buns, he took off his own coat and wrapped it around my shoulders. He pulled me against him, and there we were, eye to eye, chest to chest, hip to hip.

"Katie," he whispered.

"Evan," I whispered back. When he kissed me, I could feel his heart beating against mine. I leaned back against the window, underneath the lanterns, the delicate wind chimes above our heads. It was as if I were breathing him and drinking him, and all of the sights and sounds of that New York New Year's Eve vanished as he held me.

FIFTEEN

Ben was standing at the closet door when I woke up, scowling at the depleted row of hangers and idly scratching his belly. I sat up in bed, yawning.

"Who do you think would want to kill Kitty Cavanaugh?" I asked.

He shrugged without turning around. Janie was, presumably, still asleep in the guest room, and the kids, I guessed, were downstairs destroying the kitchen in their quest for breakfast.

He pulled out a shirt, a suit, and a tie. "I don't know," he said, pulling on his pants. "That's for the police to worry about."

"You really think Stannie Bergeron's going to crack this case? He could barely figure out our alarm system."

Ben put on his shirt, tied his tie, looked in the mirror, and tugged the knot slightly to the left. "Well, neither could you."

"Touché," I grumbled, flinging back the covers. "When are you coming home tonight?"

"Late," he said. "Sorry. I've got a town hall meeting in Massapequa."

"Better you than me," I said. "So you don't have any theories? Insights? Anything you can share with me before you leave for the wilds of Long Island?"

He shook his head, then fingered a scrap of toilet paper stuck to a shaving cut on his chin. "I didn't know her at all, and I've only seen him once or twice on the train."

"Well, the train. There you go. What was his job?"

Ben turned his back to me, tossing last night's shirt into the closet, where it would join the knee-high pile of clothes I'd been meaning to take to the dry cleaner's for the past two weeks. Possibly three. "I'm running out of shirts." This remark was delivered under his breath, at a volume just loud enough for me to hear.

"I'll drop off the dry cleaning this morning." I hopped out of bed, bent over, and scooped dress shirts into my arms, hoping that the view would entice him to stay a few minutes longer.

"Insurance," said Ben. Score one for my black silk underwear. "His father runs a maritime insurance business—they do boats, shoreline properties, summer camps with lakes—and Philip worked for his father. What I heard is that he wasn't very aggressive about bringing in new business. He liked the perks of the job and the title, but he wasn't very good at the work itself. Business wasn't booming."

"Ah." I imagined Philip in an impeccably tailored suit rolling into the office after ten, leaving for lunch at eleven thirty, and spending the afternoon on the golf course.

"Gotta go," he said, bending down to kiss me. "You and the kids have a wonderful day."

"See ya," I said to his back.

The Red Wheel Barrow was closed that morning—teachers in-service day, I thought—so I bade a reluctant farewell to Janie, who was headed back to the city. Then I fed the kids, helped them get dressed, and drove them to the park, where the mommies were assembled, bundled up and huddled together underneath a forbidding gray sky.

It looked, for a moment, like one of those children's games where you have to figure out what's missing in a picture. There was Carol Gwinnell, in her fringed poncho and hoop earrings, and Lexi Hagen-Holdt in head-to-toe fleece and spandex Nike, and Sukie

Sutherland in dark red lipstick and leather driving gloves, standing beside the bench where Kitty had customarily sat.

I made my way over slowly. The ladies were listening to Marybeth Coe run down the theories that were making their way through the town. Kitty Cavanaugh had been the victim of a gangland-style hit. Kitty Cavanaugh had been bludgeoned by terrorists. Kitty Cavanaugh had been strangled to death with her BabyBjörn and left stiffening on the kitchen floor.

"I still think it was feminists," Sukie Sutherland said. She'd lowered herself onto the bench and was fiddling with her cell phone in between sips from her spirulina smoothie. She wore wool trousers that hung from her hipbones and put her flat, cashmere-sheathed belly on display. Her soft leather boots and shearling coat were a painful contrast to my own sneakers and sweatshirt. "And I don't care what it says in the Constitution, I say anyone who made a threat about her over the Internet should just be rounded up and arrested."

"It's the Bill of Rights, actually," I murmured. Unlike my husband's murmur, mine wasn't loud enough for anyone to hear. Carol Gwinnell inched closer to Sukie. Lexi Hagen-Holdt shifted so that her back was almost, but not quite, turned to me. "We're going with the motion-activated security system," she announced.

"We installed electronic gates this morning," Marybeth Coe piped up. She lowered her voice. "And I hear the Raglins actually hired a bodyguard." A noise moved throughout the clutch of mommies, and it wasn't a snort of disbelief. It was, instead, the sound of the women rummaging in their paisley silk diaper bags for paper and pen, or Palm Pilots, to scribble down where this bodyguard had been obtained and whether more were available. I sighed and shoved my hands in my pockets as the mommy circle formed, with me, as always, on the outside. I'd planned on stretching my term as queen for a day to at least the end of the week, but Sukie had clearly usurped me. Both Channel Six and Channel Ten had led their six o'clock newscasts with interviews, in which Sukie (who, I noticed, hadn't been so debilitated with shock and grief that she'd been unable to slip into Mr. Steven's salon for a blowout), recited her sound bites: *Kitty was kind, Kitty was brilliant, Kitty was a wonderful mother, and what a horrible loss this was for us all.*

"Mommy." Little Peyton tugged on Marybeth Coe's arm. "I'm hungry!"

Ten seconds later, half a dozen mothers opened up half a dozen insulated snack bags and removed half a dozen studies in healthful eating. Peyton nibbled from a Tupperware container full of steamed edamame. Charlie Gwinnell munched vegetable puffs, while Tristan and Isolde snacked on soy nut spread on nine-grain bread. My three kids trotted over and stared at me expectantly. I made a show of rummaging in my tote bag like I'd actually remembered to put something in there, or like the Snack Fairy had visited during the night. All I found were two cough drops and half of a melted Nestlé Crunch bar.

"Um . . ."

"Here," said Sukie, briskly distributing sandwich quarters. "I packed extra."

When the kids were eating, I sidled over to Carol Gwinnell, hoping that the only other mother on the playground who wore a size that wasn't in the single digits might feel some kind of natural affinity, and tapped her shoulder.

"Do you know a good lawyer in town?"

She rezipped her Ziploc bag of cut-up bell peppers and handed her son Charlie a paper napkin. "What kind?"

"Someone who does wills." The lies came easily, once I got going. "Ben and I did one after the kids were born, but now . . . with everything that's happened . . . I mean, not to be morbid, but there are some things we've been meaning to update, and I guess now with everything that's happened . . ."

She nodded, pale blue eyes round and serious.

"Do you know a guy named Kevin Dolan?" I asked, ever-so-casual as I invoked the name of Lisa the sitter's lawyer and Philip Cavanaugh's friend.

"Kevin, sure," she said, helping Charlie onto a swing. "He's got offices in that big old Victorian on the corner of Elm and Main. He's a nice guy." Carol licked her chapped lips and inched closer to me. "Sukie told me you were talking to Kitty's sitter."

I gave a noncommittal nod.

"And you talked to Phil?"

"I dropped off a pie. I wanted to tell him how sorry I was," I said, deciding to leave out for the time being the way Philip had seemed desperate to find out whether his dead wife had been happy while trying to maneuver me onto the marital bed.

Carol's bracelets jingled over the low voices of the mommies murmuring, talking about which channel was giving the story of Kitty's murder the best coverage and how many reporters had called their houses. Every once in a while someone's voice would rise sharply. "Peyton! Stay where I can see you!" "Tate! No eating dirt!"

"Did he try anything?" she whispered.

I feigned shock. "Who? Phil?"

Carol's milky skin flushed as she licked her lips again. "He's got kind of a reputation."

I widened my eyes and lowered my voice. "Did he ever try anything with you?"

Carol's blush deepened. Her head bobbed once, up and down, as she dragged one purple ballet slipper along the bumpy rubberized mat beneath the slides. "He's tried something with everyone."

I amped up the disbelief. "Lexi? Marybeth?"

Carol shrugged, then ran her fingers through her fine red hair. "He tried to kiss me at a Christmas party three years ago. But we were under the mistletoe, so maybe . . ."

"Wow. Poor Kitty."

She nodded vigorously and gave Charlie's swing an extra-emphatic shove. "It's so sad. Just so sad."

Sophie ran up to me, tugging my hand. "Mommy, Sam and Jack are blocking the slide from everyone."

By the time I coaxed the boys down the slide, Carol had rejoined the mommy collective. I spent twenty minutes by myself pushing Sophie on a swing while she sang "Peggy's Pie Parlor Polka" six times in a row. Finally, I cajoled Sam and Jack off the teeter-totter, got everyone into the van, drove to the nearest minimart, and bought juice boxes and the kind of prepackaged peanut-butter crackers so loaded with preservatives and hydrogenated fats that a single glance at the nutritional information would cause the average Upchurch mommy to swoon.

So the whole town knew that Philip Cavanaugh had wandering eyes and a vagrant tongue and that he hadn't set the world of maritime insurance on fire. I pulled out of the parking lot, feeling a frisson of pleasure that was immediately followed by a crushing wave of guilt. The pleasure was at the realization that pretty Kitty Cavanaugh's life hadn't been as beautiful and put together as it looked from where I was sitting. The guilt was for the pleasure. She was dead, I thought, turning onto Main Street. She was dead, and her little girls would grow up without a mother, and only a horrible person would feel happy about any of that.

Kevin Dolan, Attorney at Law, worked out of a lovely white Victorian with leaded-glass doors and a discreet painted wooden sign on the corner of Elm and Main. I smoothed on some lipstick, twisted my curls into a bun, and made sure the Cat in the Hat Band-Aid on my ankle was covered by my sock before leaving the car.

"Can I help you?" the receptionist asked as I led Sam, Jack, and Sophie inside what must have formerly been a parlor, arranged them in chairs with needlepoint cushions in front of a marble-mantel-topped fireplace, and gave them my very best behave-yourself stare.

"Hi, I'm Kate Klein Borowitz," I said, tossing Ben's name into the mix, hoping it would lend some gravitas, along with the extra syllables. "I was a friend of Kitty Cavanaugh."

"Such a tragedy," the receptionist murmured from behind a desk that looked like a genuine antique. She was in her fifties, with carefully styled gray hair, a maroon blazer, and a pleated maroon and white plaid kilt.

"I know that Kevin was a friend of the family," I said. Then I unfurled the guaranteed-to-get-me-in excuse I'd come up with on the way over from the playground. "I was wondering if he'd have a moment to speak with me about a speech I'm working on for her memorial service."

She gave a sympathetic nod, pressed a button on the phone, murmured briefly, and said, "He'll see you now."

I patted the kids and gave them a look that promised dire consequences if they failed to sit quietly or made a raid on the bowl of Hershey's Kisses set on one of the many delicate end tables. "You guys behave yourselves," I said cheerfully, in a tone that wouldn't give the receptionist any reason to expect that they wouldn't. "Mommy will be out in a minute."

I turned toward the office door. The receptionist put her hand on my forearm. "I just want you to know he's been terribly upset by this," she whispered. *And if you upset him any more, I'll throw your kids in my oven and roast them for dinner,* her look promised. I nodded, walked through the office door, and found Kevin Dolan, short and round-shouldered in a too-tight Oxford shirt and a too-long tie, sitting behind a heavy oak desk.

He had an egg-shaped head on a plum-shaped body, plump cheeks, twinkly brown eyes, and a warm smile. Not a matinee idol, but very appealing: the guy who'd be voted class clown or, alternately, get a few degrees in political science and hire my husband to help him run for the Senate. I could see why his receptionist wanted to protect him. There was something sweet about Kevin Dolan, something that reminded me of my own boys.

"Hello!" he said, bounding out of his seat, shaking my hand, pulling out a wooden chair for me, and waiting until I sat down before heading back around his desk.

"Thank you for talking with me. I'm Kate Klein."

"Happy to help. I heard that you were the one who . . ." He lowered his voice and stilled the knee that had been bouncing up and down. "That must have been terrible."

I nodded and decided that honesty—relative honesty—would be the best policy with this sweetly solicitous man. "I didn't know her all that well, but our friends—the other mothers—we'd like to do something in her honor."

He drummed his fingers on the desk, crossed his legs, and bounced one foot briskly up and down. "That's a wonderful idea."

"So tell me," I said, pulling out my notebook. (Kevin raised his eyes at the glitter on the cover but said nothing.) "How would you describe Kitty? If you could pick three words to remember her by, what would they be?"

"Devoted," he said. One hand slipped into his pocket and started jangling his keys. He didn't seem nervous, though. Maybe he was just one of those natural twitchers—the kind of guy who'd squirm in his seat through the credits before a movie and have to get up at least twice to stretch his legs during the film. "She was the most devoted mother I've ever seen."

Devoted, I wrote, trying to quell the pang of disappointment. Well, what was I expecting? That the first of his three adjectives would be "unfaithful"?

"Devoted to her kids?" I said.

"Devoted to her children, to her marriage, to her home," Kevin said, tapping the edge of a manila folder on the desk and slipping it into a drawer. "Her house was—is—beautiful."

House beautiful, I wrote. "I know."

"Three words isn't enough. Kitty was smart, she was pretty, she was . . ." His voice stopped abruptly. He ran his hands rapidly over his close-cropped curls. "Well, you knew her. What would you say? What words would you use to describe her?"

"Intimidating?" I said. It was a risk, but it paid off. The corners of Kevin's eyes crinkled as he smiled.

"You thought so?" he asked.

She scared me to death, I almost said, before I realized how that would have sounded. "Well, it's like what you were saying. She was devoted to her children, she had the beautiful house. For the rest of us . . . I mean, some mornings I'm just struggling to make sure my kids are in clean clothes, never mind whether they match, never mind whether my house looks neat . . ."

His chair creaked as he rocked forward. "I don't think Kitty wanted to intimidate anyone. But she did take parenting very seriously."

"Do you know why?"

He gave me a friendly smile. "Well, I guess most parents around here take it pretty seriously."

"I know. I mean . . ." I took a wild guess. "Had something happened to one of her kids that would make her be so . . . so rigorous about it? I know that sometimes that can be kind of a wake-up call . . ." My voice trailed off as Kevin's smile turned to puzzlement. "I mean, once one of my twins rolled off the bed . . ." Now he was looking at me not only with puzzlement but with concern as well. Another minute and he'd be calling the Department of Family Services. "But never mind me!" I said. My voice was too loud in the warm little office, with framed antique needlepoint samplers on the walls and autumn sunlight pouring in through the sparkling windows. I tried again. "Can you tell me anything about her work for *Content?*"

He shook his head. "She played her cards close to her vest." He leaned back in his chair, folded his hands across his belly, stared at the ceiling, then rocked forward. "I knew her ever since she married Phil—but now, with all that's come out, I wonder if I ever knew her at all."

"You and Phil were friends for a long time?"

"Since high school," he said, nodding. "We're local boys. We both grew up here, and after school, we came back to stay."

I nodded and I wrote it down, and snuck another peek at Kevin. His brown eyes were bright and interested behind a pair of horn-rimmed glasses, and his chins lapped gently over his collar. *Such a nice guy,* the girls had probably said about him in high school. Of Phil Cavanaugh they would have said, *He's dreamy.*

"So how did she meet Philip? Was it in New York?" I was hoping he'd throw me a bone, some scrap of information about Kitty's pre-baby, pre-Upchurch life, something that would give me a sense of who she really was besides a perfect mother with perfect hair and a perfect house.

"No. Here. He ran into her at the office, right after he'd started working with his dad."

"And how about before she met Philip?" I asked. "Do you know anything about her life before she came to Upchurch?"

"I know she was writing, and living in New York," he said. "Trying to get her career off the ground. I think she did freelance pieces, edited a hospital's newsletter." I asked which one. He shrugged, then shook his head and apologized.

"Do you remember where she lived? What neighborhood?" I asked. "I used to live in the Village."

"She never talked much about it," he said. He shifted in his seat, crossed and uncrossed his legs.

I gave him a variation of Phil's question to me. "Was she happy there? Or was she happier here? Was this—you know, kids, house, playground, carpools—was this what she wanted?"

He gave me a smile and rocked back in his chair again with his hands cradling his belly. "I don't know if she loved New York," he said. "I think it was kind of the usual thing. Bad boyfriends, bad bosses. Aren't there a whole bunch of books with pink covers about stuff like that?"

"So nothing out of the ordinary."

He smiled. "Not that I know about. She never did time in a Thai prison for drug smuggling or anything like that. As for Connecticut . . ." He rocked back and forth, looking sad, I decided. No—nostalgic. Wistful.

"I don't know," he finally said. His voice thickened. "I think—I'd like to believe—that she was happy here."

The wheels of his desk chair squeaked against the sheet of hard plastic underneath them. "She was one of my favorite people," he blurted in a voice that sounded completely different from his initial how-can-I-help-you bonhomie. "I just can't believe something like this would happen. In the city, maybe, you'd expect it. But out here?"

A flush crept from the gaping neck of his shirt up to the soft line of his jaw. *She was one of my favorite people.* Aha! I could imagine how this had played out—handsome Philip and his plain, pudgy sidekick, handsome Philip with his beautiful wife, and Kevin nursing a secret, unrequited crush on her for all those years. Had Kitty encouraged him? Had they exchanged passionate glances over the years, his soft brown eyes meeting her astonishing blue ones across the Fourth of July barbecue, the Halloween candy bowl, the Christmas eggnog? Had they consummated their love? Was it Kitty's revenge for Phil's sticking his tongue down the neighbor ladies' throats underneath the mistletoe for all those years? Had Kevin begged her to leave Philip, saying her husband wasn't good enough to kiss the ground she walked on? Had Kitty refused, knowing that a divorce would tarnish her perfect-mother glow? And had Kevin shown up at her house one crisp October morning to try to convince her one last time . . . then grabbed a butcher knife off Kitty's kitchen counter, saying, *If I can't have you, no one will?*

Kevin blinked, rocked forward, and looked at the grandfather clock in the corner. "I don't mean to rush you," he said, bounding to his feet.

I stood up, scrambling for my coat. As I bent forward to scoop my bag off the floor, I saw the photograph on his desk and felt the breath freeze in my throat. There was a petite, dark-haired woman standing on a beach, wearing a sleek black maillot cut high on the hip. Her bare feet were planted in sand as fine as sugar, and turquoise waves foamed in the background, but I wasn't as interested in the scenery as I was in her smile, her heart-shaped face, a slightly crooked left incisor. She was the same woman from the photograph hidden in the back of Kitty's drawer. *K and D, Summer '92, Montauk.*

"Is this your wife?" I asked, striving to sound casual. "She looks so familiar. I must have met her somewhere. Diana?"

"Delphine," said Kevin. "She teaches Pilates. She's got a studio downtown."

"Did she maybe do a demonstration at the Red Wheel Barrow?" I babbled. "I just know I've seen her from somewhere."

"I'm not sure," he said, looking past me, up at the clock.

"Were she and Kitty friends?" I blurted as I heard the sounds I'd been dreading—a scream, and then a crash, and Sophie's cry of "Stupid baby!"

I thought I saw him flinch the tiniest bit, but his voice was steady when he spoke. "We were all friends," he said. I took my cue, shook his hand, thanked him for his time, and promised to keep in touch.

SIXTEEN

"Maybe I'm overthinking," I told Janie after I'd finally gotten her on the phone an hour later. The kids and I were back home in our kitchen. After the debacle in Kevin Dolan's waiting room, I'd picked up the glass and the Kisses, written a check for the bowl, fed the kids a late lunch, then settled them at the table with a bowlful of blueberries and the Candy Land board.

"You?" Janie said, from her desk at *New York Night.* I could hear her fingers rattling over the keyboard. "Never. I won't hear it."

"But I think," I said, flicking the spinner and moving my piece three squares, "that maybe she was having an a-f-f-a-i-r with this lawyer who was her husband's best friend."

Janie had the courtesy to sound interested. "Do tell. Only no more spelling. Takes too long. Do you know pig Latin?"

I took the phone into the bathroom instead and gave Janie a whispered recounting of my conversation with Kevin, whose gaze had gotten all misty when he'd talked about Kitty's happiness, and whose wife had apparently known the deceased back in 1992. "He said that Kitty was one of his favorite people."

"Well, you're one of my favorite people," Janie said. "Doesn't mean I want to sleep with you, then kill you."

"Still, it's something. More than what the police have." I ticked off the suspects on my fingers as I talked. "Could've been the sitter, because she was sleeping with Phil."

"Or Phil could have hired someone to do it, so he could be free to pursue a life of happiness with the sitter," said Janie.

"Laura Lynn Baird had a motive. The book advance money," I said. "Or maybe it was Kevin Dolan, because he was in love with her and couldn't have her."

"You know this just from talking to him?"

"Well, it's a guess," I said. "And it could've just been some random Internet crazy who was stalking her online."

"Keep digging," said Janie. "Don't get frustrated. Gotta bounce," she said, hanging up as her other line rang.

"Mommy," Sophie asked as I returned to the game, "who made Mrs. Cavanaugh dead?"

Oh, dear. "Were the kids talking about that on the playground?"

She squinted at me. "No, Mommy, you were talking about it on the phone with Aunt Janie the Fabulous."

I smiled in spite of myself. "Did Aunt Janie tell you to call her that?"

"She says it's her name," said Sophie.

"Tristan talked about it," Jack said in his husky voice that always sounded a little raspy from disuse.

I tried to pull Sophie onto my lap, in the manner of comforting mothers from Norman Rockwell pictures. Sophie shot me a you've-got-to-be-kidding-me look and wriggled away. I cleared my throat. "Yes, well, Mrs. Cavanaugh did . . . um . . . well, she's dead, and the police are looking very hard to find the person who did it."

"Somebody made her dead," said Sam, his voice indistinguishable from his brother's.

"Why?" asked Jack, flicking the Candy Land spinner.

"Well . . ." I took another deep breath and felt my eyes prickle with tears. *Was she happy?* Philip Cavanaugh asked. "Nobody knows yet." I brushed hastily at my eyes, hoping the kids wouldn't notice.

"Why are you crying?" Sophie asked.

"Because what happened is very sad."

Sam handed me his napkin, then stared at me with his big brown eyes. "Why?"

"Well . . ." My voice trailed off as the three of them stared up at me. "She was somebody's mother," I finally said. My lips trembled as more tears came to my eyes. Whatever I'd thought of Kitty—her politics, her marriage, the choices she'd made—that much had been true.

SEVENTEEN

On that New Year's Eve night, after we'd made our escape from the Lo Kee Inn, I maneuvered Evan down the stairs to the subway, onto the train, up the stairs, into our building, and onto the elevator. The whole trip was a blur of delicious kisses and declarations delivered in fragments. *You feel so . . . I can't believe . . . I want . . . I need . . .* He slid his hands under my sweater. I brushed my lips against the pale strip of skin at the back of his neck that I'd noticed the first time I'd seen him. He plunged his hands into my hair, pulling until it tumbled over my shoulders. We couldn't get enough of each other. Every time I'd seen that phrase in a book, I'd rolled my eyes, but now I knew exactly what it meant.

"Do you know how long I've thought about touching you?" he whispered, kissing my neck in the elevator. I felt like I would swoon—another cliché. I felt my heart open like a flower. He had thought about touching me. If the world ended that very night, I'd go happily, knowing that.

We'd staggered down the hallway, his arm over my shoulder, as I'd fumbled for my keys. "I b'lieve you're trying to seduce me," he said as we stumbled through the door. Then his coat was gone, my shoes were off, and we were making our way to my bedroom, slipping, almost falling, banging into the walls, knowing we'd have bruises in the morning and not caring a bit.

Yes, I thought as he flopped down on top of my bed and buried his face in my pillow. I lay down beside him, waiting for him to roll over and say my name, to look at me with his laughing eyes, to kiss me again and say, *It's you, you're the one.* Instead, for the longest time, I didn't hear anything at all . . . and when the prone figure next to me did start making noises, they were not whispered words of love. They were snores.

"Evan?" I nudged him gently. Nothing happened. I shook his shoulder. His snores got more emphatic. I leaned down and kissed his cheek. Then I bit his earlobe lightly. Then I bit it harder. He didn't wake up.

I lay down beside him, unbuttoned the top two buttons of his starched, pleated shirt, closed my own eyes, and tried to sleep. Every few minutes Evan would thrash in the bed, rolling fitfully from side to side, almost dislodging me. I eased myself upright and sat beside him, cross-legged, watching his chest rise and fall and his eyes roll underneath his eyelids. "I love you," I whispered into the darkness.

At three in the morning, a full bladder won out over my romantic plans to stay beside him all night long, daydreaming about our future happiness and watching him sleep. I tiptoed out of the room and down the hall, and almost screamed when I felt a hand on my shoulder.

"What's going on?" Janie whispered. Her Tina Turner wig was crooked, and her leopard-print sleep mask was shoved high on her forehead.

"He's sleeping," I whispered back.

"He's passed out," Janie said. "Which is generally what happens when you try to drink New Jersey. Meanwhile, I've been up half the night, sick with worry!"

The door to her bedroom opened, and an Asian guy in a baseball cap slunk out, giving Janie a shamefaced wave before sidling past us. I raised my eyebrows.

"Sick with worry?"

"I *was* sick with worry," she said. "Where is it written that you have to be sick with worry by yourself? And you ditched me, and the audience wanted an encore. What was I supposed to do?"

"You sang with that guy?"

"Um." Janie bit her lip as her bedroom door opened again and two other guys gave her brief, embarrassed nods and slipped out the door.

"Jesus, Janie. Your bedroom's like a clown car." I made a show of looking, wide-eyed, at her door. "Do you have a midget in there?"

"Never you mind," she said. "I needed Ikettes. You really can't do 'Nutbush' without them. And that's not even the point!"

I walked past her to the bathroom. When I emerged, Janie beckoned to me from the couch. I sighed, knowing she wouldn't take no for an answer. She tossed me a blanket—a little something in shahtoosh Sy had sent as a housewarming gift—and I pulled it over my legs.

"So?"

I took a deep breath and couldn't keep myself from smiling. "He likes me."

"Of course he *likes* you, Kate. That was never the question. The question is, does he plan to break things off with Michelle?"

My smile faded. We hadn't talked about Michelle. Come to think of it, we hadn't talked about much of anything. We'd been too busy kissing. But didn't actions speak louder than words?

"I should go back in there."

Janie shook her head in disapproval. "Roll him on his side," she said, and gave me a hug. "That way he won't choke on his own vomit."

I eased my bedroom door open. Evan was sitting hunched on my pink and cream comforter, looking miserable and haggard in the shaft of the street light that slipped in underneath the blind.

"Kate," he croaked, giving me an apologetic wave.

I swallowed hard, suddenly dizzy, and took a desperate stab at our formerly easy banter. "Well," I said. "This is awkward." I sat down beside him, reached out tentatively, and touched the tender spot on the back of his neck. He shivered. *No,* I thought. *That wasn't a shiver. That was a flinch.*

He rubbed his hands over his face, then scrubbed at his hair, all without meeting my eyes. I heard him take a deep breath. Time seemed to slow down, in order to give me a chance to permanently engrave every detail of the scene in my mind, so I'd be able to have it at my fingertips and replay it, over and over for the rest of my life. I saw the shadows my little lamp cast on the wall, and the way the streetlight turned the stubble on his cheeks to silver. I saw that his cummerbund had gotten twisted, and how his gaze stayed on his hands as he started to talk.

"Kate," he said again. I pushed myself off the bed. I thought of my mother, how she'd lectured me about my posture: *Shoulders back, Kate! Chest up! Don't slouch! It doesn't make you look any smaller!* So I threw my shoulders back. I stuck my chest out. I squeezed the muscles in my midsection I'd worked on so hard when I'd been singing, stabilizing myself from my core, and I braced myself, knowing before he opened his mouth what he was going to tell me, and how badly it was going to hurt.

"I'm sorry," he said, sounding wretched—almost as wretched as I felt. "I didn't mean for this to happen. You're my friend, and I . . ." I heard his throat click as he swallowed. He rubbed his hands over his face again. "I'm not the kind of guy who does things like this."

I looked at him, knowing I could have made it easy—*Oh, it's okay, no big deal, it was New Year's, we'd been drinking, no harm, no foul, go back to your fiancée and let us never speak of this again.* I held myself perfectly still, refusing to let him see me tremble, but I couldn't stop the tears from sliding out of my eyes.

"I thought . . ." My voice broke, and I sounded like a sad little girl. "I thought you . . ."

He looked up at me miserably. "Oh, Katie. You're terrific. But Michelle and I . . . well, you know. If I were single . . . if I'd met you first . . ."

She cheats on you! I wanted to shout. *She cheats on you with a shampoo model and I've got proof! She'll never love you like I do!* The words froze in my throat.

"I never meant to hurt you," he said. He shifted on the bed, raised one hand to his forehead, and rubbed it slowly. "You deserve someone wonderful . . ." He licked his lips.

"You're wonderful," I said. My lips felt numb, my tongue felt thick. *We're wonderful together.* But I knew if I said that, then I'd start begging, and if I wasn't going to leave this bedroom with Evan as my boyfriend, I was at least going to leave it with my pride.

"Katie," he said. "Are you going to be okay?"

"Oh, sure." I forced myself to say the words, and give them a light-hearted spin.

He rubbed his forehead. "I should go. Maybe Michelle left a message at home . . ."

Or maybe you should start calling shampoo models, I thought but did not say. Instead I held the door open for him, letting light from the hallway pour into the room. He got up off the bed slowly, and I followed him down the hall. At the front door he turned to me and started to say something. I busied myself at the kitchen sink so I wouldn't have to look at him, and turned both taps on full blast so I wouldn't have to hear.

For the next three hours, I cleaned out my closet, shoving all the clothes that didn't fit into garbage bags, performing the act as if it were penance for having asked the universe for too much.

At six o'clock, I showered, got dressed, and threw handfuls of clothing and clean underwear into a duffel bag. I pulled my coat out of the closet, my hat and scarf and mittens. I made sure I had my wallet and my cell phone, and I pulled my passport out of the shoebox in the closet where I kept it hidden.

I walked out of the apartment, down the hall, and stood in front of Evan's door, balled my trembling hands into fists, and counted to ten, giving him one last chance to come to me, to tell me that he was wrong, he was sorry, he loved me more than he could ever love her, that we were supposed to be together, and that I was the one. The door stayed shut. I made myself keep walking to the elevator, made myself press the button, made myself walk out onto the cold, dark street.

I caught a cab at the corner of Greenwich and Jane. "Where to, hon?" the cabdriver asked. "JFK," I told him. I rested my head against the cool glass of the window and watched the city slide by: buses and cabs, trash cans overflowing with empty green champagne bottles, spent streamers and Happy New Year foam headbands crumpled in the gutters. The British Airways counter was open. I used my credit card to book myself on the first flight to Heathrow. My mother was in London, and even if she wouldn't talk to me or console me, London was the first place I could think of, and the farthest I could run.

EIGHTEEN

The next afternoon, after feeding the kids lunch and putting them down for a nap (actual sleep for the boys, lying quietly on her bed leafing through a copy of *Vogue* she'd convinced me to check out of the library for Sophie), I surfed over to DieLauraLynn.com, one of the just over 1,700 websites, blogs, and online magazines devoted to the proposition that the media's latest blond conservative darling was misguided, wrong, silly, stupid, narcissistic, overly ambitious, dangerous to women the world over, and personally responsible both for the postmillennial death of feminism and for young girls' eating disorders. This site was the one that had broken the news that Kitty Cavanaugh had been ghostwriting for Laura Lynn Baird. It had an unflattering picture of Laura Lynn on the home page, with devil's horns protruding from her blond mane and animated flames issuing from her miniskirt. The words "Liar, liar, pants on fire: Laura Lynn's ghostwriter revealed!" scrolled in boldface eighteen-point red print across the bottom of the page.

I clicked the link to enter the site and was whisked to a collection of all of the articles written about Kitty Cavanaugh's death and the revelation that she'd been penning "The Good Mother." I scrolled through slowly, jotting down notes, biographical data—Kitty's maiden name (Verree) and hometown (Eastham, Massachusetts, just as on the postcard I'd seen). At the bottom of the page was another link. "Media click here," it invited. When I clicked, an email popped up, preaddressed to tara@radicalmamas.com, with "Media Request" written in the memo line. I backspaced over "Media" so that all that was left was "Request." It was three fifteen, which meant I had fifteen minutes until Sophie roused her brothers and the three of them came down the stairs, demanding a snack or a trip to the park, or, God help me to endure it, another game of Candy Land.

"Hello," I typed. "I am . . ." My fingers paused. I am what, exactly? *A married mother of three trapped in a whitebread Connecticut suburb with too much time on her hands who just wandered across her dead neighbor's body* came to mind.

"I am a graduate student in women's studies," I typed instead, figuring that it had been true at one point in my life. "I am working on a paper giving a feminist critique of ghostwriting as a publicly sanctioned act of female self-erasure." There. That sounded nonsensical enough to actually be true. "I'd like to ask you some questions about Laura Lynn Baird and Kitty Cavanaugh. You can reach me at this number between 8:30 and 11:45, Monday, Wednesday, and Friday." I added my phone number, typed my name, and hit send before I could lose my nerve.

Sophie wandered down the stairs with her Uglydoll tucked under her arm and her brothers trailing two steps behind her. "Nook," she requested—her babyspeak for "milk." I lifted her into my arms, sniffing her hair in search of a sweet, innocent whiff of Johnson & Johnson's No More Tears. Instead, I got a noseful of something expensive and probably French, since Sophie liked to tear the perfume samples out of the magazines.

The telephone rang. I tucked it under my chin and scooped Sophie against my hip. "Hello?"

"Monday, Wednesday, and Friday between eight thirty and eleven forty-five?" an amused young woman's voice asked. "I just had to call now to figure out whether you were in prison."

"Not prison," I said. I helped Sophie and the boys into their booster seats and went to the refrigerator to find them a snack. "No, I'm a, um, part-time student with three kids, and those are the hours that they're in nursery school," I said, pulling out three pudding cups and plunking them down on the table.

"Three kids in nursery school," the voice said. It was an arch, ironic voice, a young woman's voice attached to—I snuck a fast look at the caller ID while I unpeeled the pudding lids—a 212 area code. "Mercy me. Anyhow, I'm Tara Singh from Radical Mamas."

"Momm*eee*!" Sophie wailed as Jack licked the top of her pudding container. I gave him a stern look and took a deep breath.

"Whoa," said Tara Singh. "Sounds like you've got your hands full."

"Yes," I said, pulling Sophie's pudding out of Jack's hands and distributing spoons. "Listen, if you'd be willing to talk with me, I get into the city quite a bit."

"Oh, you do not," said Sophie, jabbing her spoon into her pudding. I glared at my daughter and tucked the phone more tightly against me. Too late. Tara Singh giggled.

"Anyhow, is there a chance we could meet for coffee or a drink?"

"Sure thing," she said. "Just let me look at my book . . ." I could picture this woman, a much hipper mother than I'd ever be, wearing a strappy tank top, low-rise jeans, and thick-soled boots, with her hair in a twist and an army-navy bag with a peace sign pin slung over her shoulders.

"How's tomorrow?"

Tomorrow was Friday. The kids had school in the morning. Then the boys had a six-month checkup with their speech therapist. They'd done a year of therapy starting when they turned two and weren't speaking more than a handful of words apiece. After nine months, the high-priced, extremely credentialed therapist had told me that her best guess was that the boys could talk but simply preferred to let Sophie do it for them.

But maybe I could get Gracie to sit, and maybe Ben could come home early enough to give them dinner. I could get dressed up in grown-up clothes, meet Tara Singh for drinks, and then have dinner with Janie. Or with my father, who, I realized with another pang of guilt, I'd been neglecting.

"Let's go somewhere fabulous," I said. Tara laughed at that, the slightly condescending laughter of a New Yorker dealing with a suburbanite whose entire knowledge of the big city came from watching expurgated *Sex and the City* reruns on basic cable.

"Somewhere fabulous it is," she said, rattling off a name and an address. "Pastis . . . Nine Ninth Avenue," I repeated, scribbling it down with a purple Crayola on the back of a brown paper bag.

"Hey, you didn't mention where you go to school."

"Upchurch Community College" rolled off my tongue as if I'd been saying it my entire life. I got off the phone just in time to prevent Sophie from punting her half-eaten pudding cup at her brothers.

"Behave," I said.

Sophie stared at me blandly. The ring of pudding around her mouth looked like lip liner. "Mommy, you are lying," she said.

I swooped down and covered her cheeks with kisses, surprising her. She giggled, then pushed me away. "Not lying," I explained, scooping up the abandoned pudding cups and tossing them into the trash. "Not exactly. I'm just telling a story."

I hadn't been exactly right about Tara Singh, but I hadn't been that far off either. The low-rise jeans I'd pictured were present and accounted for. The strappy tank, in a pretty blush pink, was topped with a fitted coffee-colored corduroy jacket. No wedding ring. One tiny pin decorated the left breast pocket. "Mommies Are People," it read.

"Thanks so much for meeting with me," I said, easing myself onto the rickety wood and wicker café chair at a table at Pastis. We were back in my old neighborhood, which was a lot more fabulous than when I'd lived there, if by fabulous you mean hot, noisy, and crammed with beautiful people, none of whom seemed to be eating anything I'd regard as a meal. As I picked up my menu, a gazelle in a pixie cut two tables over considered a plate of green beans.

"My pleasure," Tara said, flipping open the menu. The green bean woman frowned at her plate, poked the beans with her finger, then summoned a waiter. "Is there butter on these?" I heard her ask.

I shifted again before deciding that getting comfortable on the tiny chair wouldn't happen in my lifetime. When the waiter came, I ordered a glass of chardonnay and, in defiance of the butterless green bean woman, a cheeseburger and fries. "Same for me," said Tara Singh. "With a Diet Coke." She replaced her menu. I pulled out my notebook. Tara grinned at it, then shook her head in mock sorrow.

"So. Laura Lynn Baird had a ghostwriter," she gloated. "A dead ghostwriter. It's like Christmas came early this year!"

"How'd you get the story?"

She gave me a mysterious smile and smoothed her napkin on her lap. "Actually, it was an anonymous tip. An email. But when I called *Content* to check it, they didn't deny it."

"When did you get the email?"

Tara fiddled with her fork. "The day Kitty died, actually."

"And you have no idea who sent it?"

She shook her head. "I saved it, of course, and I forwarded it to the cops, but so far . . ." She shrugged again. I wrote it down.

"You've been following Laura Lynn Baird's career for a while, right?"

Tara nodded, still smiling, with her plum-painted lips parted to show square white teeth. There wasn't a single line on her coffee-colored skin. I wondered how old she was—twenty-three? Twenty-four? Awfully young to be a mama herself. "I know what you're thinking," she said.

I raised my eyebrows and waited.

"Do I think Laura Lynn could have killed Kitty Cavanaugh? The answer is maybe."

Maybe, I wrote.

"I wouldn't put anything past that bitch," Tara said. "Up to and including homicide. She was crazy—and not just because crazy makes good television. She was . . ." She grinned even wider and performed a gesture I hadn't seen since my own days on the playground: pointed her index finger at her head and twirled it in tiny circles.

"Nuts," I said.

"Institutionalized," Tara said. "Just before her father died. She checked herself into some clinic in Pennsylvania for a month. Her people said it was exhaustion. Please," she said, rolling her expressive eyes. "If you're exhausted, you go to sleep, not to Happy Meadows."

I scribbled down the words *Happy Meadows* and made a mental note to ask my old snitch Mary Elizabeth whether she'd heard anything about this.

"Well, actually, the paper I'm writing is about erasure as subversion. You know, women writers through history who've chosen to use pen names, or male names, or write anonymously, as a way of undermining the patriarchal . . . hierarchical . . ." Shit. Seven years ago I could've slung this bullshit with the best of them. "Anyhow. You really think that Laura Lynn could have done it? She'd be a pretty obvious suspect."

"Even though she'd be a completely obvious suspect, even though she'd be killing the goose that laid the golden egg. I'm telling you, bitch is ca-ra-zee." She tapped her straw on the table until it burst out of its white paper wrapper. "Did you hear about the time she threw a can of Diet Coke at Chris Matthews's head?"

"Um . . ."

"I know it sounds like an urban legend, but it wasn't. It happened. We've got streaming video of it on the Web site."

"So I guess the question is, does she have an alibi?"

"Sure," said Tara. "Of course she did. The day Kitty got killed, she was addressing Women United for America's Future in Washington."

"Hmm," I said, writing it down.

"I've got an alibi too, in case you're interested," she said, making a sour face. "God knows the cops were."

"Well, if you've got a Web site called Die Laura Lynn dot com . . ."

Tara's peals of laughter rang out across the room, causing the green bean lady to scowl at us. "Please," she spluttered. "Do you think I'd really be that obvious?"

Good point.

"And just because Laura Liar has an alibi, it doesn't mean she wasn't involved."

"But why?"

"Maybe Kitty wanted what was hers," she said, twirling the straw wrapper between her fingers until it was thin as thread. "Maybe she asked for a cut of Laura Lynn's salary . . . or a byline. Maybe she threatened to go public—tell the world that not only was Laura Lynn not writing that wretched column, but the closest Laura Lynn ever came to caring for her own child was holding him during photo shoots."

"So . . ." I put the pieces together. "You think that Laura Lynn could have hired someone to have Kitty killed?"

Tara grinned again. "Sure. She could have waved ten thousand tax-free dollars in front of some broke-ass Young Republican who'd run up a bunch of credit card debt. Why not?" She sat back, looking satisfied, as a waitress delivered our burgers. "And Laura Lynn was a major right-to-lifer—oh, excuse me, she was an advocate for preborn Americans. Don't you love that? Preborn Americans? I wonder what that makes us. Postborn? Anyhow. Right-to-lifers and gun nuts—plenty of overlap in that Venn diagram, and Laura Lynn was their patron saint." She nodded as she picked up her burger. "I could imagine her getting in touch with one of those wack jobs, showing them Kitty's picture and saying, *This woman's an enemy of the preborn.* Or that she'd threatened Laura Lynn. Or that she was having sex with contraception." She burbled more laughter. "Sure, I could completely see it going down that way."

"And what about Kitty Cavanaugh?" I asked.

"You're writing about erasure?" Tara asked, and I nodded. "Well, she's your girl. She doesn't have much of a paper trail," Tara said. "Grew up on Cape Cod. Graduated from Hanfield in ninety-one, and then I couldn't find anything until ninety-five, when she started writing for a hospital newsletter. She did some pieces for women's magazines—*Redbook, Cosmo*—in the nineties. Mostly health-related stuff, stories about young women with breast cancer, 'Ten Diet Tips for Strong Bones,' like that. Nothing political at all, as far as I can tell. She got married in 1999, moved to Connecticut, and then she started ghosting for Laura Lynn." She took a bite of her burger, wiped her lips, and looked at me. "Did you know her at all? Did she believe that shit, or just write it?"

"I don't know," I said, setting my own burger down and feeling like I actually knew less about the mysterious Kitty Cavanaugh than I had when I'd thought she was just another inferiority complex–causing Upchurch supermom.

"You want to know the weird thing?" Tara asked. She shifted in her seat, smoothing the lapels of her jacket. "She looks . . . kind of nice, in her pictures. Not like Laura Lynn, who always looks like she's on the verge of spitting. Kitty looked like someone you could be friends with, you know?"

I nodded, thinking about my own Kitty sightings: Kitty in the park, Kitty in the supermarket, Kitty nodding hello at the soccer field or running the cookie-decorating table at the Red Wheel Barrow holiday craft fair with a kind word for every child. And hadn't she always been friendly to me . . . and my kids? She'd always smiled. I remembered that now. I'd thought she'd been smirking at my cheap, sloppy clothes, at my fractious children, at how chaotic our lives seemed next to her own, but maybe her smiles had been just smiles. Maybe my own insecurities had gotten in the way of our actually getting to know each other, and maybe even becoming friends.

"Kitty used to live in New York, right?"

"Bunch of places," Tara said. "Park Slope for a while, then Chelsea, then the West Village."

I flipped a page in my notebook and heard Kitty's voice on the telephone. *We have a mutual friend . . .* "Did you ever come across the name Evan McKenna in conjunction with Kitty? Or Laura Lynn Baird?"

Tara shook her head. "Why? Who's he?"

"Nobody," I said, and flipped my notebook shut. "He's nobody."

After finishing my burger, showing Tara my kids' pictures and admiring hers, and thanking her for her time and her insights, I walked out of the restaurant, pulled out my cell phone and finally returned Evan McKenna's call. My message was short and sweet: "Evan, it's Kate Klein. I need to speak with you." Then my cell phone number. Then "Goodbye."

I put the phone in my pocket and looked around through the swirling crowds of people along the cobblestones on Gansevoort Street. They all seemed to be twenty years younger than I was, their bright chatter rising like snowflakes in reverse into the starless black sky. The boys wore knit caps with pom-poms on top—a new fashion, one more I'd missed—and the girls all seemed to be wearing skinny striped knit scarves that they'd twined around their necks in double and triple loops. I looked down at myself: three-year-old navy wool coat, Janie's sweater, canvas tote bag, scuffed black boots. Then I sighed and started uptown to meet my father.

NINETEEN

"Birdie," my father said, opening the Met's backstage door and folding me into his mothball-scented embrace. He held me at arm's length and looked me up and down while I smiled under his scrutiny. "You look great. Come on," he said, swinging his oboe case beside him as we walked to the subway. He slid his Metrocard through the sensor once for himself and once for me. "Are you hungry? Did you have any dinner?"

"I did, but I'll keep you company," I said. Back at the apartment, I carefully removed the razor blades he used to make his reeds from the dining room table and hung my coat over the back of the chair that had always been mine. Nothing ever changed here. The piano was still draped in the same fringed scarves, still topped with the same framed photographs; the walls of the dimly lit living room were still lined with pictures of my mother—publicity stills, or shots of her on stage, in costume. I tossed my coat on the plush pink love seat, and gathered up two months' worth of newspapers and takeout menus. My father set the table. I emptied the dishwasher and checked the fridge for the staples that would satisfy me that he was keeping himself fed. There was a desiccated packet of deli turkey, a container of olives rimed in blue mold, two slices of petrified bread, and a box of baking soda.

"I've been eating at the diner," he said. He'd pulled off his jacket and bow tie, and his suspenders hung down around his knees. "And there's milk. See?" He waved the carton at me, and I nodded my approval. The doorman buzzed up, my father went to the door, and a few minutes later the kitchen table was covered with steaming cartons of spareribs, dumplings, chicken with broccoli, spicy green beans, and fried rice.

"How's the investigation?" my father asked, popping a water chestnut into his mouth.

"The police still haven't caught anyone," I said. I sipped from my water glass, and as he ate, I filled my father in, working backward from my cheeseburger with Tara to Philip's desperate question. "He wanted to know if she was happy."

My father's eyes were wide and soft underneath his glasses. "Was she?"

I cracked open a fortune cookie, one-handed. "I don't know. She always seemed so put together when I saw her. Now I think she might have been just as lost as I am in Connecticut. She may have been having an affair. Or maybe her husband was. Lots of mystery."

My father poked a single chopstick into the fried rice, and when he looked up, his eyes were worried. "Why are you so interested? Is it because you were the one to find her?"

"Well, there's that." I swept the jagged cookie pieces into my palm. "I don't know. Maybe she reminds me of myself a little. She used to be a writer, she used to live in New York." I cracked open another cookie and told him what Tara Singh had told me. "She actually lived in my old neighborhood. I think she might have known Evan McKenna."

"Your friend Evan?" he asked.

I got up without answering and started closing the containers of food, thinking that somehow hearing his name out loud from someone who really did love me hurt even worse than thinking it. "It probably has nothing to do with it. Maybe they were just old friends. Or maybe she hired him to find out whether her husband was cheating." I sniffed the carton of milk he'd brandished so proudly, winced, and dumped it down the sink. "How's Mom?"

"She'll be home soon," he reported. "She's teaching a master class this spring."

Bitter words—*good for her*—rose in my throat. I pressed my lips together and took a breath. "That should be nice. I'm sure you miss her. I know my kids do."

He looked at me carefully. I turned my back and stacked the food containers in the refrigerator. I was remembering the way I'd run to her in London, hoping, I guess, that she'd magically turn into the kind of mother I'd seen in movies or on TV—loving and solicitous, offering sympathy and strong English tea. Instead, she'd tossed a room service menu at me and hurried into a chauffeured car that would whisk her to lunch with executives at the European offices of her record label.

He shook his head. "You know this won't be forever. She just wants to sing for as long as she can. Someday we'll get her back."

"Someday," I repeated. I'd been hearing it my whole life. *I'll be back by summer . . . I'll be home for Christmas . . . Of course I'll be at your graduation, honey, I wouldn't miss that for anything!* Lies. Not that she'd meant to lie, but something always came up—another performance, a recording opportunity, travel difficulties. Something always made her break her word.

My father reached for my hand. "She loves you very much."

"I know she does," I said.

He stared at me, puzzled. "Birdie, what's wrong?"

"Besides running across dead bodies?" I gave a short, bitter laugh. "I don't know. Connecticut, I guess."

"What about it?" he asked. He filled the teakettle and flicked on the gas. "Hot chocolate?" he asked, and I nodded yes.

"It makes Stepford look like a hotbed of revolution." I told him about the birthday party I'd botched, about Marybeth Coe and her baby's diaper-free existence, about the formidable playground gang. I didn't tell him the rest of it: that Ben was hardly ever home and was usually either on the phone or online when he was; that I was having more sex with the shower attachment than I was with my spouse; that all the other mothers seemed content to while away the hours playing Candy Land or doing crafts with their kids, while I'd feel like screaming and running out of the house after fifteen minutes of either activity, which led me to the conclusion that there was either something wrong with all of them or, more likely, something wrong with me.

"These women," I said. "They have the most beautiful gardens you've ever seen—planned, laid out, perfectly weeded and watered. They hang wreaths on their doors, and not just for Christmas, either. They've got spring wreaths, and Easter wreaths, and Thanksgiving wreaths, and probably last-day-of-school wreaths. Their houses look like they could be in one of those magazines: *Traditional Home, Colonial Home, Whatever Home.* They all had careers, but none of them ever talk about them, let alone say they miss them. They never want to talk about anything but their gardens, and what room they're redecorating, and their kids, and I . . ." I cleared my throat. "It's high school all over again." Only at least this time, I reasoned, nobody'd stuck a sanitary napkin to my chair. Yet.

My father set my hot chocolate in front of me. I wrapped my hands around the musical notes dancing up and down the chipped china. I'd bought this mug for him for some Father's Day more than twenty years ago.

"So you're looking into Kitty Cavanaugh's death?"

I took a sip of hot chocolate, then set my mug down. "I'm actually more interested in her life," I said. "I'm trying to figure out who she used to be before Upchurch."

"Be careful," my father said sternly.

"I'll be fine," I said, with more confidence than I felt.

TWENTY

It was almost one in the morning when the train pulled into the Upchurch station. I was the only one to get off. I pulled my coat tight against me and shivered as I hurried off the platform. The parking lot was empty except for my minivan, glowing a ghostly silver under the sodium lights. My heels sounded as loud as gunshots as I racewalked across the pavement, wishing I'd remembered a scarf. There was something fluttering underneath my minivan's windshield wiper. A parking ticket? I wasn't even sure they gave them out in Upchurch.

It wasn't a parking ticket. It was a note tucked into an envelope with my name on the front, a note written on a sheet of lined paper that looked like it had been ripped out of a notebook. The words printed in thick black letters read, "Stop asking questions or you will be next."

I whirled around wildly, my heart hammering, as if whoever'd stuck the note on my car might have hung around to see my reaction. There was not a single other car, or person, to be seen, but I thought—or imagined—that I could hear footsteps approaching me, slowly at first, then faster and faster.

I grabbed my keys, unlocked the car, got behind the wheel, slammed the door, and locked it. Then I stared in the rearview mirror, frozen in horror, imagining I saw a hunched figure rising out of the backseat, arms extended . . . Nope. Just the kids' car seats.

"Okay," I whispered to myself. "Okay." My hands shook as I pulled out my cell phone. Who to call first? Ben? What could he do, at one o'clock in the morning? Wake up all three kids and come to fetch me?

"Calm down, Kate," I whispered. I pulled Stan Bergeron's business card out of my tote bag and dialed his pager. After I'd punched in my number, I hung up and wrapped my hands around the wheel until they stopped shaking, jerking my head around to the left and the right and the left again, imagining I heard footsteps approaching or saw someone coming toward me, or heard something rustling in the backseat.

The chief of police sounded sleepy. "This is Stan Bergeron, returning a page."

"Stan, it's Kate Klein. I'm in the parking lot at the train station. Someone left a note on my car. 'Stop asking questions or you will be next.' "

"Stop asking questions about what?"

My heart sank. "About whether the Montessori preschool in Greenwich is any good," I snapped.

There was a pause.

"About Kitty Cavanaugh," I said, hearing my voice rise toward a shriek.

Stan sighed as he realized he wasn't going to get to go back to sleep. "Meet me at the police station. Bring the note with you," he said.

"I touched it," I told him.

"Beg pardon?"

"To read it. I touched it. So my fingerprints are on it."

Stan stifled a yawn. "We'll deal with it. Come on down."

Stan offered me coffee but couldn't figure out how to work the pot. I plugged it in, measured water and grounds, and slumped behind the desk where I'd sat the day I'd found Kitty.

"You're not the only one," he said, not unkindly, pushing a notebook and pen across the desk so that I could write down exactly what had happened.

"Huh?"

"Alexis Hagen-Holdt was in here this afternoon. She thought someone was following her when she was jogging and almost ran her off the road."

"Oh, God."

"Yeah. Her neighbor down the street has a sixteen-year-old son who just got his license. We're pretty sure that was the culprit." He plopped down in the chair across from me with a sigh. "Everyone's nervous."

"Can you blame us?" I smoothed my shaking hands against my knees, and set about writing my field report, listing everyone I'd talked to, from the ladies on the playground to Laura Lynn Baird to Tara Singh and even my father in New York. It was after three in the morning by the time I drove home, with Stan trailing me in his cruiser. He escorted me to the front door. I carefully punched our code into the alarm system's keypad and eased the door open.

Stan waved his flashlight into the foyer. The beam of light strobed off the piles of abandoned toys and kids' shoes, casting each kicked-off sneaker and discarded Barbie in flickering shadow. "Do you want me to come inside?" he whispered. I shook my head.

"I'll be okay."

I shut the door, locked it, reset the alarm, and crept up the creaky staircase, holding my breath as I eased past Sam and Jack's room, then Sophie's. Six more steps and I'd be home free. Five . . . four . . . three . . . two . . .

"Mama?"

Shit.

"Sleep," I whispered to my daughter.

"Story," she whispered back, pulling a book out of the stack on the table by her bed.

I sat on her little canopied bed. Sophie was wearing a pink flannel nightgown. Her fine brown hair fell in tangles around her cheeks. She scooched over to make room, then leaned against me. "'In the great green room,'" I began.

"'Was a telephone,'" said Sophie. She hooked Uglydoll, also dressed in a miniature pink nightgown, under her arm and flipped the pages.

"'Goodnight comb and goodnight brush, goodnight nobody, goodnight mush.'"

"Mama, who is Nobody?" Sophie asked, pointing at the blank page.

Me, I thought. I was thinking of the couples I'd seen on the street back in the city, skinny scarves looped around their necks, laughing into the darkness. I was thinking about Janie, with her highlights and her handbags and her fingers rattling over the keyboard, smart and competent, running her life, instead of the other way around. I thought about my mother in London tossing the room service menu at me and telling me she had to go without even asking what had brought me there and why my eyes were still red and puffy from all the crying I'd done on the flight. I thought of Ben standing in the doorway looking down at me as I crouched on my knees in front of the bathtub, not looking at me so much as looking through me.

Instead, I said, "I don't know, sweetheart," and finished the story. "'Goodnight stars, goodnight air, goodnight noises everywhere.'" I kissed my daughter and then, at her insistence, her doll and eased over the creaking floorboards down the hall to my bedroom. If Ben woke up, I would tell him the truth. Either way I'd have to tell him. If someone was slipping threatening notes underneath the windshield of our car, if I was in danger, or the kids were, my husband needed to know. Three more steps. Two more. One . . .

My cell phone buzzed in my pocket. Down the hall, one of the boys cried out in his sleep. I pulled it out, fumbled, almost dropped it, then brought it to my ear. "Hello?"

I knew what I'd hear next: a low, growling, clotted voice, the voice of every monster under the bed, and it would say, "I left the note on your car, Kate. You thought your locks and your alarm kept you safe, but you're not safe. I'm in your house. *I'm in your house right now . . .*"

"Kate?"

Even after all this time, even after all the kids, his low, warm voice still made my stomach do a slow flip-flop. I could see him as he'd looked that New Year's Eve, with his eyes half open and his hands tangling in my hair.

"Evan, where are you?" I whispered. I backed into the kids' bathroom, pulled the door shut, and sat down on the toilet in the dark. "The police need to talk to you."

"Kate . . ."

"Kitty Cavanaugh's dead and she had a note with your number by her phone and the police know that you were the last one to call her and now someone left a note on my car tonight, 'Stop asking questions or you will be next.' "

"Kate, slow down."

I took a deep breath and closed my eyes in the darkness.

"Where are you?"

"Newark airport. I just got back from Miami."

My stomach did another somersault. I pictured palm trees, white sand, Michelle in a thong bikini.

". . . been in touch with the police there," he was saying. "I'll be there—in Upchurch—tomorrow afternoon. Can I see you?"

"I'm married," I blurted.

"I know." Evan paused, and when he spoke again it was in the low, teasing tones I remembered from all of those takeout dinners and Scrabble games (and, more recently, from many of my sessions with the showerhead). "But I can still see you, can't I?"

I leaned forward on the toilet seat, clutching the phone in one sweaty hand. But before I could answer, Evan said, "Are you all right, Katie? You don't sound like yourself."

"I have to go. My kids are sleeping," I blurted, without thinking how ridiculous that sounded—it was the middle of the night; of course my kids were sleeping, and what did he mean about not sounding like myself? How did he even know who that was anymore? I hung up, turned off the phone, then crept back down the stairs to double-check that the alarm was working and that every door and every window had been locked.

PART TWO

The Ghost Writer

TWENTY-ONE

It was a six-hour flight from London to New York, and I'd gone a little nuts in the duty-free shop, buying two paperback novels with candy pink covers, comically bewildered British heroines, and the promise of a happy ending by page 375; four glossy magazines; three Cadbury milk chocolate bars; and one half-bottle of red wine I was fully prepared to slip into the bathroom to chug. I had a silk eye mask and a pair of Scottish wax earplugs. Finally, in case of dire emergency or an unexpected crying jag, I had two of the prescription painkillers I'd saved from the summer before when I'd had my wisdom teeth pulled.

On the plane, I'd slipped off my shoes, pulled the blanket up to my chin, unwrapped the first candy bar, and flipped open one of the magazines when a tall, stooped man with a pleasant, narrow face sat down beside me.

"Hi."

He was about my age, and his voice, and orthodontically perfected teeth, were unmistakably American. I gave him a faint half-smile, nodded, and turned toward the window with the magazine spread open in my lap. "Your Most Intimate Health Questions Answered," read the headline. Evidently the editors of British *Cosmo* believed that many of my most intimate health questions involved itches in places you couldn't scratch in public.

The guy was undeterred by my cold shoulder and the words

"yeast infection" in large pink letters on the top of the page. He stowed his laptop underneath the seat in front of him, wriggled out of his leather jacket, and inquired, "Is that any good?"

"I'm learning a lot." I ostentatiously flicked another page and wondered whether I'd actually have to scratch myself to get him to leave me alone.

He clicked his seatbelt closed. "Are you from New York?"

I made a noncommittal noise. *Why, God? Why me?* I eased one of the painkillers out of my pocket.

"You look so familiar," the guy continued. I turned and looked at him: brown eyes, close set, underneath thick black eyebrows. Beaky nose in a thin face, and a nice-enough smile, narrow shoulders and knobby wrists. Nobody was ever going to mistake him for a pop star.

"Just one of those faces, I guess." I slid the pill into my mouth and washed it down with a slug of bottled water.

"You know, one thing I never get used to over here: no ice in the water."

I half nodded and turned toward the window. Ten days with my mother had given me a bunch of new diva tricks—the dismissive yawn, the vacant stare, the sudden switch to another language.

"You have to ask for ice if you want it in your water," he continued. "You go out to eat, they pour you a glass half full of warm water. Who wants to drink that?"

"Look," I said, deciding that if I didn't take proactive steps, I'd be listening to this dolt talk about his beverage preferences until the drugs kicked in.

He mistook my movement for friendliness, smiled, and stuck out his hand. "Ben Borowitz."

"I have a gun," I replied, and opened my purse to show him.

He pulled back, thrusting both hands in the air as if I were a cop who'd told him to stick 'em up. Of course, the instant the words were out of my mouth, I felt guilty. I touched his wrist gently. He jumped in his seat.

"Hey."

He ignored me, grabbing the in-flight magazine and flipped to a feature about Memphis barbecue.

"I don't really have a gun," I said, opening my purse wider. "It's just a compact. My mother bought it for me on Portobello Road." Reina and I had spent an afternoon shopping, with my mother striding grandly along the rainy street in ankle-length skirts and a necklace of gumball-sized pearls, waiting to be recognized; me in jeans and a bulky raincoat trailing after her, praying that if she was, she wouldn't introduce me.

He risked a glance sideways, and I pulled out the compact to show him. "See?"

"I can see that you don't want to be disturbed," he said, with his gaze fixed rigidly on his magazine.

"Yes, but I shouldn't have scared you. I'm sorry. I've just . . ." Oh, God. I felt my eyelids prickle and my throat start to close. "I've been going through kind of a hard time."

He reached into his pocket and pulled out a handkerchief. An actual cloth one that smelled clean and felt starchy when I pressed it beneath my eyes.

"I'm sorry I bothered you," he said. "It's just that you really do look familiar."

I shrugged and sniffled, readying myself for a game of Jewish geography or New York City where'd you go/who do you know. "I grew up on the Upper West Side and I went to Pimm for high school."

"Did you live on Amsterdam Avenue?"

I nodded, turning toward him.

"Did you ever take saxophone lessons?"

"No. Voice." I took another sip of water, imagining I was already starting to feel drowsy. "But there were saxophone teachers in my building."

"I took sax lessons," he said. "Maybe I saw you."

"Maybe you did." I tried to give him his handkerchief back.

"No, keep it. It's yours," he said, and smiled. "But you'll have to give it back. Will you have dinner with me?"

I nodded. He had a nice smile, I thought . . . or maybe that was just the medication talking. Then I closed my eyes, and when I woke up, we were on the ground at Kennedy Airport and my head was on Ben Borowitz's shoulder. He'd tucked my blanket around me and was having a quiet consultation with the pretty British flight attendant about the best way to remove drool from his leather jacket, which he'd bunched up and placed under my cheek. "Sorry," I murmured thickly. "No, no," said Ben. "Don't worry." He had a car waiting. Could he give me a ride home?

I let him put me in the car. A week later, we went out for sushi. I asked the right questions about his life, his job, his friends, and his hobbies and made myself nod and smile in all the right places, and I only slipped into the bathroom twice to check my messages at home to see if Evan had called. *Suitable,* I thought, leaning across the table to clink sake cups with the man who, two years later, would become my husband. He is a suitable man. We'll have a suitable life together. I knew that what I felt for Ben wasn't even close to the passion I'd felt for Evan. But look where passion had gotten me. Suitable, I figured, would suit me just fine.

Ben and I honeymooned in Saint Lucia and moved into his apartment, two bedrooms at Sixty-fifth and Central Park West, and for three years we were happy. Well, I was reasonably content, with my job and with Janie. Being married felt a lot like being single, with the addition of a very large, sparkly diamond and the very minor issue of being unable to date other men. Not that I was seeing much of my husband. Ben appeared to have spent all of whatever free time he would ever have wooing me. Now that he'd sealed the deal, he worked nights, weekends, and all summer long, except for the occasional weekend when he'd drive out on Saturday to visit me and Janie at Sy's house in Bridgehampton, spend the whole day poolside, and drive back Sunday with his entire face sunburned, except for the patch of white around his ear where he'd held his cell phone.

Then came Sophie. Ben went back to work two days after she arrived. I didn't complain, but it was hard not to notice that Janie and my father both took more time off than my husband did (Reina flew in long enough to kiss the baby, then flew back to Rome). After ten days, my father went back to the orchestra, Janie went back to *New York Night,* and I was left alone, exhausted and bewildered, with an eight-and-a-half-pound shriek machine and a supercompetent baby nurse who, regrettably, spoke only Russian.

When Sophie was twelve weeks old, I went to visit Dr. Morrison for my twice-postponed postbirth checkup.

"How are you doing?" he asked genially as I stuck my feet into the stirrups.

"Uh . . ." Honestly, between dealing with a cranky newborn, a husband who was never home, a mother who kept promising to return, then changing her mind, and Sveta the baby nurse, who communicated via grunts, gestures, and angry shakes of her head, I was having a hard time stringing together more than two words at a time.

"Knees apart, please. What are you planning on doing for birth control?"

I laughed weakly. "Never have sex again?"

He chuckled twice as he rummaged inside me. Then his eyebrows drew down. "Huh."

"Huh what?" I asked. I knew I should have been more worried, but honestly, lying on my back with my colicky baby thirty blocks away was the most restful experience I'd had since Sophie's arrival. It was all I could do not to doze off.

"I think we should step into the ultrasound room."

I struggled to think. "Why? Is there, um, something still in there?"

"Follow me," he said. Five minutes later Dr. Morrison had smeared goo on my belly, pressed the ultrasound wand against it, and located not one but two heartbeats. "Congratulations, Mom!" the nurse had had the nerve to say. Lucky for her, she had quick reflexes. The shoe I threw at the ultrasound monitor barely grazed her shoulder. I'd gone running out of the office and down the hall and into the elevator with my pants pulled on but not zipped or buttoned, my sneakers shoved onto my feet, unlaced, and the examination gown flapping in back and sticking to the ultrasound gel in front.

Ben had answered his phone on the third ring. "Ben Borowitz speaking."

"Motherfucker!" I'd yelled so loudly that the flock of pigeons on the corner had taken flight and the homeless guy going through the garbage can and mumbling to himself had looked up and said, quite lucidly, "Lady, you nuts."

"What?"

"I'm pregnant," I said, and started crying. "Again. With twins!"

"You got pregnant . . ." His voice trailed off. "I didn't think you could get pregnant when . . . I mean, it's so soon!"

"Tell me about it," I sniffled.

He cleared his throat. "So what are we going to do now?"

I shoved my hair back from my cheeks and pulled the gown tight against my shoulders. "Have three kids, I guess. But you're going to have to help me."

"I will," he promised.

"You can't just say you're going to come home early and not come home, or that you're going to do the laundry and not do it. I'm . . ." I wiped tears off my cheeks with the hem of the gown. "I'm kind of not making it here."

"I'll help you, Kate. I promise I will."

He'd meant it at the time. At least, that's the belief that I'd clung to after the boys came along and the baby nurse returned and my mother was once again missing in action. Ten days after my

C-section, Janie and my father were once again back at work and I was alone in the apartment with a very unhappy eleven-month-old and two newborns. The trouble was, as Ben patiently explained to me over and over again, he was building a business, cementing his reputation, setting himself up for the halcyon, hazy days somewhere in the future when he wouldn't have to work every day and most nights and almost every weekend. "I'm doing this for us," he'd say, and I'd nod and say, "I understand."

As long as I had New York, and my father, and Janie, I thought I'd be fine. The kids would grow up eventually. They'd go to nursery school, then school school. Someday I'd get to the point where I could talk to them and they'd answer back. I could work part-time. I could reclaim my pre-baby life and have some kind of balance again.

Then I got stroller-jacked.

The kids and I were on our way back from the Museum of Natural History, where we'd spent twenty educational minutes inspecting the exhibit on life under the sea, an equal amount of time changing diapers, and forty-five minutes in the gift shop. It was unexpectedly warm for February, with a clear blue sky and a gentle breeze that promised the joys of spring. Sam and Jack, who'd emerged from my womb good-natured and easygoing and hadn't changed much in the intervening years, were in their stroller, fast asleep. Sophie, who'd emerged from my womb red-faced and shrieking inconsolably and hadn't changed much either, was wide awake and standing on the board I'd affixed to the back of the stroller.

"Mommy, why are wheels round?" she asked as we strolled along Central Park West.

"Because if they were square, they wouldn't turn!"

Sophie considered this. "Why?"

"Well, they turn because that's what wheels do! That's how they get you places!"

"But why—"

But before Sophie could finish, a man in a stained baseball cap popped out from behind a dumpster, grabbed the stroller's handlebars, and wheeled it swiftly into a dark alley I'd never noticed before.

"Hey!" I screamed as Sophie hopped nimbly off the board and wrapped her arms around my legs.

"Be cool, be cool," he said, pushing the stroller against the dumpster and fumbling in his pocket. My heart froze as I saw the gun.

"Gimme your bag."

I peeled Sophie off my legs, held her against me, bent over, and fished the diaper bag out from underneath the stroller.

"No, your *purse.*"

"I don't have one!" I said. "I don't carry a purse, I just stick my wallet in the diaper bag." I thrust the bag out at him, feeling dizzy and sick. "Please don't hurt my babies."

He dumped the diaper bag out on the pavement. Wipes and diapers and boxes of raisins came tumbling down, along with my wallet, which he shoved in his pocket. "Jewelry." I handed over my watch and bracelet, and tried to yank my wedding band off while forcing myself to look at him, his face, his body. He was five ten or so, maybe a hundred and sixty pounds, a pale white guy with dirty blond hair in faded jeans and a leather jacket.

"Now give me the stroller."

"What?"

He glared at me. "Get the brats out of there and hand it over."

"Stand still," I whispered to Sophie. She grabbed my legs again, and I lurched forward and unfastened the boys with shaking hands, still unable to quite believe that this was happening.

I lifted the boys into my arms. The thief pressed the red button underneath the handlebars. Nothing happened. He peered at the print on the foam grips.

"This says, 'Easy one-hand fold.' "

"Yeah, well . . ."

He pushed the button again and jiggled the stroller up and down. Still nothing. He kicked the cross-braces.

"No, not that way," I said, trying to adjust approximately sixty-three pounds of toddler in my arms. "No, Mumma, no!" Sophie wailed as Jack's foot bounced off her shoulder. "No more baby touch!"

"You've got to press and push up on that bottom bar at the same time."

"This one?" he asked, gesturing toward one of the crossbars with his gun.

"No, no, the one underneath." I pointed with my chin. Jack and Sam, unbelievably, were still asleep, but Sophie seemed to have figured out what was happening.

"Mumma, why dat man takin stroller?"

"He needs it, I guess," I said, shifting the boys in my arms. Sophie shrieked at a volume that would have done her grandmother proud.

"Uglydoll!"

Shit. *Chapter Forty-three,* I thought to myself. *In which I am sold into stuffed slavery and Sophie is left inconsolable.*

"Um, excuse me? Sir?"

"Uglydoll!" Sophie blatted as both boys opened their eyes, looked at their sister, and started to wail. The mugger had finally managed to collapse the stroller and had lifted it over his shoulder.

"Could I just get my daughter's toy out of the basket?"

"Buy her another one, rich bitch!"

"Uglydoll is special!" Sophie wailed.

"Uglydoll is special!" I repeated. "I mean, I can't just buy her another one!"

He heaved a sigh and stopped. I hurried forward as fast as I could with Sophie still attached to my leg, worked one hand free, and rummaged through the basket underneath the folded-up stroller as quickly as I could. Juice box, deflated toy basketball, plastic container full of cheddar cheese crackers . . .

"Uglydoll!"

I finally located the doll and handed him to Sophie. She popped her thumb in her mouth and clutched the doll, glaring up at our mugger, who cocked an eyebrow at the four of us.

"Anything else?"

I slumped backward against the Dumpster. "No," I said, watching my four-hundred-dollar German-engineered stroller vanishing from my life forever. "No, that'll be all."

Rich bitch, I thought, shaking my head. I shoved what I could back into the diaper bag, carried the kids to the sidewalk, hailed a cab, and called my husband.

By three o'clock that afternoon, Ben had collected us at the police station. His brow was furrowed, his lips were pinched, and his eyes were furious. "That's it," he said. "That's it for the city. We're leaving as fast as I can get us out of here."

I opened my mouth to protest and found I was too wrung out and shaky to come up with coherent arguments as to why we should stay. By four o'clock Ben was on the phone with real estate agents. The next week he put our apartment on the market, and the week after that he ushered me into our very own Montclaire and handed me the keys. Goodbye, New York City; hello, Upchuck, Connecticut.

Even before we'd moved here, but certainly more since the great relocation, I'd find myself daydreaming about how my life could have turned out differently. What if I'd tried harder with Evan? What if I'd held out for the big love instead of settling for a man I merely liked?

No point in wondering, I thought, dragging myself out of bed too early the next morning as my kids clamored for pancakes and my husband clamored for his dry cleaning. If there was no Ben, there'd be no kids, and I couldn't imagine my life without them. Still, as I distributed plates and clean shirts, I couldn't keep from thinking about what would have happened if the British Airways computer that had assigned me my seat had put me one row forward or one row back, or if I'd gone to Paris or Miami Beach instead of London to tend to my broken heart, or if I'd slipped my eye mask on a minute earlier and Ben Borowitz had never seen my face.

TWENTY-TWO

The Upchurch Town Hall, according to the plaque set in a hunk of granite in front of the building, had been built in the Year of Our Lord 1984. But whoever had done the construction had taken the town's Colonial history seriously: instead of padded flip-up auditorium seats with armrests and cushioning, the high-ceilinged room was lined with high-backed hardwood pews that would have done a luxury-averse Puritan proud and that were, judging from the shifting and squirming going on, a tad too narrow for the modern-day behind.

Not that there was any room for me to squeeze mine in. Kitty's memorial service was slated to start at ten a.m., but evidently, all the other citizens of our fair town had gotten a memo instructing them to show up no later than nine forty-five. By the time I rolled into the room at a very respectable nine fifty-three—with my hair combed, and wearing lipstick I'd applied in the rearview mirror—every seat of every row was taken, as was each of the three dozen or so folding chairs set up around the room's perimeter.

I circled the room, then edged my way into a corner. Carol Gwinnell waved to me from her seat three rows back from the podium. She was wearing a dove gray skirt, a white silk blouse, black pumps, and, in place of her usual clusters of bangles and bells, a simple pair of diamond studs. Next to her was Sukie Sutherland, in a pale beige suit and a double strand of pearls. Next to Sukie sat Lexi Hagen-Holdt, with her hair neatly French braided, in a long-sleeved light brown T-shirt dress that stretched against her shoulders and tights that showed off the curves of her calves.

I stood in a corner in my black skirt and dark blue sweater and wished I'd gotten the memo about muted earth tones. "Let us pray," intoned Ted Gordon, the town's Congregationalist minister. Everyone dropped their heads. I dropped mine too, so fast that I could hear my neck creak. "Oh, Lord, we ask that you welcome our sister Katherine Cavanaugh into your arms. We ask that you comfort her grieving family, her loved ones: her husband, Philip, her daughters, Madeline and Emerson, her parents, Bonnie and Hugh . . ."

Parents? I couldn't remember whether any of the obituaries had mentioned parents. The "she is survived by's" had only included her husband and her daughters. Tara Singh's website had featured Kitty's maiden name and hometown but had said nothing about a mother or father . . . and Bonnie was the name I remembered from the postcard in Kitty's bedroom.

I raised my eyes as far as I dared and scanned the crowd. There were a dozen couples who were the right age to be her mother and father. I looked in the front row, but I could only see Philip, and the girls in matching navy dresses, and a well-preserved older couple whose male half was the spitting image of Philip, if Philip were thirty years older and had spent a good portion of that time enjoying marbled steak and twelve-year-old Scotch.

"Lord, we ask you to lift up this community," Reverend Gordon continued. The reverend had curly hair, round shoulders, and an earnest look on his full face. He looked, I thought, struggling mightily to keep from bursting into inappropriate laughter, exactly like the guy who'd played Flounder in *Animal House,* which made it a little difficult to take him seriously. "Let us be a light to one another, a comfort to the grieving family," he said, cheeks quivering with sincerity. "Let us be patient and loving as we travel through this terrible time as a community, and as the police continue their quest to bring the perpetrators of this horror to justice."

Reverend Gordon leaned forward and gripped the edge of the podium tightly. His gold wedding band twinkled underneath the lights.

"What can we say about Kitty Cavanaugh?" he asked. "A brilliant thinker. A loving mother. A caring, devoted spouse."

A ghostwriter. A woman who spent three afternoons a week in New York City doing God knows what.

Reverend Ted paused and and looked down at us all warmly. "What can we say," he asked, "about a thirty-six-year-old woman who died?"

I think that my jaw must have sagged open. *I know my eyes widened.* I am certain that I whispered the words *Oh, no, he didn't!* under my breath. A murdered woman's funeral, and Flounder's quoting *Love Story*? Didn't Kitty deserve better than that? I looked around for someone who I could share that observation with, but all I heard were quiet sobs and genteel sniffles.

As it turned out, there was a great deal that Reverend Ted had to say about a thirty-six-year-old woman who died. He praised Kitty's warmth as a mother, her skills as a homemaker, the excellence of her homemade strawberry rhubarb pie, which had twice taken ribbons in the church's annual Spring Fling Bake Fair. He spoke in only the broadest, blandest terms of the "thought-provoking articles" she'd written, left out entirely the fact that she'd written them for somebody else, and made a single passing reference to Kitty's book, "which has died along with her." I eased my right foot out of the high-heeled pump I'd foolishly chosen and waited for any mention of Kitty's pre-Upchurch life—a college friend, a hospital newsletter editor, a New York City roommate. It never came. There wasn't another word about her parents, or a single mention of anyone from her childhood or college or New York City. It was like she hadn't existed until she married Philip and moved to Upchurch; like she'd written herself into being. Or rewritten, I thought, putting on my right shoe and slipping off my left one.

"And now," Reverend Ted said, gazing down at us benevolently, "if any of Kitty's friends would like to speak?"

The big, high-ceilinged room was silent except for the occasional sniffle or the shifting of one stockinged leg against another. Flounder gazed at the audience expectantly. I found myself unexpectedly on the verge of tears as Kitty's in-laws stared stoically ahead, poster children for the stiff upper lip society, and Marybeth and Sukie murmured softly to each other but made no move toward the stage. Wasn't anyone going to say anything? Didn't she have any friends? If I bought the farm, I was sure that Janie would give a kick-ass speech in my honor, that she'd make me sound funny and loving and competent and that she wouldn't mention the day Sam had rolled off the bed and Jack had fallen out of his car seat and I'd had to go to the emergency room twice in eight hours. And unlike me, Kitty had actual praises that could be sung about her. There were women here who'd seen her devotion to her daughters first-hand. So why wasn't anyone singing?

Finally Kevin Dolan made his way to the stage and whispered into Reverend Ted's ear. I exhaled, thinking that at last someone was going to say something on Kitty's behalf, as Kevin whispered and pointed. Into the crowd. Toward the back of the room. At me.

"Kate Klein?" the reverend asked. Heads turned. A flurry of whispers made its way through the aisles, as the blood drained from my face. I shook my head. Reverend Ted appeared not to notice. "Kate Klein!" he said, and then tried for the first semi-joke of the morning. "Come on down!"

I shook my head more vigorously and mouthed the word *no,* while keeping an appropriately sedate expression cemented to my face. My *no* didn't register. Hands gripped my arms and I found myself propelled down the aisle in my too-tight shoes. Then, somehow, I was up on the stage, with Kevin Dolan guiding me gently toward the podium. "I'm sorry," he murmured. "I must have heard you wrong, but didn't you tell me you were working on a speech for her memorial?"

Busted, I thought, as my head bobbed up and down, a movement completely independent of my will. *Oh, Kate, you are so completely screwed.* I held the edges of the podium in a death grip and stared out at the crowd—three hundred of my Connecticut contemporaries—with not a single thought as to what I was going to say.

I swallowed hard, then began, "Kitty Cavanaugh was . . ."

"Louder!" called someone in the back row.

"Can't hear you!" added someone else.

I cleared my throat and adjusted the microphone, wincing at the squeal of feedback, and tried again.

"Kitty Cavanaugh was a good mother, a good wife. As we've all heard," I added limply. "And she was doing important work—the work of . . ." *Spending secret afternoons in New York City and possibly cheating on her husband, who was undoubtedly cheating on her.* Oh, God help me. I swallowed hard. ". . . investigating what it means to be a good mother, a good wife, a good person in our times. We might not all have agreed with what she had to say . . ." I wiped my forehead, as someone in the back row sucked in an outraged breath. "But maybe we can all agree that being a parent is hard. Really, really hard. Harder than those books make it sound, harder than the movies make it look. And at the end of the day, I think Kitty will be remembered for being brave enough to ask those hard questions, to try to find her own answers, to not give a damn if they flew in the face of what we'd been raised to believe." I swiped my sleeve against my forehead again and felt sweat trickling down my back and soaking the band of my bra. I probably looked like Albert Brooks in *Broadcast News.* Memories of the handful of times I'd seen Kitty—really seen her—flashed uselessly through my mind. Kitty in pink linen, smiling at her daughters; Kitty sprawled out dead on her kitchen floor with blood turning her silk blouse the color of old Bordeaux.

Sing, I thought. *Sing her praises.* "So . . . so maybe we can all sing a song. In her memory." I whipped my index finger discreetly over my upper lip and realized that, in spite of years of voice lessons and listening to every jazz recording ever made, in spite of growing up with one of the world's preeminent sopranos as a mother and one of the country's top oboists as a dad, I couldn't remember the melody to one single song. Not a single lyric, not a single note. Nothing. My mind was absolutely blank. Except . . . I drew a deep breath. "If you're happy and you know it, clap your hands." My voice cracked on the last word. The audience stared at me, dumbfounded. Reverend Ted's broad brow was furrowed. Kevin Dolan's jaw dropped. Finally Lexi Hagen-Holdt and Carol Gwinnell patted their hands together and began to sing.

"If you're happy and you know it, clap your hands."

A few more halfhearted clappers joined in, their faces politely expressionless, their voices cultured and soft.

"If you're happy and you know it, then your face will surely show it," Reverend Ted joined in, in a serviceable baritone.

"If you're happy and you know it, clap your hands," sang Kevin Dolan. The final pairs of claps rang through the audience like stones falling into an empty well. "Thank you," I murmured, and limped back down the crowded aisle, which parted as the other mourners leaned—no, cringed—away from me.

I staggered past them, drenched with sweat, and went back to the wall I'd been leaning on. The woman beside me leaned over to touch my hand. "That was . . ." Her lips worked for a few seconds. "That was really something."

I nodded weakly. Really something. I just bet it was.

"To conclude," said Reverend Ted, "We will hear from Kitty's family."

Oh, no, I thought, as my breath caught in my throat. Philip Cavanaugh was making his way unsteadily through the crowd with his daughters. One was on his left side and one was on his right and they were guiding him, like tiny navy blue tugboats guiding a freighter into port. *Oh, no. Not this.* I fumbled in my purse for a tissue and settled for a wadded, chocolate-streaked napkin from Dairy Queen. I'd never cared much one way or the other about Lady Di, but I still had vivid memories of her funeral—that casket with the folded letter on top reading "Mummy" that had had me sobbing like I'd lost my own mother (who was actually performing in Denver at the time, perfectly safe). What if it had been me, and Sophie and Sam and Jack were left with just their father? I thought of the letter on the van the night before and couldn't stop myself from shaking, as Philip Cavanaugh paused and wiped his eyes. His eyes were sunk deep into his head. His lips were grayish and trembling. His cheeks were hollow; new loose skin beneath his chin wobbled as he walked.

He climbed one step, then two. His heel caught on the third step and he stumbled, almost falling, before he reached the podium. I heard Lexi Hagen-Holdt gasp, and saw Carol Gwinnell pat her shoulders. The dark-haired woman seated in the front row next to Kevin Dolan—Delphine, I presumed—sobbed quietly into a handkerchief. Philip reached out one finger and touched the microphone lightly, as if to make sure it was still there.

"Kitty was . . ." His voice was a low, toneless rasp. He cleared his throat and tried again. "Kitty was . . ."

Much too loud, this time, or he'd gotten too close to the microphone. There was a booming echo, then a muffled thump. Philip Cavanaugh leaned forward and buried his face in his hands.

"This is too much," muttered the woman on my left. Then Reverend Ted was there, gently guiding Philip back down to his seat. The two girls remained, standing in front of the microphone, miniature Kittys with perfect posture and shining brown hair combed back neatly from their pale faces. They looked at each other, and finally, one of them—Madeline or Emerson, I had no idea—stepped forward. "We loved our mother very much," she said.

The clock ticked. Lexi Hagen-Holdt cried. Philip Cavanaugh's breath rasped as he struggled for composure and Reverend Ted patted him ineffectually on the back. The other little girl stepped up to join her sister.

"She was the best mother in the world."

The lobby was a logjam. Philip, propped upright by his parents on one side and Reverend Ted on the other, stood like a waxen effigy with a hand on each of his daughters' shoulders. I scooted behind them as quickly as I could, given the blister situation, trying not to hear my reviews ("Who was that . . . that large woman, and what on earth was she thinking?" one chic, rail-thin woman inquired of another). As I watched, Kevin and Delphine Dolan approached Philip. Kevin wrapped his arms around Phil's shoulders. Phil closed his eyes, and Delphine Dolan, whose makeup was in ruins, stood by his side, wiping at her eyes. When Phil reached for her arm, I thought I saw her flinch.

I pushed through the doors and beat almost everyone out to the parking lot. Once I was there, I ignored the faces and concentrated on license plates. Eastham, Massachusetts, the obituaries had said. Eastham was where the unsent postcard I'd found was supposed to go. Connecticut plates are blue and white; Massachusetts plates are red, white, and blue. I saw three cars with Massachusetts plates: a little green lozenge of a Saab hatchback, a Cadillac SUV with a booster seat in back, and—I held my breath—a four-door Honda, probably five years old, which made it easily the oldest car in the lot. It was gray, with a ding in the driver's door and a bumper sticker reading "Give Peace a Chance."

I stood off at what I hoped was a polite distance between the Honda and the Saab and held my breath as—finally—one of the older couples I'd seen inside approached the gray car. The man was white-haired and frail, with pale skin and watery blue eyes behind oversized eyeglasses. The woman was short, small and slender, with curly gray hair cut close to her head, in a loose green sack of a dress, a necklace made of chunky glass beads, and Birkenstocks over black tights. She wore no makeup, not even the Upchurch woman's casual swipe of Sugar Maple lipstick. Definitely from out of town.

I picked my way across the gravel parking lot to their car. "Excuse me, are you Kitty's parents?" I looked at the woman, struggling to remember Kitty's maiden name. "Bonnie Verree?"

They looked at each other before the woman answered.

"Yes. I'm Bonnie Verree. Kitty was my daughter."

"I'm Kate Klein," I said, holding out my hand.

"We heard you speak," she said. She took my hand in hers, which was small and warm. She had the same blue eyes as Kitty, but that was where the resemblance stopped. I couldn't see any of her daughter's fine features in Bonnie's friendly, button-shaped face . . . and Kitty had been easily eight inches taller than her mother.

"You're the painter," I said.

She stared at me curiously.

"I was in Kitty's house . . . those beautiful seascapes."

"Oh," she said. Her husband clamped one blue-veined hand on her shoulder.

"We need to get going," he said. "There's terrible traffic on ninety-one."

I nodded, then blurted, "I wanted to tell you how sorry I was for your loss."

"Thank you, dear," she said.

"I was the one who found her," I began, then shut my mouth, realizing, with mounting horror, that it sounded almost as if I were bragging. *Hooray for me, I found your daughter's corpse!*

"That must have been horrible for you," Bonnie said.

I gave a small nod, as if to suggest that I was the kind of sophisticated soul who stumbled across exsanguinated neighbors regularly. "I wish I'd known Kitty better," I said slowly, trying to think of a way to ask about that postcard. *Happier than I can even believe.* "I mean, we saw each other all the time, at the playground, and, of course, I read *Content,* so I've seen the articles she wrote . . ."

The words "articles she wrote" had a galvanic effect on the couple. Hugh's pale, lined face turned red. Bonnie pulled her hands away and looked at me helplessly. Her husband stalked to the driver's side of the car and shoved the key into the lock so hard I was surprised that I didn't see it pop out on the other side of the door.

"I'm sorry for your loss," I blurted again.

Bonnie shook her head as her husband reached over the gearshift and pushed her door open. "You don't understand," she said, in a voice so quiet I had to lean forward to hear it. "Hugh and I lost Katie a long time ago."

I was so stunned by what she'd said and by what she'd called Kitty, that I stood there as if I'd been frozen as Bonnie slammed the door and Hugh put the car in gear and came within six inches of driving his Honda over my toes. He stomped on the gas, squealed out of the parking lot, and pulled onto Main Street without pausing to look for oncoming traffic.

I staggered backward. My heel caught, and I'd almost hit the ground before someone grabbed my elbows.

"Are you all right?" a man's voice said.

My heel buckled underneath me and I fell down onto the gravel. "Ow!" When I pushed myself upright, my ankle throbbed, and my palms oozed pinpricks of blood.

"Sorry. Thank you," I said. The man who'd tried to catch me was in his fifties, short and wiry and entirely bald, with brown eyes, a narrow face, and a nut brown tan. He reminded me a little bit of an otter, something small and sleek and better suited for the water than the land.

"Jesus," I said, hoping that a few deep breaths would get my knees to stop shaking. "Meet the parents."

The man gave a perplexed shrug and extended his hand. "Joel Asch," he said.

The name was familiar, but it took me a second to remember what Laura Lynn Baird had told me. *Content*'s editor in chief, who might have been sleeping with the deceased.

"You were Kitty's friend," I said.

He nodded. "I tried to be," he said, watching as I brushed bits of gravel off my hands.

"Did you two know each other a long time?" I asked.

He turned his head toward the town hall doors, where mourners clad in taupe and gray were filing out, murmuring quietly to each other. "Would you like to get a cup of coffee?" he asked. "I've got some time before I have to go back to the city."

TWENTY-THREE

Ten minutes later Joel Asch and I were seated at a table at Brookfield Bagels, a gray-shingled cottage with yellow-and-white-striped awnings and half a dozen round wooden tables for two, where six bucks could get you a watery cup of coffee and a warm, squishy circle of dough the exact texture of impacted Wonder Bread. Joel Asch took one bite, winced, and set it aside.

"I know," I said, lowering my voice, "they're awful, aren't they?"

"They're . . . not good," he said. He looked as if he was debating whether to force down his mouthful of faux bagel or spit it into his napkin. He finally decided to keep chewing.

"So tell me," I said. "How did a stay-at-home mom from Upchurch end up writing for one of the most important magazines in America?" With my fulsome compliment still hanging in the warm, yeast-scented air, I reached into my bag for my notebook.

Joel Asch smiled at me indulgently. "You wouldn't be angling for her job, now, would you?"

I shook my head. "I keep pretty busy here," I said.

"Well," he said. "I was Kitty's professor in college, and we'd kept in touch over the years. Kitty was actually the one who brought Laura Lynn to my attention. I caught her a few times on CNN. Her ideas intrigued me. The battle between stay-at-home mothers and mothers who work. The contested ground of maternity in America."

I nodded and wrote *contested ground.* "As a mother myself, I have to tell you, that's a fascinating subject." As a mother myself, it was doubtful I'd ever find time to read about it, given that I was too busy living it, but flattery couldn't hurt.

"So I called Laura Lynn, and she was eager to be associated with *Content.*"

"Of course," I said, in a tone that implied that you'd have to be a pederast or a space alien not to want to be associated with *Content.*

"But she was busy. The demands on her time were such that it became clear that she would need . . ." He twirled his plain gold wedding band around one thin brown finger. "A certain level of assistance. And I'd seen plenty of Kitty's work in college."

Seen her work, I wrote. The plot was thickening. At least, I hoped it was. "What subject did you teach at Hanfield?" I asked.

"I was a guest lecturer there for a semester. I taught a course in politics and the press." He carefully rolled up his empty cream cheese packet. "Kitty impressed me. Her mind impressed me. The clarity of her writing. The singularity of her focus."

"Mmm-hmm," I said, wondering whether *singularity of focus* wasn't professorspeak for *nice rack.* Kitty must have been a tasty morsel as a coed—that bittersweet chocolate hair tied back in a headband, that fresh face and perfect body in jeans and a Hanfield sweatshirt.

"She was very bright," he said. "And a hard worker, and she turned in her papers on time. I helped her find her first job, writing the in-house newsletter for St. Francis Hospital in New York. When it became clear that Laura Lynn needed help, I called Kitty and asked if she'd be interested. Then I set up a lunch for the two of them to meet, and that was that."

That was that, I wrote. My heart was pounding. He'd met her in college, admired her mind, kept in touch with her over the years, found her not one but two jobs in the ultracompetitive New York City market. If that didn't spell *affair* I wasn't sure what did . . . which meant that horrid Laura Lynn had hit the nail on the head. "I have to say, I'm amazed she found the time to write. Kids can be pretty overwhelming."

He gave an indulgent chuckle. "That's what my wife tells me."

I laughed along with him, thinking that his wife and I probably had a lot in common—high-powered husbands who were hardly ever home, men who liked the concept of a wife and children more than they seemed to enjoy the reality of kids who'd cry at the slightest insult or stubbed toe, clamor for junk food or crappy plastic toys and on bad days whine ceaselessly at bedtime, bathtime, mealtime, and many times in between.

"How did they work together?" I asked.

"They did a lot by email, and on the phone. Laura Lynn would call her from airports or greenrooms or wherever she found herself. They'd talk about a theme, hammer out an outline, then Kitty would write a draft, Laura Lynn would approve it, and Kitty would email it to me."

"She didn't come into the office?"

He shook his head, looking pained, and a little suspicious. "Well, the other writers . . ." He reached into his pocket for a travel pack of aspirin, shook two loose, considered, and added a third. I filled in the blank myself: the other writers at *Content* probably had no idea that Laura Lynn Baird wasn't writing "The Good Mother" herself, so having Kitty show up in the office would have come as an unpleasant surprise.

"What about her politics?"

He gulped his pills and gave me a blank stare. I tried again.

"Laura Lynn had very strong opinions about working mothers." This earned me blank stare, the sequel. "She felt that mothers shouldn't work outside the house."

"That's not a very nuanced reading of her work," he demurred. I plowed ahead, thinking that there'd be time for nuance later, after I'd figured out who'd killed Kitty and was now leaving notes suggesting that I was next in line.

"I guess that what I'm wondering is whether Kitty felt the same way about working mothers."

Joel Asch unfolded his paper bag and smoothed it on the table. "You knew her, didn't you? Weren't you close?"

I tried for another chuckle. "Well, you know how it is. Mostly we wound up talking about what kind of peanut butter our kids liked."

Ha ha ha, laughed Joel.

"How about in college? Hanfield had lots of conservatives, right?" I knew it did, from my time online, and from my own college years, when it had been notorious as a breeding ground for budding Phyllis Schlaflys and Pat Buchanans. "Did Kitty participate in any of that?"

"I can't say that I remember specifically."

"So why would she want to go to work ghostwriting—"

"Assisting," Joel Asch said with a grimace.

"Fine. Assisting a woman who was writing things she didn't necessarily believe?"

Joel Asch took a furious bite of his bagel. I watched as his teeth sank into the mush. "Entrée," he muttered.

"Excuse me?"

"It gave her entrée," he said, biting off each word. "Writing for *Content* gave her a certain cachet, a certain éclat, a certain—"

"Please let your next word be in English," I said.

He frowned at me. Then his face relaxed. He tilted his chin back and gazed at the ceiling. "Fine," he said. "English. Fine." His expression grew wistful. "She was funny, too, you know. Kitty was. Do you know what she called this place?"

"What, Brookfield Bagels?"

"No," he said. "Upchurch. She called it Land of the Lost."

I felt my heart contract in sympathy as I realized that behind the perfect-mother mask Kitty had been disconcerted by her hometown, just like I was. And funny. Who knew? "So why did she move here?"

I expected another shrug or blank look or some variation on my own story: *she's here because it's where her husband wanted to be.* But Joel Asch surprised me.

"I think she ended up here for the same reason she was willing to work for *Content* and shape prose she might not have necessarily agreed with," he said.

"Cachet," I quoted, "éclat."

His thin lips lifted in a faint smile. "Status. That and the ability to move in the right circles," he said. "I'm not sure there's a French word for it. Access, maybe. She could have access to people in high places, attend the right charity benefits, the right fund-raisers. If she picked up the phone and said, 'I write for *Content,* I'm doing research for Laura Lynn Baird,' she could get senators on the line. Even presidents."

"And she didn't care that she didn't have a byline?"

He suffered through another bite of bagel and shook his head. I was starting to feel desperate, and he was starting to look antsy. "Look," I said. "I'm not trying to pry, or snoop, but I'm scared. We all are. The police haven't arrested anyone. All of the mothers are jumping at shadows. Anything you could tell me . . . anything at all . . ."

"I'm sorry," Joel said. Then he looked at his watch. "I wish I had some answers for you, but I should really get going." He pushed himself away from the table. I followed him out the door.

"Do you think one of Laura Lynn's readers could have had something to do with it?" I asked, as we made our way to the parking lot. Joel walked fast, and I struggled to keep up. My ankle was killing me, and my feet must have swollen while I was sitting. It felt like I was walking on knives. "I know she got hate mail."

"Laura Lynn got hate mail," he corrected. "I would forward it to her. She wanted to see it, no matter how crude, or threatening, or laden with misspellings."

I hurried after him as fast as I could, thinking that as far as Joel Asch was concerned, *threatening* and *laden with misspellings* were probably equally frightening. "Did Kitty see the hate mail?" I asked. "Did she know about it?"

He rubbed at his pate, then jammed his hands in his pockets and pulled out his keys. "I really wouldn't know," he said. Which, I realized, wasn't exactly an answer. I reached for his shoulder, and he spun around, exhaling impatiently. The sun stretched out our shadows in the Brookfield Bagels parking lot. It was high noon, which was appropriate—and upsetting. I was going to be late to get my kids again.

"Look," I said. "Forgive me if I'm confused. Maybe being home with kids has fogged my brain a little, but this doesn't make sense. You helped Kitty Cavanaugh get two jobs, one of which was a pretty big deal, and now she's been murdered. This beautiful, brilliant, hardworking, funny woman. Dead. Don't you want to find out who did it?"

"Of course I do," he said quietly.

"Were you sleeping with her? Is that why you gave her the job?"

His shoulders stiffened as he glared at me. I heard the thrum of traffic on Main Street, the faint babbling of the brook that ran behind the bagel shop. The cool breeze stirred my hair. I braced myself, thinking he'd laugh or storm off or get in his car and drive.

"No," he said. "I wasn't sleeping with her. For heaven's sake, she was young enough to be my daughter." He took a deep breath, tossing his keys from his left hand to his right. "I appreciate that you're interested in the details of her death. I wish I could be more help." He paused, then went on awkwardly. "I'm sorry you lost a friend."

He extended his hand and, after a minute, I shook it and told him, "I'm sorry too."

TWENTY-FOUR

It was twelve-ten when I made it to the Red Wheel Barrow. Sam and Jack were sitting side by side in the center of the red wooden bench outside the principal's office. Sophie was standing in front of them, little hands balled on her hips, her somber face drawn into a frown. "You're late again, Mommy," she said.

"I know," I said, digging into my bag for my wallet and bracing myself for yet another go-round with Mrs. Dietl.

I found her seated behind a gray metal desk. There was a painted ceramic apple in one corner, a monogrammed silver letter opener in the other, and a coffee can with a slit cut in its lid between them. "You do realize that this is the fifth time you've been late this semester," she said, when I'd smiled weakly and told her how sorry I was. "If this continues, we're going to have to have a serious talk about your arrangements."

"I'm sorry," I murmured again as I jammed my thirty-dollar fine into the coffee can and went to collect my kids.

"Please try not to let it happen again!" she called.

"Don't mess with my toot-toot," I muttered under my breath. Sophie giggled, but Mrs. Dietl, who'd overheard, was not amused. She hurried down the hall after us, beaded eyeglass chain swinging against the shelf of her bosom, gabardine skirt swishing, and sensible shoes squeaking over the linoleum.

"If you find that you are unhappy here, or that we at the Red Wheel Barrow are, as an institution, unable to meet your family's needs, there are other nursery schools, and most certainly other children who'd be happy to take your places," she said.

"I know," I said, turning back to look her in the eyes. "I'm sorry." The hell of it was, she was right. There were other parents, lots of them, who'd be tripping over each other for the privilege of paying nine thousand bucks a semester so some overbred, overeducated teacher could watch their kids fingerpaint. I slapped on a smile, swore on my life that it would never ever ever happen again, and finally got the kids out of the red clapboard building with the bright white trim and into the van.

"We're hungry," Sophie whined as I started driving home, down a street lined with maple trees whose branches arched over the road to create a shimmering canopy of crimson and gold. The whole scene was straight out of an inspirational greeting card, the kind I'd never buy and never send. It felt as foreign as the moon. Back in New York, I'd known every inch of my neighborhood: the newsstands and salad bars, the hole-in-the-wall coffee shop, the guys at the dry cleaners, and the girls at the little grocery store who'd saved my ass more than once by going into the overstock room for more Pampers after Sam decided he'd only wear the ones with Elmo on them, even the homeless guy who'd called me "pretty mama" when I wheeled the babies by.

"Sit tight," I told them. Sophie groaned and clutched her belly.

"Hungry," said Sam, or possibly Jack.

"Just another minute," I said. And then, in absolute defiance of everything Upchurch in general and the Red Wheel Barrow school in particular represented, I drove to McDonald's and ordered three Happy Meals, distributed the goodies in the parking lot, and started the trip home. "Playdate," Sophie mumbled through a mouthful of chewed potato, already sounding groggy from the combination of nitrates and sodium and whatever McDonald's puts in its milkshakes.

"Huh?"

"We're supposed to go to Tristan and Isi's house for a playdate," she said.

Oops. I called Sukie Sutherland. "We're running late, but I fed them lunch!"

"No problem," she said, in her chipper, good-mommy lilt. "We're going to make Thanksgiving centerpieces and bake flaxseed muffins."

"Sounds great!" I said.

In the Sutherlands' driveway, I wiped the telltale ketchup stains off the kids' hands and faces, told them to be good, and deposited them in Sukie's pristine entryway. I drove back home, past the Chamberlains' house, then the Langdons'. As the minivan rounded the curve, I saw a man standing in front of my driveway, with his hands in his pockets and an amused look on his face. Faded blue jeans. Broad shoulders. Black hair curling past his earlobes. Evan McKenna, standing not fifty yards from my front door.

My first impulse was to hit the gas and keep going. My second impulse was to stomp on the gas and hit him. I imagined his body flying in the air like one of Sophie's dolls, and how I'd disengage the child safety locks, roll down the windows, shriek *That's what you get for breaking my heart!* and drive off into the sunset, just like Thelma and Louise, only with a minivan instead of a Thunderbird, and minus the dying.

Instead, I screeched to a halt by the curb, took a millionth of a second to be grateful that I'd combed my hair that morning and waxed my upper lip the day before, flung open the passenger's side door, and said, "Get in the van!"

Evan gave me a lazy smile. "Is this a dramatic reenactment of *Silence of the Lambs?*"

"Just get in!"

He shrugged, pulled off his cap and tucked it into his back pocket, then swung himself into the seat beside me. As soon as he'd slammed the door, I screeched away from the curb, fast enough to lay twin tracks of rubber that my husband was certain to notice when he came home. My heart was thudding in my ears and hands shook as I stomped on the brakes for the stop sign at the end of the road.

"Hi," said Evan.

I hazarded a look to the right, where I found him looking at me with the same easy sweetness I'd remembered from all those years ago. His cheeks were red from the cold, his thick eyebrows were unruly as ever, and his clever mouth curved as he smiled.

"What are you doing at my house?"

He shrugged. "I told you, I had to talk to the cops, and I figured, since I was in the neighborhood . . ."

I gripped the wheel as hard as I could to make my hands stop shaking. "You can't just show up at my house and hang around in the middle of the street! What about the neighbors!"

"Katie." He pulled off his sunglasses and had the nerve to smirk. "This is an innocent visit from an old friend. It's not like we were doing it in the road."

I felt my face flush and suddenly became aware of my thighs pressing against each other. They were naked underneath my skirt because I hadn't been able to find a pair of tights or pantyhose. I thought I could hear the silk lining of the skirt whisper over my skin as I moved. Worse, judging from his smile, I thought Evan could hear it too.

"And I have some information about our mutual friend."

"Tell me," I said, and started driving. Okay. This could work. He'd spill the beans and I'd dump him at the train station. The entire transaction would take fifteen minutes—twenty, tops. It wouldn't be enough time for me to fall in love with him again.

"Boy," he said, "you must think I'm easy."

"Evan . . ." I don't think about you at all, I wanted to say. Lie. Whatever.

"Have you had lunch yet?" he inquired. "Because I could use some lunch." He sniffed. "Smells like french fries in here."

"That's just my perfume." I spoke without looking at him. Bad things would happen if I looked at him. It would be like looking at the sun.

"Come on, Kate. I haven't seen you in years." He touched my shoulder. "I missed you, you know," he said quietly.

I turned left onto Main Street faster than I had to and said nothing. I didn't trust my voice.

Evan shrugged and turned to look out the window, taking in my new town: the white clapboard church with its spire piercing the cloudless blue sky; the old Victorians dripping with gingerbread trim that had been converted into banks or law offices; the brick-and-glass town hall; and the Olde Main Street Apothecary, where the half-deaf pharmacist would make you shout your name and your prescription across the counter until everyone in town knew that you were in there for Xanax or Rogaine or Viagra.

"Wow," he said. "It's not exactly Atlantic City, is it?"

I held myself perfectly still and said nothing. *I would have run away with you,* I thought. *If you'd ever really asked.*

Evan continued to evaluate the scenery. "Two Talbots?"

I lifted my chin. "One of them is Talbot Petites."

"Ah. Well, there you go." He rubbed his head. And I could smell his clean scent of soap and laundry detergent and something else, faint and sugary, that had always reminded me of campfires and graham crackers, the memory of sweetness in my mouth underneath a black sky pricked with stars. "You like it here?"

"It's fine."

"How's Janie?"

"Great. Perfect. Never better. She's a big-shot editor at *New York Night* now." I pulled up at the town's blinking yellow light. "How's

Michelle?" I snuck another glance sideways. Evan had turned back toward the window. "Did she ever marry you?"

He shrugged. "We got married. It didn't last."

His hands were in his lap, palms up. His face was grave. "I'm sorry," I made myself say.

"I tried calling you . . ."

"Was your phone not working, or was it your fingers?" I asked lightly.

"But first you were in London, and then—"

"And then you moved away! By the time I unpacked and got over the jet lag, you were gone."

"We didn't move," Evan said patiently. "We got kicked out. You didn't know?"

"Didn't know what?"

"Janie bought the building and evicted us."

I stomped on the brake at the traffic signal in front of the Super Shop Mart and stared at him, torn between shock, disbelief, and awe at what Janie had been able to pull off. "She did what?"

"Bought the building," Evan repeated. "Then she told us she was turning it into co-ops and gave us ten days to leave."

"Jesus. Is that legal?"

"She said if she ever saw me again or heard that I was trying to get in touch with you, she'd have both of my legs broken. And she tried to have me deported."

The car behind me gave a polite *toot-toot.* I started driving. "I know you're kidding. You're a U.S. citizen!"

"Yeah, well, you know that and I know that. Apparently the INS was a little confused on the matter. Janie found some other guy named Evan McKenna who was living illegally in Brooklyn . . . ah, never mind. Long story. It all worked out." His lips twitched upward. "Except for the other Evan McKenna. They packed his ass back to County Cork."

"I hope you don't expect me to feel sorry for you." My voice was tart, but my eyelids were suddenly prickly with tears. "You didn't even call me after 9/11. Everyone called everyone after 9/11. There was an article about it in the *Times.*" I swiped at my eyes as the Range Rover behind me honked its horn.

"I wanted to," he said. "I wanted to call." He pulled his seat belt away from his chest, then let it snap back, thumping gently against him. "But I saw you that summer. I saw you in Central Park, at the zoo. With another guy. You looked so happy, I thought, why make trouble?"

I snorted and flicked on my turn indicator so hard that the shaft almost snapped off in my hand. I remembered the day he was talking about: a beautiful August afternoon. I'd met Ben on his lunch hour and we'd bought slices of pizza, then strolled over to eat them and watch the sea lions have their lunch. It had been a lovely day . . . but still, like every time Ben and I went out in New York City, there was always a part of me that couldn't help scanning the crowds, waiting for Evan to emerge, cock his eyebrow at me, hold out his arms, and say, "I made a mistake, Kate. We belong together."

"What kind . . ." My voice was wobbling. "What kind of trouble did you want to make?"

He didn't say anything as I swung onto the highway and merged into traffic heading north toward Hartford, and when he started talking again his voice was so quiet I had to strain to hear him.

"I thought about you a lot, after that night," he said. "I still do."

I looked over to see if he was smirking. Maybe this was his idea of a good joke to play on a lonely, overwhelmed, out-of-place mother stuck in a suburb she despised. No smirk. He was looking at me, his green eyes narrowed. "Do you think about me?"

Only every day. "Every once in a while. But what does it matter now?" I asked, hearing the despair in my voice.

He sighed. " 'If I could turn back time,' " he sang.

I stared at him in mingled amusement and horror. "You're quoting Cher?"

" 'If I could find a way,' " he continued.

"Oh, please, " I said. "How about you just buy me lunch?"

He sat back in his seat, looking pleased. "Works for me," he said.

TWENTY-FIVE

I took Evan to the least sexual, least suggestive place I could think of, which was the Chuck E. Cheese's two towns away from Upchurch. We weren't likely to see anyone I knew, and if we did, well, who'd conduct a tryst in broad daylight at a theme restaurant that catered to six-year-olds?

"Nice," Evan said, holding the door, then touching my elbow lightly as we walked up to the hostess's stand. "Very atmospheric. Can we play whack-a-mole?"

"I'm married," I said crisply, in a tone that belied the way my knees were trembling. "The only one whacking my mole these days is my husband."

"Maybe skee-ball, then," he said, with an agreeable shrug. I risked a quick sideways glance. He'd gotten a few wrinkles in the corners of his eyes, a few silver hairs lacing the black curls near his temples, all of which only served to make him even more appealing, which was unfair on a celestial level. Lord knows my wrinkles and gray hairs had done little to improve my looks.

"Welcome to Chuck E. Cheese!" said a beaming, ponytailed girl behind a yellow and orange plastic podium. She held paper party hats in one hand and plastic leis in the other. "Are you here for Trevor's birthday party?"

Evan shook his head. "Yes, we are," I said, and helped myself. I put the party hat defiantly on my head and stared at Evan until he shrugged and put on his hat too. Now I'd be able to look at him without wanting to undo the last seven years of my life and/or haul him into the bathroom for a quickie.

We sat down on two plastic stumps in front of a kid-sized plastic table and ordered a cheese pizza and a pitcher of soda.

"So," said Evan, looking me over. The party hat wasn't working, so I tossed a plastic lei across the table and wondered if I could ask the waitress for a clown nose. Maybe that would do the trick. "How'd you wind up in Connecticut, anyhow?"

"My husband," I said simply. "He thought it was safe here."

His eyebrows lifted. His curls hung over his forehead, almost to his eyebrows and, as always, I wanted nothing more than to reach out and brush them away. "And you just went along with him? Left your job? Left Janie?" He shook his head. "I'm surprised she didn't just buy Connecticut to make you move back."

"I had children. Have. Have children. Here." I pulled out my little monogrammed leather folder where I kept two-year-out-of-date pictures of Sam, Jack, and Sophie. "See, these are my twins, Sam and Jack. Of course, they were newborns in this picture, they're three now, and this is Sophie . . ." I flipped through the pictures, then placed the folder under my left hand, like a Bible, for strength.

"They're adorable," he said. "Do you like it here?" I couldn't think of what to say, as our waitress bounced over with the soda and two cups. He poured for both of us.

"I . . ." I picked up my plastic cup and drank. "I miss . . ."

He refilled my cup. "The city?"

"The pace of it. The energy. Being able to just walk out my door in the morning and be somewhere, you know? Without having to get in a car, or set up a play date. I miss first-run movies—I mean, not like I've got time to even go to the movies anymore. I miss my job. I miss watching Mark try to throw his chair every Thursday. I miss takeout, and taxis, and sample sales, and the Cowgirl Café, and Magnolia Bakery, and window shopping on Fifth Avenue, and tennis in Riverside Park, and. . . ." *You.* I shut my mouth. Then I shut my eyes. "It's a big change, living here," I said. When I opened my eyes he was staring at me, studying my face carefully.

"You know, nothing was the same after you left."

The waitress slid a steaming pizza onto the table. I pulled off a gooey slice and took a big bite, wincing as the molten cheese scalded the roof of my mouth. "You were the one who left," I pointed out, as soon as I could speak again.

"I know. What I meant was . . ." He shifted on his seat and handed me napkins. "When you were living down the hall, when I was hanging out with you and Janie. I think, sometimes, that was the happiest I've been."

"Why not?" I tossed my hair, puckered my lips, and blew on my pizza. "You had everything. You had the two of us to keep you fed and amused, and you had Michelle to go home to every night. What man wouldn't have loved that?"

He picked up his own slice. "You're not being fair."

I twirled mozzarella around my finger. "What, to Michelle?"

"No, to yourself. How do you know you weren't the one I would have rather gone home to every night?"

"Because I threw myself at you! I had such a crush . . . I did everything but staple a Welcome mat to my private area . . ."

Evan started laughing. "Your private area?"

I felt my face flush. "That's what Sophie calls it," I mumbled. "Her private area."

"She's a cutie," Evan said. "She looks like you."

I felt my eyes well with tears for the umpteenth time that day. I saw Madeline and Emerson Cavanaugh standing on the stage of the Upchurch Town Hall. *She was the best mother in the world.* "Yes," I said, and nodded helplessly. "My little girl." I wiped my hands, then my eyes. No more, I decided. No more of this. It's the road less traveled, and there's no point in even thinking about it again.

I sipped from my cup and got myself together. "You knew Kitty."

Evan nodded, crumpling his napkin. "From New York. She was

a client. Every once in a while she'd give me a name of a man and ask me to do a background check. Basic biographical stuff—where they lived, when they'd gotten married, if they'd had kids."

"What kind of names? How many? Was this for *Content*? What was she looking for?"

"Hey, hey, easy, easy," he said. He gave me a smile, then pulled a notebook out of his back pocket. "I think I checked out maybe half a dozen men for her, starting in 1998."

"All men?"

"All men. Most of them lived in New York, one was an ophthalmologist in Maine, one was down in D.C."

"Why was she investigating them? What did she want to know?"

"Like I said, all she asked for was basic biography—stuff you can probably find out on the Internet these days. In terms of why . . ." He exhaled in frustration and spread his hands on the table. "I know she was doing some writing, and some of them were pretty big deals—politicians, college professors—but not all. But the thing is, with clients, with this kind of work, you don't always ask, and they don't always volunteer. Kitty didn't."

"And then she called you again?"

"Two weeks ago," he said. "We caught up for a few minutes, and then she said she was getting to the end of her investigation."

"What investigation?"

Evan gave another maddening shrug. "Like I said, don't ask, don't tell. She said she was pretty sure she'd found what she was looking for, but there were a few loose ends she needed to tie up, and was I still doing investigative work. I told her I was; she said she'd be in touch. She had another name, but not one she felt comfortable emailing or saying over the phone. So I waited." He shook his head and crumpled another napkin. "The next call I got was from the police, saying she'd been murdered." He leaned forward. "I asked her if she knew you."

The restaurant was spinning. "You knew I moved to Upchurch?"

He shrugged. "I keep up."

"How? I know Janie doesn't talk to you."

"Give me a little credit, Kate. It is my job. And your wedding announcement was in the *Times,* so I knew your new last name."

"What did . . ." I took a deep breath, trying to shove away the thoughts of Evan caring enough to find out my new last name and my new hometown. "What did Kitty say about me?"

"That she only knew you from the playground, but that you seemed smart. Funny. Good with your kids."

I swallowed hard. "She said that?" Of all the things I'd expected Kitty to say about me, *smart, funny,* and *good with her kids* would not have topped the list the way *incompetent, clueless,* and *in desperate need of a personal trainer* might have.

"So she never gave you the name?"

He shook his head.

"What about the men she had you look up before?"

He tore a page from the notebook and handed over a sheet of paper with four names. One of them I actually recognized—Emmett James, a literary critic and poet who taught at Yale.

"I couldn't find all of the records. Here's what I've got. This guy's the doctor in Maine," Evan said, tapping the page. "He makes instruments," he said, pointing to the name David Linde. "And this one . . ."

I leaned over to see the last two words on the page and felt things start to go gray again. "Bo Baird?"

"She had me check him out ten years ago," Evan said. "Before she started working for Laura Lynn. Before Laura Lynn was Laura Lynn, come to think of it."

I stared at the page. "So what's the connection?"

"I don't know. All I know for sure is that Bo Baird didn't do it—"

"But maybe Laura Lynn did," I said, wiping my sweaty palms against my skirt. "Or it had something to do with money, because Laura Lynn got a major book advance."

We paused for breath and looked at each other. I pulled my notebook out of my purse.

"Who have you talked to?" he asked.

"How do you know I've talked to anyone?"

He smiled. "Because, Katie, I know you. I know how you operate. No way could you resist this."

"Sure," I grumbled, trying hard to ignore the warm glow that hearing him say my name had ignited in the pit of my belly. "I'm the same as I ever was. Just with less sleep."

He tapped the blank page with his pen, smiling his merry smile as he looked at me. "Give it up."

I flipped to the first page of my notebook and told him everything: how I suspected that Philip Cavanaugh might have been sleeping with the sitter and God only knew how many other neighborhood ladies; how Delphine Dolan had been a friend of Kitty's prior to her move to Upchurch and how Kevin Dolan seemed to be carrying a torch for the deceased. I told him how Laura Lynn had told me that Joel Asch had gotten Kitty her job because they might have been sleeping together, and how my interview with Joel made me think that was a definite possibility. I told him all about my meeting with Tara Singh and Philip Cavanaugh's question, *Was she happy?* Then, after a minute of hesitation, I told Evan about the note on my car. His eyes got gratifyingly wide.

"Whoa." He scribbled something down, then looked at me. "So what's the plan?"

I toyed with a lock of my hair and tapped my pen against a blank page. "Nail down the infidelities. Who was Philip sleeping with? Who was Kitty sleeping with?"

"Good," he said. "Very good. We should also take another look at the gentlemen on my list."

We. He'd said *We.* My heart soared, then sank just as quickly. There was no *we.* I was married. Married with three kids, and a house in the 'burbs. No *we.* I shouldn't even think of the letters *W* and *E* in combination.

"Let me take the men," I said. "I'll get Janie to help. You take the neighbors. The Dolans, specifically, and Philip Cavanaugh, and Joel Asch. See what you can dig up on him."

He nodded and wrote it down. "What's your plan?" he asked.

I doodled hearts along the border of the page as I thought. It took me a minute to realize I already had the perfect opportunity to ply my neighbors with drink and ask them pointed questions about Kitty Cavanaugh's life and times. "Ben and I are having a holiday open house for the people he works with on Saturday. I can invite the neighbors too."

"That'll work," said Evan. I could see—or imagined I could see—admiration in his eyes. I lifted my hair from the nape of my neck, shook out the curls, and let them tumble down my back, noting the way his eyes followed my movements.

"What should I wear?" he asked.

I pulled off my party hat and gave him my very best go-to-hell look. "You, my old friend, are not invited."

TWENTY-SIX

Before the boys' birthday party disaster, I'd considered myself a pretty fair hostess. I'd thrown parties when I lived with Janie, simple affairs involving the purchase of ten-pound bags of ice, cases of beer, and whatever wine we could find on sale that didn't come in a box.

Things slowed down once I was married. There was our wedding, of course, but that had been much more of Ben's mother's show than mine. Lorna Borowitz had been happy to let my father book a string quartet for the ceremony and we'd spent six chatty weekends in a row schlepping from one bridal salon to another, but she'd been reduced to horrified silence when Reina offered to sing "Ave Maria" as I came down the aisle. "I can do something Jewish!" Reina had offered, a little belatedly, long-distance from Sydney. "'Hava Nagila'? 'Kol Nidre'? Something from *Fiddler on the Roof*?" "Thanks but no thanks," Lorna had finally managed. Reina had contented herself with humming along in loud harmony to the string quartet's rendition of "The Wedding March" until I'd glared at her from underneath the chuppah, and she'd shut up.

After that, parties in our apartment had been extremely low-key, especially once the kids arrived. We'd invite Ben's partners and their girlfriends of the month over for takeout Thai on Sunday night, or we'd buy lox and bagels and invite Lorna, Ben's brother Mark, and his girlfriend for brunch. The one time I'd invited my

New York Night friends over after the babies had come hadn't gone well. Half a dozen reporters and fact-checkers had shown up after midnight, expecting to find the fete in full swing. Instead, they'd arrived to Dan Zanes on the stereo, me with an armload of wide-awake two-year-old, and Janie rummaging past the wine and champagne in frantic search of a sippy cup. The guests hadn't enjoyed themselves; the kids hadn't slept; and I woke up to shrieks of horror the next morning when Sophie discovered that someone had taken an adult-sized poop in her potty.

This time, I was going to get it right. No Cheetos, no board games, only the finest in food and flowers. My only concern was that, as the week went on, the guest list seemed to have snowballed slightly out of control. Ben had invited two dozen of his work colleagues for postelection armchair quarterbacking. I'd added the Dolans and the Sutherlands, the Coes and the Gwinnells, and then once word got around every other mother on the playground, plus her husband, plus the houseguests some of them had asked to bring along. Then I'd casually mentioned the affair to my father and he'd been eager to attend, along with Reina, who, as luck would have it, was in town. I'd invited Janie, her father, and his new wife, and I'd even extended the olive branch and asked Mrs. Dietl at the nursery school to attend.

The dozens of details—renting linens and extra chairs, ordering flowers, emptying the living room of three contractor's trash bags full of toys, had left me little time to obsess over Kitty Cavanaugh's murder, or Evan McKenna's reappearance. Our only post-pizza contact had come via email, where he'd written to say he was looking into the Dolans, Joel Asch, and Philip Cavanaugh. I polished the good china, rented a fifty-cup coffee urn, and bought five hundred dollars' worth of wine and liquor from the package store on Old Post Road.

By Saturday night, the house was gleaming (thanks to the cleaners I'd hired), the kitchen was redolent with the smells of a dozen delicacies, from single spoonfuls of sherry-laced cream of mushroom soup to miniature duck-confit puffs (all provided by Glorious Foods and trucked in from Manhattan), my kids were arrayed in their freshly pressed finery (pressing courtesy of Gracie the sitter, finery thanks to Janie's personal shopper at Barneys).

My best friend had arrived at six p.m. sharp, looking stunning in a full-length fur coat over a slit-to-there black skirt and steel-blue satin top, both undoubtedly made by some designer I'd never heard of, whose wares I could neither afford nor pull up past my knees.

"BFF," she said, embracing me, then pulling a wheeled calfskin-covered suitcase into the foyer. She was sporting a pair of extremely high black heels that twined around her calves with black satin ribbons, and large quantities of both eyeliner and perfume. Her hair looked freshly colored, her teeth were a glaring white, and there was a pair of Chiclet-sized platinum-set diamonds flashing from her earlobes, in case the cumulative effect of all that high-maintenance gloss wasn't blinding enough.

"What's with the luggage?"

"Oh, just a few things for the kiddos. And I might be staying awhile," she said. I picked up the suitcase and led her up the stairs. The kids thundered down the hall to meet her and ran into her arms.

"Who loves you more than anyone else in the whole world?"

"Aunt Janie!"

"Who brought you fabulous presents?"

"Aunt Janie!"

"Who dumped the guy with the toupee because she found crab medication in his bathroom?"

"Aunt Janie!" screamed Sam and Jack. Sophie, who wore a red velvet party dress with a matching bow slipping out of her fine brown hair, wrinkled her nose.

"Were his crabs sick?" she asked.

"Yes!" I said brightly, shooting Janie a murderous look. "But I'm sure they're feeling better now!" I handed the kids off to Gracie, led Janie into my bedroom, and shut the door behind us.

"Sorry, sorry, sorry," she said, and flopped onto my bed, lying spread-eagled on my beige down comforter. I was dying to ask whether she'd actually bought our entire apartment building with the sole aim of tossing Evan and Michelle out on the street, but if I brought it up, she'd know that Evan and I had been in touch, and God only knew what she'd do to him then. Or to me. Or both of us.

"So it's okay if I stay awhile?" Janie asked.

"Like I could stop you if I tried."

"Good. Because I'm actually on assignment."

I wriggled my black skirt over my hips and started pawing through the mismatched shoes on the shelf of my closet in search of the velvet ballet slippers I'd remembered seeing up there. "Huh?"

She grinned, sat up, and started reeling off headlines. " 'Fear and Loathing in the Suburbs'! 'Murder and Mayhem in the Promised Land'!" She paused for the pièce de résistance, her eyes wide and sparkling. " 'Momicide'!"

"That's the worst title I've ever heard. Are you doing this for *New York Night*?" I asked, knowing that the magazine's coverage rarely strayed beyond celebrities and what they were snorting.

"They're branching out into hard news," Janie said smugly. "They're very interested in a piece about people who left the city in order to be safe and ended up not so safe." She crossed her legs, admiring her shoes, before scowling at mine. "Is that what you're wearing?"

I looked at myself: calf-length gored black skirt, gray cashmere sweater, black ballet slippers. "This isn't good?"

She studied me. "Um. Do you have a scarf? Or a necklace? Or an entirely different outfit?"

I shrugged. Janie started flipping through the hangers. "I miss you," she grumbled. "You know I can't stand this time of year. Too many tourists."

I pulled on the black silk camisole she'd handed me—I hoped she'd find something for me to wear on top of it—and went into the bathroom to start drying my hair. "Is your father coming?"

Janie said nothing.

"You invited him, right?"

She bent over to retie her shoes. "Little problem there."

I blew dust off my curling iron, then plugged it in. "What now?"

"You know he got married again?"

I nodded. Janie sighed. "Well, he and the new missus kind of aren't speaking to me."

I shook my head wearily. "What did you do?"

She shuffled her feet. "They were flying back from their honeymoon on Sunday, and I called customs and told them that she had pot in her suitcase."

"Jane Elizabeth Segal!"

"Well, it was my birthday, and my father always takes me out to dinner on my birthday, just the two of us, and I figured if she was being questioned by the police, he'd be free!"

"Did they arrest her?" I twirled my bangs with the curling iron, wincing at the sizzling sound of not-quite-dry hair hitting the hot tongs.

"Nah, they just held her," Janie said sulkily. "For eight hours. Sy canceled dinner anyhow." She rolled her eyes. "He said he wouldn't feel right eating when his bride was in the pen."

"So chivalry isn't dead!" I uncurled my hair and studied the effect. Hmm. Not bad.

"No, but they're both pissed. She didn't actually have any drugs in her suitcase, but she did have a bunch of stuff she'd bought and didn't declare."

"Oops."

"I think she's a shopaholic. It's a real addiction, you know," she said, and tossed me a black beaded wrap that I didn't remember buying and figured had to be hers.

"Tell you what," I said, my tone casual as I picked up the curling iron again. "I'll apologize to Sy on your behalf if you run a few names through LexisNexis for me."

"Sure." she said, sounding relieved. "Just don't tell Sy I was drinking or anything."

"Were you?"

"No, but if he thinks I was, he'll try to pack me off to that boot camp in Jamaica that was just on *60 Minutes.*"

"I don't think you can send adults there against their wishes."

Janie frowned darkly. "Sy has his ways. Now, who are these people I'm investigating?"

I avoided her eyes in the mirror as I handed her the piece of paper Evan had given me. "Just some people that Kitty Cavanaugh might have been asking questions about."

"And you got these names where, exactly?"

I turned my gaze back to the curling iron and the mirror. "I have my ways too."

Janie shook her head. "Fine. Although let me just say that Evan McKenna was bad news then, and he's bad news now." She blinked, looking at my reflection in the mirror. "Don't panic, but I believe your bangs may be on fire."

I combed water through my smoking hair and handed over my brush and the curling iron to Janie as the kids raced into the room and jumped up and down on the bed. I slipped on the wrap and considered my reflection in the mirror, thinking that there was a point where baby weight became just plain weight, and that I'd probably passed it sometime after the twins had turned three. "Sophie, what are we going to do with your mother?" Janie asked.

"I don't know," Sophie trilled, bouncing up and down. Her red velvet bow fell out of her hair and landed on Ben's pillow. "She's hopeless!"

"Okay," said Janie, pointing at Sophie with the hairbrush. "You, stop bouncing. You two," she said, pointing at Sam and Jack, "stand right here. You're my assistants. You," she said to me. "Sit down."

Sophie stopped bouncing and tried to clip her bow onto Uglydoll's ear. The boys lined up at the end of the bed. I sat in front of the bathroom mirror.

"You should really use your powers for good instead of trivial," I told Janie as she started in on my hair. "Imagine what you could do in the Middle East."

"Have you ever been to the Middle East?" Janie asked, grabbing my chin in her fingers and turning my face left, then right. "It's a very inhospitable climate. Not good for my complexion. Tissues," she said, pointing her hairbrush at the boys, who hurried to comply. I closed my eyes and let her work. When I finally snuck a quick look in the mirror to make sure I didn't look ridiculous, I saw my hair curling in soft ringlets around my cheek. It was so pretty that I wondered if I could reproduce the look myself. Then I realized that the chances of my having twenty free minutes every morning were about as likely as space aliens landing on my lawn.

The doorbell rang. "Ooh, why don't you guys go see who it is?" Janie suggested, handing each of them a gift-wrapped package on their way out the door. The kids thundered down the stairs. Janie set down the hairbrush and reached for her handbag.

"So what's the game plan for tonight?" she asked.

"I'm going to talk to Delphine Dolan, who knew Kitty in ninety-two. You've got three assignments," I said, sliding my cosmetics back into the vanity drawer. "First, find out whether Philip Cavanaugh was running around with the sitter, and whether he's the kind of guy who could kill his wife, or hire someone else to do it."

"Gotcha," said Janie.

"Secondly, see if you can pick up any gossip about whether Kitty was sleeping with someone named Joel Asch. He was Kitty's editor at *Content*."

"Joel Asch," Janie repeated. "What's thing three?"

I brushed gloss onto my lips, smacked them together, considered the effect, then rubbed most of it off with a hand towel. "Keep an eye on the downstairs toilet. It gets clogged sometimes," I said.

"Sitter, shitter, editor." Janie said merrily. "Got it. Oh, and look. I brought us a present."

"What?"

Smiling conspiratorially, she slipped her hand into her beaded bag. "Guess!"

"I have no idea. After-dinner mints?"

Janie rolled her eyes and grinned at me, opening her fist. Two little white pills lay in the center of her palm.

"What is that?"

"Ecstasy!" she said. Her hazel eyes were shining. She looked as proud as a kid who's brought home her first A paper.

"Janie," I said slowly. "Why did you bring Ecstasy to my party?"

She made a face. "In case things get boring."

I held out my hand. "Give 'em here."

Janie put her hands behind her back. "It's like truth serum. I'll slip one in Philip Cavanaugh's drink, and—"

"He'll kill you?" I said.

Janie bit her lip. "I was thinking more that he'd make a pass at me."

"Janie, that's what he does when his inhibitions *haven't* been lowered. I don't think we want to know what he'd do under the influence."

"Fine." Janie pouted, putting the pills back in her bag, taking my arm, and pulling me down the stairs toward my party.

TWENTY-SEVEN

Marybeth Coe and her husband brought champagne. Carol and Rob Gwinnell came with a bottle of wine and a Dora the Explorer video for the kids. Jeremy and Al, Ben's partners, brought their wives, a big box of Belgian chocolate, and lots of gossip about the Democrats' dismal performance on election day. Ted Fitch, New York State's attorney general and my husband's number-one client for the next election cycle, arrived with his nose reddened either from the cold or, from the smell of it, Irish coffee at a previous party.

"Hello, Kate!" he said, throwing his arms around Janie, who gently detached herself and pointed him in my direction.

"Oh, Kate, of course!" he said, giving me a professional smack on the cheek before striding off to press the flesh and find the bar.

Kevin Dolan introduced me to his wife, Delphine, who murmured, *"Bonsoir,"* in a throaty voice and wriggled out of her coat to reveal a skimpy black dress displaying cleavage both fore and aft. I watched in wonder as the gaze of every man at the party swung toward her as if their eyes were ball bearings and her ass crack had been magnetized. *Hoo boy,* I thought, as my mother burst through the door.

"Kate, *darling,*" said Reina, automatically readjusting my wrap. "You look *lovely*!"

"Thanks, Mom," I said, knowing that I should feel grateful. At least she hadn't hugged Janie. "Hi, Dad."

"Hello, Birdie," he said. He kissed my cheek and handed me a bouquet of red carnations.

Reina walked from the foyer into the living room, where two dozen lit candles twinkled from the mantel. She flung her cape over a chair. "Where are the *children*?" she demanded, as if I were keeping them locked away from her on purpose. "I brought them *presents*!"

"Great! I'll just . . ." My mother and I wrestled briefly over the wrapped package in her hands. Reina meant well—at least, that's what I told myself—but her grasp of age-appropriate playthings was shaky at best. She usually bought my children expensive gifts that they could either choke on or kill each other with. This time it wasn't so bad. She'd purchased porcelain French *poupées,* with rouged cheeks and painted hair. Sam got a circus master, Jack got a lion tamer, and Sophie's doll wore a pink silk leotard and balanced on a wire.

"They're beautiful!" I said, relinquishing them to Reina, who raised her eyebrows indignantly, took a minute to nod at a few of the other mothers, and located the stairs. Then she yodeled for her grandchildren in a manner guaranteed to stop all conversation and cause any dog within a mile radius to howl.

By the time I'd hung up her cape and another armload of coats, put my father's flowers in a vase, and handled a refrigerator space crisis, the foyer had filled up again. Lexi Hagen-Holdt's cheeks looked flushed above her loose black velvet sack of a dress, and her husband, Denny, kept a proprietary grip on her elbow. Denny was a beefy guy with reddish blond hair and a crushing handshake. He owned car dealerships in Darien and Danbury, selling Range Rovers to men whose only actual off-road experience would come after they'd had a few too many drinks with dinner and overshot the driveways of their four-million-dollar homes.

"You want to be careful with those luminarias," Sukie Sutherland whispered, grabbing my arm as I was on my way back to the closet. "I heard they can start housefires." Outside the frosted windows, the paper bag luminarias the kids and I had set out that afternoon were glowing a warm orange gold, tracing our driveway in a curving line of light. The forecasters had called for unseasonable cold and flurries. As I watched through the window, I saw a few big, fat flakes drifting lazily onto the ground.

"Everything looks great," Ben said, squeezing my shoulders as he passed me. He'd been thrilled when I'd agreed to host the party. Besides the tax write-off, I think he saw it as a shot at social redemption in the wake of the boys' birthday party.

The doorbell rang, the door opened and closed and opened and closed, and there, at last, with his hat in his hand and snow dripping from his scarf, was the not-so-merry widower.

"Philip!" Even with the bustle of a dozen other guests, I sounded like I was shouting. "I'm so glad you came!"

"Thank you for having me," he said. His voice was subdued. His blond hair was combed back crisply from his temples, and he smelled like sandalwood and lime. I held out my hands for his dark blue wool overcoat as his gaze descended from my face to my breasts—in the camisole that, I realized, was dismayingly low-cut—and stayed there.

"How have you been?" I asked.

He gave me the universal shrug of *as well as can be expected.* "I'm taking the girls to Florida for a while," he said. "My parents have a place down there, and I think a change of scenery . . ."

I nodded, took his coat, told him where to find the bar. "I'd like you to meet my mother," I concluded, as Reina reappeared by my left elbow. "Philip Cavanaugh, Reina Danhauser."

Philip turned so that he was staring at her breasts instead of mine and inclined his head slightly. "La Reina?" he asked.

My mother batted her false eyelashes. "Hel-*lo,*" she said.

"I'm honored," said Philip, bending slightly from the waist, hovering over her hand as if he might kiss it. "Honored to meet you."

My mother simpered and seemed not to notice that Philip's bow gave him a perfect view of her cleavage and that he was taking full advantage of that view. I had to give Reina credit: even at fifty-seven, her brow was unfurrowed (probably thanks to the regular ingestion of sheep's embryos and the occasional Botox or collagen touch-up), her lips were full, her ivory skin was flawless over her wide cheekbones and broad forehead, and her hair had been dyed a glassy, lacquered-looking black. She didn't look a day over forty-five. And she'd probably look pretty much the same until she died—probably on stage.

"Now, what can I bring you to drink?" Philip smiled at her, then turned toward the bar. As soon as he was out of earshot, Reina grabbed my shoulders.

"Did you see that man?" she demanded. "Did you *see* him?"

I detached myself. "He's Kitty Cavanaugh's husband."

"The dead woman?" Reina breathed, one crimson-nailed hand fluttering over the creamy expanse of her bosom. I wasn't sure whether being a murder victim's widower increased Philip's appeal or detracted from it.

"The dead woman," I confirmed. "And don't be too impressed. He oozes charm like a slug oozes"—Hmm. What did slugs ooze?—"slime."

My mother pursed her lips. "I thought he was delightful."

I nodded, smiled, and excused myself, thinking that my mother would have found Jeffrey Dahmer charming if she'd learned he'd bought her latest CD.

In the living room, Janie was leaning beside the fireplace, one arm resting casually on the mantelpiece, chatting with Philip. As I watched, he lifted a lock of her hair between his fingers, and both of them laughed. Across the room, I saw the muscles in Lexi Hagen-

Holdt's calves flutter and clench. Leave it to Lexi to find a way to exercise while sitting still.

At eight thirty I was on the verge of congratulating myself for a job well done. The house was full, both bartenders were busy, the caterers were circulating with their platters full of treats, and the neighbors and the politicians appeared to be getting along swimmingly, even though all of the politicians were Democrats and I had to believe that most of my neighbors were not. At eight fifteen the kids had made their entrance, to a chorus of *oohs* and *aahs.* Ben lifted Sam in his left arm and Jack in his right and made the rounds, giving the boys more attention than they'd had from him in the entire month. Sophie requested her seltzer in a champagne glass and refused to go back upstairs. "We're having fun!" she said, from her perch on her grandfather's knee. Then she tossed her head back and giggled, an obvious homage to Aunt Janie. She'd even tied hair ribbons around her legs.

"I know, honey, and everyone liked seeing you, but now it's getting late—"

Sophie waved me away with one imperious hand. "Reina says nothing good ever happens until after ten o'clock."

"Well, that's an interesting point of view, but your mommy thinks that eight thirty is a good time for brushing your teeth and pajamas."

"Oh, Kate, let them stay a little longer," my father interjected. There was a lamp next to his chair, and I noticed in the light how sparse his hair had gotten. "I've got her," he said, resettling Sophie on his lap. "You just enjoy yourself!"

I sighed, filled Gracie in on the situation, and mingled, sipping a glass of red wine, sampling from the platters that came past me, watching Delphine Dolan from the corner of my eye, waiting until she was alone (although, given her attire and the male attention it was attracting, I wasn't sure she would ever be alone). The food was delicious, and way too rich. After a bite of smoked salmon, a sliver of paté, a few miniature dumplings, and three spoonfuls of sherry-laced mushroom soup, I was starting to feel sick.

But I had a mission. When Kevin kissed his wife's cheek and headed toward the crowded bar, I made my move.

Delphine was sitting by the fire in a wingback chair with her showy legs crossed. Her dark hair was in an upsweep, her eyes had been shadowed dramatically, and she looked much too sophisticated for our preppy, well-scrubbed suburb. I watched as she toyed with the wedge of lime in her drink, then rested her pointed chin in her hand.

"Hello," I said.

"Bonjour," she replied.

"Can I get you anything?"

"Non, non," she said, shaking her head and smiling politely. "Everything is *magnifique*."

I licked my lips, hoping there was at least the residue of the lip gloss I'd mostly wiped off, and bent down beside her. "I know that you and your husband were close with Kitty."

She nodded. Her heart-shaped face looked pretty even as she frowned, but her eyes were troubled.

"Did you and Kitty spend a lot of time together?"

She looked up at me curiously.

"I mean, my best friend Janie and I, every summer we try to take a trip together." *Lie.* Every summer we meant to try to take a trip together, but then something would come up—one of my kids would get sick, or Ben would get busy—and I'd wind up bailing. "Even though I've got kids now and she doesn't, we try to get together. We go to the mountains . . . or the beach . . . But I know Kitty didn't like to leave her girls."

Delphine seemed to freeze. Then she tapped her wineglass against her perfectly white, tiny front teeth. The noise, a tiny chiming, was clear as a bell in the suddenly silent living room. Her eyes filled with tears. "Everyone talks about how Kitty was such a good mother. She was better than that," she said. Somehow, her voice sounded less French . . . and very sad. "She was—"

But I never got to find out what Delphine thought Kitty was, because one of the waitresses, a pretty girl with red hair in a ponytail, tapped my shoulder. "Mrs. Borowitz? Your phone was ringing."

I excused myself and tucked my cell phone under my ear. "Hello?"

"I sent you a present," said the voice on the other end.

I hurried down the hall past the bathroom to the basement door, which I closed firmly behind me, and hurtled down the stairs in the dark. "You can't call me here!" I whispered.

"Well, I've been trying mental telepathy, but it doesn't seem to be working. How's the party?" Evan McKenna asked.

I fumbled for the light switch, and heard two of the three bulbs pop when I flicked it on. "Fine."

His voice was low and intimate. "Wish I was there?"

"Oh, you'd love it. It's the bash of the century. And I really should get back." I pulled my wrap tightly around my shoulders.

"Fine," he said. "Your present should be there tomorrow."

I drew in my breath, imagining what Evan McKenna could be sending me.

"Hanfield yearbooks," he said. "Two for you, two for me. I thought we could see if anyone looked familiar."

"That's. Well." *That was smart* was what I wanted to say, but I didn't want to encourage him. "Can you do me a favor?"

"Name your pleasure," he said. I squeezed my eyes shut and pressed my thighs together.

"Delphine Dolan," I managed to say.

"The lawyer's wife," said Evan. "The one whose picture was in Kitty's bedroom."

"Well, she's here, and she's being"—I paused, savoring the word I was about to use, one of my favorites from my days as Evan's assistant investigator, his partner in crime—"hinky."

"Hinky," he said. He sounded amused. "I'm on your case. You go have fun," he said. I hung up the phone and paused, trying to compose myself. The basement was full of the kids' cast-offs, the car seats and snowsuits they'd outgrown, trash bags full of baby blankets and clothes that I'd been meaning to take to Goodwill. In the weak glow of the single working bulb, the high chairs and bouncy seats cast misshapen shadows on the walls.

I fluffed my hair and made my way up the stairs. My heart was beating too fast, and the doorknob felt cold in my hand. When I turned it, it stuck.

I tried again. Nothing doing. Had someone locked the door behind me? I knocked, softly at first, then louder. "Hello?" I twisted the doorknob back and forth and thumped my first against the door. "Janie? Ben? Hello?" Something scurried across the basement floor on little scratching feet and vanished under the wall. I swallowed a scream and pounded on the door again. "Ben?"

Finally, the doorknob turned, and I half fell into the hallway. "What happened?" asked the redheaded caterer.

"I don't know." My heart was thudding in my chest, and I felt faint. "Someone must have locked it accidentally." I assured her I was fine, replaced the telephone in its cradle, gulped down half a glass of wine, and returned to the living room, meaning to grab my husband and tell him that we needed to find an exterminator, preferably one who worked weekends.

Janie pulled me into a corner and whispered in my ear, "Don't freak out, but we may have a small situation."

"What? Is it the toilet?" She shook her head gravely. "Are the kids okay?"

"The kids are fine," she said, taking me by the hand and dragging me into the kitchen, where the caterers were pulling plastic wrap off trays of miniature éclairs and petit fours and slices of candied fruit. The tip of her pink tongue flicked out and wetted her lips, and she fiddled with her earrings.

"Okay," she said. "I know you told me not to use the Ecstasy, but

Philip asked for my number, then he wanted me to show him around the rest of your house, so I just figured—"

"You gave Philip Ecstasy."

Janie started wringing her hands. "I crumbled up one of the pills and dropped it in his glass, which was right on the mantel, and the next thing I knew—"

"You gave Philip Ecstasy." I thought that repeating it would make it seem more real, and give me some notion of what to do about it. So far, no luck.

Janie's shoulders were shaking, and it took me a minute to realize that she was laughing, not crying. "Janie, what?"

"Your . . . your mother . . ." she gasped.

I felt a chill wash over me. "Oh. Oh, no. No, no, no, no."

"She grabbed the glass before I could stop her, and I said, 'I think that's Philip's,' and she gave me this look like I was trying to steal it and said something in Italian, which you know I don't speak . . ." She raised her hands and mimed surrender.

"Oh, God." I swallowed hard and took off back down the hallway. Through my panic, I noticed things in flashes—a silver platter full of crumpled napkins and half-empty wineglasses, a black streak on the wall where Sophie had rammed her Tiny Tykes scooter, Sukie Sutherland and Marybeth Coe huddled outside the powder room, looking amused as they whispered.

Back in the living room, Denny Holdt was standing with his hands clasped behind his back, studying the knot of Ben's guests—politicians and consultants—that had formed in front of the TV. The Gwinnells were on the couch in front of the fireplace with my father and Sophie. Lexi, with both hands wrapped around the goblet of her wineglass, looked desperate to be in motion again. And in the center of the room . . .

"What *is* this fabric?" Reina asked, red lips pursed as if for a kiss, one crimson nail tracing her plunging neckline. She had Philip's jacket pinched between the fingers of her other hand and, as

I watched in horror, she pressed her palm against his chest and stroked as if she were petting a large and docile dog.

"Er, I think it's just wool," Philip said. "Maybe a wool blend . . ."

"Marvelous," Reina said dreamily.

Okay, Kate. Be calm. "Mom, can you come help me in the kitchen for a minute?"

"Per che?" she asked, quite reasonably.

"We have to get her out of here," Janie whispered in my ear.

"Let's go upstairs and get the kids in bed." I grabbed my mother's elbow and tried to get her moving. Nothing doing. It was like trying to relocate a five-foot-nine-inch chunk of granite. As if in slow motion, I watched Reina's free hand float through the air and come to rest on Philip's cheek.

"You're a *handsome* man," she announced.

"That's very kind of you to say," said Philip, edging backwards. No dice: Reina still had his lapel pinned between her fingers, so when he backed up, she came forward, giving him a moony grin.

"Mother . . ." I said.

"Mrs. Klein," Janie attempted.

"You remind me of a tenor I once knew in Barcelona."

My father got to his feet, frowning. "Reina?"

"He was a beautiful young man. Sang like an *angel.* After the performances he'd walk me back to the hotel . . ." She skimmed her fingers over the creamy skin of her bosom. *Oh, Lord,* I thought, as my father's face went pale.

"Mom," I hissed. She ignored me, staring up at Philip.

"Would you like to hear me sing?" she asked, batting her eyelashes.

"I . . . um . . ."

That was all the encouragement Reina needed to launch into one of her favorite arias. She breathed deeply, causing her bosom to swell dangerously against her neckline, then parted her painted lips. *"Sempre libera degg'io/Folleggiare di gioia in gioia . . ."*

"Oh, Lord," I breathed, and cringed against the wall. Delphine's bottom had been thoroughly upstaged. Every single party guest was staring at my mother. Reina's voice was lovely as ever, crystalline perfection, and so loud that I feared for my chandeliers.

"Vo'che scorra il viver mio/Pei sentieri del piacer . . . ."

I caught my father's attention and made frantic upward gestures with my hands. He nodded, lifted the twins into his arms, and headed for the stairs. Meanwhile, Reina continued to sing and clutch Philip's jacket. As I watched in horror, her hand wandered down his lapel and came to rest on his chest. I marched across the living room and grabbed her other hand, cutting her off mid-syllable, and eased her out of the living room to a smattering of applause and Sophie's request for an encore of "O Mio Babbino Caro."

"Here," I said, filling a glass at the kitchen sink. "Drink this."

Reina stared at me in confusion.

"Go," I whispered to Janie. "Go get something."

"What?" she asked, wiping tears from her eyes. "Techno music and a *Cat in the Hat* hat?"

"Ka-ate?" Reina trilled. "Why did you bring me in here?"

"Drink your water, Mother," I said again and then, as casually as I could, "Hey, are you taking any prescription medication?"

She blinked. "Why?"

"Oh, just curious!" I said.

"Reina?" I turned and saw Ben and my father entering the kitchen. Roger looked worried. Ben just looked furious. "Is everything all right?" Ben asked.

In an ideal world, there would be some easy way to tell your husband and your father that your best friend has accidentally given your mother an illegal designer drug. In real life, I couldn't even figure out how to start, so I decided to go with an all-purpose "Reina wasn't feeling well."

"I'm fine!" my mother protested. "I was just talking to that handsome man. Philllip," she slurred. My father's eyes met mine above Reina's head. *Is she drunk?* he mouthed.

Reina tossed her water glass into my sink, where I heard it shatter. She didn't seem to notice but rewrapped her fringed gold velvet scarf around her bare shoulders, and adjusted her black satin corset-style top. "I'm not thirsty!" she said.

"Reina . . . ," said Ben.

"I'm all *tingly*!" she announced. I handed her over to my confused-looking father and pulled Ben into the pantry.

"Listen," I whispered, "don't panic, but there's a small chance that Reina might have taken some Ecstasy."

"Ecstasy?" my husband thundered. "Where would she get Ecstasy?"

"It's kind of a long story, but . . ." I could feel Ben's glare like acid on my skin, and I felt sick with shame, knowing that, along with everything else, I'd made a botch of another party. Illegal drugs were even worse than sugary punch and pin the tail on the donkey.

Meanwhile, Reina pulled the pantry door open, her lipsticked mouth drawn into an O of dismay. "I took *Ecstasy*?" she squealed.

"You should call it E," Janie said. "It makes you sound hipper."

Ben's lips were pressed into a tight slit of disapproval. "We should probably take her to the hospital." He grabbed my mother's arm, nodded at my father, and marched the pair of them down the hall.

The rest of the guests gathered to watch them pass, poking their heads out of the living room with glasses in their hands and stricken looks on their faces.

"Is everything all right?" Carol Gwinnell asked.

"Fine," Ben said shortly, shoving his arms into his overcoat and checking his pocket for his keys. "Kate, I'll call when I can. Enjoy the rest of the night, everyone," he called, and then the room was quiet again as the tires of Ben's car squealed down the luminaria-lit driveway and onto the street.

In case you were wondering, having your husband and your parents leave in the middle of a holiday bash to drive to the nearest emergency room tends to put a damper on the festivities, and curtail any investigative activity you might have planned. People hurriedly set down their glasses and began retrieving their coats and hats and scarves, shaking hands and kissing cheeks and rushing out of my house to the safety of their cars, where, presumably, they'd fire up their cell phones and begin the postmortem.

I slumped on the sofa, kicked off my shoes, and wished I were dead as the caterers gathered half-empty wineglasses and crumpled napkins from the tables. When I looked up, Janie had pulled Sukie Sutherland and Marybeth Coe over to my couch. "Girl talk!" she said. "Stop sulking, Kate." Then she turned to Sukie and Marybeth. "I need you guys to tell Kate what you told me," she said.

The two of them exchanged a guilty glance. Marybeth rocked back and forth in her heels. Sukie fiddled with a button on her coat.

"It's just gossip," she finally said. "I'm not sure I feel right—"

"I promise that we'll take whatever you say in the utmost confidence," Janie said solemnly, which only made Marybeth and Sukie even more fidgety.

"I don't want this printed," Sukie said, looking at Janie, who nodded.

Sukie sighed. "That man," she finally said. "The one your husband works for."

It took me a minute to figure out who she was talking about. "Ted Fitch?"

Sukie nodded. "I knew he looked familiar, but I couldn't place him for a while."

I leaned forward, hanging on every word.

"I saw him in the city," Sukie said. "With Kitty Cavanaugh. They were at Aquavit together, having lunch . . ." Sukie rubbed her hands along her coat, looking unhappy. "And Kitty was crying."

TWENTY-EIGHT

Ben was gone before I woke up on Monday morning. A note stuck to the coffeepot said that my father had called, my mother was fine, that they were both resting comfortably at home, and that I shouldn't expect him for dinner.

"Really, it wasn't a total loss," Janie said, pouring the kids their cereal and me my second cup of coffee, then raising her eyebrows and waving the bottle of Bailey's over my mug. I groaned and shook my head, knowing that not even infinite rivers of alcohol would ease the shame of Saturday night. And how was I going to face the other mommies at the Red Wheel Barrow drop-off? I groaned again, wondering if I just left my kids on the corner they'd be able to find their way to school by themselves.

The good news was that Janie had solved the mystery of Phil and the sitter. The other mothers had filled in the blanks. Phil and Lisa had indeed been having a thing, but it had ended the year before after Lisa had gotten herself saved at some sort of campus rally and turned her life over to Jesus, who, presumably, frowned upon both extramarital liaisons and murder.

"Now," Janie asked, "what are we going to do about Ted Fitch?"

"I have a plan." I was starting to tell her about it when the doorbell rang. I opened the door to find the delivery guy glaring at me.

"Package," he grunted, with an expression suggesting I'd personally ruined his morning. He shoved the electronic clipboard at me and tugged at the hair growing out of the mole on his nose while I signed. I took the box inside, thinking that it was typical of Upchurch not even to have the obligatory hot deliveryman for the housewives' delectation, and ripped it open. Inside were the yearbooks Evan had promised. I flipped through the pages while Janie noted the name in the return address window.

"Oh, dear," she said. "Him again."

"I've been meaning to ask you. Did you really try to have Evan deported?"

Janie fussed with her hair and rearranged the collar of her men's striped pajamas. "I made a few calls."

"And you bought the whole building just so you could kick him out?"

She set a bowl of cut-up berries on the table. "Real estate always holds its value."

"Good to know." I poured myself a bowl of bran flakes and started flipping more carefully through one of the yearbooks.

On page 139 I found a teenage Kitty with her arm looped around another girl's shoulders. Both of them were grinning around bright orange mouthguards, and they had field hockey sticks over their shoulders. "Kitty Verree and Dorie Stevenson celebrate another victory," the caption read.

Janie peered over my shoulder. "Who's that?"

I swallowed a mouthful of bran paste, thinking that Dorie looked an awful lot like a big blond in a pink suit at Kitty's memorial service. "I should probably go see Reina today."

"Oh, please. A little Ecstasy never killed anyone." Janie paused, considering. "Crystal meth, maybe. But Ecstasy . . ."

"What's crystal meth?" Sam inquired.

"Come on," Janie said to the kids. "Let's go upstairs and get dressed for school. Aunt Janie has to work today. Can you guys say *Pulitzer*?"

I cleared the table, loaded the dishwasher, poured myself more coffee, and fired up the computer. I was lucky. The Hanfield alumni website revealed that Dorie Stevenson '91 was working as a financial analyst for Dow Jones in Princeton. She was a high-powered analyst too, judging from the number of people I had to speak with before Dorie herself got on the line.

"Kitty and I hadn't really been in touch in years," said Dorie, who had the kind of high, breathy, boop-boop-be-doop voice you wouldn't necessarily associate with finances or analysis. "I was so shocked to hear what had happened to her."

"Would you have time to talk with me?"

She paused, and I could hear her wondering why. "This probably sounds weird," I said. "I'm just one of the other mothers in the neighborhood. But the police haven't arrested anyone, and I guess I'm trying to find out about her just so I feel like I'm doing something, you know?"

"I guess," Dorie answered. "But I'm not sure I'll be too much help."

"I'd still love to talk to you." We made a date for eleven o'clock the next morning. There was no nursery school, and I was pretty sure I could shanghai Janie into taking the kids to their skating lesson in the morning and get a sitter for the afternoon. I hung up the phone, sponged off the table, and headed up the stairs to figure out what I could wear that would get a Dow Jones analyst to take me seriously.

"First thing about Kitty is that she was gorgeous," Dorie Stevenson said on Tuesday. "Second thing—she had no idea how pretty she was." She licked her bee-stung lips, shook her platinum blond curls, and took an enthusiastic bite of the chocolate croissant she'd plucked from the silver platter the secretary had brought us. Her eyes rolled ecstatically. "That," she pronounced, "is the shit."

I nodded and wrote down *gorgeous.* I'd left home at six in the morning, telling Ben I had a check-up with Dr. Morrison. "Fine," he'd said, without lifting his eyes from the op-ed page. "Happy Pap smear!" Janie caroled as I scurried out the door.

I nodded and smiled, thinking that for once I'd gotten the clothes right. My blue suit and brown crocodile loafers made me look as if I could have worked there, and the styling product guaranteed to eliminate the frizzies had actually worked.

Dorie Stevenson worked in an office that had been done in shades of peach and cream. Her desk, our chairs, and the platter with the pastries all looked like genuine antiques. She was from Memphis, she'd told me, and I could detect a hint of a southern accent still softening her breathy speech.

I helped myself to an almond horn, poured cream into my coffee, and said, "You should have seen her in Upchurch. She was the perfect mother with the perfect home, and she always looked . . ."

Dorie smiled, then swallowed another mouthful of croissant. "Let me guess. Perfect?"

I nodded. "Was she that way in college?"

She patted her lips. "Not at first." She nibbled at her croissant and toyed with the cameo pin at her collar. "Like I told you, she was my roommate. We were best friends for a while, but after sophomore year . . . well, we were kind of moving in different circles, I guess you'd say. I saw her, but . . ." She shrugged again, and washed down her mouthful of pastry and chocolate with a sip of cappuccino. "Starving," she told me. "I lasted"—she glanced down at the gold watch adorning one plump, pale wrist—"eighteen hours on the South Beach diet this time."

"Ah."

"Nineteen is my personal best. Russian peasant stock." She shook her head and took a bite. "If there's a nuclear war, I'll live forever. All the skinny little model types? Forget it."

I nodded and took a bite of my almond horn. Sixty years ago, Dorie Stevenson would have had the kind of body men would drool over—lush hips, an equally luxurious bosom, rounded arms and thighs. In our enlightened age, she probably lived her every waking moment in despair or on a diet. On a diet, or breaking one, I thought, as Dorie hummed and sighed ecstatically over the last bite of croissant, then used one moistened fingertip to lift each buttery morsel from her plate.

"God, that was good," she breathed. Her eyelids fluttered. She licked her lips and straightened up in the curved, dainty chair. "Okay. So. Kitty."

"She was beautiful," I prompted.

"She was beautiful, and extremely prepared," Dorie said. "Both of us started school a week early. Hanfield had a special program for . . . God, what did they call us?" She closed her eyes. "Ah! Economic diversity initiative admits." Her eyes flew open, and she smiled. "That meant we were poor, but God forbid anyone say that. So they brought us in early—all the poor kids on scholarships, plus all the minority students, even the ones who'd gone to Exeter and had parents who were professors at Yale—and made us all go camping."

"Camping?"

"That was how they were going to—oh, hang on, this one I remember—'facilitate our transition into the university environment.' And probably make sure we knew how to use silverware and whatever." She gave a rippling laugh, but I imagined I could hear the hurt underneath it.

"So you and Kitty were roommates?"

"Tentmates, for starters," Dorie said. "They took us to what was basically some professor's backyard—not exactly the wild blue yonder—but Kitty came with topographical maps of the region and her own flint box. She told me she'd spent the summer reading up on survival guides so she'd know what mushrooms were poisonous and how to find north from the moss on the trees." She shook her head. "She had food in her backpack too. I never forgot that. Like she thought they weren't going to feed us. She had those ramen noodles, and cans of bean soup . . ." Her big blue eyes filled with tears. "So she'd be ready. Ready for anything."

Ready for anything, I wrote, as Dorie looked at the ceiling, eyelids fluttering, one hand fanning underneath them.

"Hanfield was not a good place for Kitty," she said.

"What do you mean?"

She sighed, shook her curls, and delicately plucked a raspberry Danish from the tray. "Have you ever been there?"

"I went to Columbia," I said.

"Then you've probably got some idea," she said. "There were girls who came to campus with their own cars. And their own horses. Girls who had everything—designer clothes, two-hundred-dollar haircuts, diamond earrings, pearl necklaces, perfect lives just waiting for them as soon as they graduated." She wrinkled her nose. "Or at least they'd have trust funds waiting."

I nodded, remembering high school and all the pretty girls at Pimm, the confidence they had exuded knowing that any obstacle life might toss at them could be overcome with the right connections and a large amount of cash. "And Kitty didn't have any of that?" I thought back to the dented Honda I'd seen in the town hall parking lot.

"She was beautiful, like I said," Dorie said slowly. "But she had"—she waved her other hand above her head—"big hair, you know? Those big poufy spiral perms? Big hair, lots of makeup, a little too flashy for Hanfield. She figured it out about a week after we got there—cut her hair in a bob, quit wearing all that gold—but you know." She shrugged her plump shoulders. "First impressions and all o' that."

I nodded, trying to imagine the perfect, polished, fresh-scrubbed Kitty I'd known with a bad perm and too much blue eye shadow. I found that I couldn't.

"Was she jealous of the other girls?"

"Not jealous," Dorie said slowly. "Not exactly that. I'd say she was very aware of what they had that she didn't. But how could you not be? You'd hear girls talking about flying to New York for the weekend so they could go shopping, or going to Switzerland over spring break. I think it was hard not to be aware of the world you were living in. It's just that . . ." She paused and brushed crumbs off her chest. "Not everyone thought to do something about it."

I leaned forward, ignoring the remnants of my own pastry in my lap. "What did Kitty do?"

Dorie ducked her head. "This part I'm not so comfortable talking about." She leaned forward, looking at me earnestly. "She was a good girl, you know? She had a good heart. And everyone does stupid things in college." She attempted a little chuckle. "That's what college is there for, right?"

"Please," I said, lifting my hand to my heart. "Whatever you tell me won't leave this room."

She sighed again and shook her head. "Older men," she said quietly.

My fingers felt icy as I wrote the words down.

"You have to understand how pretty she was, how bright. She was sweet and smart, and she was . . ." Dorie ran her finger around her plate again as if she'd uncover the right word on its rim. "If you got sick, she'd be the one to take care of you. She could make chicken soup on a hot plate, and she could sew. If something got ripped, she'd sew it back up. She was . . ." She fanned at her eyes again, sniffling. "She could have had any guy on campus after she'd figured out the hair thing, any guy her own age, and instead she'd be going with"—Dorie's lips pursed in an unconscious gesture of distaste—"guys in their fifties."

Oh my, I thought, scribbling madly. "Did she ever date a visiting professor?" I asked. "A man named Joel Asch?"

Dorie sat bolt upright in her chair. "You know about that?"

I nodded. Dorie twisted her napkin. "It was ridiculous," she said. "He'd send roses to our dorm room, write poetry—really terrible poetry. Kitty and I would laugh about it. Mister Big-Shot Editor from New York City, and the best he can do is 'Your eyes are like cornflowers.' And I'd ask her, 'Kitty, why? Why him?' I mean, I could get it if it was, like, some Harrison Ford type, some older, sophisticated, good-looking guy to, you know, take her shopping and teach her the ways of the world."

"Joel Asch didn't do that?"

Dorie laughed—a brief, angry snort. "Well, he took her shopping, all right. Bought her a pair of pearl earrings. She was so proud of them, she wore them every single day for the rest of the school year. And I guess he gave her a job too. At least that's what I heard. Like I said, we didn't stay friends. She knew I didn't approve of what she was doing." She set her plate back on the coffee table. "My father left my mother for another woman—a younger woman—so you can imagine I wasn't real happy to see her running around with some other woman's husband. I was," she said, and sighed, "a woman of very high ideals at the time."

"Do you remember the names of any of the other men?"

She shook her head again. "I made it a point not to ask. She knew I didn't like it, so she kept me away from it. When they called, she'd take the telephone into the hall, and she'd have them pick her up at the library—not that they'd have wanted to come to the dorms, I guess." She patted her lips with a pale pink linen napkin and looked at the peach-and-pale-green cloisonné clock on her desk.

"When you asked her why, did she tell you?"

Dorie flashed me a rueful smile. "She said she had her reasons. I told her whatever she wanted, whatever she was looking for, there were other ways to get it, bright as she was. Good as she was." Her eyes filled with tears again. She blinked, dabbed at them, then fanned her lashes. "I should have tried harder. Poor Kitty. And those poor baby girls."

TWENTY-NINE

"Hi, Kate!" Ben's assistant was a willowy young thing with shoulder-length auburn ringlets, four holes in each ear, and a master's in public policy from Georgetown.

"Melissa! It's great to see you!" Young Melissa was looking lovely in a short, forest green suede jacket, mini-kilt with black tights, and kitten-heeled pumps. "I was just in town doing some shopping and I thought I'd stop by to see if Ben was free for coffee."

"Oh, sorry," said Melissa, apparently failing to notice my lack of shopping bags, or failing to realize that the offices of B Squared Consulting were in the financial district, a good sixty blocks away from the department stores and the boutiques on Fifth Avenue. She bounded back behind her desk and tapped the control pad of her PowerBook. "He's at the Civil Liberties luncheon. He should be back by four."

"Oh, no." I feigned disappointment, knowing, of course, that Ben wouldn't be in. I'd consulted his schedule before I'd left that morning. "Listen, don't tell Ben, but I've been thinking of . . . thinking of . . ."

Melissa leaned forward, her revoltingly dewy skin aglow with anticipation.

"Redecorating!" I said. "He's had that carpet forever!"

Her smooth brow furrowed. "Actually, I think it was replaced last year."

"Oh, right, of course. Not the carpet. The desk!" I said, trying my damndest to remember exactly what kind of furniture Ben had in his office. "That old thing!"

Melissa looked puzzled. "I think it's an antique."

Oh, God, could I please catch a break? "Exactly! Which is why it would work so much better at the house in Connecticut than here!" I responded, edging backward toward Ben's office. "I'm just going to take a quick look and, um, maybe some measurements . . ." I started rummaging in the butter-colored Marc Jacobs satchel Janie had lent me, as if I were searching for a tape measure or fabric swatches. "I'm going to use the executive washroom too." I gave her a sheepish, just-us-girls smile. "I don't think my sushi's agreeing with me."

Dear Lord, I thought as I bolted for Ben's office and locked the door behind me. Why did I doubt that in all of her adventures Miss Marple had never once obtained an important clue by pretending to have the shits?

"Call if you need anything!" Melissa said sweetly.

"Will do!" I replied, seating myself on Ben's Aeron chair and adjusting it so the armrests weren't cutting into my sides. I tapped the mouse, praying that Ben hadn't logged out before he'd left for lunch. He hadn't.

I started a search for any files that contained the words *Ted Fitch.* Then I held my breath while the flashlight wagged back and forth and Cheerful Melissa answered the phone on the other side of the door. My cell phone's zippy disco ring tone startled me so badly I almost fell off the chair.

"Hello?"

"Kate?" Janie's voice was small and worried. "Listen. Quick question. Your kids are toilet trained, right?"

"Yes," I said. "Mostly. Almost entirely. Why?"

"No reason!" she said. "Everything's fine. Gotta go."

"Ten files found," the helpful Microsoft paper clip finally announced.

"Wait, Janie. If you're out and the boys have to go, you can take them into the bathroom with you. It's no big deal."

"Perfect!" she said. "No worries! See you soon!"

I put down the phone and clicked on the first file.

"Fitch bio." I hit print. "Fitch position papers." I printed them too. "Schedule Sept." "Schedule Oct." "Schedule Nov.-Dec." Why not? And finally, pay dirt. "Fitch oppo." Which, as I knew from watching *The War Room* (which Ben, of course, owned on a bootlegged DVD, complete with James Carville's barely comprehensible audio commentary), stood for opposition research—everything Ben's team had dug up on their candidate so they could be prepared when the other side found it. Thirty-seven pages. Yikes. *Print.*

I heard knocking above the printer's whir. "Kate?" Melissa caroled. "Is everything all right in there?"

"Just printing out some measurements!" I called back merrily. I saw the doorknob turn back and forth.

"The door's locked," Melissa noted. *Fabulous,* I thought, scooping pages out of the laser printer. It's a wonder, I thought, what a Georgetown degree can do for a girl's powers of observation.

"Yeah, just hold on . . . I'm, um, temporarily indisposed."

Melissa was sounding worried. "Please don't touch anything, 'kay? Ben hates it when people move things on his desk."

"Oh, don't worry," I called. "I've got printer privileges!" Jesus. Printer privileges. Who had I become?

Melissa was working the doorknob so hard I was surprised it didn't spin off in her hand.

"Let me just finish up in here!" I flung open the door to Ben's bathroom, flushed the toilet, and sprayed Ben's can of cinnamon-stick air freshener vigorously around the room. "Printing complete," said the computer. As it spat out the final page, I scooted behind Ben's desk, closed all the files, shoved the printed pages into my purse, flung open the door, and almost ran smack into Melissa.

"Whew. Sorry about that."

She stared at me with her nose wrinkled. I couldn't blame her.

The place smelled like a potpourri bomb had exploded. "Is everything all right?"

"Fine!" I said, clutching my purse to my chest and sidling rapidly toward the elevators in the manner of a constipated crab. "You just might not want to go in there for a little while."

"Did you get what you needed?"

Oh, God, I thought as the blood drained from my face and pooled in my extremities. So much for Miss Marple. She's onto me. She knows. "Excuse me?" I said.

"The measurements," Melissa said, staring at me as if I'd been hitting the crack pipe, or the air freshener were affecting my brain.

"Yes! I'll be able to find something just perfect for that space!" I said, grinning like an idiot. "Do me a favor and don't mention this to Ben. I want it to be a surprise."

She nodded dubiously, and not wanting to push my luck, I scurried down the corporate gray and ivory halls, down the elevator and out the revolving front door to the sidewalk, where I hailed a cab and made my way to Grand Central Station to catch the four-fifteen train home. Once I'd purchased my ticket and curled up in a corner on the rattling Metro-North train, I pulled out the sheaf of Fitch papers. The first paragraph was dry as dust. The next two pages could have cured insomnia. Speeding tickets. A fifty-dollar fine for leaving his Christmas tree on the curb. Be still my heart. But on page four I hit pay dirt, and it was better—and worse—than I could ever have imagined.

THIRTY

The house was quiet when Ben's car pulled into the driveway at seven o'clock that night. I'd sent Janie and the kids to dinner and a movie, and arranged myself in the living room, awaiting his return. I was still neatly dressed in my blue suit left over from my reporter days. My hair was pulled back from my face, and I had a stack of damning Ted Fitch papers in my lap.

"Can I have a word with you?" I called politely to my husband as he was hanging up his coat. My heart sank as I got a good look at what he had in his hand.

"Upchurch Woman Remembered by Friends," read the *Gazette*'s headline. And there was a picture of me at the podium, with my jaw hanging open and my hair a frizzy corona around my head, looking about the size of one of Jupiter's moons.

"I ran into Stan Bergeron at the gas station," Ben said. My heart sank even further. "He wanted to know if you'd recovered from all of the excitement the other night. So I asked him what excitement he was talking about—"

I swallowed hard. "I was going to tell you—"

"Which is how I came to find out that someone's been making threats on your life."

"—but you're hardly ever home and I just couldn't figure out how."

We both paused to take a breath and glare at each other. Ben

pinched the bridge of his nose and started rubbing the reddened skin there. He'd acquired a bit of a belly since we'd moved, and it pushed at his black leather belt as he breathed. "Okay. Let's start at the beginning." He waved the newspaper at me. "You were at Kitty Cavanaugh's memorial service—no, excuse me. I beg your pardon. You *spoke* at Kitty Cavanaugh's memorial service."

"That was kind of inadvertent," I mumbled.

His black eyebrows drew down. "Did somebody put a gun to your head and say, 'Give a speech or I'll shoot'?"

"Pretty much. Except for the gun part."

"You're going around asking people questions—"

My neck tensed as I glared at him. "I used to be a reporter, remember? That was what I did for a living!"

"Asking questions about whether rock stars had genital warts," Ben said. "It's not exactly the same thing."

I lifted my chin. "It was never about the genital warts," I said, with as much dignity as I could muster. "It was occasionally about the herpes. And that's beside the point. Whatever you think of my subject matter, I used to be a reporter."

"But you're not anymore!" Ben shouted. "For God's sake, Kate, you're not a journalist, you're not a detective, you're not a private eye, you're just a housewife!"

I slammed the stack of pages onto the table and stalked into the kitchen, where I started pulling food out of the refrigerator: a carton of eggs, a can of black beans, a bunch of grapes. Ben followed me.

"I didn't mean it like that."

I ignored him. "Do you want dinner?" I asked, pulling out mustard, mayonnaise, turkey, and cheese, before realizing that we were out of bread and the sandwich I'd formerly been craving wasn't going to happen.

"I just want you to be safe. That's why we moved here, remember? You can't do things that put your safety in jeopardy. You can't do things that put our children in danger."

I whirled around, flushed with indignation and sick with shame, knowing, deep down, that he was right, and that I couldn't admit it, because once I did, my investigation, and the way it made me feel alive, after seven years and three kids—alive the way I'd been when I was still holding on to the possibility that someday Evan McKenna would love me—would be over. I'd be right back to my life, my grindingly boring little life, where I didn't fit in, where I had no friends, where the time between now and the day when the kids would spend full days in school stretched out interminably, and I didn't think I could take it.

So I said, "Do you honestly think I'd do anything—anything ever—that would hurt the children?"

"Well, let's see," Ben said, with his voice getting louder and his lips getting pale. He raised one finger. "You've got a friend who crushes up illegal drugs in people's drinks—"

"Oh, that is so unfair," I fumed.

He raised another finger; a prosecutor giving a devastating summation. "You're running around town asking people questions about something that's none of your business."

"A friend of mine was murdered," I said, pointing to a spot in front of my own refrigerator. "Stabbed to death, in her kitchen, in our town. Doesn't that make it my business?"

"She wasn't your friend!" Ben yelled. "You barely even knew her! I don't know why you won't just stay out of it! Take care of the kids. Take care of yourself. Find a hobby if you need something to do with your time."

A red fog descended in front of my eyes. "Something to do with my time?" I repeated. "Do you have any idea what I do all day? Do you have any idea what your kids do all day? Any idea at all?"

He stuck out his jaw and glared at me. I pushed past him, pulled a frying pan out of the island in the center of the kitchen, flicked a blob of butter into its center, and turned the stove on high.

"While you're thinking that over, here's another question," I said, cracking two eggs and sliding them onto the bubbling butter. "Why are you working for a rapist?"

Ben's face twitched. "What are you talking about?"

"You know what I'm talking about. And if you don't, take a look at those pages I printed out." I reached for a spatula. "They should refresh your memory."

Ben went to the living room and came back with the pages in his hand. I slid my eggs on a plate and plopped down at the table. He sat down across from me and flipped through the sheets, then stared at me, shaking his head. I hadn't seen him look this outraged since the fourth night of our honeymoon, when I'd had six vodka and cranberry juices and taken his suggestion that we try something new in bed as an invitation to stick my pinkie up his ass. (As it turned out, he'd been thinking more along the lines of me on top.)

"This is proprietary information," he finally said, with his thumb and index finger working at the bridge of his nose.

"Ben. I always thought you were . . ." I groped for the right words. "I thought you had integrity."

"He said it was consensual," Ben said wearily. When he shut his eyes, the skin of his eyelids looked bruised.

"He choked her!" I said. "How consensual could that have been?"

"That's her story, which was never corroborated. There was no police investigation. No doctor's report."

"You think this woman"—I glanced at the name on the pages to make sure I got it right—"this Sandra Willis made it up? You think she was lying?"

Ben tilted his face up and stared at the ceiling, as if the crown molding had suddenly developed the capacity for conversation. "I think that whatever happened, happened a long time ago. I think that there's such a thing as a youthful indiscretion."

I stared at him, stunned. "Are you kidding me? A youthful indiscretion is when Sam leaves his Legos out. A youthful indiscretion is not raping a Vassar coed when you're twenty years old, then getting your father to pay everyone off so that it never hits the paper."

"Stop!" he boomed. "Stop right now, Kate. You don't know the whole story."

"What don't I know? What else is there? A sequel?"

His lips had gone so white they were almost invisible, and his voice was clipped. "Edward Fitch is a war hero. His work as attorney general has been unimpeachable, and when he's elected senator, he's going to serve the people of New York with distinction."

"Sure," I said, stabbing at my eggs. "Just keep him away from Poughkeepsie. Does his wife know about this?"

"I have no idea. Why? Are you planning on calling to enlighten her?" He picked up the portable phone and tossed it into my lap. "Why not?" He raised his voice to a savage, lisping Valley Girlish uptalk. "Hi, you don't know me? But my name is Kate Klein, and my husband works for your husband? Anyhow, I was in the city shopping? And I happened to stop by my husband's office?" He lowered his voice. "Which, by the way, I'm amazed you managed to find."

"What's that supposed to mean?"

He raked his fingers through his hair. "Let's just say you haven't been the most attentive spouse when it comes to my professional life."

"That is so not what this conversation is about."

"The other wives stop by," Ben persisted. "They take an interest. Al's wife even brings him dinner when he's working late."

"Al lives in TriBeCa. And his wife's had so many face-lifts that she's practically got eyes in the back of her head."

"That's beside the point," Ben snapped. "She brings him dinner."

"Well, forgive me for not zipping into Manhattan to bring you a freakin' pot pie!" I stood up from the table, dumped my plate into the sink, and turned on the water.

"So, assuming that you weren't bringing me that pot pie, what were you doing in my office? Why the sudden interest in Ted Fitch?" Ben asked.

I set the frying pan, still unwashed, on the drying rack. "Ted Fitch and Kitty Cavanaugh knew each other."

Ben pushed himself away from the table. "Oh, great," he said, his voice rich with contempt. "Just great. It's not bad enough that you're running around investigating our neighbors, but now you're harassing my clients too?"

I felt like he'd punched me in the solar plexus, but my voice sounded steady. "Sukie Sutherland saw them talking in a bar before she was murdered. Kitty was crying." I waved the stack of papers in his face. "And I bet I know why."

Ben's face was pale, and his voice was calm, but I saw his knuckles whiten as he gripped the edge of the counter. "Kate," he said, "you can't be serious."

"Does he have an alibi?" I shot back.

He lifted his chin. "I'm not even going to dignify that with a response."

"Fine," I said, and kicked the dishwasher shut. "I'll find out for myself." I grabbed the phone and raised my voice to the mocking falsetto he'd deployed so effectively. "Hi, this is Kate Klein? And given your history of choking women who don't want to have sex with you? I was just wondering if you could tell me where you were the day Kitty Cavanaugh was killed?"

His fingers dug into the flesh above my elbow. "If you say one word to my client," he snarled, "one word, other than 'Hello,' 'Goodbye,' and 'Congratulations, Senator—' "

"You'll what?" I wrenched my arm away. "Rape me?"

He let go of me, looking horrified. "Kate."

I grabbed the papers and shoved them into my borrowed purse. "Sleep in the guest room," I said.

Upstairs, I slammed our bedroom door, yanked off my clothes, pulled on my nightgown, and dove under the covers with my stack of printouts on the fascinating life and times of Edward Jeffords Fitch, fifty-seven-year-old graduate of Yale and Harvard Law School, winner of the Bronze Star in Vietnam, assistant district attorney, district attorney, state's attorney general, and, if my husband had his way, the next Democratic senator from the great state of New York. *Had he done it?* I wondered, staring at the camera-ready visage that accompanied the story the *Times* had run when he'd announced his candidacy. Had he been the one to bury that knife in Kitty Cavanaugh's back? Would Ben try to find out? Did Ben even care what the answer was, as long as it didn't impinge on Ted Fitch's electability?

I pulled the covers up to my ears and listened as the car door and then the side door slammed and my husband and best friend fumbled through the kids' bedtime routine. "Mommy," Sophie kept saying. "I want the mommy."

At nine o'clock, after the final request for a glass of water and another story was denied, Janie tapped gently at the door.

"Everything okay?" she whispered.

I opened the door and flopped back on the bed with my face in a pillow. "Yes. No. I don't know."

"Okay," said Janie, flopping down beside me. Her streaky hair was gathered in a ponytail, and she'd borrowed a pair of my cargo pants that hung loosely around her waist. "Glad we're clear on that."

I handed her the Fitch file, then gave her the fifteen-second synopsis. Janie's eyes got wider and wider. "Wow," she said, and "Whoa," and, finally, an astonished and extremely gratifying "Oh . . . my . . . God."

"So what now?"

"We find out if Ted Fitch has an alibi." I flung myself onto my back, thinking, *Then I figure out how I wound up married to someone who'd work for a man like that.*

THIRTY-ONE

When I dragged myself out of bed the next morning, there was no sign of Ben anywhere. His overcoat had vanished from its hanger, his briefcase had departed the closet floor, and his space in the garage was empty. There was, however, a note stuck to the refrigerator under a magnet reading "Number One Mommy." "Kate," it read, with an angry-looking slash after my name. "Don't do anything. Don't call anyone. I will try to answer your questions within the next week." No signature. No "love."

No thanks, I thought, crumpling the note and shoving it into the pocket of my bathrobe, remembering the little-girl lisp he'd used the night before. I'll get what I need myself. Then I dialed the Red Wheel Barrow to tell them the kids would be absent and called upstairs to Janie to tell her we were going on a field trip.

It's amazing what happens to people's peripheral vision when confronted with two women and three kids on a crowded train. Suddenly, it's as if all those businessmen and women with briefcases and laptops can't see past their copies of the *Wall Street Journal* and volunteer to give up the empty seats beside them. Last summer, I'd taken the train to Boston with all three kids to meet my mother and drive up to Tanglewood. Sophie was walking, the boys were in a double stroller, and there was not a pair of empty seats to be found.

After lurching through three cars, I ended up squatting with all three kids and their portable DVD player on the floor by the luggage bay. Once I'd gotten the boys out of their stroller and *Elmo's World* on the screen, the woman whose raincoat and attaché case were sprawled over the empty seat beside her favored us with a bright smile. "What cuties!" she gushed. I returned her smile and bit back what I wanted to say, which was "You know what makes them even cuter? Somewhere to sit!"

I've lived and learned. That morning Janie and I got the kids onto the southbound train to New York and were confronted with the customary sight of lots of busy businesspeople taking up two seats apiece.

"Hmm," said Janie, scowling down the rows with her paper cup of coffee in her hands, teetering in three-inch-high heels (white kidskin, to match her utterly child-unfriendly coat and handbag). Her hair was in a chignon, and she was towing her little wheeled suitcase behind her. "Excuse me!" she said to the businessman on the BlackBerry to her left and the woman chattering on her cell phone in the seats across from him. "Hi. We're traveling with three small children, and I'm wearing really high heels. Would you two mind doubling up so we could sit down?"

The two of them looked at her, then at each other. Then the man looked back down at his BlackBerry, and the woman resumed her conversation. "Hel-lo!" said Janie. "Do you not speak English? Women! Children! Very high heels!"

"Not to worry," I whispered over my shoulder. "Follow my lead." I was dressed to impress, or at least, I was as impressive as I ever got. Janie had flat-ironed my hair into submission, and I was wearing my best black wool pants and a black sweater—size XL, so it fit.

"Okay, Sophie!" I said brightly—and loudly—plopping my daughter down in the raincoat-draped seat next to a red-faced man in a navy blue suit. "You sit right here," I said, winking broadly.

"Mommy's just going to walk for a little while and find a place for Jack and Sam!"

Mr. Blue Suit was so startled that he actually hung up his phone. "Ma'am?" he said, with fear in his eyes. "You're not going to just leave her here by herself?"

"Oh, not by herself!" I said, pulling a juice box out of my diaper bag with a flourish. "Now, Soph, this is for you. Try not to spill it everywhere like you did last time."

With a noise that would be phonetically rendered as *harrumph,* Mr. Blue Suit gathered his newspapers, his briefcase, his raincoat, and his phone, and went to sit beside one of his fellow travelers. Janie caught on fast.

"All right, Sam," she said, parking him next to a guy in gray flannel. She handed him markers and a coloring book and gave him a big wink. "I know you're excited about those brand-new big-boy underpants, so don't forgot to call me if you think you have to go. I'll be sitting back there . . . somewhere . . ."

The gray flannel guy muttered, "Oh, Jesus," and practically ran to the club car. Janie grinned at me, and before we knew it, we had two entire rows of seats all to ourselves.

"I can't believe that," Janie said, shaking her head. "What is wrong with these people?" She raised her voice and got to her feet. "Women and children, people! Women and children get seats first!"

"Janie."

"Didn't any of you see *Titanic*? Honest to God!" She sat down, took a deep breath, a sip of her double espresso, then got back to her feet. "Shame on all of you!" she yelled, as the car's passengers flinched and shoved their noses a few inches deeper into the morning papers. I tugged Janie back down beside me.

"Okay, we appreciate that, but we have to concentrate now." I passed Sophie a compact, a blush brush, and my iPod, and pulled the Fitch file out of my purse.

"So," said Janie, taking another sip of coffee. "We can skip that list of names, 'cause we think Ted Fitch did it."

"He's a definite possibility. He had a motive," I said. "Or at least we know that Kitty and Ted knew each other, which meant that he'd be familiar enough for her to open the door and let him in. He had opportunity," I continued. "I checked his schedule. The day Kitty died, all he had was a dinner event. Hundred-dollar-a-plate fund-raiser with the Kiwanis in Westchester."

"A hop, skip, and a jump away from Upchurch," said Janie.

"History of violence," I said. "That Sandra Willis he . . . um." I looked at my kids. The boys had their curly heads bent over a coloring book. Sophie had the earbuds stuffed in her ears and was brushing sparkly powder onto her cheeks. "Interfered with."

"Charming fellow," Janie said. "I am so not voting for him." She pressed her freshly painted lips together as the train rattled along the tracks. "Motive," she said. "Say he was upset about something Laura Lynn had published and Kitty had written. No matter how angry he was . . ." She checked her reflection in the scuffed plastic of the window. "I mean, would he interfere with her, or just write an op-ed?"

"He'd actually have one of his staffers write it," I said absently. "But maybe he wasn't about her writing."

"Maybe it was a crime of passion!" Janie's eyes lit up. "Ooh, ooh, this is good!" She reached into her bag and removed a notebook—an official reporter's notebook, I saw with a pang—and started writing. "They were having an affair!"

I lowered my voice, hoping Janie would follow suit. "Let's not get ahead of ourselves."

"We know she liked older men, right? So they were having an affair," she continued, "and he told her he'd leave his wife, but then he changed his mind and Kitty wouldn't take no for an answer and that's why she was crying in the restaurant, and he said, *Just lay low until the election is over,* but she said, *No, I can't lay low, I won't live a lie, I'm having our baby, Ted—"*

"Janie, the kids," I whispered, starting to laugh in spite of myself.

"A little Fitch! A Fitchlette!"

"I bet that's the kind of thing they would have noticed in the autopsy," I said. To no avail. Janie was on a roll.

"*I won't be ignored, Ted,* she told him. *You have to give our baby a name,* she said, and when he realized that she wasn't kidding, that she was going to take her story to the tabloids—"

"Or *Content.*" I said, caught up in Janie's tawdry tale in spite of myself. "She wouldn't have to go to the tabloids. She could've just written her own story for *Content.*"

"Or maybe," Janie said, pausing dramatically, "she was going to tell *you.* That's why she called you that night! That's why she wanted to see you! She knew you were a writer and," Janie said, pausing at last for a breath, "she knew that you knew me."

"How did she know that?"

Janie wrinkled her nose. "You don't speak of me constantly?"

"I do," piped Sophie.

I stared at my daughter, suddenly realizing that she'd probably heard every word we'd said and understood most of them. I made a lip-zipping gesture to Janie, who nodded but kept scribbling notes.

"He killed her," she whispered, once Sophie appeared to be engrossed in her makeup again. "And his unborn son—"

"Or daughter," I chimed in.

"And he thought," said Janie, "that the secret had died with her—"

"Until Kate Klein, ace investigator, cracked the case and sent him to the electric chair!"

Janie high-fived me, then wrinkled her nose. "Of course, if he goes to jail, Ben's going to lose his biggest client. But I'm going to get a great story."

• • •

The public post–Election Day wound-licking known as the Rally for America was sponsored by two of New York City's biggest labor unions and the New York State Democratic Committee and was being held on the plaza across from City Hall. The five of us waited for a minivan taxi, which deposited us in a throng of bundled-up true believers, many of them toting red, white, and blue signs reading Voters for Change and presumably eager and willing to spend the next eleven months doing whatever it took to ensure that the Democrats wouldn't get their asses handed to them yet again.

The day was cold but clear. The sky above us was a pale blue, and the streets were filled with workers on their lunch break and holiday shoppers bustling off to the pre-Christmas sales. The air smelled like honeyed peanuts and hot dogs. Janie inhaled blissfully, and the kids followed suit.

I stared at the dais and picked out Ted Fitch immediately. He was nicely color-coordinated with the signs and the patriotic bunting: his nose was red, his hair was white, and his overcoat was a good, solid navy blue, a garment I'd bet that my husband had vetted with a focus group of female voters between the ages of thirty-four and fifty-four.

Ted was third on the roster, after Deputy Mayor Michael Suarez and the state's comptroller. The deputy mayor was, in my opinion, too handsome to waste himself on the people's business and should have gone into acting instead; the comptroller was a sixtysomething career politician who'd spent forty years of her life in Albany and, as a result, looked and sounded half dead. Janie and I shepherded the kids into the concrete basin, where a friendly ward leader gave them each a balloon. Janie tied one around each kid's wrist, I pulled out my notebook and a pen, and Ted Fitch launched into his standard stump speech.

"I *am* Ted Fitch and I *will* be the next senator from the great state of New York!" he boomed to a sprinkling of applause. I studied his long, angular face, his aquiline nose and thin lips, as Ted zipped through his talking points: the diversity of our great nation, the oppressiveness of the current regime, how a new day was dawning in America, and how he needed the support of true believers—true Americans, all over the nation—to make the dream a reality. "Thank you all for all of your support, and God bless America!" he concluded. There was more applause, a little more enthusiastic, as he collected handshakes and cheek pecks from the other dignitaries, high-fived the ten-year-old they'd procured to sing the National Anthem, and made his way offstage.

"Stay here," I told Janie. I shoved my notebook in the pocket of my black wool pea coat and threaded my way through the crowd to the line of Town Cars idling along the curb behind the stage. The drivers were leaning against the doors, smoking and talking. The first three I asked shook their heads, but I hit pay dirt with the fourth. By the time Ted Fitch had glad-handed his way down the stairs and his staffers were walking him back to his car, I was standing there waiting for him.

"Well, what a pleasant surprise!" he said, hugging my shoulders and giving me a hard, bloodless buss on the cheek. Up close, Ted didn't look as good as he did in his campaign posters, or as rested as he'd been at our party. Bags had bloomed underneath his eyes and there was white stuff crusted in the corners of his lips.

"Can I borrow you for a minute?" I asked.

"Of course!" he replied, in the bluff, hearty voice of a man getting ready to spend the next year shaking hands, kissing babies, and acting inordinately interested in everyone he met. "What can I do for you?"

I stepped close to him and said quietly, so his pair of fresh-faced staffers wouldn't hear, "Can we talk somewhere in private?"

Ted Fitch nodded, puzzlement spreading over his face. "Is the car all right?"

I didn't have time to regret saying yes until I'd slid awkwardly along the length of the big back seat and the door had closed with a heavy clunk behind me. I'd wanted privacy, but the tinted windows and black leather interior were making me feel like I'd locked myself into a crypt, with Ted Fitch beside me.

"Water?" Ted asked. I shook my head as he opened a bottle of his own and downed a fistful of pills. "Echinacea, zinc, vitamin C, ginkgo biloba," he explained. "Gotta stay strong out here!"

I nodded. He gulped, blinked, swallowed more water and more pills. "So, Kate! Is everything all right? Is this about Ben?"

I shook my head and smoothed my hands along my pants, suddenly wishing we were outside in the fresh, cold air. "I wanted to ask you about Kitty Cavanaugh."

I was watching him carefully, to see if he'd blink, or twitch, or touch his ear, or shout out, "Yes! I killed her!" His face gave nothing away. "The writer. Such a tragedy," he said. "Wasn't she a neighbor of yours?"

"She was. And a friend of yours," I prompted.

He shut his eyes in a gesture somewhere between a long blink and a short wince. "We knew some of the same people," he said carefully.

I shifted my body on the seat, feeling a drop of sweat work its way between my breasts and soak into my waistband. The heater was blowing stale, warm air in my face, and its roar made me feel like I was shouting. "I know how busy you are—"

"That husband of yours!" Ted Fitch said, with a ready-for-my-close-up guffaw. "He keeps me hopping!"

"Kitty was murdered," I said, speaking fast, feeling my entire body start sweating, knowing I needed to get the words out before I lost my nerve completely. "The police haven't arrested anyone. I know that you and Kitty were together at Aquavit having lunch before she was murdered. I just want to know . . ." *Okay, Kate. Stay calm.* "I want to know what your relationship was."

Ted Fitch blew out an explosive, mint-scented breath. "You think I'm involved in her death somehow?" He glared at me, all traces of be-nice-to-the-soccer-mom wiped off his features, replaced by what was almost a caricature of annoyance. "What gives you the right? Are you a detective now?"

I shook my head. "Just a housewife," I said softly.

Ted Fitch gave a disgusted growl and reached for his door handle. "I don't have time for this nonsense."

I wiped my hands on my legs again. "Sandra Willis," I said.

He let go of the handle and slumped back in the seat as blood turned the tips of his ears bright red and his cheeks and nose angry maroon. "Jesus," he said softly. "Jesus Christ. You and Ben must have some pillow talk."

"This didn't come from Ben," I said. It was true enough. "I used to be a reporter." Which was also true.

He sighed. "So the papers have this now. The—uh—the incident with Miss . . . uh . . ."

"Sandra Willis," I said again. "I don't think the papers have anything. That isn't my concern. I just want to know about Kitty."

He unscrewed the top of his water bottle, then screwed it on again. "I don't think we should discuss it," he said.

"Yeah, well, Sandra Willis didn't think she wanted to have sex with you, but you didn't let that stop you, right?" As soon as the words were out of my mouth, I knew that they'd been a mistake.

His face contorted again. "Get out of this car right now." This time he reached across me, his forearm as unyielding as a two-by-four against my breasts, and grabbed my door handle. He shoved the door open a few inches before I managed to slam it shut.

"You were together before she died. What were you talking about? Why was she crying? Were you having an affair? Was she . . ." *Pregnant,* I was going to ask. In spite of my best intentions, Janie's story had taken hold in my brain. Ted Fitch, purple-faced and breathing hard, sat back on his side of the car.

"You want to know?" he asked in a strangled voice. "You want to know what she wanted?" He shoved his hand into his hip pocket.

Oh, God. This time I was the one who grabbed for the door handle. "Maybe we can continue this some other time—"

He grabbed my hand and yanked me back down in my seat. "You want it?" he asked. His face was twisted as he threw a balled-up piece of paper at me. "Here. Here you go. Now get out."

It wasn't until I finally got the door open and half stepped, half staggered out onto the sidewalk that I realized what he'd thrown in my lap. Money. I unfolded the crumpled twenty with shaking hands as the door slammed and the Town Car drove away.

"Hey!"

Janie hustled over with the kids and their balloons. "Is this friendship finally paying off?" she inquired. Then she got a good look at my face. "What happened?" she asked. "Are you okay?" I shook my head, and she lowered her voice, putting one hand on my shoulder and studying my face. "What now?" she asked.

"Now," I said, and took a deep, shuddering breath, giving all three kids a group hug, "let's get some lunch and go shopping."

We spent the day at our favorite New York hangouts, pretending everything was fine—that I'd never moved to Connecticut, that nobody had gotten murdered, that I hadn't been shoved out of a car after a politician had tossed twenty bucks in my lap. We had hot fudge sundaes at Serendipity 3, where Janie and I had decided to live together, and we let the kids spend Ted Fitch's twenty at Dylan's Candy Bar. After a trip to the Museum of Natural History to look at the whale and a stop at Rockefeller Center to watch the ice skaters, the kids were wiped out from the combination of sugar and activity. Janie dropped us off at the train station. "I'll look into the list," she promised, pulling a sticky Sam and a sleeping Jack off of her shoulders and handing them over to me. "Call me when you get back to Pleasantville."

The four o'clock train back to Upchurch was almost empty. I set the boys down to sleep on a nest made of our coats, and I tucked

Sophie at a window seat with my scarf and hat for a pillow. She still had a lollipop clutched in one sticky hand. I detached it as gently as I could and kissed her candy-sweet cheek. "Bug off," she said, swatting at me with her eyes half-closed.

I settled myself in my own seat and pulled out my notebook, to try to make sense of the day. *You want to know what she wanted?* he'd asked, and tossed money at me. *Kitty wanted money,* I wrote, then added a question mark. I thought of Dorie Stevenson's soft Southern twang. *A pair of pearl earrings that she wore every day . . .* I scribbled frantically, equal parts enthralled and exhausted. Maybe Kitty had been having sex with men for money. Maybe that was what they could give her that the college boys couldn't. And if Philip really had been a disaster at work, as Ben had told me, maybe she needed money, still.

I felt my pulse quicken as I imagined it: Kitty adding up the cost of private school tuition and a six-figure mortgage, the cars, the clothes, the vacations for sun or skiing, the dozens of things you'd need to survive nicely in Upchurch, and realizing the only way she could have it all was by supplementing her ghostwriting with the occasional discreet afternoon assignation that would end with a few hundred dollars on the nightstand. I wondered whether Dorie knew, or had suspected, what her old roommate had been up to. I wondered how Tara Singh would feel to find out that her mortal enemy's ghostwriter had had feet of clay, and various body parts for rent.

Back in Upchurch, the garage was empty, and the house was dark. I gave the kids chicken nuggets for dinner, bathed them, read them the story of Little Red Riding Hood, and put them to bed. I was sitting down on the couch with my notebook and my nuggets when the phone rang.

"Hello?"

"Kate?" It took me a minute to attach the deep voice to Denny Holdt's face. "Sorry to bother you, but I was wondering whether you'd seen Lexi lately."

I thought. "At the party. Before that, at ice-skating lessons." She'd had Brierly bundled up against her chest in her brightly colored Guatemalan wrap while Hadley practiced skating backwards. Lexi and the baby both had on red-and-gold wool caps with earflaps pulled down over their blond hair. She'd turned down a sip of my vending machine hot chocolate, pulled a bright green Granny Smith apple from her pocket, and eaten that instead.

"Yeah," Denny said gruffly. "She didn't come home last night."

Oh my God, I thought, remembering what Stan had told me in the police station, how Lexi had thought she was being followed. "Are the kids all right? The baby?"

"No, no, the kids were with a sitter. Brierly's right here with me. And Hadley . . . Hadley, stop that!" There was a shout, then the sound of something crashing. When Denny came back on the line, he sounded a little breathless. "Sorry, he keeps swinging off the balcony."

"Was there a note, or a message?"

"Nope. Nope, nothing. I got home at eight o'clock and the kids were in bed, asleep. The sitter said she didn't know where Lexi was going, and she hadn't said when she'd be back. Nothing was touched, nothing was taken. There's no suitcases missing, or clothes or anything. Her purse is gone, and her car, but her jewelry's all here, and—*Hadley, what did I tell you about that?*"

Another thump, a screech, and noisy tears. It was longer before Denny got back on the line.

"Sorry."

"I think you should call the police," I said.

"I did," he replied. "They say they can't do anything until she's been missing for forty-eight hours, even with . . . with everything else that's been going on."

"Do you have any idea where she could have gone?"

"Her mother hasn't heard from her. Her sister hasn't heard from her. She's not answering her cell phone, so I'm calling all of her friends. *Hadley, you stop that right now!*"

More thumping, more screaming. I pictured Lexi at my party,

her shoulders tensed and calves twitching as she watched Philip touching Janie's hair. "Forgive me for asking this."

"No. No, please, whatever it is . . ." His voice dropped. "If it'll help them find her . . ."

I talked quickly, before I could lose my nerve. "Were you and Lexi having any problems?"

There was an uncomfortable, bristly pause. "We were fine," he said stiffly.

"Fine. Fine. Listen, is there anything I can do to help? Anyone I can call?"

"No," he said. "No, you were last on my list."

Figures, I thought as Denny Holdt hung up without saying goodbye. I turned the phone over in my hand for a minute, then dialed the Cavanaughs' number. Philip answered on the fourth ring.

"It's Kate Klein. I just got off the phone with Denny Holdt."

"Denny told me," said Philip. "It's horrible." He sounded like he meant it too. His tone was what you'd expect from a sincerely worried neighbor, as opposed to someone who'd chopped Lexi up into little pieces and stored her remains in freezer bags. Then again, did I really have any idea what a mass murderer would sound like?

"How are you?" I asked.

"Oh, keeping busy," Philip said. "I'm taking a leave of absence from work, and I'll be meeting the girls down in Florida tomorrow."

I nodded, remembering. "They're there with your parents?"

"My mother," he said. "My father's going to stay up here to hold down the fort."

I told him to travel safely, to give his daughters my best wishes and those of my children. Then I hung up the phone and wrote *Philip to Florida* in my notebook, thinking that I wouldn't have been the least bit shocked if it turned out he wasn't traveling alone.

Upstairs, Sophie had kicked off the covers and lay spread-eagled on her sheet in her pink-and-white-striped pajamas, miniatures of Aunt Janie's, with an identically attired Uglydoll in the crook of her arm. Sam slept on his left side, Jack on his right, nestled together in the bottom bunk bed, the way I imagined they had when they were still inside of me. I tiptoed over their trucks and blocks and bent to kiss their cheeks. Then I crept back downstairs, picked up the phone, and called Carol Gwinnell, the least intimidating of the fast-dwindling pool of Upchurch supermoms, to ask if she'd heard the news about Lexi.

THIRTY-TWO

"I heard," Ben began, forty-five minutes later, "that you saw my client today."

I looked up from my computer, where I'd been scrolling through more of Laura Lynn/Kitty's columns, and raised my eyebrows. "Beg your pardon?" I asked politely.

He exhaled impatiently. "At the rally, Kate."

"Oh," I said, tapping away without meeting his eyes. "Oh, yes. We had a conversation."

"Well, I had a conversation with him too," Ben said, slapping a slim manila folder down on the desk beside me. "Most of it was spent trying to convince him not to fire B Squared Consulting."

"You still want to work for him?" I asked. "I guess I shouldn't be surprised."

"You're unbelievable, do you know that?" he growled.

"Yes, but being unbelievable isn't a crime. Does your guy have an alibi?" I asked.

Ben pointed at the folder. "At the time of Kitty Cavanaugh's murder he was having lunch."

"And there were witnesses to this lunch?"

Ben paused. "His mistress."

"Bully for Ted," I said. I closed the computer and looked at the pages. There was a picture of an apartment building, a photocopy of a driver's license belonging to one Barbara Downing, hair blond, eyes blue, height five five, age thirty-six. I wondered if, in private moments, he called her Barbie. I flipped through the pages, looking for other pictures, but found only a few grainy long-lens photos of the candidate exiting his Town Car and entering the apartment building. "What, no nudity?"

Ben winced.

"And just because he's got a mistress, and just because she'll swear to whatever he tells her to swear to, doesn't mean he didn't do it."

Ben's nostrils flared. "You think he found the time to drive to Upchurch, murder a woman, clean himself up, and be back in the city for his three o'clock briefing before his dinner in Westchester?"

"Some days," I said sweetly. "I take the kids to the Red Wheel Barrow in the morning, do three loads of laundry, pick up your dry cleaning, get the oil changed, swing by the grocery store, pick the kids up again, and feed them lunch in the car so we can get to Craft Circle at one-thirty. It's all about time management. If you told me I had to throw a murder in there somewhere, I'm sure I'd figure out how." I gave him a big, cheesy grin and turned back to my computer.

"You still think he did it?" Ben demanded.

"I'm not convinced he didn't. And either way, there was something fishy going on between the two of them. Unless throwing money is, like, his kink." I could tell from Ben's confused expression that whatever Ted Fitch had told him about my ambush at the rally, it hadn't included his tossing twenty dollars into my lap.

"Kate . . ." Ben shook his head wearily and returned the pages to the folder.

"Nor," I continued, "is the news that he has a mistress exactly a balm to my soul." A lofty moral pronouncement from a woman who'd once found Play-Doh in her pubic hair, but it was true. I walked into the living room and started dismantling the pillow fort the kids had built the day before and replacing the cushions on the couch. "Remind me again why you're working for him?"

"Because he's the best candidate out there," Ben said. I stared at him. He shrugged. "Because everyone's dirty." He raked his fingers through his hair. "If it's not women, it's alcohol. If it's not women or alcohol, it's a kid in jail, or rehab, or a messy divorce and an angry ex-wife trying to sell her story to the tabloids." He rubbed his temples. "Bill Clinton changed the nature of the beast," he said. "Post-Nixon, you'd have to be a choirboy to try to get elected, because the press was going to put you under a microscope. Anything you'd ever done or even thought about doing was going to be front-page news. Now"—he shrugged—"now it doesn't matter what you've done, as long as you've got thick skin and a nice smile."

I fluffed the last of the pillows, then squatted down to pick blocks up off the floor. "Do you think Ted killed Kitty Cavanaugh?"

He shook his head without any hesitation. "We aren't friends, but I've spent a lot of time with him. I could see him getting ugly. I could see him losing his temper, getting abusive." He looked down; he appeared frail and exhausted. I could see blue veins pulsing in his wrists. "He wasn't too happy with me today. Or with you. He's a yeller, maybe a shover. But I can't see him stabbing someone to death."

I tossed the blocks into the toy chest. "So if he didn't do it, who did?"

Ben ran his fingers wearily through his hair again. "Can't you just let it go?"

"Can't," I said, getting up from the couch and smoothing the pillow where I'd sat. "Won't," I added.

"Why not?"

"Because women in this town—women just like me—are disappearing and dying." I gathered crusty paint brushes and construction paper from the coffee table. "Lexi Hagen-Holdt's missing now. Her husband just called."

He looked at me with narrowed eyes. "So what, you're going to investigate that too?"

I felt my temper flare but kept my voice light. "Why? Would what be a problem for you?"

He just shook his head.

"Look, I'm . . ." I set down the arts and crafts equipment, groping for words. "I'm good at this, Ben. And I've never been really, really good at anything."

He rubbed his eyes. "What are you talking about? You're a good mother."

Only insofar as our children still have all of their limbs, I thought. "Not by Upchurch standards. I'm barely adequate. And that's the thing. I was a good-not-great singer, but not in the same league as my mother. I was a good writer, but not as good as Janie." I put the paint brushes in their glass bottle. "I'm good at this. Or I think I could be."

He stared at me. "You want to keep doing this?" he demanded. "You think this could be"—the incredulity in his voice was almost too much for me to stand—"what, a career?"

"Well, I don't know! Maybe! I mean, the kids are going to be in school all day, at some point. I'm going to have to find something to do. I'm not just going to take yoga classes and, and volunteer at the art museum!"

"Why not?" Ben asked. "That doesn't sound so bad to me." He gave me an appraising look—my backside in particular. "Maybe you could join a gym."

"I'm not going to dignify that with a response," I said.

I stood in front of Ben and held out my hand for the pictures of Ted Fitch's playthings. He gave another sigh, handed them over, muttered, "I give up," and plodded past me. I heard him walk past our bedroom and the door of the guest room open, then close.

I was in bed half asleep when my cell phone buzzed. I answered without looking at the screen to see who was calling. "Hello?"

"Kate?" asked Evan. "Is everything all right?"

My breath caught in my throat. *Nothing,* I thought. *Nothing is all right.* "Everything's fine," I said.

"I've got something for you," he said.

I sat up straight in the bed. "What?"

"It's about Delphine Dolan."

"What?" I asked again.

"I think it would be better if I told you in person," said Evan. "Can you meet me for a drink?"

I told him to give me a couple of days. "Don't call me," I said. "I'll call you."

THIRTY-THREE

"They lost your Pap smear?" Ben asked over breakfast three days later. "How?"

"I don't know. It happens sometimes, I guess. But Dr. Morrison said he could squeeze me in as long as I got there by nine."

My husband shook his head. "You really need to find a doctor in Connecticut."

"But I love Dr. Morrison!" I attempted an expression of dewy maternal remembrance and tried to squash the guilt rising through my body, because the truth was that a doctor's appointment was once again not on my agenda for the day. "I could find a doctor here, but it wouldn't be the same. Dr. Morrison brought our babies into the world."

Ben stared at me. "Are you feeling all right?"

"I'll feel fine once I get this taken care of."

I dropped the kids off at nursery school. Carol Gwinnell had told me she'd be happy to take the boys home with her after school, and Gracie was going to take Sophie for a manicure as a special treat, then drop her off at Carol's.

Ben and I rode the train to New York, together, sitting side by side on dingy orange-and-gold-striped plastic seats. Ben folded his newspapers into precise thirds. Once he'd finished the front page, he handed it, without comment, to me. "Upchurch Mother Missing," read the *Gazette* headline, beside a picture of Lexi with newborn baby Brierly in her arms. The front-page story didn't tell me anything I hadn't heard from Denny. Lexi was still missing, the cops were still looking, and a toll-free number had been set up for anyone with information to call in, no questions asked. I stared out the window, thinking about Kitty and Lexi, Joel Asch and Ted Fitch, Philip Cavanaugh and Kitty's parents, who'd lost their daughter before she'd died.

"Coffee?" Ben asked.

"Please," I said, and watched as he handed me his cup, then unfolded his long body from the seat and moved, sure-footed in his blue suit and red-and-blue striped tie, down the aisle to throw out the paper. He'd added the artificial sweetener that I liked and had wrapped the cardboard cup with paper napkins. But when he sat back down again, his thigh brushed against mine, and he immediately pulled it back and said, "Excuse me." I wanted to reach out for his hand, to say, *Let's forget this. You skip work, I'll blow off my fake Pap smear, we'll go to a museum and then to the Oyster Bar for lunch. We'll get a room at the Plaza and make love until we have to catch the six-eleven home.*

The words stuck in my throat and stayed there as the train pulled into the station. I stared at his profile, his shock of dark hair and thick eyebrows, the same well-formed mouth and chin all three of our children had inherited. If he really thought I was waiting for the kids to go to elementary school so I could enjoy mornings at the gym, lunches where I'd spear a few lettuce leaves and air-kiss my friends, afternoons whiled away at Saks or Nordstrom's, buying formal gowns for black-tie parties where I'd do more air kissing and lettuce spearing and suffering in high heels, he didn't know me. Which made hooky and hotel sex more than a little unlikely.

"Good luck with everything," Ben said, gesturing euphemistically toward my nether regions.

"Wait," I said, but he'd already disappeared into the crowd thronging Grand Central Station: men in overcoats and women whose sneakers squeaked and left drippy gray prints on the wet marble floor. I sighed, then walked down the stairs to the subway to my first stop: breakfast with Janie.

Janie had ordered an assortment of breakfast sandwiches and bagels. She'd spread them across her desk, along with Saran-wrapped slices of blueberry-yogurt loaf and bottled water, when I arrived at the offices where I'd formerly worked.

"Help yourself," she said. She was wearing imposing horn-rimmed glasses that said Prada along each earpiece and had clear plastic lenses. Janie had perfect vision but would occasionally accessorize with eyeglasses when they suited her purpose. I nibbled at egg and cheese on a bagel and looked around. The *New York Night* newsroom hadn't changed much in the five years I'd been away. The mouse gray carpeting had been replaced with something in a subtle hunter green pattern, and the battered metal filing cabinets had been moved from one wall to another, but other than that, it was the same old place.

I watched as Sandra the book editor sipped from her promotional *Man Show* water bottle and scowled at some sucker's novel, as our former boss Polly, who hadn't aged a day, purchased pretzels and orange soda from the vending machine.

"Hey!" Janie snapped her fingers in front of my face. "Are you there?"

"Sure. Sorry." I collected myself as she pulled a folder out of the top drawer of her desk. "What have you got for me?" I asked as Mark, the managing editor, yelled what looked like the word *motherfucker* into his headset and kicked the trash can across his office floor.

"Well, I've had a busy two days." She straightened her glasses and opened her folder. "David Linde," she began, sliding a picture of a sixtysomething-year-old guy with wary blue eyes and a gray ponytail. "A luthier living in Eugene, Oregon. Said he had no idea who Kitty Verree-slash-Cavanaugh was. Didn't recognize her picture."

"You emailed it to him?"

"I showed it to him."

"In Oregon?"

"Sy lent me his jet. Have you ever been there?" she asked. "It's supercute!" It was one of the things I loved about Janie—the way she could talk about the entire Pacific Northwest like it was an evening bag she was considering buying.

"He never heard of her," I said as my heart started sinking and my sex-for-money-with-older-men story began to unravel.

"That's what he said. And I ran through his whole history," Janie said, flipping to a new page of notes. "They were never even in the same place at the same time, as far as I can tell. He's been living in Oregon for, like, twenty years, and the last time he was in New York City was before she was born."

"Maybe Kitty made house calls," I said, but I was flailing, and I knew it.

"Not to worry. It gets better," Janie said, sliding David Linde's picture back into the folder. "This," she said, pulling out another photograph, "is Harold Saccio. Ophthalmologist in Maine."

Harold Saccio had tufts of curly gingery hair poking out from behind his ears, heavy glasses, and a blobby pink nose. If he was a shade or two darker, he'd be a dead ringer for my kids' Mr. Potato Head.

"Hung up on me when I mentioned Kitty's name."

My fingers tightened on the edge of the picture. "Interesting."

"Didn't answer my subsequent eighteen phone calls."

"Wow."

"Then he pulled his lab coat over his head when I greeted him in the parking lot of his office building and threatened to have me arrested for trespassing."

"You went to Maine too?"

"Maine is also very cute," said Janie, adjusting her glasses. "So he tried to blow me off. At which point I very charmingly indicated the news van that was parked across the street and said he could either speak to me in private, off the record, or I'd give them the go-sign and they could film him doing the walk of shame back to his Mercedes."

My jaw dropped open. "News van?"

"Friend of a friend," Janie said modestly. "Guy who owed me a favor."

"You know guys in Maine?"

"I get around," she said modestly, and flipped her shining hair over her shoulders. "So, back to Harry Eyeball. We drive to a diner in Portland, and he starts mumbling." She made a face. "The guy talked like an auctioneer, and he had an accent, and he was all sweaty and kept taking off his clothes."

"Huh?"

"Jacket, suit jacket, tie . . ." She winced. "I was terrified he'd keep going. I said, 'What do you know about Kitty Cavanaugh?' and he starts going on about what happened was a long time ago, it was a youthful indiscretion, blah de blah blah, doesn't wish to discuss it, it was a bad time in his life, and he's sorry, and he's happily married now."

My palms and the small of my back started sweating. "So he knew Kitty."

"In New York."

"When?"

She shook her head. "I couldn't pin him down. Couldn't even get him to say Kitty's name. He just kept saying that what happened only happened once, in New York City, and that it was all in the past. I don't know whether the past was when Kitty asked Evan to look him up, or, you know, two weeks ago. And then, when I started really pushing for details—like when he met her, who hooked it up, how much it cost . . ." She sighed. "He got on the phone with his lawyer and said if I had anything else to ask him, I'd need a subpoena. And he stuck me with the check!"

"Bastard," I said. "And after you came all that way to see him."

Janie nodded, sliding Harold's picture back into the envelope. "Bo Baird's dead, of course, which takes him off the suspect list."

"Him, but not Laura Lynn," I said, thinking out loud. "What if she found out that her father knew her ghostwriter, in a biblical sense?"

"Knew her and paid her," Janie said. "I think it's at least worth mentioning to our pal Stannie."

"What about Emmett James?"

Janie made another face. "That didn't go very well," she said, and pulled the fourth photograph out of the envelope. If the other two men had been in the full flower of middle age, Emmett James was waiting at Death's bus stop. He was tiny, in pleated black pants and a loose-fitting white button-down shirt, with wisps of white hair floating around a head pink and innocent as an egg. Tiny, blue-veined hands were folded in his lap.

"Emmett James," Janie said. "Professor emeritus of English literature with a concentration in modern British and American poets. Ninety-two years old, lives in New Haven, and he's in a wheelchair. So, not to generalize about the differently abled, but I don't think he's our killer . . . and I can't imagine him paying for sex. At least not in this century."

I studied the photograph. "Did you ask him about her?"

"I did," Janie said. "Or should I say, I tried. The guy's really, really old." She sipped from her cup of coffee. "He started quoting this poem for me. We were in his office, which was, like, floor-to-ceiling books, and this high little window, absolutely no light. It was all very Gollum and the ring."

"What poem?"

"It's by Sharon Olds," she said, handing me the final page from her folder, a single-spaced printout of a poem titled "Why My Mother Made Me."

I read:

Maybe I am what she always wanted
my father as a woman,
maybe I am what she wanted to be
When she first saw him, tall and smart,
standing there in the college yard with the
hard male light of 1937 . . .

I stopped reading. "Nineteen thirty-seven?"

"I'm telling you, he was out of it," Janie said. "I felt bad for bothering him."

I nodded, skimming the rest of the poem, looking for clues, or some reference to prostitution. I got nothing.

I lie here now as I once lay
in the crook of her arm, her creature
and I feel her looking down into me the way
the maker of a sword gazes at his face
in the steel of the blade.

"What's it supposed to mean?"

"Probably nothing," Janie said. "I mean, the guy was like a jukebox. Press a button, a poem would come out."

"Did he have one for you?" I asked.

She ducked her head modestly and quoted, "She walks in beauty, like the night."

"Very nice." I swept the pictures and the poetry into the folder. "I can never thank you enough for doing all of this for me."

"Well, it's for me too. My story."

"If there is one," I grumbled. "It's probably going to turn out that the mailman did it." I got to my feet, shoving the folder into my WGBH tote bag, which I'd carried to prove that I was absolutely, positively not trying to impress Evan McKenna.

Janie stood up and put her hand on my shoulder. "Hey."

I looked up. "What?"

She looked deep into my eyes and solemnly intoned, "Do you ever have that not-so-fresh feeling?"

"Huh?"

She sighed, nudged me back down into a chair, and sat down. "I'm worried about you. Only I don't know how to talk about it. As you know, I'm not very maternal, so I've been watching television."

"You've been watching television commercials," I said.

Her eyes flashed. "And a *Hallmark Hall of Fame* movie, which I want credit for. Those are two hours of my life I'm never getting back." She grabbed my hands, looked into my eyes again, and said, "Seriously, Kate, I'm worried about you."

"I'm fine," I said.

"How are things with Ben?" she asked.

"They're fine."

"And the kids? No, wait, let me guess," she said, scowling at me with a look of absolute aggravation. "They're fine too."

I looked at my best friend, twisted a lock of hair around my finger, and came clean. "Ben told me I needed a hobby," I said. "He said I'm a housewife, not a detective."

"Oof."

"Do you think I need a hobby?"

Janie pulled off her glasses and folded them carefully in the cylindrical leather case that said Prada. "I think," she finally said. "I think that I want you to be careful. I think if anything ever happened to you, or your kids—"

"Janie!"

"Well, have they found Lexi Higgy-Whoosit yet?" she demanded.

"Hagen-Holdt," I said, and shook my head. "Nothing's going to happen to us," I said, but even as I spoke the words, I wasn't sure I believed them. There was a line of the poem stuck in my head. *A tall woman, stained, sour, sharp . . .* Was that Kitty? Was it me?

"I love you," Janie said, leaning across her desk to give me a hug. "I just want you to be safe. Safe and happy."

"Love you too," I said. But even as I was hugging her, even as I was thanking her for everything she'd done, I was glancing to be sure that the photographs and the mysterious poem were secure in my bag, and I knew that I wouldn't be able to stop now, not even if I wanted to.

THIRTY-FOUR

I got to the bar of the Time Hotel fifteen minutes before noon, when I'd arranged to meet Evan, and saw that we would have the place to ourselves. There were a dozen low, round tables, circles of polished stone surrounded by overstuffed, squishy rectangles. All of them were empty. The lights were low; the room felt warm after the wind outside. Two televisions hanging over the bar were tuned to celebrity poker. I checked my coat, put my hat and mittens in my bag next to Janie's file, went to the ladies' room, and studied myself in the mirror. The lights were unforgiving. My skin was sallow, my hair was a wreck, and the only thing I had in my purse to remedy the situation was a single tube of lipstick that could very well have dated back to the time when I'd still held out hope that Evan and I could someday be a couple. I sighed, wet a paper towel and rubbed it above my lip and underneath my eyes. Then I broke out the lipstick, carefully shaded my lips, then smeared some on my fingertip and adding a judicious swipe across the top of each cheekbone. I looked down at the lipstick, a pearly pink color, and wondered whether it could serve as eyeshadow too.

I risked another look in the mirror and wished I'd put on more makeup before I'd left the house. I wished I'd gotten my legs waxed. I wished I'd let Janie talk me into that Japanese hair-straightening treatment. I wished I'd worn a different outfit, something other than khaki cargo pants and a black sweater that I thought had looked pretty good when I'd left the house. I wished I'd had time to go shopping. I wished I hadn't let Sophie record over my Yoga for Weight Loss tape with *Elmo's Adventures in Grouchland.*

This is ridiculous, I thought. I was a grown-up, a married woman, the mother of three, not some foolish fourteen-year-old meeting her junior high crush in the band room during lunch. I popped a mint into my mouth, smoothed my hair, hummed several restorative bars of "I Am Woman," and pushed through the bathroom door.

Evan was standing at the bar green eyes shining, looking just the way I'd remembered him, most recently in sessions involving my shower nozzle, just the way he had, all those years ago, before he'd broken my heart, before the kids had come, before my husband had started making unilateral decisions about where we'd live and what I'd be permitted to do with my time. Before I became invisible. *Goodnight nobody.*

"Not much of a lunch crowd," I said as I made my way through the empty tables toward him.

"Kate," Evan said, and smiled, looking me over, taking me in. His hand was shaking slightly as he picked up his glass and walked toward a table in the back corner of the room. I eased myself down, feeling my face flush and my heart pound. Evan took the seat beside me and set his drink on a napkin.

"Whatcha got?" I asked.

He grinned at me. "You go first."

I shook my head. "Tell me about the Dolans," I said.

"Well, Kevin wasn't having an affair with Kitty. From everything I've been able to find out, he's completely devoted to his wife and has been since they got married."

I nodded, feeling disappointed that my theory about Kevin pining for Kitty wasn't true, but happy that at least one Upchurch marriage seemed to be on solid ground.

"However," Evan said, "Delphine Dolan doesn't exist."

"What?"

He pulled a piece of paper out of his pocket, a photocopy of a marriage license between Kevin Dolan and Debbie Farber.

"Debbie Farber?"

"Born in Hackensack, New Jersey. She must have changed her name, or just started calling herself Delphine." He refolded the piece of paper. "Now you go."

I wriggled around on my rectangle and told him about Lexi Hagen-Holdt's disappearance and about Ted Fitch—what he'd said, what he'd done, what I'd learned about him (leaving out that I'd learned it by sneaking into my husband's office under the pretense of redecorating).

"You think Kitty was a hooker?" Evan asked, as a waiter brought us glasses of water and I ordered what I knew would be an eight-dollar soda.

"I think that at one point in her life she might have been sleeping with men in exchange for things," I said, remembering the pearl earrings Dorie had told me about, and wondering why a woman like Kitty would have sold herself at all, and why she would have sold herself so cheaply.

"So, a hooker," said Evan.

"Not that official," I replied.

"What?" he asked. "She didn't join the union?"

I groaned and closed my eyes.

"Stop thinking so hard," he said, and placed one warm hand in the center of my back.

In my head, I shoved him away in a firm but good-natured fashion, I opened up Janie's folder, and we moved on to a further analysis of the men they'd both investigated. In my head, I pushed myself to my feet, picked up my bag, and thanked him with a brisk handshake and a promise to keep in touch. In my head, I caught a four o'clock train back to Upchurch, and made it home in time to prepare my family a healthful dinner of lean protein and whole grains, to bathe my children individually, scrubbing the tub in between each child, to read them bedtime stories, dispense hugs and kisses, and be in my own bed by ten o'clock, where I would rekindle marital relations with my husband in a flurry of apologies and promises of immediate improvement.

In real life, I let Evan tilt my head back. I closed my eyes and opened my mouth, and when he pressed his lips against mine, gently first, and then with more force, I kissed him back, leaning into his body, feeling the warmth of his skin, so close I could hear his heart beating, and it was just like I'd felt the first time he'd kissed me. The dim bar, the Time Hotel, Kitty Cavanaugh's murder and possibly illicit double life, the whole city, the whole world receded like a wave, leaving just the two of us with our arms around each other.

Evan drew back, breathing hard. "We could get a room," he said.

I pulled away. My lips were swollen, my cheeks felt flushed, my whole body was shaking with yearning, and I knew that if we stayed here another minute with him kissing me like that, I would lose all power to reason.

"No." I got unsteadily to my feet. "I can't."

"You can," he said, and held my hands. "You can do whatever you want. I wish . . ." His voice trailed off as I wiped my lips off with a paper napkin soaked in ice water. "I wish it had all happened differently with us."

If wishes were horses, then beggars would ride. I yanked my red wool hat down tight over my hair and slipped on my red wool mittens. The left one snagged on the stone of my engagement ring. "I have to go home."

He nodded. "Will you call me?"

"I . . ."

He stood up and readjusted my hat, then kissed the tip of my nose. "I'll be thinking about you," he said.

"Goodbye, Evan." I said, knowing that I'd be thinking about him too.

PART THREE

Goodnight Nobody

THIRTY-FIVE

Carol Gwinnell's house smelled like apple pie when I knocked on her door at five thirty. "Mommy!" my kids cried, pelting across her kitchen floor and wrapping their arms around my legs. Carol waved at me from the stove.

"Did you guys have fun?" I asked.

"Yes!" said Sam.

"Yes!" said Jack.

"Thank you for a lovely afternoon," Sophie said politely, before grabbing my hand and looking meaningfully toward the door.

"One second, honey. I just want to say thank you to Mrs. Gwinnell."

"Oh, you're welcome! Come any time!" Carol said. She lowered her voice as my kids pulled on their coats. "Nobody's heard anything about . . . anything. Call me when you get home, all right?"

"Do you think the same person who"—I dropped my voice to a whisper—"killed Kitty had something to do with Lexi too? Who did they know in common?"

Carol crinkled her nose, and her earrings chimed faintly. "Only everyone. Same school, same church, same friends, same pediatrician, same gym . . ." She peered past me, into her family room, where the television was tuned to CNN, with the volume muted. "I've got to get dinner started. Call me when you're home, okay?"

I promised that I would, then led the kids to the car, with Carol standing in her lit doorway, with a red-and-white gingham apron around her waist, watching us drive away.

"Charlie doesn't flush the toilet when he's done," Sophie whispered as I buckled her into her seat and handed her and each of the boys a single piece of Halloween candy that I'd kept in the glove compartment for an occasion just like this.

"Well, that's not very nice."

She waved her hand, already bored with the conversation. "Can I have kimchee for dinner?"

"Sure," I said. "Sure."

I got home, locked the doors behind us, and called Carol to check in. I fed the kids dinner (turkey hot dogs for the boys, kimchee that I'd mail-ordered from Zabar's for Sophie), gave everyone a bath, and read *Cinderella,* which the boys pretended not to like.

At eight-thirty, when everyone was sleeping, I took a shower, pulled on a baggy, frayed nightgown and a pair of touch-me-not panties with the elastic missing from one leg, and crept into the kids' bedrooms and made sure they were tucked in, sleeping, safe. When I slipped under my own covers and closed my eyes, I felt sure it was just for show, that I'd no more be able to sleep than I'd been able to keep myself from kissing Evan McKenna, but when I woke up, sleet was splattering against the windowpane, my kids were squabbling about something, and judging from the wrinkled pillow and crooked comforter on the guest room's bed, my husband had come and gone without my even noticing.

"Oh my God," Janie squealed on my cell phone. "You didn't!"

"I didn't," I said as my stomach rolled over lazily. I cut up slices of cinnamon toast and set the plate down in front of my children. The enormity of what I'd come so close to doing hadn't really hit me until that morning, but it had hit with a vengeance—either that, or the guilt had weakened my immune system. Ever since I'd woken up, my stomach had been aching and I'd been running to the toilet every ten minutes, much to my kids' amusement. "But I wanted to."

She paused. "I could still have him deported," she said.

"Don't worry. I'm never going to see him again." I'd decided that much on the train ride home. I wasn't cut out for adultery. I felt wretched, sick with guilt . . . and logistically, it wouldn't work. The sneaking around I was already doing had taxed me to the limit. There was no way I could think up any more fake excuses to get me into the city. Ben might buy that Dr. Morrison's office had lost my Pap smear once, but not twice.

"Do you still love him?" asked Janie.

I groaned in response.

"Do you still love Ben?" she asked.

I groaned even louder. "What does it matter?" I asked. "I'm married. I've got kids."

"I think that they let you get a divorce these days even if you do have children. Not that I'm encouraging you to get a divorce," she added hastily.

"Of course not," I said. I reached for my glass of flat seltzer and forced myself to take a sip. "It was a one-time-only thing," I said. "I needed his help."

"And he helped you."

I managed another sip of seltzer. Then I made my way to the bathroom on trembling legs and sat on the toilet, wondering how this had happened, how I'd turned, overnight, into the kind of woman I swore I'd never be. A liar. An almost cheater. Someone who'd toss away a marriage and break up a family for cheap thrills in a hotel. "He found out Delphine Dolan doesn't exist."

"Huh? She looked pretty real at your party."

"It's not her real name," I said. "She used to be Debbie Farber."

"Oh," Janie said. "Well, in that case, call Stan and tell him to arrest her right now."

I said goodbye, hung up the phone, and went back to the

kitchen, where the kids were squabbling about the crayons, or the dollhouse, or the identical books of stickers I'd bought them in New York. "No," Sophie screamed, waving a piece of toast like a judge's gavel. "No, you poopy baby, give it *back*!"

Kate Klein, this is your life, I thought, and tried to sort out the latest skirmish in the Crayola Wars.

I built a fire in the living room fireplace and played three games of Chutes and Ladders and four of Candy Land. I heated up canned chicken soup for lunch, knowing that every other mother in Upchurch, including my pie-baking pal Carol Gwinnell, was probably feeding her kids homemade.

When the weak sun broke through the clouds, I washed hands and faces, left the dishes in the sink, and piled everyone into the minivan. The ground was still wet, but the temperature had climbed into the low fifties, and there was a balmy wind blowing. I figured we should play while we could. The forecasts were already calling for six to eight inches of snow that weekend.

There were two news vans clustered at the corner of Apple Dell, where Lexi lived, and a third that I saw out of the corner of my eye parked in front of the Cavanaughs' house on Folly Farm Way. At the park, the Upchurch mommies stood in a tight knot by the swing set, talking in low voices, eyes constantly darting left and right to make sure no bundled-up pitchers with big ears were listening.

"Did you hear?" Rainey Wilkes asked. She had her daughter Lily crammed into a BabyBjörn, even though Lily was almost two—a good year and at least ten pounds over the recommended guidelines. Between her powder blue down snowsuit and the constraints of the Björn, poor Lily couldn't even wiggle her arms.

"Is it Lexi? Did anyone . . ." I swallowed hard. I couldn't bring myself to say *find her,* because it sounded like I was talking about a lost dog—or a body. "Did she come back?" I asked instead.

Rainey shook her head. "I heard they've called in the FBI.

They're searching the woods around her house." She paused, swallowed hard, and lowered her voice. "They've got dogs looking too. I saw them out this morning."

I pressed my mittened hand against my lips. I couldn't help but imagine Lexi the way I'd found Kitty—sprawled on her belly in a pool of cooling blood, a knife protruding from between her muscular shoulders.

I sank down on a bench. Sam and Jack, in the matching red tasseled caps Janie had bought them, were playing some kind of elaborate pirate game behind the swing sets. As I watched, they waved imaginary swords at each other and roared. Sophie, in her pink tasseled cap, had been roped into a round of hide-and-seek. Carol Gwinnell sat down beside me, clutching her embroidered purse in her lap.

"Rob wants to put the house on the market," she said. She reached into her bag, releasing a puff of patchouli scent, and I caught a glimpse of something unthinkable—a red and white pack of cigarettes. She pulled out a butterscotch candy, unwrapped it, and popped it in her mouth. "It's like everything's gone bad here." Her laughter was high and shrill. "I can't stop eating. I went through an entire bag of M&M's last night."

"Where will you go?"

She shrugged, crumpling the cellophane candy wrapper in her fist. "Maybe White Plains or New Canaan. Someplace with good schools, not too far from the city." She leaned in close. "We aren't the only ones," she said. "I called a Realtor and she said I was the third one so far, that day." She reached into her bag again. "Butterscotch?" she asked.

"Thanks." I sucked my candy, feeling miserable and numb, and listened to the whispers swirl around me, as the supermommies of Upchurch digested the new knowledge that their little Eden wasn't paradise after all. The truth was, the talk was almost comforting. It took me back to my days in New York, when the other mothers were as bewildered and exhausted as I was, where every week it seemed like someone else's marriage was in trouble, where husbands lost their jobs or complained ceaselessly about the ones they had, where wives entertained giggly crushes on their obstetricians or their plumbers or an old boyfriend who'd come back into town, looking better than he had a right to.

"Mommeeeee!"

Every single one of us whirled around. Sophie was crumpled at the base of the slide, clutching her stomach.

I got up and ran faster than I'd run in years, right through the steaming puddle a few feet in front of Sophie, and swept her into my arms.

"What? What happened?"

"My tummy is all bad," she moaned. Then she gagged and threw up, all over the shearling jacket I'd finally purchased so that I'd look just like everyone else on the playground.

"Oh, Soph, I'm sorry. Come on, let's get you home." I piled the three kids into the car. "Are you guys all right?" I asked Sam and Jack.

"Tummy hurts," Jack said. Sam clutched his belly and groaned. Oh, boy, was this going to be an action-packed afternoon.

I swung by the minimart and sat in the parking lot with my head in my hands. Bring the kids in? Leave them in a locked car for the two minutes it would take me to buy chicken broth and saltines?

I couldn't do it. I put the car in drive and headed home, where I spent the next four hours ferrying sick children in and out of the bathroom, washing clothes and sheets, and eventually, spot-treating the rug in the boys' room after Sam didn't make it to the bathroom in time.

By five o'clock, all three kids had fallen asleep. I transferred a load of laundry from the washer to the dryer, shucked off my foul-smelling sweater, and turned on my computer.

I told myself I was going to spend five minutes looking at the news—the *Upchurch Gazette*'s website, maybe even CNN.com—to see if there was any updates about missing mothers of Upchurch. "You have one new message," said my email. My heart stopped when I saw what was on top of my in-box. "From: Evan McKenna. To: Kate Klein. Subject: You."

As always, Evan was short and to the point. "I miss you," he'd written. "When can I see you?"

Oh, God. Oh, God. I hit delete, then hit empty trash, and then, for good measure, hit delete temporary files. Then I hit restart and waited for the computer to chug through its shutdown. I had to tell him to leave me alone. But what were the moral and ethical consequences of breaking my promise never to speak to him again in order to tell him that I never wanted to speak to him again?

I stood at the foot of the stairs, listening, and didn't hear a sound. So I took my cell phone into the garage, far enough away so that I felt I wasn't soiling my hearth with infidelity, but close enough to hear the kids if they needed me. I sat on the cold concrete with my back against the minivan. Finally, I punched in his number.

Evan answered on the first ring. "Kate," he said.

I felt my mouth tighten even as my knees trembled at the sound of my name in his mouth.

"Please don't email me," I blurted.

"O-kay," he drawled. "So how are we going to keep in touch? Smoke signals? Singing telegrams?"

"We're not going to keep in touch," I said. My delivery would have done credit to any number of kick-ass action movie heroines. I almost sounded like I meant it. "We have no reason to keep in touch."

"Not even for the simple exchange of information?"

I leaned against the car. "What kind of information?"

"A nice little tidbit about Delphine Dolan, aka Debbie Farber," he said. "It's good. And some information on your vanished neighbor."

"Tell me."

He chuckled. "I have to tell you, Kate, I'm feeling a little used here."

"Tell me!"

"Well, thing is, it's not as much of a 'tell' as it is a 'show.' Meet me at the end of your street at midnight tonight."

My mind whirled. "I can't . . . Ben's been coming home late . . . all the kids are sick . . ."

"Fine, then. Midnight tomorrow."

"Evan. Evan!" I was talking to a dial tone. "Shit." I turned to go back in the house. And there was Sophie, with Uglydoll, a plastic stethoscope looped around his neck, in her arms and strands of sweaty hair clinging to her cheeks.

"You said the S word," she said.

"I did," I said, feeling queasy with guilt. "That wasn't so good."

"Why are you in here?"

"I had to make a phone call, and I didn't want to wake you guys up." I took her hand. "Are the boys downstairs?"

She nodded gravely. "I said to color."

Sam and Jack were sitting at the kitchen table, coloring in unnatural silence. "Hi, guys!" My voice sounded too loud and too bright to my ears. "Is everyone feeling better?"

Wan nods from around the table.

"Is anyone ready for a snack?"

Sam shrugged. Jack nodded. "Rice Krispies treats?" asked Sophie.

Thank God she was still at an age where affection—or at least silence—could be bought for puffed rice and marshmallow goo. "You're not going to throw up anymore?"

Sophie answered for all of them, looking up at me soberly. "No, we won't."

I let Jack pour the Rice Krispies. Sam measured the Fluff. Sophie stirred, counting out loud with each turn of the spoon. "One, two, three, four, five, six, Evan." *Oh, God.* Had I heard her wrong?

Had she overheard me? What if she said it in front of Ben? Had I ever even told my husband I'd once hoped Evan would be more than friend? Or maybe I'd heard wrong because I was guilty and paranoid, and Sophie had said "seven" after all. But maybe—

"Mommy?"

Sophie stared up at me with the mixing bowl in her hand. "Sorry, honey," I said, and started spreading Rice Krispies treats into the pan.

THIRTY-SIX

"Hello?"

"Hello, is this Bonnie Verree?"

"Yes," said the voice on the other end of the line.

"I'm not sure you remember me. My name is Kate Klein."

"If you're happy and you know it, clap your hands," she said instantly. Okay. So she remembered.

"I'm sorry to bother you, ma'am." I was actually more sorry about a host of other transgressions, from my makeout session with Evan McKenna to turning her daughter's memorial service into a singalong, but no time for that now. It was Sunday morning. Ben and I had taken the kids to make-up music class, and Ben had actually offered to go in with them while I stayed back in the minivan with my cell phone. (I'd told him I wanted to make a few calls to the neighborhood ladies to see if there was any word on Lexi.) "I was wondering if I could talk to you about Kitty."

"Why?" she asked. "What else is there to say?" Her voice sharpened. "Is this about the ghostwriting?"

"No. It's about her."

I drew a question mark in my notebook. "I guess I feel responsible, in a way. I found her. And nobody's been arrested yet. And I . . ." This was the hard part. "I think that maybe we could have been friends. We had so much in common. We both used to live in New York."

"Kitty loved it there," Bonnie said. Her voice was wistful.

"Did you know she called Upchurch the Land of the Lost?"

"It doesn't surprise me," her mother said. Then she sighed. "We still live in Eastham. Same house Kitty grew up in. Call before you come, and we'll talk."

I thanked her profusely, hung up the phone, and was making notes of our conversation when there was a *tap-tap-tap* at the window. I jumped in my seat and bumped my head on the moon roof.

"Ow!"

I turned and found myself looking at the composed visage of Sukie Sutherland. She was tapping her manicure on my car window. I rolled it down halfway.

"Everything okay?" she asked.

I smiled weakly. My hands were shaking.

"Want some tea?" she asked, pushing her cup of herbal brew through the window. It smelled like boiled cat piss.

"No, I'm good." Sukie wore a cream wool hat and a matching muffler, an unpuked-upon shearling coat and high-heeled leather boots completely unsuitable for the snow.

Her smile widened. "Well, then. See you for the goodbye song."

"See you," I said. She waved her fingers and walked away. I sat in the driver's seat for another minute, wondering what excuse, gynecological or otherwise, I could conjure up to get a day's worth of time in Cape Cod.

That night I lay in bed, my insides knotted, a Ruth Rendell paperback in my hands, watching my husband, who'd made his triumphant return to the marital bed (or at least the marital bedroom), hang up his pants. He turned them upside down by the cuffs, shook them, studied them, then shook them again, making sure the creases were just so.

"How's your book?" he asked. His shoulder blades drew together underneath the white cotton of his undershirt.

"Fine. Thank you for taking the kids to class."

"You're welcome," he said stiffly. He gave the pants a final shake and clipped the cuffs to the hanger. "Do you think you'll be able to take in the dry cleaning this week?"

"Sure."

"I would appreciate that."

"Ben, come on!" I tossed my book to the foot of the bed. He picked it up, closed it, and set it neatly on the nightstand. I gathered my hair at the nape of my neck and said the four words that could stop strong men in their tracks: "We need to talk."

Ben's face was set as he hung his pants in the closet.

I breathed deeply and began the delicate process of tricking him into taking me where I needed to go. "I know things have been a little tense between us lately."

My husband snorted, perhaps in appreciation of my understatement. His expression was distant, his dark eyes looked sad. I blurted out the apology I'd rehearsed over Rice Krispies treats the day before. "I'm sorry that I got so caught up in the Kitty Cavanaugh thing." *And I'm sorry I lied to you about backing off, and I'm sorry I've been sneaking into New York behind your back, and oh yeah, I'm sorry I kissed Evan McKenna.*

The straight line of his back seemed to soften incrementally. "Well, I'm sorry too."

Sorry for what? For moving us out here, for being condescending about how I spent my time, for calling me a housewife in need of a hobby, for not looking at me or listening to me in weeks?

But if there was an elaboration, Ben wasn't sharing. He began the careful process of putting his shirt back on a hanger. Fine. Onward. I gathered the covers up around my chin, obscuring the low-cut nightgown I'd worn for the occasion, which didn't seem to be having its desired effect.

"I was thinking that it would be nice if we could go away somewhere for Thanksgiving."

His back stiffened again. "You just decided this now?"

"We could go somewhere close. Just a little trip. Maybe Vermont? We could see if any of those little bed-and-breakfasts have room. Or," I said casually, "have you ever been to Cape Cod?"

"Once," said Ben. "A long time ago. My father took me when I was a kid. We rented a canoe, I think." His expression softened, and I felt, if possible, even worse than I had when I didn't know I'd be trading on one of my husband's approximately three memories of his father, who'd died when he was just eight, to get a chance to talk to Kitty's parents on their home turf.

"I bet it's really quiet this time of year. We could walk on the beach. Build fires. The kids would like it. It's even educational!" I said, slipping in a little fact I'd picked up on the Internet that morning. "Did you know the pilgrims landed in Provincetown before Plymouth Rock?"

Ben seemed impressed. "Really?"

"Yeah. But then they decided it was too gay."

I thought I saw the hint of a smile before he shook his head. "It's really not a good time for me to go away." He walked into the bathroom and closed the door. "I've got too much ground to make up with Ted Fitch."

I winced. "But it's Thanksgiving!" I called. No answer. "Even politicians get to spend the day with their family!" Still nothing. "Or their mistresses!" Ben made no reply. I rolled over, balling my pillow underneath me. "Look, you always said, 'Just be patient, Kate, it won't be like this forever.' And I have been patient. But Sophie's going to start full-day kindergarten next year, and the boys are getting bigger, and we've never taken a vacation as a family." I lay there, listening to the *plick . . . plick . . . plick* sound of his flossing his teeth through the door, feeling lousy for invoking my children for my own nefarious purposes. Ben turned off the bathroom light, pulled on his pajama pants, and got into bed beside me.

"You know, Brian Davies has a house there, and he owes me one. I'll ask him about it in the morning."

"Great!" I said, and kissed one prickly cheek.

He rolled toward me, smiling. "Want to show me how grateful you are?" he asked, grabbing my left breast through my nightgown. As his fingers brushed my nipple, I felt Evan's lips against mine, his warm hand on my back. I pushed my husband away.

"I can't," I said.

Ben's expression of desire quickly became a frown.

"Because of the Pap smear," I explained. "I'm still bleeding a little bit . . . It's not a big deal, but you know. I'm still kind of crampy."

"Oh, oh, all right," he said hastily. I lay back, relieved and guilty, thinking that there was nothing like the the phrase *still kind of crampy* for stopping the male libido in its tracks.

"I'm sorry," I said. Ben didn't answer. A minute later, he was flat on his back, full lips parted, snoring.

I flipped my pillow over, then kicked at the comforter, searching for a comfortable spot and failing to find it. I looked at the clock. Eleven thirty-eight. *No,* I thought. *Absolutely not.* But it was as if my brain had left my body and was hovering somewhere overhead, near the imported Italian chandelier the decorator had chosen, watching as my body flung back the covers, tiptoed across the room, pulled on the cargo pants I'd left conveniently hanging over the back of the armchair beside our bed. *This isn't happening,* I thought, even as my body pulled on a long-sleeved pink T-shirt with a deep V neck and no bra underneath, and I tiptoed down the stairs.

I'll just talk to him, I told myself as I slid my sockless feet into my boots, shrugged on my shearling coat, disarmed the alarm at the front door, locked the door behind me, stepped into the frosty night air, and padded across the lawn. I'll just hear what he has to tell me, and then I'll tell him not to come again. That is, if he's even here.

But I couldn't stop my heart from beating faster when I saw the car with its lights off parked at the end of our cul-de-sac, couldn't stop myself from walking faster, then jogging, then running with my hair streaming behind me, breasts bouncing underneath my haphazardly cleaned shearling coat. I heard every little sound—my boots crunching through the crust of ice that had formed over the snow, my breath puffing out into the cold night air. I felt my blood singing as I got closer to the car. I saw Evan's face through the windshield, smiling in the faint light of the dashboard, and above him, I could see every star in the sky.

I had honestly intended to keep things businesslike. I'd imagined starting off with an absolutely unflirtatious "So, what've you got for me?" I'd certainly thought I'd at least keep my coat on. But when Evan opened the door, the look on his face was so tender, so full of desire, that I found myself with my coat unzipped and my tough-cookie question unasked, as he pulled me into in his arms.

"No," I said, after the first kiss. "Don't," I told him sternly as he slid his hands up my shirt and groaned to find my bare breasts. "Cut it out!" I managed, and wriggled back to the safety of the passenger's seat.

"Kate."

Both of us were breathing hard. The windows were silvery with condensation. I looked down to keep from looking at him—the flush of his cheeks, his black hair, his eyes, the blue-green almost swallowed by his pupils. That was when I saw the manila envelope with my name on it.

I swallowed hard once, then again, and finally managed to croak out the words in a low, rough voice, "What've you got for me?" They sounded a lot less businesslike than they had in my head.

"Lexi," he said. "Lexi Hagen-Holdt. I made some inquiries and hit pay dirt with the groundskeeper at Upchurch Country Day. Lexi went running every morning, when her son . . ." He pulled his notebook out of the glove compartment.

"Hadley," I supplied.

"Right. Hadley was in nursery school. Lexi would put the baby in a jogging stroller and she'd do six, seven miles. Except the two months before Kitty died, she started taking a little detour over to the school's equipment shed. There'd be a car in the parking lot. Blue Mercedes sedan, registered to—"

"Philip Cavanaugh," I said. I was imagining Lexi and Philip grappling with each other on top of folding gymnastic mats, surrounded by half-deflated basketballs and ripped volleyball nets while little Brierly slumbered in her stroller. Lexi would probably find all that sporting equipment a turn-on. "So where's Lexi now? Down in Miami Beach with Phil?"

He wiped his lips with the back of his hand. "No action on her credit cards since she disappeared. No calls from her phone. But that's not all . . ."

"What?"

"Delphine Dolan, née Debbie Farber. She's got a record."

"For what?"

"Solicitation." As soon as he said the word, I felt the hair at the back of my neck stand up. This was it. The missing link. "She was arrested three times in New York. Loitering, creating a public nuisance, and solicitation for the purposes of prostitution. And she did some editorial work under her former name." He flipped open the clasp of the envelope and slid a magazine into my hands. I peered down at the title. *Eager Beaver.* The spring '89 issue.

"Oh, my."

"Page thirty-seven," he said.

I flipped to the pertinent page and found an extremely naked Delphine Dolan, sporting a huge late '80s perm and a tiny stripe of pubic hair, posing with a pair of well-endowed, muscular fellows. The gentleman underneath her had a tattoo of a scorpion on his forearm, and the man to her right had a reddish brown mullet. When I flipped the page, Delphine had two of her fingers jammed in a place where ladies of refined breeding don't typically stick their digits—at least not when photographers are nearby.

"Keep going," said Evan. "She's got a tattoo of a heart on her *tuchus.*"

"Oh, lordie me," I said. Then, "So what now?"

"Get her alone. Ask her some questions," said Evan.

"She teaches Pilates," I said. "I bet I could sign up for a private lesson, have a little heart-to-heart with her."

"Just not when she's got you hooked up to one of those machines. You have to be careful."

I closed the magazine. "Can I keep this?"

He lifted an eyebrow. "Is married life that boring?"

"I . . ." I ran my fingers over the glossy words *Eager Beaver.* "I don't want to talk about married life," I finally said.

"Fine," he said. "Let's not talk." His fingers were warm against my cheek as he turned my face back toward him. I wanted to touch every inch of him—his ears, his chin, the silky skin of his neck. *Evan McKenna.* I could hear myself speaking his name in a voice I didn't recognize as my hands roamed across the span of his back and his hands tangled in my hair.

Suddenly, the world turned blood red and violet blue. There was a single angry *blip-blip* from behind us. I squinted through the fogged-up rearview window, but Evan figured it out faster. "Cops," he said, tugging my shirt down. "Let me handle this."

"No, Evan, let me . . ."

We opened our doors at the same time and went tumbling out into the cold darkness, me with my thin T-shirt barely pulled down, Evan with his plaid shirt unbuttoned three buttons too far.

Stan Bergeron regarded us in the glow of his flashlight. "Evening, Mrs. Borowitz."

I waved weakly.

"Mr. McKenna."

"Evening, Officer," he said.

"Stan, I can explain this," I said. At that moment, my copy of *Eager Beaver* slithered off the passenger's seat and fell out onto the road with a sad little flapping sound. Stan trained his flashlight on it. "I can explain that too!" I said frantically. "Delphine Dolan's in there!"

Stan considered the magazine. "I doubt she'd fit," he said.

I tried again. "Lexi Hagen-Holdt was having an affair with Philip Cavanaugh!"

Stan merely nodded. From the look on his face I could tell that this wasn't a revelation.

I tried again. "Do you know that Delphine Dolan changed her name and has a record of prostitution?"

Stan turned off his flashlight. "Do you know there's a curfew?"

"Huh?"

"A curfew. Nobody's supposed to be out after midnight, hanging around in parked cars." He shone his flashlight on Evan's license plate. "It's mostly for the teenagers." He wrote something in his notebook and shone the light on us again, taking in our dishabille.

"Mrs. Borowitz was just going home," said Evan.

"We were just talking," I said helplessly. I looked down and was horrified to see that I was wringing my hands. "And listen, Stan, if you run into Ben at the gas station, there's no real reason he has to know about this. Not that anything was going on. I mean, I know how this looks, but—"

"I'll walk you to your door, Kate," Evan said.

Stan shook his head. "No, sir. You're coming with me."

Evan stared at him, looking puzzled. "I just want to tell her goodnight."

Stan turned his flashlight on again. I heard a click, then a jingle, and I realized that he'd pulled out his handcuffs. "Either you come quietly," he said, "or I'll call for backup and we'll arrest you."

Evan's voice was incredulous. "What for?"

"There's the curfew, for starters," said Stan.

"You're going to arrest me for being out after midnight?"

"And your alibi," Stan continued.

"What about his alibi?" I asked.

"What about my alibi?" Evan echoed. "I told you where I was, I gave you my plane tickets, the receipts from the hotel—"

"Trouble is," Stan said, "the hotel said you weren't actually there all four nights. You were checked in all four nights, and you paid for all four nights, but I finally got someone in housekeeping to return my call, and it turns out that on the day of Kitty's death you never slept in the room."

My body went icy. I turned in slow motion and looked at Evan, who'd raised his hands. "It isn't what you think," I heard. And, "I was staying with a friend." And finally, the time-honored refrain of cheaters—and maybe killers—throughout time, the world over: "I can explain!"

"Why don't we get this sorted out at the station?" Stan asked. He turned back to me. "Goodnight, Mrs. Borowitz."

"Fine." Evan glared at Stan, then turned to me. "Don't worry, Kate. This is all a big misunderstanding."

I stared at him as Stan ushered him into the patrol car. "I'll call you!" Evan said softly. The car pulled away, leaving me standing there shivering in my unzipped winter coat, with Evan's car parked in front of my house and a pornographic magazine lying on the road beside it. Then I picked up the magazine, turned and ran across the yard, opened the door, rekeyed the alarm, and kicked off my boots. *Bad dream,* I whispered. *Bad dream, bad dream, bad dream,* I thought, as I crept up the stairs and made sure each of my children was still sleeping. In the morning, I peeked through the bedroom window with my heart hammering. Evan's car was gone, and my spirits lifted briefly as I indulged in a brief fantasy that maybe I'd imagined the whole thing. But when I pulled my coat on for another trip to the supermarket, *Eager Beaver* was still stuffed in my pocket, and the sleeves still smelled faintly of bile.

THIRTY-SEVEN

"Mommy!" said Sophie, straining forward as much as her car seat would let her.

I stifled a sigh, plastered a patient smile on my face, and turned around. "Yes, honey?"

"Jack and Sam want to know if we're there yet."

I turned around a little more to see both of the boys in question dozing in their respective seats. "Soph, they're sleeping."

"They told me," she said stubbornly. "They're curious." She'd learned the word *curious* the week before and had been using it almost constantly ever since. I bit my lip to hide my smile. Sophie had dressed Uglydoll in a pink crocheted bikini, even though I'd told her over and over that, while we were going to the beach, it was too cold to swim, and plus, wasn't the doll supposed to be a boy? "Look," I said, pulling out the TripTik that my husband was using to supplement the MapQuested directions. "We're on this road," I said, pointing at I-195. "We have to take it until we get to this road . . ." I pointed at Route 25. "Then we'll go over a big bridge."

Sophie's eyes got wide.

"And then we'll be in Cape Cod?"

"Yes, but we'll have to keep driving until we get to the part of Cape Cod where we're going to stay." I pointed to a blue dot on the map. "Truro. Right here, on the wrist of the arm."

"Oh." She considered this for a minute, then started kicking rhythmically at the driver's seat in the approximate vicinity of Ben's kidneys. I knew I should have told her to stop. Instead, I closed my eyes. I'd called Stan from the Red Wheel Barrow parking lot on Monday morning and learned that Evan had been released early that morning.

"So his alibi checked out?"

"Seems to have," Stan rumbled. "We'll be checking with a party in West Palm Beach."

"A party in West Palm Beach," I'd repeated, picturing a bronzed bombshell in a bikini.

Stan paused. "You're an adult," he finally said. "I don't want to tell you your business."

"Stan, nothing was happening, I swear—"

"Just be careful," he said. I promised him I would. Still, I'd spent what felt like every waking minute thinking about Evan, while Ben put in fourteen-hour days in an effort to ensure that Ted Fitch wouldn't bolt and that he'd be able to take a four-day weekend. What if the last seven years of my life (and the three kids who'd come during them) had all been a mistake? What if I was supposed to be with Evan all along? What if he was all those things the love songs were about: my one and only? Then I heard Janie's voice in my head, telling me that Evan was interested only in the chase, the thing he couldn't have, whether that was me or Michelle or somebody else. And what was I supposed to do about it now?

I closed my eyes. When I opened them again, we were pulling down a steep, curving driveway surrounded by bare brown branches dusted with snow.

"Here we are!" said Ben as he rolled up to the garage of a big modern house that looked like three gray shoeboxes turned on their sides.

I looked at the oversized sliding glass front door. "Are you sure?"

"Here." He passed me a sheet of paper with a printed picture of the house. I consulted the photograph, then looked at the house, its grayed, weathered façade broken here and there by oversized square windows. "Yup, that's it." I paused. "Cheerful place."

"Brian says the house turns its back on the world," Ben said, putting the car in park. All three kids had fallen asleep. We sat quietly for a minute, listening to the ticks of the cooling engine and the wind. "It's beautiful inside," he said.

"I'll take Brian's word for it," I said, getting out of the seat and inspecting the empty garden beds, divided into neat rectangles and covered with mulch, each one absolutely empty.

"Come on," said Ben. He'd gathered all the suitcases and duffel bags and our six bags of groceries, including a twenty-pound turkey, and started ferrying them to the front door. He must have made up his mind, or written himself a memo—*Try harder with wife*—because he'd been on his best behavior for the entire ride up. He'd stopped before I'd asked him to, purchased my preferred traveling snacks (Dunkin' Donuts coffee and roasted sunflower seeds), and kept the kids entertained by singing along to every song on *Dogs Playing Polka.*

"I'll bring everything inside. Why don't you go explore."

"Okay." I crunched across the gravel path and slid open the sliding front door. There were three bedrooms downstairs, linked by a hallway of creamy tile. Sunshine spilled through the doors and through the oversized windows in each of the bedrooms, making warm golden squares along the floor.

I climbed the stairs. "Oh, wow." The entire second story—living room, kitchen, dining room—were all one open space lined with floor-to-ceiling sliding glass doors that looked over the blue-green water of Cape Cod Bay.

"Look at that view," Ben said. I jumped a little as his cheek brushed against my neck.

"Our bedroom should be down this hall." He took my hand and led me into a big, high-ceilinged room. To my right more sliding glass doors looked out over the empty garden beds and the rolling green hills we'd driven through to get here. To my left, through another wall of doors and high windows, was a small deck, with a double chaise longue. Beyond that was the water again, gentle waves lapping at a shore lined with seaweed and driftwood. "And look at this!"

The bedroom had its own bathroom, with a sunken Jacuzzi big enough for two, and a toilet in its own snug little stall. "You can poop while you're looking at the ocean," I said.

Ben's hands slid off my shoulders. "That was beautifully put, my bride."

Getting rid of the rest of my family the morning after Thanksgiving hadn't turned out to be hard at all. I'd told Ben I needed a few hours to scrub the pots and pans and maybe take a walk. He'd nodded approvingly. "Don't work too hard," he said, causing the fishhook of guilt that had taken up permanent residence in my chest to give a painful twist. "Take a break," he told me and kissed my cheek. "Everything was delicious." I managed a weak smile as he piled the kids into the car for a trip to the pirate museum in Provincetown. As soon as the minivan had pulled out of the driveway I dumped half a bottle of detergent into the turkey pan and the dish I'd used to bake Ben's mother's sweet-potato-and-marshmallow casserole, filled the sink with hot water, and picked up the telephone.

"We're right on the border of Wellfleet and Eastham," Bonnie Verree told me.

"Could I walk there?"

She considered. "Maybe ride a bike," she said, and told me how to get there. "It'll take you half an hour," she said.

"Give me an hour," I said. "I have to make sure I remember how to ride a bike."

I imagined I could see her smiling as she answered, "Some things you don't forget."

Gone for bike ride, I wrote on a note that I stuck on the refrigerator. I dashed to the bedroom, pulled on the jeans and sweatshirt and hiking boots I'd packed, along with my freshly cleaned shearling coat, my red wool hat and wool mittens. Thank God the bike I'd glimpsed in the garage had air in its tires and a recently oiled chain. I pushed it up the steep driveway with the cold air stinging my cheeks, swung my leg over the seat, and wobbled away, gaining speed as I coasted down a narrow ribbon of blacktop lined with towering brown-leafed trees and blueberry bushes.

After ten minutes I pulled off my hat and mittens. Ten minutes after that, breathing hard at the crest of a hill, I took off my coat and bundled it onto a rack over the rear tire with a bungee cord the last rider had left there. Fifteen minutes more and I was coasting down another long hill with my hair flying behind me, made a sharp left, and pedaled through Wellfleet's tiny downtown, out to Route 6, then onto a bike path, which led one to the Verrees' back door.

Bonnie and Hugh lived in a little Cape Cod–style house with silvery cedar shingles. The kitchen's fake-brick linoleum floors and yellow Formica countertops, the dark wood kitchen table and Tiffany-style light fixtures looked to be circa 1975, but everything was neat and clean, and there was strong coffee brewing in the battered percolator. The paintings on the walls were in the same style as the one I'd seen in Kitty's living room: bright, representational seascapes in rich, inviting colors—deep azure blue of the ocean, golden sand, bright red and orange umbrellas, white seagulls punctuating the sky.

Bonnie set a basket of blueberry muffins on the table. "Frozen berries," she said, as I gathered my sweaty hair into a bun at the nape of my neck. "I picked them myself last summer." She poured coffee into a pair of heavy clay mugs and sat across from me at her table, looking at me expectantly.

"I've found out some things about your daughter," I began, and wrapped my hands around the mug. "Some of them are . . . well, they're a little . . ."

She nodded, bending her head as if readying herself for the guillotine. She wore a loose-fitting purple jumper, a white turtleneck, a necklace of rough-hewn purple stones, thick blue wool socks underneath leather sandals. Her eyes looked wary, and her face was set in tense lines, as if she was awaiting more bad news. "Go on," she said.

"It looks as though . . . that is, some people are saying . . ."

"Just tell me," Bonnie urged. "I don't think there's anything I can hear that'll make me feel any worse."

Don't bet on it. "I think that she might have been involved in prostitution."

Bonnie stared at me with her blue eyes wide. Then she bent over sharply at the waist. I saw her shoulders shaking, heard the tiny gasping sounds she made. It wasn't until she straightened up, wiping her eyes, that I saw that she hadn't been crying at all. She was laughing.

"Kitty?" she gasped, her round frame shaking with mirth. "My Kitty? Prostitution? Oh . . . oh, that's just . . . oh my," she said, and doubled over again, leaving me sitting in a spool chair, blushing furiously, completely without a clue.

When Bonnie finally regained her composure and wiped her eyes, she told me she was sorry. She could see, she told me gravely, that I must have put a lot of thought into my investigation. She was even pretty sure how I'd been misled. "The older men, right?" she asked.

I nodded dumbly.

Bonnie sighed and wiped her eyes again. "She wasn't having sex with them, and she wasn't taking their money. Whatever else she might have been, Kitty was the most moral person I ever knew. She never wanted a single thing from any of those men except the truth," she said, and pushed herself back from the table, walked over to the coffeepot, and refilled her cup.

"The truth about what?"

Bonnie sat down heavily at the table and said, "Kitty was looking for her father."

I think my jaw must have dropped as the pieces fell into place:

Kitty's unwillingness to tell Dorie what she was really after with those older men; Kitty crying over lunch with Ted Fitch; Joel Asch looking at me with what I now knew must have been regret on his face, looking at me and saying that it wasn't what I thought, that, after all, he was old enough to be her—

"Father," I said. I looked at Bonnie. "But . . ."

She shook her head shortly. "Kitty wasn't mine," she said. "She was my sister Judith's daughter."

There were about a hundred questions I wanted to ask. I settled on the most obvious. "Do the police know?"

Bonnie nodded.

"What happened?"

Bonnie ran her fingers over her necklace. "This was the sixties," she began, "which I think should explain a lot of what I'm going to tell you." She lifted the stones from her chest, then let them fall back again. "My father—our father—was a police officer. Officer Medeiros. Very strict. Judith and I had to be home by ten on school nights, eleven on weekends; we couldn't date until we were sixteen; we couldn't drive, couldn't go anywhere unsupervised, couldn't do anything . . ." She shook her head. "It didn't bother me much: I was a homebody, even back then, and I didn't have boys beating down my door. But Judy . . ." She sighed and shook her head again, and I thought I saw Kitty in that pained, rueful gesture.

"How about your mother?" I asked.

"Gone," said Bonnie. "Breast cancer. Judy was eleven, and I was nine."

"I'm sorry," I murmured, and tilted the coffee in my cup.

She nodded. "I think my father wouldn't have held on so tightly if he wasn't afraid of losing us. And that's what happened with my sister. The tighter he held on, the more he told her no, the more she'd just find another way. She'd climb out her window and smoke cigarettes on the roof, or she'd sneak out the cellar door and go to parties with her friends. When she was eighteen, she left for good."

"To New York," I guessed, and Bonnie nodded.

"She wanted to be a painter." She pointed at the pictures on the wall. "All of these were hers."

I studied the pictures more carefully. All of them were seascapes, with turquoise water and honey-colored sand, views of the ocean at sunrise, or during the daytime, dotted with umbrellas. None of them had any people. There was just the sea and the sand and the birds in the sky.

"Could she make a living at it?"

Bonnie sighed. "On the Cape? I think so. She could have found a gallery in Wellfleet or Provincetown to show her work. She would have done fine. Judy was beautiful." Bonnie said. "She had long dark hair, almost to her waist, and she was tall with a nice figure. That might have made up for some of what she was lacking in talent. She was good for here, but I don't think she was good enough for New York." She rubbed her fingers against the red-and-white checked tablecloth. "I think there are a lot of beautiful girls in the world, and a lot of them moved to New York City in the 1960s wanting to be artists or singers or actresses or models or something. Judy's paintings were good, but they weren't very fashionable. Everyone was doing abstracts. None of the galleries wanted pretty pictures of the ocean. If she'd researched it ahead of time . . ." Bonnie sighed. "Well. Judy never thought about the odds. She dropped out of high school as soon as she turned eighteen and went to live in the Village. It broke my father's heart . . . but it was about the most romantic thing any of our friends could imagine."

Even almost forty years after the fact, I could hear bitterness in Bonnie's voice, sadness mixed with a little sister's grudging admiration for what her big sister had gotten away with.

"Here," said Bonnie, pulling a photograph out of a drawer at a wooden desk against the wall. I looked and saw a tall, slender girl with long dark hair like Kitty's. She wore a peasant blouse that dipped low enough to show off her smooth, tanned skin and a miniskirt cut high enough to show coltish legs.

"That was taken when she was seventeen," Bonnie said.

"So what happened in New York?" I asked. "Did she support herself?"

Bonnie shrugged. "My father sent her money, but I wasn't supposed to know about that." I wasn't sure whether she could hear the bitterness in her voice. "Judy sent letters home to us, about the walk-up she was living in, her roommates, the restaurants where she was working. She'd send postcards with pictures of the city—Central Park, the Empire State Building." She stretched out her hand for the photograph. I gave it to her, and she slid it back into the drawer. "She lasted seven years down there, and when she came home, she was six months pregnant."

"Had she gotten married in New York?"

Bonnie shook her head. "Judy talked a good game about how marriage was an instrument of the bourgeois oppressor, how she wanted to experience different men the same way she wanted to experience different cities, how she never wanted to be tied down, but I shared a room with her. I was the one who heard her crying at night. After a while, she told me that she'd fallen in love with the baby's father, but that there were complications." She ran her hands through her silvery curls. "He was a very important man, she said. And married, but trying to get out of it. Once he did, they'd be together. He loved her, she told me, and she knew they'd be together." Her voice cracked, and she pressed her hands against her eyes.

"Did you . . ." I began.

Bonnie shook her head. "She never told me his name." She straightened her shoulders. "I wish I had a picture of Judy when she was pregnant with Kitty," she said. "She never got bloated or blotchy or had her fingers swell. I know it's a cliché, but she just glowed. Like she'd swallowed one of those candles she was always burning, or like she knew some secret, some big, delicious secret that she'd never have to tell."

"Wow." I'd never glowed when I was pregnant. The best I'd been able to manage was a certain fresh-scrubbed, rosy-cheeked look, usually after I'd splashed cold water on my face after a vigorous bout of vomiting.

Bonnie sighed. "Even nine months pregnant, there wasn't a boy we'd known in high school who didn't want to take her out. They'd stop by the house with treats for her—scented candles, journals, an embroidered pillow she'd seen in some head shop in Hyannis, a crate full of lobsters—"

I must have made a face, because Bonnie looked at me sharply and said, "Lobsters aren't free. And that was what Judy wanted when she was pregnant. Not ice cream and pickles, but lobster with lemon juice." She smoothed the tablecloth again. "She didn't care for any of them. She was just waiting for the man back in New York City. And after she had Kitty, as soon as she was able, she left the baby here and went back to New York."

I couldn't believe it. "She just left?"

Bonnie shrugged. "Her big-shot boyfriend was paying her rent in the Village. He wanted her there to be available for him. She went back to wait."

"He wanted her, but not the baby," I said.

The table trembled as Bonnie got abruptly to her feet and put her mug in the sink. Weak wintry light filtered in through the white cotton curtains at the window, etching the lines of her face in shadow. "Judy was a fool," she said roughly. "She thought he really would leave his wife and marry her and give Kitty his last name. She died believing that."

"What happened?" I asked, even though the pain in the pit of my stomach was telling me that I already knew how the story had ended.

"When Kitty was seven . . ." Her voice caught in her throat. "Oh, you should have seen the two of them together. Kitty loved her mother so much. She would just light up when Judy came home, and whatever Aunt Judy gave her—a little plastic snow globe with the Empire State Building inside of it, or a mug that said 'I Love

New York'—she'd act like it was treasure. She'd sleep with Judy's things next to her pillow."

I nodded, feeling my eyelids prickle, seeing my own children in my mind, the way they'd go running to the door whenever Aunt Janie arrived with gifts.

"We gave her an allowance. Two dollars a week. She never spent a penny of it. We'd take her to the penny-candy stores in Provincetown, or to the mall in Hyannis, and she'd never buy herself a single thing. She'd make birthday cards for me and Hugh, she'd make our Christmas presents. Hugh used to tease her. He called her his little miser. But I knew what the money was for. When she was old enough, she told me, she was going to buy a bus ticket to go to New York City and live with her Aunt Judy."

"Did Kitty know that Judy was her mother?"

She slumped in her chair. Even her gray curls and the straps of her dress seemed to droop. "We always meant to tell her," she said. "When she was old enough to understand. Hugh and I just never could agree on when that was. Kitty found out when she was twelve. One of my father's old friends told her," she said bitterly. "Came over for Christmas, got in his cups, and said it was high time that Kitty knew the truth."

"How did she take it?"

"She was angry. She asked why we'd lied to her. Then she asked why her mother didn't want her," Bonnie said. "What was I supposed to tell her? What was the answer to that? Judy was dead by then." She looked down at her hands. "She died of an overdose. Heroin."

"Oh," I said.

Bonnie's eyes shone with unshed tears, and her lips trembled as she spoke in a monotone. "The police told us it was an accident or maybe . . . maybe not an accident. They told us the drug hadn't been cut, that she'd taken enough to kill a dozen men. It never made sense to me," she said, shaking her head. "I know Judy did some . . . some things that weren't legal. I know she smoked pot, I know she took mushrooms, but heroin never made sense. She was so afraid of needles. She'd faint in the pediatrician's office every time she had to have a shot, and that week—the week she died . . ." She pulled a fistful of tissues out of her pocket and used one of them to blow her nose. "She called me and told me that he was finally going to be with her, and I found a postcard in her purse after she . . . after she." She gulped, wrapping her arms around her chest. "That she was happy. That they were going to be together."

Together, I thought, remembering the postcard I'd pulled out of Kitty's desk drawer. *We are finally together. Happier than I can even believe.*

"What was his name?" I asked.

Bonnie shook her head. "She never told me," she said. "And once she was . . . after she . . ." She gathered herself. "Once Judy was gone, we waited for someone to come to the apartment . . . or the funeral." She brushed angrily at her eyes. "Maybe he was lying to her. Maybe Judy just got tired of waiting. No matter what happened, Kitty was never the same after she found out. We lost her," she said. "She got good grades, didn't cut class, didn't run around with boys, but it was like living with a boarder. She barely spoke to us, and when she did, all she wanted to talk about was Judy—where she'd been, who she'd known, how she'd lived, how she'd died. There was always a coolness toward me, and she was even worse with Hugh—like she blamed him more for not being straight with her. I don't think she ever really trusted anyone after that. Not us, certainly. Not her husband. No one," she said, as her voice trembled, then broke. "No one except her girls. They'd come here . . . in the summer . . ." She was sobbing now, gasping between her words, like Sam or Jack or Sophie after they'd fallen down and gotten hurt. "I took them to the beach, I took them swimming, we'd pick blueberries and go clamming . . ." She covered her eyes with her small, shaking hands and sat there for a moment, breathing deeply, until she could look at me again.

"Kitty made it her mission to find him," she said.

I nodded, remembering the words of the poem Emmett James had recited to Janie: *"I lie here now as I once lay/in the crook of her arm, her creature/and I feel her/looking down into me the way the/maker of a sword gazes at his face in the/steel of the blade."* Kitty had grown up to become her mother's sword.

"She'd ask me questions, over the years: did I recognize this name or that one; did I remember if Judy ever went away for vacations," Bonnie said. "I knew what she was getting at. If there was a man who'd taken her mother's life—directly or indirectly—well, then, that man should pay." She rocked back and forth in her chair and twirled her beads around her finger again.

"Was Joel Asch one of the possibilities?"

"He was," said Bonnie, nodding. "He'd known Judy in the Village. And even after Kitty told me that he wasn't, she said he was good to her. He must have felt responsible, somehow—like he couldn't save Judy, but he could help her daughter. You know he gave Kitty a job." She shifted in her chair, smoothing her dress around her hips.

"The columns," I said. "The ghostwriting."

" 'The Good Mother,' " said Bonnie, shaking her head. "I think that maybe it soothed something inside of her to write those things about mothers who left. She loved Judith, but how could she not have been angry? Her own mother left her. I think that would be a hard thing for any child to think about."

It was my turn to nod, remembering some of the invective in "The Good Mother," the gleefully venomous way it eviscerated women who felt it was acceptable, even laudable, to work outside the home, to leave your babies for even an instant, to deprive them of an endless soak in the warm bath of mother-love.

"Hugh was furious about those columns—after all, I'd worked. I told him what Kitty said—that writing 'The Good Mother' was cathartic. And it was the means to an end," Bonnie said. She wiped at her eyes. "She told me, the week before she died, that she'd found out something big. That she'd come to the end of it. I told her to be careful. Kitty promised me she knew what she was doing . . ." She shrugged helplessly, her voice breaking. "I should have told her not to," she said. "I was as much of a mother as Kitty ever had. I should have told her that the past was the past and her future—her girls—they were what mattered. I should have made her stop."

THIRTY-EIGHT

"Mommy, Mommy!"

I wheeled the bike down the driveway and saw Sophie stagger across the deck, straining to carry a purple plastic bucket with water sloshing over the top and onto her jeans and puffy purple down coat, with one brother on each side. Her hair was in pigtails, and her fingernails were each painted a different shade of pink. "Daddy took us to a bakery after the museum and we had hot chocolate and crullers and sticky buns and then we went down to the beach and I got a baby crab and now we're making leftover turkey sandwiches!"

"Excellent!" I said, bending down for a look. I had ridden home thinking of Kitty like some Greek goddess, tall and noble, striding through the streets of Manhattan. I pictured New York City's movers and shakers clutching Kitty's hands with their moist palms, lifting her glossy chocolate hair to admire the pale curve of her neck, while she looked them over, taking inventory, looking for the tilt of her own eyebrows or the shape of her nose, eyes shining and expectant as she spoke her mother's name.

"Her name is Princess Fiona," Sophie said.

"Great, but how do you know she's a girl?"

Sophie considered the question, then considered the crab. "Because she is beautiful. Mommy, can she come home with us?"

"Well, maybe she can stay up on the porch while we're in Cape Cod, but I don't think she'd like Connecticut."

"Why not?"

"Well, she'd miss the ocean, don't you think?"

Sophie scratched her nose, then bent over the bucket. "Princess Fiona, would you miss the ocean?" she asked.

Ben smiled at me wearily from behind the glass door. Three hours later, once each sandy child had been stripped, showered, dressed, fed, and put down in one of the darkened downstairs bedrooms for a nap, Ben and I sat together on the couch, in the living room overlooking the ocean. He'd lit a fire in the fireplace, and we were almost but not quite holding hands.

"Am I still in the doghouse?" I asked.

"Some doghouse," he said, and sipped from a mug of whiskey-laced coffee. The waves rolled in and out, and above them, white clouds, tinged faintly pink, floated low in the periwinkle blue sky. The sunset was sure to be spectacular. I turned my own cup in my hands. The whiskey and the warmth of the fire after the brisk bike ride were making me sleepy. I wished I could stretch out on the couch underneath a blanket, turn off all the thoughts about Kitty Cavanaugh and Delphine Dolan, Bonnie Verree and her sister Judith, not to mention Evan McKenna, and just drift.

Ben set his cup down on the coffee table. "Kate, there's something I want to discuss with you."

My heart froze. *He knows.* Someone saw me at the Time Hotel, or spotted Evan's car at the end of our street. I swallowed hard and tried to prepare for the accusation, delivered in a dry and toneless voice; followed by reiteration of his quite reasonable demands of a helpmeet and spouse (not to get involved in harebrained murder mysteries, à la meddling kids in *Scooby-Doo,* not to almost have sex with guys I'd known back in New York, not to fling accusations of murder at his most prominent clients or make up lies to cover for any of the above).

"What's that?" I managed to ask.

Ben turned toward me, setting one hand on my upper arm. "I've been feeling bad about giving you such a hard time with the Kitty

Cavanaugh thing." He slid his arm around my shoulder. "You miss using your mind," he said. "I understand that."

"I love being a mother," I said reflexively.

"But the kids are kids," Ben said. He patted my shoulder. "There's only so far a conversation with a four-year-old will get you." I held my breath as he nuzzled my cheek. "So here's what I've been thinking," he said. "How would you like to come work for me part-time?"

"I . . ." I pulled myself out of his arms and stared at him, certain that I'd heard wrong. "What? What would I do? I haven't exactly endeared myself to Ted Fitch. And I don't really know anything about politics."

"Well, it's not rocket science," he said with an indulgent chuckle. "You could answer the phone, help with the mail—"

"Help with the mail," I repeated. "So I'd basically be, what? An intern?"

Ben's expression—and the speed with which his hands made their retreat—suggested he was beginning to appreciate the magnitude of his error. "Oh, no, not an intern. You'd be sitting in on all of the strategy meetings, helping to implement the media plans—"

"Lucky me!" I said lightly. "Now, would I bring coffee too, or is that someone else's job?"

He turned away, sighing. "Kate, I'm trying to help you. I'm trying to help us."

"I just don't think it would be a good idea, me working for you. Besides, politics really isn't my thing."

"What was your thing, exactly?" Ben asked. "Dead celebrities?"

"Genital warts, actually," I said.

"Okay," he said stiffly. "Why don't you go lie down for a while? Relax. Take a nap."

I eased the bedroom door shut, lay down on the salmon-and-turquoise cover, closed my eyes and tried to let the whiskey do its work. Fifteen minutes later, when Ben slipped onto the bed beside me, I kept my eyes closed and my breathing slow and even.

"I love you, Kate," he whispered. I murmured sleepy nonsense words back. The space between us seemed to stretch out until it was as wide as the ocean outside the windows. I held myself still until I felt him sigh and roll off the bed. After he closed the door I counted to one hundred before pulling my cell phone out of my pocket and tiptoeing into the bathroom to make my call.

"Dude, I can barely hear you," Janie complained when she answered.

"I know," I said. "The reception here is really bad." So bad that I'd ended up crouching in the center of the Jacuzzi tub before I'd gotten enough of a signal to make the call. "Can you check something for me?" I asked, and told her everything Bonnie had told me, including Judith Medeiros's last name and the year and circumstances of her death. "You've got friends in the police department, right?"

"But of course," said Janie. "I've got all the major precincts covered. Let me guess: you want to find out if her accidental death was really accidental."

"Anything," I said. "I want to find out anything. And are you by any chance free on Monday morning?"

"You know I don't like Mondays," said Janie. "Or mornings."

"Trust me," I said, heaving myself out of the tub. "It's for a good cause."

THIRTY-NINE

I hadn't spent more than ten minutes in Delphine Dolan's nine a.m. Monday morning Pilates mat class before I knew that I was going to die there. Judging from the panting and wheezing beside me, my best friend was going to die right along with me.

"Toes pointed, fingertips straight, please, squeeze ze core, head up, and one! Two! Three!"

"How many do we do?" I grunted at Marybeth Coe, who was on her back beside me.

"A hundred," she said serenely. I couldn't help but notice that she wasn't panting or sweating or turning purple and looking like she wanted to die. She just had a nice healthy glow. "That's the name of the exercise. The hundred."

"Nine! Ten! Eleven!"

My midsection was on fire as I fluttered my arms up and down. I'd never felt pain like this. Not even during labor with Sophie. Not even the first time I'd coughed after my C-section with the twins.

"Eighteen! Nineteen! Twenty!"

Delphine Dolan stalked up and down the rows of supine women, clad in a black capri-length catsuit so tight that I thought if I stared hard enough I'd be able to see her tattoo. A complicated arrangement of straps stretched across her taut shoulders and tanned, lean back, leaving her slender arms bare. Her shiny brown hair was in a French twist, of course, and not one drop of sweat had made its way through her foundation. The nails of her long, prehensile toes were painted pale pink, and a thick circle of diamonds glittered on her ring finger. She'd come a long way since Hackensack.

"Thirty-one! Thirty-two! Thirty-three!"

"Merde," Janie gasped, shooting me a look that let me know I'd pay for dragging her out of Manhattan to the workout from hell.

"Forty-six! Forty-seven! Forty-eight!"

My plan had been to take one class, then corner Delphine in the parking lot or the locker room and ask her some questions about Kitty. Clearly, that plan needed revising. After class, assuming I survived that long, I wouldn't be in a position to corner anyone. I'd probably have to be carried out on a stretcher.

"Sixty-three! Sixty-four! Sixty-five!"

I tried to distract myself by focusing on Sukie Sutherland's legs—long and lean, with perfectly pedicured toes. Where, I wondered, for the millionth time since I'd moved to Upchurch, where did these women find the time?

"Eight-eight! Eighty-nine! Ninety!"

Please, God, I prayed as I pumped my arms. *Please don't let me die in a Pilates studio in Connecticut surrounded by women I can't stand.*

"And . . . one hundred! Arms over head, deep inhale up, and slowly exhale, and sit up," Delphine commanded. We did, all fourteen of us. I noticed, with some dismay, that I was the only one who'd sweated through my sports bra. "Arms over head again, deep breaths . . ." I stretched and breathed, then reached forward, as Janie pushed herself onto her hands and knees. She hung there for a moment, wavering, then collapsed back down on the mat.

"C'est fini?" she whispered.

"I think so," I whispered back. Sukie Sutherland shot us a dirty look. I pretended not to notice as we stretched. "You okay?"

Janie nodded, although she looked a little green. Delphine sashayed across the room, long legs pumping, bent over, giving us all a view of her admirable ass, and punched a button on the CD player. As the soothing strains of Enya filled the room, she dimmed the lights, bade us *"Au revoir,"* and exited through the door to the locker room.

I pushed myself to my feet. My arms felt like overcooked spaghetti; my legs felt like Jell-O, and my midriff ached so profoundly that I found myself taking shallow breaths to avoid the agony of a full-on inhalation. "Janie!" I hissed.

She was flopped forward, belly-down on her mat. "Can't . . . move," she said weakly. "You . . . go on . . . without me. Needs . . . of the many . . . outweigh . . . needs . . . of the few."

"For God's sake," I whispered, grabbing her hands and yanking her onto her feet, a move I was certain hurt me more than it hurt her.

We pushed through the swinging door that led to the mauve and pink locker room. Delphine Dolan was standing in front of the row of sinks and the floor-to-ceiling mirror behind them, unpinning her hair. The catsuit lay in a tangled bundle at her feet. She was absolutely naked.

"'Allo, Kate!" she called cheerfully, as if we'd been out for a Sunday afternoon stroll, as if we were both fully clothed and she hadn't spent the last hour and fifteen minutes trying to kill me. " 'ow did you like the class?"

"It was something," I managed to say, trying desperately to avoid my own sweaty, sweatpanted reflection in the mirror. Delphine Dolan had the most perfect body I'd ever seen: creamy skin, perky breasts, a slender waist, thighs without a hint of a ripple or pucker, and pubic hair that was still waxed into a tiny landing strip. I had a moment's panic when I didn't see the little heart tattoo I'd noticed on the pages of *Eager Beaver,* but then I saw that in the place where it had been in the picture was a patch of poreless, shiny skin. She'd probably had it lasered away. Maybe around the time she decided to be French. "Do you have a minute? There's something I wanted to ask you about."

"What's that?"

"Kitty Cavanaugh," I said. "It'll only take a few minutes."

"A few minutes"—Delphine favored me with a kindly smile, perhaps because my face was still the color of an eggplant—"*alors,* I do not have." She looked pointedly at the clock above the changing room door. "I must meet Kevin for *le brunch.*"

Le brunch. Okay. There was laying it on thick, and then there was laying it on with a trowel.

"Maybe some ozzer time?" Delphine said, charming smile still in place.

"Maybe now," said Janie. "Debbie."

Delphine's smile wobbled. *"Pardon?"* she said, tilting her head at what she probably thought was an inquisitive and charming angle. I saw her eyes flick toward the door. She was probably trying to make sure that we were still alone in the locker room and nobody had heard what Janie had just called her.

"Debbie Farber," Janie recited, snapping the straps of her black and purple scoop-neck shirt that matched her purple and black yoga pants. "Born nineteen seventy-two in Hackensack, New Jersey. Dropped out of high school at fifteen. First arrested at sixteen. Shoplifting, grand theft auto, assault with a deadly weapon, loitering for the purposes of prostitution."

"It was my mother's car!" Delphine muttered, and there wasn't a trace of Paris in her accent. It was now juiciest New Jersey. "She just reported it missing because her new husband hated my guts! And I wasn't a prostitute!" She lifted her head and glared at us, and when she spoke it was with enormous, if slightly misplaced, dignity. "I was an *escort.*"

Janie's snort reverberated throughout the locker room. I elbowed her, then said, "We don't care about that. We just want to talk to you about Kitty. You knew her."

Delphine clasped her hands in front of her breasts as if she'd just realized that she was naked.

"Come with us," said Janie. "Quick cup of coffee. Won't take a minute."

Delphine raised her head. Displeasure had twisted her fine features into an ugly mask. "And what if I won't?"

"Then," Janie said, "we'll tell a few of your clients with little asses and big mouths what your real name is, and what you used to do for a living. Maybe they'll be a little more impressed than we are with the distinction between 'prostitute' and 'escort.' " She handed Delphine her cell phone. "Call your husband and tell him you're going to be late for *le brunch.*"

"Look," said Delphine twenty minutes later, slender forearms folded on an orange plastic table. She'd refused to go anywhere in Upchurch, had nixed Greenwich and turned Darien down flat, so we were sitting in a booth at a McDonald's in Lakeville, just off I-84. I'd treated myself to a hot apple pie. Janie had ordered a Big Mac and fries. Delphine had declined coffee, tea, bottled water, and a sip of the eggnog-flavored milkshake I'd bought to go with my pie and was sitting with nothing in front of her except for a paper napkin.

"Kitty got in touch with me regarding one of my clients back in New York," she said.

"Who?" Janie and I asked at the same time.

Delphine shook her head. "Doesn't matter. He wasn't who she was looking for, and he had a stroke five years ago. He's not your guy. You know about . . ." She let her voice trail off.

I nodded. "Bonnie told me."

"Bonnie," Delphine said. Her eyes were clear underneath the mascara and her voice without its French accent was pleasant and low. "She was nice. Kitty and I went up there for Thanksgiving once, when we both lived in New York." She wrapped her hands around her elbows. "I used to tell her that I had a father and believe me, he was no picnic. But she couldn't stop looking. For her, it was like"—she pulled two fresh napkins from the dispenser and started shredding them—"a compulsion. Like she couldn't help herself."

"So how did the two of you wind up here?" I asked.

"We were friends in the city," Delphine said. "We'd go to the gym together, and we'd go out after for a coffee or a smoothie, and we'd talk. She was nice."

Delphine's face was drawn as she spun her diamond ring around her finger.

"I tried to help her," she said, lowering her eyes. "Sometimes in . . . in my line of work I'd come across the name of a man Kitty was interested in, and I'd set up a meeting. She'd help me out too. She helped me get health insurance, and when I got in"—she toyed with a tendril of glossy hair, then with the strap of her catsuit—"in some trouble once, she helped take care of it. She said girls like us needed to look out for each other."

"Girls like us?" I repeated.

Delphine nodded as her slender fingers worked at the napkins, tearing them into confetti. "You know. Girls who were alone in the world."

"So you met each other in New York," I prompted.

"And then she met Philip through his father. She had to interview him for some piece she was researching about reforms in insurance law. She and Philip got married, and they introduced me to Kevin." A genuine smile played around her lips for an instant at the thought of her husband. "I went for speech classes and everything so I'd sound—you know. Like I fit in here. But I didn't do so well at them, so . . ." She shrugged. "Now I'm French!"

"How nice for you," said Janie.

I glared at her as Delphine lifted her index finger to her mouth and started nibbling at the nail, looking all of sixteen. "I should have done better by her. I told her she was too good for him, but she didn't want to hear it."

"Why?" asked Janie. "Why was she too good for him?"

"Because he cheated on her constantly," said Delphine. "Cheated on her. Lied to her. Slept with anything with a pulse while she supported them. He . . ." She lowered her eyes, and I took a guess.

"He hit on you?"

"On everyone," she said in a flat voice. "And she wouldn't leave.

She said her girls deserved two parents who loved them and lived together, and that no matter what happened, she wouldn't leave. I told her he was making a fool of her. I said that instead of wasting her time chasing after some father who obviously didn't want to be found she should have been paying attention to her husband and her girls. After that . . ." Delphine pressed the pads of her fingertips against the delicate skin beneath her eyes. "Things were never right between us after that." She patted her eyes and looked down at the shredded remains of her napkin. "I pray for her," she said. "Every night. I pray that before she died, she found what she was looking for."

"Well, that was a whole load of nothing," I complained, as soon as Janie and I had dropped Delphine off at her studio and were alone in the car again.

"Au contraire, ma soeur," said Janie. "For one thing, it's always interesting to spend time with a working girl. For another, she gave us a major clue." She grinned at me, pulled into the Brookfield Bagels parking lot, and whipped out her cell phone.

"What?" I demanded. "What clue?"

" 'Some piece about insurance law,' " Janie quoted. "Please. Even *Content,* which is Sominex on a page, wouldn't print anything that dull. What was the name of Kitty's husband's business?" When I told her she punched in the number for information. "Yes, in Connecticut a listing for Upchurch Marine Insurance?" She paused as she was connected, then told the receptionist, "Hi, I'm calling for Philip Cavanaugh?" She paused, then spoke once more. "Senior," she said.

My entire body broke out in goose bumps. "You think maybe Philip's father . . ."

Janie held up one finger for silence. "Hello, my name is Janie Segal of the carpet Segals. Do you insure dinghies?

"Oh Lord," I groaned.

"As soon as possible," Janie said crisply. "Yes, three o'clock will be fine. I'll see you then." She hung up the phone and I stared at her with my mouth hanging open.

"Do you think that maybe he was *her* father too? Do you think that she and Philip . . . oh, my God."

"It's extremely *Flowers in the Attic,*" Janie said. She applied lipstick, then smacked her lips together and flipped the mirror shut.

I sank back into the passenger's seat. "Oh . . . my . . . God."

"Buck up, little camper," said Janie, swinging out of the parking lot. "I'm making us an appointment, and we're going in."

"So!" said Philip Cavanaugh Senior, settling his bulk behind his burled walnut desk three hours later and smiling at us with teeth so white and even that they could only be dentures. His face was a preview of coming attractions, a glimpse at what his son would look like thirty years down the road—the blue eyes rheumy and bloodshot, the hint of a gut blossomed into actuality, and sagging jowls flushed with broken capillaries. His suit was expensive but threadbare; one of the shoelaces on his worn black wingtips had broken and been tied into a knot. "You're having . . ." He pulled on half-moon spectacles and peered down at the form Janie had filled out. He'd missed a spot shaving that morning; there was a strip of gray stubble on his chin. "A dinghy insurance emergency?"

While he looked at Janie, I looked around. I'd expected more of a maritime theme in the office—a pirate flag fluttering in front, maybe, or crisp white and navy pillows on the couch, or windows shaped like portholes. At least a few nautical touches. Instead, Philip Senior had gone for rich guy generic: heavy dark wood, paneled walls and leather, with a humidor in the corner. It would have been impressive, save for the fact that business clearly wasn't booming. The secretary's desk out front was empty except for a rotary-style telephone. The waiting room was empty, and the walls were bare except for pale squares where pictures used to hang. The only car in the parking lot was the ten-year-old Jaguar I recognized from Kitty's memorial.

"Not really," Janie said. "My dinghy's actually insured already."

He blinked at us. His eyes were set deep into twin pouches of flesh, and threaded with red. "Oh?"

"We were hoping to speak with you about your daughter-in-law," I said.

He pulled off his half-moon glasses and polished them on his tie. When he replaced them, his gaze had sharpened. "I recognize you now," he told me. "You're the young lady who spoke at Kitty's service."

I bit my lip and nodded.

Janie jumped right in. "Were you Kitty's father? Because, honestly, if you were, and then she married your son, not to judge, but—"

"Janie!" I hissed.

Philip Cavanaugh's liverish lips worked for a minute, and his bulky body seemed to deflate inside his suit. "I wasn't," he said.

"But you could have been," I said.

He seemed to gather himself, straightening his back and glaring at me. "I knew her, but only briefly. Kitty told me that her mother had had a long-term involvement. Judy and I . . ." he shook his heavy head. "It wasn't a lengthy thing."

"Tell me how Kitty found you," I said.

He shook his head heavily. "The same way you did. The phone book. She came to see me nine or ten years ago, telling me she needed background for an article. We had offices in New York then . . ." He looked around unhappily, as if he were just then realizing that he didn't have those offices anymore. "She asked intelligent questions. Took notes. At the end of an hour, she slid an envelope across the table. There was a photograph inside."

"Judith," I said.

He nodded slowly. "We had been acquainted. Back in New York."

"So what happened then?" asked Janie.

"Kitty asked me to take a blood test," Philip Cavanaugh Senior said. "She told me that her intentions were honorable—that she wasn't after money, just information. Medical background and what-not." He looked up at us slyly. "Well, of course I had my suspicions."

"You thought it was a shakedown," said Janie.

He nodded unhappily. "I told Kitty I needed time to think. Explained that it would be awkward: I'd already been married to Flora, of course, and we'd had Philip. As soon as she left, I got on the phone with my lawyer. Eric Brannon. Old family friend. I told him the specifics of the situation. He drafted an agreement, sent it overnight."

"What did it say?"

"That she promised not to sue me," Philip said. He pulled off his glasses again and looked at me like that should have been self-evident. "That if I was the . . . er. Uh." He gathered himself, face flushed, jowls wobbling. "Father. If I was, I'd make an effort to . . . I believe the agreement said 'integrate her into the family unit.' "

I nodded, wondering how well that would have gone. *Hi, Flora! Hi, Phil! Meet my love child from the sixties!*

"The agreement also promised, er, certain financial recompense. She turned me down. She wasn't interested. Not in the money, not in meeting anyone. She just wanted to know the truth."

He walked over to the cut-glass decanters on a dark oak table beside the humidor and poured himself a slug of Scotch. "It was all moot. The blood test came back negative," he said, with relief still visible on his face. "I told her I was sorry. She took the news well enough, I thought. Didn't cry or get emotional. She shook my hand and thanked me for my time. I should have known . . ." His voice trailed off again. "I was so relieved, you see, not to be the . . . that it wasn't me. I should have known I was getting off too easily."

"What happened?" asked Janie.

Philip Senior adjusted his bulk. "My son came into the office that day and saw her," he said.

"Ah." I could imagine how that would have gone—Philip Cavanaugh Jr. walking into his father's office and seeing tall, slender Kitty, with her blue eyes and shining hair. And what would she have seen, looking at him? A man who'd grown up with every luxury, every privilege—a mother and a father; money, and the comforts it could buy. He would have looked at her with longing, with lust. She would have looked at him and thought, *He has my place in the world. That's where I belong.* "Love at first sight," I said.

"For my son," Philip Senior said, nodding sadly. "He chased her. Even when he was going with other girls, she was the one he really wanted. And he got her," he said heavily, and shook his head again.

"And then, it all went wrong," Janie intoned, in the manner of a VH-1 *Behind the Music* narrator.

Philip appeared not to notice. Maybe he wasn't a *Behind the Music* fan. "I don't know how he ever convinced her—what he said that made her think that he was what she wanted, that Upchurch was what she wanted. But one day we were all having brunch at the club—Flora, my wife, and Philip, and some little girlfriend he was with—and in comes Kitty. She walks right up to him like there's nobody else in the room—like there's nobody else in the world—and she says, 'I accept.' I didn't even know he'd proposed." He shook his head, fumbling with his glasses.

I could imagine that scene too—Kitty in a linen dress, bittersweet brown hair in a flippy ponytail, stepping lightly in high-heeled sandals. She'd look around at the people, at the china and the crystal, the gold watches and diamond rings, the sedans in the parking lot. She would consider the heavy carpets and the chandeliers and the clipped greens of the golf course through the window, and maybe she'd imagine her mother's life and death, the promise someone had made to her, then broken, and how her own life, and her childrens' lives, would never be like that with a man like Philip Cavanaugh by her side.

"I should have warned him," Philip said bleakly. "I should have told him that there was history. Night after night, I lie awake and think of what I could have done . . . My poor granddaughters." He glared at us, his mottled cheeks flushed and his heavy hands splayed on his desk. "Did you get what you came for, young ladies?" he asked, in a voice laced with sarcasm and sadness.

"All we want to know is who killed her," I said.

He shook his head. "Not me, if that's what you're thinking. And if you want my best guess, it's this: Kitty was looking for her father, and she found him. Or he found her."

I stared at him until he snorted and pushed his blotter across his empty desk. "The police have checked my alibi. And I have no motive. She was my son's wife. My daughter-in-law. The mother of my grandchildren."

"She was also a threat to your reputation," I pointed out. "Kitty was born in 1969. You were already married to Flora when you were acquainted with Judy Medeiros."

"It would have been embarrassing," he admitted. "But I would have survived. Men do." He swept one thick pink palm across his leather blotter. *True enough,* I thought.

FORTY

That night at the dinner table, Ben poked his fork suspiciously into his pasta, twirling a few strands around its tines. "Was this frozen?" he asked.

I nodded. He sighed, probably adding another black mark to the growing column underneath my name. *Doesn't listen. Isn't thin. Puts children in danger. Serves Trader Joe's heat-and-eat fettuccine Alfredo to me after a hard day at the office.*

I looked at him. His eyes were tired, and he had a strand of pasta stuck to his chin. "It's not bad," he said. He reached across the table, trying to take my hand, but only succeeded in knocking over Sophie's milk.

"Daddy!" she said, scowling at him. I got up for the paper towels. Janie tossed me a sponge and Ben poured Sophie more milk, then bent down to help me with the cleanup. The boys, giggling, decided that the sight of their parents on their hands and knees swabbing up two percent was the absolute height of hilarity and dumped their glasses out too. "Boys," I said. I straightened up and knocked my head on the edge of the table, sending Janie's Diet Coke tumbling onto my head.

"Ow! Fuck!" I said, wiping soda out of my eyes.

"Mommy said the *F* word," Sophie announced.

"Kate, are you all right?" asked Janie, bending down with concern on her face and a sponge in her hand.

"How do people drink this stuff?" I asked, picking up the empty can and picturing the first person I'd interviewed: Laura Lynn, her spindly hand shooting through the door, her emaciated frame and crisped hair, her ice bucket full of the very beverage currently blinding me, and the silver-framed picture front and center on the living room bookshelf. A picture of her father.

"Flowers in the Attic," I said softly. "Oh, my God."

"What, Kate? What is it?" Janie asked.

"Are you all right?" asked Ben.

"Not a brother, but a sister," I babbled. "Do you remember Bo Baird?"

"He was on the list Kitty gave . . . on Kitty's list," Janie said, wisely reluctant to invoke Evan's name in front of my husband.

I jumped to my feet. "And Tara Singh told me there'd been rumors about Laura Lynn having some kind of breakdown after her father's death."

Ben thrust three fingers in the air. "How many fingers do you see?"

"Bo Baird!" I repeated, and ran past him to my laptop, which I'd left set up in the breakfast nook. "Ben, were there ever any rumors about him and an out-of-wedlock child? Or using drugs? Heroin?"

"What?" Ben followed after me, still with the gallon of milk in his hands. "Kate, slow down! Who's Tara Singh?"

I ignored him. "He died in a hotel room in Boston with another woman, right?"

"Should I call an ambulance? Are you having double vision?"

I looked up from the keyboard long enough to glare at him. "My head is fine and I'm asking you a question!"

He put the milk down on the island in the middle of the kitchen and began speaking in a dry, lecturing-to-the-freshmen voice. "Bo Baird was infamous for his infidelities, but I never heard anything about an illegitimate child or heroin. Now tell me what you're talking about, or I'm calling the doctor."

"She's Kitty's half sister," I muttered. It all made sense. Kitty wasn't just Laura Lynn's ghostwriter, she was her half sister and, coincidentally, a walking, talking condemnation of everything two generations of conservatives stood for, the illegitimate sister of a woman who thought single mothers signaled the end of Western civilization—as well as a fellow writer with a legitimate claim on her seven-figure book advance. I snatched my keys and purse from the breakfast bar. "Come on, Janie!" I called. Janie picked up her purse from the breakfast bar and ran after me as the kids stared.

"I'll be back soon! Drink your milk, kids! And, um, brush your teeth, and don't give your father a hard time!" I ran for the garage door with Ben on my heels.

"Where are you going?" He grabbed my shoulder and spun me around, and I couldn't come up with a single thing to tell him. Loose filling? Female trouble? Jury duty that I'd just remembered at six thirty on a Monday night?

Janie placed one hand calmly on his cheek. "Something suddenly came up," she said.

"We have to go," I said. I wrenched myself free and threw myself behind the wheel of the car. As I pulled out of the garage and zoomed down the driveway, Ben was standing in the doorway, watching me. His hands were in his pockets, and there was a look I couldn't read on his face.

Laura Lynn Baird opened her door, saw my face, and started to close it. Janie jammed her stiletto-clad foot inside. "Let us in or we're calling the cops."

"And telling them what?" Laura Lynn demanded in her clipped voice. "I should call the cops on you."

"Never mind the cops. We'll call the press," I said. "We'll tell them that Bo Baird fathered a child out of wedlock."

Maybe it was wishful thinking, but I saw the blood drain from Laura Lynn's face. "You're crazy," she said, baring her lips so that I could see her teeth before she shoved the door shut. I pushed back, remembering Kitty's body on the kitchen floor, her two little girls saying, *She was the best mother in the world.*

"How'd it feel to have your own sister killed?" I asked. "I bet that would make a hell of a story for *Content.*"

Laura Lynn's scrawny body sagged against the doorjamb. "She wasn't . . . I didn't . . ."

Janie pushed past me, then grabbed Laura Lynn's arm and goose-stepped the smaller, scrawny woman into the living room, where all three wide-screen TVs were on, one tuned to CNN, one playing MSNBC, the third frozen on a close-up of Laura Lynn's own face. "Ma!" Laura Lynn screeched in the direction of the stairs. "Give the baby his bath!"

Ma shouted back something I couldn't hear. In the living room Laura Lynn, breathing hard, positioned herself on the couch. She was wearing another in her series of Chanel suits—this one was caramel, with gold-colored fringe—but her feet were bare. There was chipped pink polish on her toes. Her stiff, processed blond hair hung in sticky spikes around her shoulders, and her face, bare of makeup, was an unhealthy red that spoke of a recent chemical peel.

Janie faced her as I stepped behind the couch and started asking questions. "What happened, Laura? Did Kitty tell you who she was? Did she say she wanted her own byline or more of the book advance money? Or maybe," I mused, as she turned on the couch, staring at me, "she was just going to write her own book. Tell her own story. A hell of a story. Right-wing newspaper magnate as the father she never knew, half sister who's a media princess, mother whose death might not have been an accident. How long until she turned into the one all the TV shows wanted to talk to?"

Laura Lynn tugged at her stiff-as-straw hair and glared at us without saying a word.

"She was your half sister," I repeated. Laura Lynn's lip curled.

"She was competition," said Janie.

"And so I killed her? That's what you two think?" She snorted. "You need to get out more." She got to her feet, blond hair obscuring radiation-red cheeks. "Why don't you start right now?"

"Fine," said Janie, easily grabbing the cordless telephone next to Laura Lynn's monogrammed ice bucket. "I think we'll just make a few calls first. The newspapers, maybe a few of those television talk shows. Or maybe," she said, extending the phone toward Laura, "I should let you go first. Why don't you give a holler to Ma upstairs. Give her a little heads-up so she can get ready for another go-round with the late-night talk shows." She pursed her lips thoughtfully. "I wonder if Judith Medeiros let your father wear her clothes too?"

Laura Lynn's eyes filled with tears. She brushed them away fiercely. "That's enough," she said. She snatched a remote control off the coffee table, waved it at the TV sets, flicked them all into blackness, and popped the top off a can of Diet Coke.

"I knew she was looking for something the first day we met," she said, wiping her mouth with the fringed sleeve of her jacket. "It was supposed to be a job interview, and all she wanted to hear about was my life. Did I have brothers and sisters, where did we go on vacations, did I ever live in New York? I didn't want to answer, but she was Joel's darling. I didn't have a choice."

Janie leaned against the bookcase and opened Laura Lynn's copy of some conservative woman's book of dating tips for God-fearing girls. "How did you figure out what Kitty really wanted to know?" she asked, flipping through the pages.

Laura Lynn kicked the bottom of the couch with her bare heel, like a little kid who'd been sent to time-out. "She told me that her mother and my father . . ." She groped for her soda, raised the can to her lips, and gulped. "I didn't believe her at first," she said. "She told me to go home and ask him. I said forget it, my father wasn't well, and I wasn't going to do anything to put his health in jeopardy. She said if I wouldn't, she'd drive up there and do it herself. I told her she'd never get through the front door."

"So then what?" asked Janie.

For the first time since we'd barged through her door, Laura Lynn seemed to falter. "I . . . my father . . . I didn't want to put him through that, through some stranger showing up with those kinds of accusations. So I lied to him," she said. "I told him my doctor needed a blood sample for my family history. He and I went into town together, saw his doctor, and I went back to New York with a blood sample. And lo and behold . . ." She crossed the room and slid one of the televisions away from the wall, revealing a safe. She twirled the tumblers and opened the door. There was an envelope inside, and a paperback book bound in plain red paper. Laura Lynn pulled both items out—I caught the words "uncorrected proofs" on the cover of the book, and the dual byline she'd spoken of: "by Laura Lynn Baird and Katherine Cavanaugh." She opened the envelope and extracted a single sheet of paper, yellow, a carbon copy of a form from Lenox Hill Hospital that had been written in triplicate.

"See here?" She pointed to a line in the center of the page and read the words in a voice rich with triumph. "Results negative."

I felt my heart contract as I scanned the form and found Bo's name, and Kitty's. "Oh."

"Yeah. Oh," she said, snatching the page out of my hand. "You can show yourselves out."

Her tone was just as furious as it had been when we'd shown up, but her face looked fragile and exhausted, like a little girl playing dress-up in her mother's suit; a little girl in need of nothing more than a good shampoo and a nap. When she plunked back on the couch, I saw that the soles of her feet were dirty. I looked at the date on the page.

"This was six years ago," I said.

She nodded.

"So if you knew that Kitty wasn't related, why let her keep working for you?"

She looked down at her lap. "I felt sorry for her, I guess. She was so perfect, so smart, but when she got going about her mother, she just . . ." She fluttered her thin hands in front of her. "Cracked. Here.

Keep this." She handed me the book. I saw the words *The Good Mother* written on the front cover in heavy black ink above Kitty's name. "I told you the truth. She was a good writer. Probably she was a good mother too."

"Too bad," said Janie as we pulled out of Laura Lynn's driveway and into the icy black night. I squeezed my eyes shut, shivering, and groaned out loud.

"What am I going to tell Ben?"

"Let me handle that," Janie said.

I shook my head, cringing at the excuse that she'd concoct, but it turned out that I didn't need to worry. By the time we pulled into the garage, the house was dark, the doors were locked, all three children were sleeping, and the master bedroom was empty. Ben had apparently chosen the guest bedroom again over the pleasure of my company, and by the time I woke up the next morning, he was gone.

By ten o'clock I'd pulled on jeans and a sweatshirt I'd plucked from the basket of unwashed laundry, dropped my kids off at Sukie Sutherland's for a playdate, and mixed a pitcher of extra-strength, very spicy Bloody Marys. Janie and I spent the morning sitting at the kitchen table, drinking.

"It's too bad," said Janie, shaking more Tabasco sauce into our glasses. "It would have been so cool if Philip was her husband . . . her brother . . . her husband . . . her brother."

I took a long sip, then pushed my glass away. Sukie said she'd take the kids until two, but it wouldn't do for me to show up tipsy and fall even further in the Upchurch mothers' esteem. If such a thing were even possible.

"Or if Laura Lynn was her sister," Janie said. "That would have worked for me too."

"Not Philip Cavanaugh," I said. "Not Bo Baird. Not Joel Asch. Not Ted Fitch. What do I do now? Just walk around New York City trying to figure out who else Judy Medeiros slept with?"

"You know I love you," said Janie. "But if that's your plan, you're on your own." She lifted her glass in a toast. "That woman had some social life."

I cut a lime into wedges and squeezed juice in my glass. "What about Judy? Have the cops told you anything?"

"It was a cold case—well, actually it was barely a case at all. Single white female and would-be artist dying with a needle in her arm didn't exactly raise eyebrows in Greenwich Village in the seventies. The coroner's report did say that she didn't have track marks . . ."

"You saw the coroner's report?"

Janie flashed me a satisfied smile.

"Can you get them to reopen the case?"

Ice cubes rattled against each other as she stirred her drink. "I'm trying."

"Maybe Evan's got more names," I said. The thought of starting from scratch, finding more men, tracking them down, asking them questions, had exhausted me before I'd begun.

"Let's start at the very beginning," Janie said. "Why do people murder? Love or money. Crimes of passion or crimes of . . . of being broke."

"Very eloquent," I sighed, feeling so drained from the disappointment and the liquor and the previous day's Pilates that even breathing was an effort. I crossed my arms on the table and rested my head against them.

"You know what? Go take a bath," said Janie. "I'll fetch the little ones."

"Are you sure?" I asked as I scrabbled for my keys and tossed them across the table.

"As long as she doesn't start talking about her nipples, I'm good. Go," said Janie, and shooed me toward the stairs.

Five minutes later, Janie backed the minivan cautiously down the driveway. Five minutes after that, I called *Content,* and this time, the snotty receptionist put me right through.

"I spent Thanksgiving in Cape Cod," I told Joel Asch. "I talked to Bonnie Verree. She told me what Kitty was looking for."

The line hummed almost imperceptibly while Joel Asch said nothing. I imagined him sitting behind a desk like the one I'd occupied at *New York Night,* some battle-scarred, scuffed-metal thing, and closing his eyes.

"I was a fool," he said roughly. "She was so *interested* in me . . ." He went silent again. My mind continued to add details to his desk; a sleek silver laptop, a fancy little stereo, a few framed pictures of his wife and kids. "I was flattered," he finally said. "And . . . oh, hell, I'll admit it. I wanted her. And I went after her. Until she told me why she was so interested. Then I felt like a fool." He laughed bitterly. "Which was only fair. I'd certainly been acting like one."

"But you tried to help her."

"I tried to be good to her," Joel said. "And I couldn't do much. A name here and there . . . an introduction to Laura Lynn Baird . . ."

And a pair of pearl earrings, I thought. My heart twisted as I imagined my own father, who would have done anything for me; who'd wanted to come to Connecticut the minute he thought I might have been in danger. I'd looked at Kitty on the playground and thought that she had everything, never guessing that I had the thing she wanted most.

"We're closing the issue tonight," Joel said, jolting me back to reality. "If there's anything else I can do for you."

"Thank you," I told him. I hung up the phone and plodded upstairs to take a bath.

Twenty minutes later, I lay in the oversized soaking tub for two that I'd only used once since we'd moved in, staring at the snow splattering onto the skylight, feeling like a complete and utter failure. Thanksgiving was over; Christmas was coming. The Red Wheel Barrow nursery school would close its doors for most of December, which meant all kids, all the time, and effectively spelled the end of my free time and my investigation. Kitty's murder was still unsolved. Kitty's paternity, and her mother's death, were still mysteries, Lexi Hagen-Holdt was still missing, and I had no idea who'd put the threatening note on my car. All of the work and worry, and all I had to show for it was one idiotic memorial speech, one imperiled marriage, and one situation involving an extremely persistent, frequently irresistible other man that I had no idea how to resolve.

So Delphine had been a hooker, I thought, as I idly loofahed my legs, and Kevin Dolan had turned out to be a suburban Pygmalion. So Kitty had been searching for her father, and answers about her mother's death, among the rich and powerful men of New York City. So my husband's client had been one of the potential daddies, and Bo Baird and Philip Cavanaugh Senior had been too.

"Love," I said. "Money." I held my breath and slid under the water, letting my hair billow around my shoulders. It all added up to a great big steaming heap of nothing. Except for Janie. At least she'd leave Upchurch with a great story. Lucky Janie. At least she got to leave.

My cell phone trilled from where I'd left it on the towel rack. I stretched my arm out of the tub and snagged it. "Hi, Janie."

"Enjoying yourself?"

I shut my eyes. "More or less."

"Good. We're stringing cranberries and popcorn for holiday garlands." She dropped her voice. "It's boring as fuck, but luckily your kids are easily amused."

"Fine. Have fun!" I tried to sound enthusiastic, and failed. "I'll see you later."

I lay back in the water and thought about the women of Upchurch, the high-test supermommies who would never really be my friends. I pictured Kitty on the playground, squatting in front of my children, her dark brown hair and classic features illuminated by the sun. Then I imagined Kitty walking into that country club, long legs scissoring underneath her dress, taking in the scene with her pansy-blue eyes, looking at Philip and Flora and Philip Junior, smoothing her skirt and smiling, sitting down in the chair that had been pulled out for her, taking her place, her rightful place, right between Philip and—

"Oh, my God." I sat bolt upright, sending water cascading down in sheets onto the tile floor, and I stumbled out of the tub, groping for the telephone.

Philip Cavanaugh Senior didn't sound happy to hear from me. I didn't care.

"I just have one more question," I said, standing naked in the bathroom, while water streamed down my shoulders and puddled at my feet.

He laughed thickly. "Sure, why not?"

"When Kitty showed up at the country club—"

"Walked in there like she owned the place," he said crossly. Ice cubes rattled in the background. Clearly Janie and I weren't the only ones consoling ourselves with drink. "Like she had a right. I wonder if her real father was Jewish?"

I let that slide. "You said Philip was there with a girlfriend. What was her name?"

The pause felt like it stretched out forever. "Chesty little thing," Philip Senior finally said. "Suzie something?"

We used to date, I heard Sukie saying, a secret smile lifting her lips, cheeks flushing under her makeup, the blush of a girl who can't believe that the guy of her dreams is smiling back at her—a blush I'd certainly worn myself, the night Evan had showed up at the Lo Kee Inn on New Year's Eve and kissed me on the street. *A million years ago.*

I hung up without saying goodbye, started to run out of the bathroom, slipped on the wet tiles and landed flat on my ass. I ignored the pain and punched in Janie's number with shaking hands. Her phone rang once . . . twice . . . three times.

"Hello?"

"Janie, take the kids and get out of there!"

"Huh?"

"Janie, listen to me. Think of an excuse and get them out of there right now. It's important!"

"Okay," she said dubiously.

"I'm on my way." I scooped my clothes off the bathroom floor, pulled on my shirt and pants, dispensing with underwear and bra, and pushed my wet feet into my sneakers. I sprinted down the stairs, praying that Janie had thought to leave her keys when she'd taken my van. I shoved my hands through the clutter on the table in the entryway hall: junk mail, old newspapers, two-week-old fingerpaintings the kids had brought home, before I found the keys on a monogrammed key chain.

I ran out the front door, sprinted through the snow, and threw myself behind the wheel of Janie's Porsche with my cell phone pressed to my ear. "I'm sorry, Chief Bergeron's not on duty this afternoon," said the same bored-sounding dispatcher I'd talked to the day I'd found Kitty, the one who'd scratched at her scalp with the tip of her pencil.

"Page him!" I screeched.

"Can you spell your name for me, please?"

I jammed the key into the ignition, stomped on the clutch, and went lurching backward down the driveway, right into my mailbox. "Shit!"

"Ma'am, there's no need for profanity."

I put the car in drive, pulled forward, backed up again around the splintered wood, and roared off toward the end of Liberty Lane.

"Have somebody meet me!" I said. "I'm going to Twelve Folly Farm Way. The woman there, Sukie Sutherland, is armed and dangerous!" I shouted.

"Can you repeat that, ma'am?" the dispatcher asked.

"Twelve Folly Farm!" I yelled. I turned left, almost hitting an SUV, whose occupant glared at me and leaned on her horn. Forty miles an hour. Forty-five. Fifty. The Porsche's suspension groaned as I ground the gears and rounded the curve just before Folly Farm Way. I dialed Evan's cell phone. ". . . 'lo?"

"Evan? Can you hear me?"

". . . can't . . . out."

"Goddamn this fucking quaint asshole town!" I yelled at the top of my lungs. Snow was splattering on the windshield, and I couldn't figure out how to work the windshield wipers.

"Okay," said Evan. "That I heard."

"You need to come here!" I screamed. "I know who did it, and—"

"Kate? Say that again!"

"Twelve Folly Farm Way!" I said over the roar of the engine. Then I hung up, slammed on the brakes in front of Sukie's house, left the keys in the ignition and the car door open, and I sprinted for the door.

I didn't knock, and I didn't ring. The door swung open as soon as I put my hand on the knob. Sukie Sutherland stood in the entryway, smiling.

"Kate!" she said, brown eyes wide but unsurprised, like I'd stopped over to borrow a cup of sugar and join her for a cup of coffee and the latest neighborhood gossip, like I was perfectly dry and completely dressed instead of standing in front of her out of breath and dripping wet, without a hat or coat or socks on a thirty-degree day in the snow. Sukie was the picture of grace and competence in her mommy uniform. Her brown hair was shining, and her neatly pressed khakis and pink pearl-buttoned angora sweater were accented nicely by the little silver gun she held in her hand. "Come on in and stand over by the refrigerator, okay, Kate?"

I followed her inside on leaden legs. "Where are my kids?"

"Kate?" I relaxed a little bit as I heard Janie's muffled voice coming from behind the basement door. "Hey, we're down here!"

"Hang on!" I shouted. Sukie leveled the gun at my heart.

"Your friend tried to make a break for it," she said, shaking her head sadly. "I would have left them alone, you know. I would have left you alone too, but you just don't quit!" She scratched her shoulder with the barrel of the gun and shook her head. "This is going to take up my entire afternoon!"

I wobbled over to the refrigerator as she directed me with the gun. I could hear Sophie's hiccuping sobs, and Janie trying to keep them calm. "If you're happy and you know it, clap your hands," I heard her sing, followed by two hesitant claps. Sukie Sutherland. A part of me had probably known it all along. Wasn't there something a little suspicious about a woman who named her kids Tristan and Isolde and alphabetized her canned goods?

"Where are your kids?"

"At Marybeth's house," she said. "I sent them over to play. They'll be there until four. That should give me plenty of time." She looked at the watch on the hand that wasn't holding the gun. "Let's see," she said, ticking off items in the manner of a woman running through her grocery list. "Get the kids in your car, get your friend in the car." She looked at me. "You've got enough booster seats for everyone, right?"

I nodded dumbly, thinking, *She's going to kill all of us and she's worrying about booster seats?* "Wh-what are you going to do?"

"Take you to the river," she said. "Drop you in the water. Such a shame," she said, brandishing the gun at me until my back was flat against her stainless-steel refrigerator. "How you killed Kitty, then cracked from the guilt and the strain of keeping the secret. Killed your kids, killed your best friend, and drove your car off the bridge. That's the part I regret," she said, grinning so I could see all of her gleaming white teeth. "It's going to be the waste of a perfectly good minivan."

"You." I raked the stiff mat of my wet hair off my forehead and tried to make my legs stop shaking.

"Me," she confirmed, nodding pleasantly, as if we were discussing whose turn it was to be Parent of the Day at the Red Wheel Barrow.

"You killed Kitty."

She nodded.

"You left that note on my car." *Keep her talking,* I thought, as my knees began to shake. *Keep her talking, and I'll . . . what? Scream? Run? Hope the dispatcher's actually going to send the cops, even though I didn't give her my Social Security number and my mother's maiden name?*

"Yep," she said, grinning like she'd just won the Nobel Prize. "And if you'd just minded your own business, instead of running around like Nancy Drew with varicose veins, you'd have saved yourself a lot of trouble. Oh, well," she added with a shrug, "your loss. It's funny, isn't it?" She tilted her head. "You always thought *you* were the smart one. So smart! So sophisticated! So much better than us dim-bulb mama bears in boring old Connecticut, right?"

"Is that what you thought?" I asked. *Nancy Drew with varicose veins,* I thought, and realized that if she didn't kill me, I was going to do my damnedest to kill her.

"All of us except Kitty." She shook her head in exaggerated sorrow. "Kitty thought you were just swell," she said.

"Sh-she did?"

Sukie shrugged. "Of course, Kitty turned out not to be such a great judge of character. She thought her husband really loved her. She thought I was her friend. Give me your hands," she said, pulling a pink and gold silk scarf out of her pocket.

I ignored her request and shoved my hands in my pockets. "Philip did love her," I said, which caused the smug expression to slide right off Sukie's face.

"He did not," Sukie said petulantly. "Not the way he loved me."

"You?" I scoffed. "Oh, please." My keep-her-talking ploy had evolved into a new strategy: *get her pissed.* Get her so angry that she'd make some stupid mistake that hopefully wouldn't involve shooting me on the spot. Not that I thought she'd actually kill me in her kitchen. She'd never get my blood out of her hand-painted Mexican tile backsplash. "You were filler," I sneered. "Kitty was the one he really wanted. And why wouldn't he? Kitty was smart. She was successful. And, seeing as how the world of work gave him problems . . ." I shrugged.

"What are you talking about?" Sukie snarled.

"Nothing everyone in town doesn't already know. Phil needed a successful, ambitious wife because he couldn't cut it. The only job he could get was working for Daddy, and even then he was a fuck-up."

"That's not true!" she screeched, leveling the gun at my chest. "He's very smart, it's just that nobody ever gave him a chance!" She stared at me, panting. Then she held up the scarf. Hermès, I'd bet. My first designer scarf. Too bad I might not live to appreciate it. "Hands together."

I edged forward toward her island with my hands dangling loose at my sides. "What were the two of you going to do after you'd eliminated the competition? What were you going to do to keep him in handmade shirts and shoes? Sell flaxseed muffins on the street? Do Pilates for pay?"

Lucky for me, Sukie lived in a Montclaire too. Her kitchen was my kitchen, minus the dishes in the sink and the crayon scribbles on the wall. I ran my fingertips underneath the granite countertop of her island and eased the top drawer open.

"We were going to be fine," Sukie said, tossing her flat-ironed locks.

"Down in Florida?" I guessed, and saw the word register in her eyes. "Is that what he was telling you? Was he talking about fun and sun in South Beach when he wasn't diddling Lexi in the equipment shed."

"Never mind Lexi," she said. A muscle underneath her eye twitched.

"Why not? What'd you do to her?" I asked. "I hope you didn't toss her off the bridge too. That's a whole lot of housewives for one river, don't you think?"

"Shut up," she said. She pointed the gun between my eyes, and I saw her arms trembling.

I shook my head ruefully while my fingers slid across cutting boards and pot lids and finally closed around something cool made of marble.

"I bet Phil kept telling you he'd leave Kitty, but that wasn't what happened, was it?"

"Kitty was a slut," Sukie said shrilly. "You don't know anything about her. She was a slut just like her mother, she never even knew who her father was—"

"But she found out, didn't she?" The muscle in Sukie's cheek twitched faster. "She found out, and *she* was going to leave *him.* No more money." I said and made a sad face. "No more book advance. Ol' Phil was actually going to have to work for a living until you did this thing for him. No more Kitty and he'd be free—with all of her money. With her life insurance and no ugly custody battle. And what does he do? Takes up with Lexi Hagen-Holdt." I shook my head again, making a great show of my puzzlement. "That's some way to treat your old sweetheart."

"You bitch!" Sukie wailed. She pulled her arm back as if she was going to belt me in the face with the gun. I brought the rolling pin up as hard as I could, slamming it into her forearm, hearing a satisfying crack. The gun flashed silver as it slid across the island into the corner. Sukie wailed and lunged at me, hands hooked into claws and aiming for my eyeballs. I stepped around the island and head-butted her chest. The air rushed out of her in a whoosh, and she staggered, then fell to the floor.

"Don't move!" I screamed, going for the gun in the corner while simultaneously trying to yank my cell phone out of my pocket. Sukie shot one leg out, kicking me hard in the shin. My hip slammed into the island and I hit the floor so hard the walls rattled. My teeth snapped shut on the tip of my tongue, and warm blood spurted into my mouth.

I screamed and got to my feet. Sukie screamed louder as she flung herself at my back, grabbing at my hair. I twisted sideways, slamming her body into the island's base. She fell off and landed hard, groaning and kicking at my legs. Until I fell down beside her. Then we were both on the floor, crawling, gasping, dragging ourselves toward the gun. Sukie's arm was sticking in the air at an odd angle, and my mouth was full of blood. I saw her fingers curl around the gun, and I shoved myself sideways as hard as I could and came down on her with all my weight, grabbing for the hand holding the gun, thanking God that I wasn't one of those hundred-and-ten-pound aerobicized mommies. The gun fell to the floor and I grabbed it, just as the front door burst open and Stan ran into the kitchen.

"Put that down, Mrs. Borowitz!" Stan shouted.

Sukie tilted her blood-streaked face up beseechingly. "Please, get her off me!" she begged. "She's trying to kill me! And she's very heavy!"

I grabbed a handful of hair and slammed Sukie's head onto the hardwood floor. It felt, I had to admit, tremendously gratifying. "She killed Kitty Cavanaugh, she killed Lexi, she's got my kids in her basement!"

"Your best friend too!" Janie yelled indignantly.

Stan stared at us, bewildered. Then he pulled out his gun and pointed it. Not at her but at me. Sukie was screaming, Janie was yelling, my kids were crying from the basement.

"She did it!" I yelled, ignoring the pain in my mangled tongue.

"Stand up," said Stan. I'd started to when Sukie's teeth closed on my thumb. I shrieked in surprise and pain. The gun fell out of my hand. Quick as a cat, Sukie snatched it. She got to her feet, looking down at the gun, then up at me, then over at Stan. Underneath the blood and the swelling that had already started, her face was pale and blank as a mannequin's. Blood was running down her face, pattering on her pink-angora-covered breasts, and I saw in her eyes exactly what was going to happen next.

As Stan held his gun aimed at us, I held out my hands. "Don't do anything crazy, Sukie, please, just . . . just give me the gun and we'll . . . we'll talk! I'll make some tea or something . . . I'll get you some ice for your arm . . ."

I could hear Janie pounding against the basement door, trying to make a game of it. "Knock, knock!" she called, and my children repeated it. "Knock, knock!"

"I loved him," she whispered.

"I know," I said. I took a step forward, then another. "I know you did, Sukie. I know how that feels."

"Loved him," she said again. Three steps. Four. I was almost close enough to touch her.

"I know."

"We could have been . . ." She lifted the gun in slow motion, with the barrel pointed not toward my head but toward hers. Her last word was almost a sigh. "Happy."

"Sukie, don't—"

"Mrs. Sutherland, please—"

Stan and I reached for her at the same instant, an instant too late. The sound of the gun was the loudest thing in the universe as she shut her eyes and pulled the trigger.

FORTY-ONE

"I don't need to go to the hospital," I told Stan after he'd liberated Janie and my children from the basement and led us all outside. The police cars I'd seen cruising our neighborhood since Kitty's murder had come screeching down the cul-de-sac, and the pink-faced officer who'd driven me back to Kitty's house after her murder was cordoning off the lawn with yellow Crime Scene Do Not Cross tape. I saw several news vans roll up behind the cruisers. I could picture the newscasters inside of them, patting powder on their faces, getting ready to tell the world how this story ended.

"You should go anyhow. You and the kids. Just to be sure." He'd wrapped a crinkly silver blanket around my shoulders, but I couldn't stop shaking. All three kids were in my arms, and Janie was standing beside me, her makeup in stark relief against skin that had gone white as the snow on Sukie's lawn.

"We're fine," I said, as two of the officers wheeled a stretcher out the front door. They'd covered Sukie's body completely with a sheet. I pressed the kids' heads against me so they wouldn't see.

"You should talk to someone," Stan said.

"I'll talk to you," I said. "You'll need a statement, right?" My teeth started to chatter.

"Do you want me to call your husband?"

I closed my eyes. *I'd never do anything to put the children in danger,* I'd promised him. I hung my head. "No."

"I'll call him," Janie said in a tiny voice that barely sounded like her own.

I dislodged Sam and Jack long enough to dig my phone out of my pocket and handed it to Janie. Sophie had her thumb stuck in her mouth. The boys looked dazed. "You guys?" I said. "I know that was scary, but everything's okay now. Mommy's fine, Aunt Janie's fine . . ." I paused to spit out a mouthful of blood, realizing too late that it wasn't the most reassuring sight.

"You should have someone look at that," Stan said. I nodded and let him herd all of us—me, Janie, Sophie, Sam, and Jack—into the back of another ambulance for the trip to the hospital.

Three hours later, I ended up with four dissolvable stitches in my tongue, a prescription for high-test painkillers, and phone numbers for three different children's therapists. The kids were taken away to some place called the family room to talk to a social worker. Janie called Ben, then managed to score some Valium and a cute intern's phone number. The five of us were huddled on my bed, and I'd swapped my wet, bloodstained T-shirt for a hospital gown, when the door burst open.

I was bracing myself for Ben, but instead, a familiar, fur-clad figure swooped into the room, with a billow of heavy perfume proceeding her.

"Grandma!" said Sophie—the first word I'd heard her speak since the scene in the kitchen.

"Grandma! Grandma!" echoed Sam and Jack.

"Kate!" Reina hurried toward my bed, coat flapping, bracelets glittering, and gathered me into her arms. I surprised myself by letting myself be gathered and, about ten seconds later, by bursting into tears.

"Oh, Mom."

"Shh, shh," she said, stroking my hair. "It's all right, it's all right. You're fine."

I was sobbing so hard that I couldn't catch my breath. "The kids," I wheezed. "The kids were in the house. Sukie had a gun—"

"Shh, shh. It's over, Kate. You're going to be fine."

"Ben's going to kill me!" I blurted, before I had time to consider my choice of words. "He told me to stay out of this and I didn't—"

"Shh, shh," she crooned. "You're fine. You're fine."

I pressed my cheek against her fur coat and tried to believe that it might be true.

She and Janie carried the kids out into the hall. The painkillers had started to turn things pleasantly fuzzy around the edges, and my limbs took on a comforting heaviness, like someone had filled them with warm sand.

"Kate."

I lifted my head slowly off the pillow. My husband was standing in the doorway. "Sorry," I said thickly.

I squinted at his face as he slumped against the doorframe. "Kate," he said. His voice echoed, like he'd been calling down to me from on top of a canyon. "I'm sorry too."

"Hot dogs!" Janie called in a hearty voice.

"Hot dogs!" said Sophie, scrambling off the couch and over to the oval oak table big enough for ten. Sam and Jack followed, holding hands, as Janie helped them into their booster seats and my mother dished out the food: hot dogs, baked beans, cut-up carrots and zucchini to dip in ranch dressing, with lemonade to drink. Everyone tucked in, and for a minute all we could hear was the low roaring of the waves as the tide rolled in, and the wind whipping silvery against the walls. It was three months since Sukie had killed herself in front of me. And the children and I had settled in at the home in Truro, the one that turned its back on the world.

"Absolutely!" Brian Davies had told me, in the too-hearty voice that people use when dealing with the recently injured or mentally ill. "Sure, you can stay. House'd just be sitting there empty, anyhow! Stay as long as you need to! Stay as long as you'd like!"

So, the morning after Sukie's suicide, I had signed myself out of the hospital, kissed my husband goodbye, and loaded the kids, plus Janie and my mother, into the minivan. We went shopping for basics: overalls and sweatshirts, pajamas and underwear, toothbrushes and hairbrushes. Reina sat in the food court with an untouched cup of hot water in front of her and her telephone in her hand staring at the people passing by like she'd just landed on our planet and had never seen a mall before. Occasionally we'd pass her and I'd catch a phrase or two in French or Italian. *Emergencia* and *famille* seemed to be figuring prominently. I bought her the kind of tea she liked, a dehumidifier, and the first pair of non-high-heeled shoes I'd bet she'd worn in years, and she took the kids to Tower Records. "They like *polka*?" she demanded, loudly enough to turn heads two stores over. "Kate, that's *obscene.*"

Before we left town I dropped Janie off back at Sukie's house. One of the cops had pulled her Porsche up to the curb, locked the door, and brought Janie's keys to the hospital. The car sat in front of the empty house, looking somehow forlorn, with snow covering its windows and a bit of yellow police tape caught on its antenna.

"I can come up next weekend," she said, hugging me goodbye.

"I could never thank you enough for . . ." *Helping me,* I wanted to say. *Believing in me.* "Being my friend."

She hugged me hard and kissed my cheek. She got in her car, I got in the van and I drove my children and my mother east, with the sun setting at our backs, a hundred and eighty miles back to the ocean.

The first weeks went by in fits and starts. We bought two cords of wood and built fires every morning and gathered around them at night, toasting marshmallows and watching movies, bundled up in blankets as the wind whipped off the sea and made the walls shudder and moan. We shopped for groceries at the Super Stop 'n Shop in

Orleans. We signed the kids up for music class in Eastham, and drove them to storytime at the libraries in Truro and Provincetown and Wellfleet, then took them out for chowder for lunch.

In the afternoons while the kids napped and Reina talked on the telephone, I'd bundle up and head to the deck overlooking the bay, feeling the rough wind in my hair as I sat on a chaise longue, thinking that I should have figured it out faster. In retrospect, it was all so clear how Sukie had been leading everyone down the wrong path. She'd been the one to tell me about Kitty's ghostwriting, and I'd bet anything that she'd been Tara Singh's anonymous tipster too. She'd given me the sitter's phone number, she'd told me about Kitty and Ted Fitch, knowing that every wrong step I made took me further away from her.

I would stare at the waves and consider Kitty Cavanaugh. What would she have said to me if she'd lived long enough for our lunch date? Would she have enlisted me in the search for her father? Did she want a friend? A witness? Would she have envied me my two parents, the same way I'd once envied her beauty, her slim figure, her shiny hair, the ease with which she seemed to manage all the things that left me confounded? And would I have told her that her focus on the past was jeopardizing her present, and that there's always a price to pay for looking back?

Only the national edition of the *New York Times* was available on the Cape in the wintertime, and I had to drive all the way to Provincetown to get it, but between those flimsy editions and a cranky dial-up Internet connection, I managed to spend those first few weeks in Truro following the fallout, the ever-widening ripples that Kitty Cavanaugh's murder had set into motion.

Sukie Sutherland had been buried on the Outer Banks of North Carolina, where her parents had retired, not in Upchurch, where she'd spent her whole life. Her husband put their house on the market the week following the funeral, then took the kids off to parts unknown.

Lexi Hagen-Holdt remained a missing person. The police had

called in a diving team from New York City, and they were dredging the Connecticut River, where Sukie had planned on taking me, for her body. The *Times* had no word on what had happened to Denny and Brierly and Hadley. I couldn't bring myself to think about them for very long.

Philip Cavanaugh had been questioned by the police to determine what he knew and when he knew it. What emerged wasn't enough to get him anything more than a stern talking-to. Yes, he'd been carrying on with Sukie, and with Lexi, and, for a while, with Lisa the sitter and Luz the personal trainer and—God help me—he'd even made a play for Mrs. Dietl, the not-so-prim-and-proper grandmother who ran the Red Wheel Barrow. Yes, he'd had what the *Times* termed "general conversations" with Sukie about his wife's work as a ghostwriter and what life might be like without Kitty, but he'd never encouraged her to do anything about it or known that she was planning on it.

As for Delphine Dolan, she'd started calling herself Debbie again and had sold her story to the tabloids. "Housewife Hooker Tells All!" blared the headline on one of the magazines Janie brought me. There was a shot of Delphine, lovely in a low-cut blue dress, and another photograph in which she was looking coyly over her shoulder, wearing nothing more than bikini bottoms and a smile.

"Her husband's standing by her," Janie read between sips of the Pedialyte and vodka she'd requested. We were bundled up on the deck, wrapped in down comforters, mittens, and hats, with the hard wind whipping off the water, reddening our cheeks and turning our fingers numb. "'I love my wife,' blah blah blah . . . Ooh, look, they're developing a sitcom based on her life!"

I nodded. "Good for Delphine."

Janie smiled shyly and handed me another magazine. I saw a copy of *Content,* with Kitty Cavanaugh's face on its front cover. It was the shot I'd recognized from her mantel. A wedding picture. Kitty was all shining dark hair and big blue eyes, a white lace veil and a white satin gown and a smile that made it seem as if the whole world was hers for the taking. "Kitty Cavanaugh: A Life," read the headline. Janie's byline was five times the size it normally was. "My first piece of legitimate journalism," she said proudly. "Sy's going to have it bronzed!"

The article was five pages long and utterly engrossing. Janie had tracked down all of the players and gotten many of them to give her quotes on the record. The one they'd used in eighteen-point type came from Dorie Stevenson. "She was the best person I knew."

It was all there: the story of Kitty's mother Judith Medeiros's life in New York and overdose death and Kitty's de facto adoption. Then came Hanfield, where Joel Asch had been her professor—"not her father, but a father figure. I wanted to help her. I hope that I did." Then, the roster of men Judy Medeiros had known, both in the biblical and nonbiblical sense. There was a prominent lobbyist and a network executive, the poetry professor and the ophthalmologist. "New York Attorney General Ted Fitch voluntarily took a paternity test in the days following Suzanne Sutherland's suicide," Janie had written. "The results were negative. The question of Kitty Cavanaugh's paternity and Judith Medeiros's death remains a mystery—one that the New York Police Department's detectives have recently reopened. If Cavanaugh herself found the answer before she died, she took it to her grave."

Our days fell into a comforting rhythm. We'd have breakfast, then take a trip to the library or the supermarket or the pirate museum in Provincetown. Lunch, then nap, crafts and coloring, a video when it rained. After dinner, we'd build a fire, and Reina would sing—sometimes opera, sometimes polka. After I'd tucked the kids in, I would lie alone in the bed beside the big windows, listening to the ocean, looking at the lights of Provincetown twinkling across the water, the stars that filled the sky. I planted bulbs in the blank spaces laid out to be a garden—tulips and daffodils and, when the weather got warmer, seeds for daisies and impatiens, petunias and pansies. On Wednesday and Friday mornings I'd drive the kids to the dock in Provincetown and we'd take the ferry into Boston, where we'd visit the offices of Dr. Birnbaum, a child psychologist. She'd usher the kids into her comfortably cluttered office, complete with dollhouse, easel, and every kind of toy, and close the door with a click. I'd sit in one of the hardwood chairs, trying not to press my ear to the door, trying to believe that Sophie, Sam, and Jack knew they were loved and that, in spite of what had happened, they were safe and would eventually be all right.

Ben came every weekend. He played with the children, went out to dinner with us, popped popcorn, sang polka, dressed and undressed Uglydoll, and watched every movie Disney ever made. At night, he would sleep in the bed beside me without reaching for me. "When you're ready to talk about this . . . ," he said late one night. I shook my head no. He'd sold our house and rented a condo in Cos Cob for himself, for the time being. He'd hired another partner, promised he'd cut back his hours, promised he'd be home more, promised we could move wherever we wanted to—another town in Connecticut, New Jersey, even New York City again, the same neighborhood, the same apartment building, if he could swing it. He wanted us to be a family again. It didn't matter where. "It'll be better," he whispered, running one finger tentatively along my cheek. "It'll be like it was before."

I kept my eyes shut and pretended to be sleeping, until I heard him sigh and felt the bed shift as he rolled back to his side.

Evan continued to call every few days. "Can I see you?" he'd ask. "We've already wasted so much time, Kate. We should be together." I put him off too. I stared at the ocean and thought about Kitty Cavanaugh's father. Was he dead or alive? Had he been following the story? Was he guilty of more than fathering an out-of-wedlock daughter?

February turned into March. "I wish I could stay," my mother told me. "But I signed a contract."

I nodded. "It's okay. You were here"—I swallowed hard—"when I needed you."

"I'll always be here when you need me," she said. She drew my hair back from my forehead and kissed me. "Remember that, Kate."

The breeze off the ocean became warmer, scented with salt and beach plums. On the weekends, Janie or Ben would watch the kids, and I would walk on the beach for hours, feeling the cool sand on the soles of my feet as I made my way past concentric circles of seaweed, piles of driftwood, the occasional decomposing fish. Some days I'd see seals cavorting fifty feet out or sunning themselves on rocks at low tide. The rocks were the most comforting thing of all. Every day, the tide would go out, and they'd reappear, the way they would all summer, the way they'd been doing for centuries before I had ever seen this beach and would continue to do after all of us were gone.

Just before Memorial Day, I reached under the front seat of the minivan to retrieve Sophie's candy necklace, and found the advance reader's copy of *The Good Mother* that Laura Lynn Baird had given me. I flipped past the blank pages at the front of the book advising that the dedication was to come, and read

Mommy & Me
by Katherine Cavanaugh
Foreword

Once upon a time there was a beautiful princess, with long black hair and rose-red lips who went off to an enchanted kingdom and came back with a baby, a little girl all her own.

When the princess died and the little girl grew up, the girl went looking for her mother, trying to understand who she was, whom she'd loved, and what each of them had become.

There are women who grow up with good mothers, women who endure indifferent mothers, and women who survive toxic parenting, absent mothers, abandoning mothers, mothers by biology only.

The woman who raised me, my aunt Bonnie, fell into the first category, as loving and supportive a mother as any child could wish.

My real mother—my biological mother, the woman who gave birth to me in a hospital in Hyannis in 1969 and moved back to New York City by herself six months later—was a mystery: a glamorous presence, a beauty, a sorceress. I spent the first years of my life trying to charm her, waiting for her to return to me the way, I'd find out much later, she was waiting for the man who'd gotten her pregnant to come back to her.

"Mommy!" Sophie held her out hand for her necklace. I tucked the book in my purse and handed it over. That night, I read more.

The man who may or may not be my father sits across from me in a midtown restaurant. His suit is black, beautifully cut, or gray, or navy blue. His gray hair is combed straight back from his forehead, or it's curly salt and pepper, thinning on top, too long in the back, or it's gone entirely, leaving the top of his head naked and vulnerable as an egg. His fingertips are blunt, the nails clipped close and coated with clear gloss. When I slide my mother's photograph across the linen-draped table, he barely glances at it before using those fingertips to slide it back. "Never saw her in my life." A dozen years, a dozen men. The Internet helps—a few keystrokes and I can download biographies from corporate Web sites or magazine profiles. I can find out where this possibility, this shadow-daddy, grew up, where he spent his summers, where he went to college, where he got married, how many children he claims. I work in a cubicle in my small town's library. I sift through reels of microfiche, yellowed newspaper clippings, laminated programs, black-and-white photographs. And I return again to the city to sit in restaurants where coffee costs six dollars a cup, and ask the only question that matters. Mine? *I wonder, staring at him over my cup as my voice launches into the speech I've given so many times before.* Are you mine? And what do you know about how my mother died?

• • •

On the first day the temperature topped seventy-five degrees, I wiggled the children into their bathing suits and slathered their pale bodies with sunblock. Janie had come to visit again. We worked together, gathering pails and shovels, towels and folding chairs and a rainbow-striped umbrella to stick in the sand. Then we descended the stairs to the beach. The boys dashed right into the little waves that lapped the sand. Sophie hung back, clutching my hand. "Come on, sweetheart," I coaxed. She shook her head but didn't resist when I scooped her into my arms. The water was shockingly cold as it flowed over my toes and ankles, but I forced myself to keep going, wading in until it was foaming past my knees . . . then my hips.

"One . . . two . . . three!" I said, and bent forward until Sophie's toes brushed the top of a wave. She squirmed in my arms, giggling, as I tossed her lightly into the air. She screamed with laughter, then collected herself and let me carry her back to shore to build a sandcastle with her brothers. I eased myself into the water until it was up to my shoulders, then took a deep breath and dunked my head. When I brushed the salt water out of my eyes and looked back to shore, the kids and Janie were applauding. I waved, then flipped onto my back and floated in the pale green ocean water, looking up at the sky. *Come home to me,* said Ben. *Come back to me,* said Evan. I closed my eyes, listening for my answer. My hair trembled in the water. My body rose and fell. The waves rolled in and out, saying nothing at all.

On Memorial Day, the telephone rang.

"Turn on your TV," said Janie.

"Which channel?"

"Doesn't matter."

I flicked on the set and saw a familiar vista—the White House, atop an emerald green lawn, underneath a sparkling blue summer sky. A podium had been set up in the Rose Garden, and the president stood behind it.

"We go live now to this unprecedented speech," said the news anchor.

The president gripped the podium. I saw his throat working as he swallowed once, twice, and then began to speak. "After careful consideration, I have decided not to seek my party's nomination for a second term as president," he said. "I have made this decision after lengthy and prayerful personal reflection, and a desire to do what is right, not only for this country, but for . . ." His throat worked again. "For my family. I have caused them pain—my wife, my children, the people who have seen me at my lowest and loved me nevertheless." He looked down at his notes, then looked up again, clenching his jaw. "I ask the media and the public to respect our privacy during this difficult time. Godspeed, and God bless America."

It was a moment before the anchor's voice came on again, and in that moment, I stared at the face on the screen as the camera lingered. I considered the high cheekbones, the cleft chin, the blue eyes that gleamed as he bowed his head over the podium. Eyes, a poet might have said, the blue of pansies . . . or of cornflowers.

"Well," the anchor spluttered, clearly off balance. "Well, Peter, I'm not quite sure what to make of this. Have we heard any news about a possible medical condition?"

"He wishes," Janie said in my ear. "Cops found the dealer last night."

"The president's dealer?"

"No, President Stuart was already a congressman then. He knew better than to buy his own junk. He had his little brother get it for him—you know, the one who spent the entire last decade in and out of rehab. Thirty years ago. Two hundred dollars of uncut China white and bye-bye, inconvenient woman and illegitimate kid."

I stared blankly at the empty podium on the television screen, picturing the note I'd found in Kitty's dresser drawer. *Stuart 1968.*

"Mommy?" Sophie tugged my hand.

"I should go." I told Janie.

"Stay tuned," she said, sounding almost giddy. "Breaking news.

Developing fast. I've got to go get my hair blown out. CNN just called."

I told her goodbye, hung up the telephone, and flicked the television into silence. Bonnie's voice echoed in my head. *She told me that she was getting to the end of it . . .* and Joel Asch's voice joined hers. *Writing for us gave Kitty access,* he'd told me. *You can interview senators. Even presidents.*

"Come on," I said. I lifted my daughter in my arms and started singing against her cheek. "Comes the measles, you can quarantine the room . . . comes a mousie, you can chase it with a broom. Comes love, nothing can be done."

"No singing," said Sophie, batting my lips away. "Don't you want to see the president some more?"

I shook my head and carried her through the glass doors out into the sunshine, down the silvery stairs that led to the water's edge. "I've seen enough," I said.

PERMISSIONS ACKNOWLEDGMENTS

Acknowledgment is made to the following for permission to reprint previously published material:

"All by Myself" by Eric Carmen, Sergei Rachmaninoff © 1975, renewed 2002 by Eric Carmen Music, Inc. All rights administered by Universal Songs of PolyGram International, Inc./BMI. Used by Permission. All Rights Reserved.

Laurie Anderson, "Smoke Rings" (reprinted with permission from the artist).

"Comes Love." Words and Music by Lew Brown, Sammy Stept, and Charles Tobias © 1939 (Renewed) WB Music Corp., Chappell & Co., and Ched Music Corporation. All Rights for Ched Music Corporation. Administered by WB Music Corp. All Rights Reserved. Used by Permission.

Goodnight Moon © 1947 by Harper & Row. Text © renewed 1975 by Roberta Brown Rauch. Illustrations © renewed 1975 by Edith Hurd, Clement Hurd, John Thacher Hurd and George Hollyer as trustees of the Edith & Clement Hurd 1982 Trust. Used by permission of HarperCollins Publishers. This selection may not be reillustrated without written permission of HarperCollins.

Horton Hatches the Egg by Dr. Seuss, copyright TM and Copyright © by Dr. Seuss Enterprises, LP 1940, renewed 1968. Used by permission of Random House Children's Books, a division of Random House, Inc.

The Feminine Mystique by Betty Friedan. Copyright © 1983, 1974, 1973, 1963 by Betty Friedan. Used by permission of W. W. Norton & Company, Inc.

"Frankie and Johnny" by Lee Bayer, Ernest W. Hayes. © 1966 by Champion Music Corporation. All rights administered by Songs of Universal, Inc./BMI. Used by Permission. All Rights Reserved.

"My Funny Valentine" by Richard Rodgers and Lorenz Hart © 1937 (Renewed) Chappell & Co. Rights for Extended Renewal Term in U.S. controlled by The Estate of Lorenz Hart (administered by WB Music Corp.) and The Family Trust U/W Richard Rodgers and The Family Trust U/W Dorothy F. Rodgers (administered by Williamson Music). All Rights outside U.S. controlled by Chappell & Co. International Copyright Secured. All Rights Reserved. Used by Permission.

"My Funny Valentine" by Lorenz Hart and Richard Rodgers. © 1937 (Renewed) Chappell & Co. Rights for Extended Renewal Term in U.S. controlled by WB Music Corp. O/B/O The Estate of Lorenz Hart and The Family Trust Under Will Richard Rodgers and The Family Trust Under Will Dorothy F. Rodgers (administered by Williamson Music). All Rights Reserved. Used by Permission

"Why My Mother Made Me" reprinted from *The Gold Cell* by Sharon Olds by permission of Alfred A. Knopf, Inc.

References to Babo and Uglydoll are granted by permission of PrettyUgly, LLC (www.uglydolls.com). All rights reserved.

ACKNOWLEDGMENTS

Thanks first and foremost to my hardworking, endlessly calm agent, Joanna Pulcini, who went far beyond the call of duty with every single sentence of this book (and also watched my daughter so I could do revisions). Joanna is the best any writer could hope for, and I'm lucky, once again, to have her as my agent and as my friend.

Thanks to Greer Hendricks, my wonderful editor, her associate editor Suzanne O'Neill, my publisher Judith Curr, Karen Mender, Carolyn Reidy, Justin Loeber, Kate Rogers, Angela Stamnes, and the whole team at Atria Books and Simon & Schuster for all of their hard work and good will.

I'm grateful to sopranos Kathleen Berger and Elizabeth Blancke-Biggs for a primer on the opera world, and to Elaine Douvas of Juilliard and the Metropolitan Opera for the lowdown on the oboe.

Ken Salikof and Nina Bjornsson were rigorous editors whose careful comments helped me along the way. Tiffany Yates was an eagle-eyed line editor.

Marcy Engelman, Dana Gidney, and Alicia Kalish take amazing care of me and my books, and I'm very lucky to work with them. Linda Michaels and Emily Gates make sure my novels see the world, and are excellent final readers.

Honi Werner graced me with yet another amazing cover, and Alita Friedman of PrettyUgly graciously permitted us to use Babo's visage on the back.

Jamie Seibert once again made my writing life possible by caring for my daughter while I wrote. Meghan Burnett was indefatigable with her assistance. Andrew Ayala and Peter Janssen gave us help when we needed it.

Thanks to all of my friends for their support while I was wrestling with this book, especially my fellow mommies, who are nothing like the ones described in this book: Susan Abrams Krevsky, Debbie Bilder, Alexa Hymowitz, Andrea Cipriani Mecchi, Carrie Coleman, Sharon Fenick and Alan Promer, Phil DiGennaro and Clare Epstein, Lisa Maslankowski and Robert DiCicco, and Craig and Elizabeth LaBan.

Thanks to my family, near and far, for love, support, and material: Ebbie Bonin, Warren Bonin and Todd Bonin, Renay Weiner, Alan and Linda Gurvitz, Joe Weiner, Jake Weiner (who's not just my brother, he's my film agent, too), April Blair, Olivia Grace Weiner, Molly Weiner, Frances Frumin Weiner, and Faye Frumin, my Nanna.

Finally, thanks to Adam and Lucy, for their love and patience.